The Labyrinth Year

About the Author

Mari Howard is a writer, painter and sometimes a poet, with a lifelong interest in the natural world. She studied in the North East and now lives in Oxford.

The Labyrinth Year

Mari Howard

HODGE PUBLISHING

Copyright © 2014 Clare Weiner *writing as* Mari Howard.

Published by Hodge Publishing,
10 Bainton Road, Oxford OX2 7AF
www.hodgepublishing.co.uk

ISBN 978-0-9564769-7-5

British Library Cataloguing in Publication Data.

A catalogue record for this book
is available from the British Library.

Cover design and typesetting:
Rachel Lawston, Lawston Design

Acknowledgments

Writing is a solitary process ... but much interaction goes into creating a book. I need to thank so many helpful and generously interested people for all their input, from giving time to brainstorm to contributing their specialist knowledge and skills, to refreshing the weary writer in so many ways.

I'd like to thank my friends and family for encouragement. At the outset, Marsha who wanted to find out what Max and Jenny did next, and convinced me that a leap into the 21st century would be a bridge too far from 1988. Liz who's supplied endless happy 'pedi-conference' opportunities, combining sharing her knowledge of medicine, and GP practice in particular, along with going on fashion sprees. Ant and Lianne who again checked the science, set me straight on life in an academic lab, and all this while planning and achieving a wedding. Many happy anniversaries, I hope!

Without Sally's amazing talents with storytelling and craft I wouldn't have met so many super mummies, grannies, a few dads, and their wide-eyed children who've inspired me with Max and Jenny's precocious offspring. Thanks to the families who've become friends. And to Sally again, for introducing me to walking the Labyrinth as a way into prayer and meditation. Several Communities (especially the Scargill Movement: www.scargillmovement.org) whose caring and fun atmosphere, combined with deep practical spirituality, contributed to Daze saying Yes to a commission from St Hildie's.

Thanks to my family, Edmund the amazing proof-reader, encourager, and brainstormer; James for introducing me to the Alliance of Independent Authors (ALLi), (and thus to Debbie Young, inspiration and blogger for ALLi among other positive talents); Ben for being involved in the production side yet again despite pressure of other work; and Nicky for heaps of encouragement, inspiration, and hugs.

And thanks to everyone who voted for *Baby, Baby* in the People's Book Prize (we didn't win but we got some wonderfully positive comments), and who's been encouraging, cheering me on. And to Bridget and Adrian, leaders of superb Writers' Weekends and so much more. A very special couple.

AUTONOMY

Jenny

JULY 1996, FRIDAY EVENING, LATE

I'm in the microscope room when Dad phones. I thank the guy who's just tapped me on the shoulder with the message, stretch, put my specs back on, slide off the stool.

I know what this'll be about. The e-mail was on my screen Monday of last week: could almost hear his voice as I read: *'Match your salary and then some? Throw in a nice car, maybe a Subaru Forester or a Honda CR-V? Suit you?'*

In the lab office, I pick up the phone, 'Hi, Dad, everything okay?'

'Hi, Kiddo: I'm looking at a blue sky here, and thinking about a week's sailing I've put in the diary. So, *have you given any more thought to Vangenics?'*

I don't want to think about any of this. For me it's late evening, for him it's around lunchtime, for both of us it's nearly the weekend. 'Mm,' I say, 'it's a great offer. But leading a team doing *ground-breaking stuff on mitochondrial DNA…* that's not really my area. We're all such specialists now: you need someone with more experience in the field. Of mitochondrial DNA.'

He should be able to accept that.

'So, what're you doing right now?' he asks, moving sideways along the conversation.

'Well, next big event is a narrowboat holiday. On the Oxford Canal. Max was offered the loan of a boat by his knee-specialist friend, and we've accepted. It's called the *Mandalay*.' I pause, awaiting Dad's response.

It's a deep throaty laugh. Not a totally unkind one. 'Good luck, Kiddo: this sounds more like a working trip than a holiday. You're packing all the right gear, life jackets included?'

'And toys, and jigsaws. And Manse Granny from Northumberland. I think we're testing our compatibility, as a couple, or something,' I joke.

'Jeez,' Dad says. 'And you're doing all that right now?'

'Well, *right* now, I'm observing some cells we've labelled with GFP—wonderful tool isn't it?'

'*Aequorea victoria*,' he responds.

'Nature is amazing,' I say, drily, 'who would've known, when the storms dumped jellyfish at Whitesands Bay and the kid who was me found them fascinating, that I'd be using their cousins' glow-in-the-dark proteins to mark faulty genes?'

'Still the same Jenny Wren. Always curious. Remember your Mom saying she had to hold you back from poking at those creatures. Not curious about coming to work in our state-of-the art laboratories, in a fantastic North American setting? Sure about that?'

'You're very persuasive, but I've got ties.'

'Aw, kiddo, to that Principal Investigator of yours? You've been working for him a long while: your contract'll be coming up for renewal.'

'It is. But I'll make the decisions, okay? Nice of you to think of me though …'

'So, where's this research going?'

'Mine? Maybe one day you'll get to know: a couple may turn up wanting fertility solutions to bypass whatever faulty gene one of them carries. If and when we've found something concrete, a definite fault or faults, a diagnosis.'

'Touché,' he says.

'I read the latest news from your friend at the genome project…' That gets him off the subject of me, until I can make excuses, appealing to the cells waiting under the microscope, and say goodbye.

A chat about *gene expression patterns* is Dad's idea of fun, I think, clearing up my work a bit later. Once he realised nature intrigued me, he turned me into another like him. The conversation, and the job offer, has been unsettling: it's woken up that feeling of frustration I have about Max: he could've been a research scientist. We could've gone off together for a few years at Vangenics. If he wasn't so committed to clinical work. Don't think about it. I chuck my gloves in the bin, take off my lab coat, and hang it up.

The Oxford University Science area never sleeps. Even on a lovely summer night in the long vacation. Outside the microscope room, as I hurry along the dim corridors and landings, machines cast long, rectangular shadows, and hum, or wink, or do both. There's always something happening, a few labs lit up, a few people completing something before they can leave.

I drive home. Magdalen Tower is floodlit; the bridge swarms with tourists. Then comes the gloom of Headington Hill. I reach my front door and remember to lock it behind me. I kick off my shoes and creep upstairs. Max grunts hello as I slip into bed. He reaches out, and takes one of my hands. 'How was it?'

'Going the right way. I had to hang around bit waiting, and I was in the office flicking through journals looking at the sits vac page, getting a feel for what's on offer if Rich doesn't obtain more funding for me.'

'Anything?'

'Not within travelling distance. You know gene expression markers? I can't help wishing there was a whole palette of glow-in-the-dark colours to use. Imagine how useful it'd be if we could mark several mutations in the same cell? Or, label different neurons in the brain? Someone's bound to be working on it.'

'Mm,' Max says. 'Zoë had a whole palette of colours on her face this evening. Alice was face-painting her with those new pens your mother sent.'

'Oh no —'

He laughs. 'It did come off, with a bit of scrubbing.' Max turns over, and pulls me towards him. 'I'd maybe enjoy chatting about fluorescent proteins, but we've a busy day tomorrow.'

My stomach tightens. 'You said, meet David for lunch: I'm going to have to go into the lab first. I'm sorry. Please don't mind fielding the girls. I'll join you all at the pub?'

He exhales loudly enough to make his point. 'As long as we all meet up.'

I say, 'Look, I *am sorry*.' He says, 'I enjoy their company. You see them every day for bath time.'

'Thank you.' Snuggling up to Max, 'I mean it. I know we don't have much time to ourselves.'

Max

SATURDAY

'You said, we'll meet Mummy and Uncle David. Can we have a drink now? Where's Mummy?' Alice, though briefly attracted by Binsey's fairy-tale thatched cottages, is far too young to be interested that Lewis Carroll drank here. Even though she likes it that *Alice in Wonderland* is an old story about a child who shared her name.

'Mummy'll be here. Soon. And there's Uncle David, look.' David, back to us, is busy with his camera, taking photos of the Perch Inn.

As he packs the camera away, we three straggle up: Alice, on her pink fairy bike, Zoë in the buggy, me with the backpack stuffed with wet wipes, woollies, sunhats, and emergency rations. 'Sorry we're late, bit of a way for the girls.'

'Great you suggested this,' he says. 'I looked at the map, and saw I could reach the Perch on foot via Port Meadow. Common land, gifted to the people of Oxford by King Alfred, and never ploughed? Pretty amazing. I passed a few cattle grazing, on the way over.'

'The ancient rights also include keeping horses. There's an annual round-up.'

'I'm tempted to investigate owning a boat on the river ... More to the point, wandering towards the Canal through Jericho—that is what it's called?—I've discovered a possible site for a project we're thinking about at St Hildegard's.'

'Is this public knowledge yet?'

'Far enough along that we're interested in affordable properties nearish the city centre. Hi, kids!'

'Hello,' Alice grins.

''lo.'

'I must apologise for Jenny,' I say, looking at my watch. 'She's had to go into the lab—big push on. Actually these past few years, there always seems to be a big push on. Rich Woods brought several of his Cambridge team over to Oxford with him, Jen's worked for him before.'

'She's happy there though?'

'Och, she's happy enough with what she's doing. Born curious. Though as I've hinted in emails, there's a few wee problems around the full-time research scientist and the mummy role. Partly the dour influences from the Manse, which I try to shield her from.'

David shakes his head, then unclips a pair of wrap-around shades from his shirt front, and puts them on. The girls are looking expectant and bored. Time to begin herding everyone towards the pub entrance, Jenny'll simply have to search for us. 'Will we go inside, find some drinks, and then, there's a playground at the back?'

Inside, we're engulfed by the seventeenth century gloom: low ceiling, old beams, tiny lead-paned windows. I keep glancing back towards the door, wishing Jenny would walk through it before we finish buying our drinks.

Instead, a tall, distinguished figure enters, briefly occluding the light. A familiar voice booms, 'Max Mullins, isn't it? And—', his tone's incredulous, 'David Robertson?'

'Anthony!' David, turning from paying at the bar, beams a friendly smile, while the Reverend Field Plowright looks distinctly cool.

AFP (as he's usually called) marvels that the two of us know each other. And again, as David explains we're cousins. His reply's a non sequitur, aimed at the bairns, 'We'll see you at Holiday Club?'

We escape. In the pub garden, giant chess is laid out on some paving. We watch a bit of a game while the girls snaffle up their juice.

AFP reappears, carrying two pints and a glass of wine one-handed on a metal tray. A packet of peanuts held between his teeth is expertly moved to a jacket pocket once he's stowed his change. Nods are exchanged. 'Not only running the neighbouring parish, an old pal of Mum's from the Christians in Golf circuit,' David remarks, under his breath.

Still no Jenny, we cross to the adventure playground. Alice, in sociable mood, munching crisps, joins a group defending a fort or Wendy house. Zoë potters around, inspecting everything with the caution of a nearly three-year-old in a new place. David (blond hair, suntan, neat jeans) watches the mêlée of playing children, and politely asks whether we have help with the kids.

'We have Ruth. A maternity leave discovery of Jen's,' I say, conscious of my more dreary weekend gear of denims and matching, worn, jacket. 'She's an ex biological scientist ... And she attends Anthony's church, so Jen reckons she'd be approved of by all the grandparents.'

'Beaut,' David laughs. 'Headleigh Parish.' He shakes his head.

I take a long draw of my drink. At this rate, food will have run out by the time Jen appears. 'Absolutely. Ruth's drawing Jen into the world of happy-clappy.'

David smiles knowingly. 'So not maintaining her steady rejection of all things irrational?'

'We allowed Alice free rein on their summer holiday programme last year: the result was her demand to join the Sunday Club. It's not Dad's drear Calvinism, of course. It's arm-waving, lightweight, simplistic. A vapid substitute for the heavy-handed approach.'

He laughs, 'Hardly a great development.'

'Not a great plan, no.' I manoeuvre the buggy a step or two further from a waste bin, where a couple of wasps are circling. 'What Jenny really thinks ... She's mostly in the crèche with Zoë, so she's spared the sermon. But, it's not good to let your children learn stuff they'll give up when they're older and then despise.'

Bad move: David turns the spotlight on me, 'Have you reached that stage?'

'Daddy?' Zoë pulls at my hand, 'Swings?'

Relief: she has great timing. 'Zo-zo, right. Let's—' I hand David my half-empty glass, and settle Zoë into one of the toddler swings, 'Okay? I'll push you.'

'You occasionally visit Hildie's.' David hasn't let it rest yet.

'Och, life's pretty noisy and full-on. Sometimes I need a refuge from the crazy world of family and general practice.' He gives me a look, and downs the remainder of his drink.

Rhythmically pushing Zoë, my eyes on Alice, I add, 'We're taking Mam on holiday, to give her a break. I'm hoping that'll work … So you: how d'you get along with AFP? You must feel vulnerable. How about the faithful who visit the Retreat House?'

'Field Plowright—oh, we don't explore below the surface of being in charge of neighbouring parishes. He's very polite, but I'm conscious of what lurks underneath, and not just about me. Plowright doesn't let women preach. If you refer to my family's attitudes, that's different.'

'Daddy, push!'

'Okay, not too high!'

'Daddy! Dadeeee!' Alice cannons into me, her face shiny with tears and snot, 'Daddy! Something hurt me!'

I crouch, she falls into my arms. 'Alice! Where? Show me? Dave— catch Zoë's swing!'

Alice thrusts her open palm under my nose. 'Here! A big, big, stripy fly. It stinged me.'

I step back to see properly, 'Oh Ally, of course it hurts, a wasp stung you.'

'Lots. And lots.'

One-handed, other arm around Alice, I pull the buggy closer. It tips over, the backpack falls out. 'Let's see what we have here.' I unzip the mouth of the bag, removing jerseys and sun hats. Tissues, wet wipes. 'Let's get rid of that snot, shall we?' Alice gulps, trying to stop crying. I hand her a tissue: she scrubs it across her face. 'What were you—?'

'I had to move the buggy, 'cos Mummy says—'

'And you put your hand on the handle, and the wasp was there?' She nods.

Alice flinches as I use some wipes to clean her grimy, red, swollen palm. Zoë, freed by David from the swing, leans over to look. 'Alice was stung by a wasp. The poor wasp was frightened so it stung her. We're making it better, though, aren't we?'

I glance around: a small gathering of concerned parents and worried children disperses, satisfied that a dad who can cope is coping. 'Getting sorted?' David asks, picking up our glasses.

'Think so. Alice, they have lots of ice here, for the drinks. Shall we go in, and ask for some? That'll make it feel better.'

'God, I can't leave you with them five minutes!' Jenny, arrived at last, sweeps her long hair behind her ears, and regards us, so obviously a woeful group: two guys in charge of two under-fives.

'You're just in time to miss the crisis,' David smiles at her, 'Shouting's over.'

She swoops in and scoops Alice up, 'Whatever was Daddy thinking about?'

'A wasp. I put my hand on it. It hurts.'

'Of course it does, baby.'

'We're getting ice for it. Inside.'

She sets Alice on the ground, and puts an arm around me, like she's suddenly realised I have actually done my best for our child. 'Sorry, babe: it takes as long as it takes. I had to wait for some samples to arrive before I could begin work. And so sorry, David, I never said hello, that was rude.'

Jenny

TWO WEEKS LATER, OXFORD CANAL

There's the most awful, juddering bump. The whole miniscule bathroom shakes, and the shower head tumbles, glancing off my skull, into the shower tray. Kerfuffle doesn't stop: thumps, bangs, tremors.

'My kids!' I grab and drag on my abandoned sweaty T-shirt and shorts, wrench open the bathroom door, and hear Max bellowing from the stern, 'Jenny! Where the hell—Jen, take the tiller for me, so I can see—'

'Tiller? We're damn well not moving. *Where are the kids?*'

'With Mam up front. We bashed into another bloody boat. I cut the engine, you keep her steady, I'm going forward, see what harm we've done.'

You've done, I think, grabbing the wretched thing. What's happened is that my supposedly competent hubby must've throttled up the engine far too much as we left the lock behind. We're slewed across the canal, nose up the bum of the boat in front. I hold her steady like that for all I'm worth.

Max moves off towards our front end. Both boats rock about in the dark greasy water. Lightning flickers, thunder crashes, obscuring the sound of oil on troubled waters. Everything stills and waits. The louring, purple sky seems only a few inches above us. Shouldn't I hear the crying of the frightened girls down the other end? The first few raindrops fall: I catch sight of something floating by.

Orange like a life jacket …

'Max!' I lean dangerously sideways, trying to see more clearly what it is. 'Max! The girls, where are they?' The downpour intensifies, 'Where's Ally and Zoë? Where's your mum?' Any response is drowned by ripping, tearing thunder. 'What?' I scream.

'Bairns are fine: Mam has them inside. I can—'

His reply's cut across by a sudden torrent of yelling invective coming from the other boat, 'Cripes! Four-Eyes and the family! What the hell d'you think you're doing? It's a public waterway, not fucking bumping races!'

It's practically as dark as night, rain is pouring down, but I'd know that voice anywhere: my stepsister Daisy.

'You jerks, they shouldn't've let you out on a canal, you can't drive!'

'Bugger you, where're my ... children?' I end lamely. *Sainsbury's*— my psychotic vision clears, my heart rate slows. That's not a child's life jacket— it's an orange supermarket bag, inflated by the wind.

I'm being over-compensating Mummy, on a guilt trip about focusing on my own ambitions. While Max, ever the peacemaker, is apologising to Daze, 'Hey, I said I'm sorry. I'm trying—'

If I could only see down the length of the boat, I might know how bad this is. Or isn't.

Granny Fee appears through the double doors, a life-jacketed child clinging each side. Relief: they really are okay. 'Mummy!'

They try to move forwards, to hug my knees: Fee, who has a plastic mac thrown over her pale blue shirt and navy slacks, keeps a firm hold on them.

'The girls are safe. We were up front in that sitting area with jigsaws, but we're fine, no bumps or bruises. Oh dear, what a tangle. Can I help in any way? And—Jenny, isn't that your sister, Daisy, on the other boat? Daisy!'

She gives Daze a friendly wave. I just want to fall through the floor, even if that means into filthy canal water. I'd hoped my stepsister and Max's mother would never, ever, have to meet again, after our wedding.

'Oh dear,' Fee continues, 'we're not very experienced over here on the *Mandalay*.'

'Evidently not.'

'But I can see you're rather an expert, pet,' Fee smiles.

Lightning flicks across the sky, suddenly rain turns to hail. The girls squeal and clutch at Grandma, and Fee hustles them inside, mother-hen style. Water runs down my specs and my face. Willow branches flail crazily, the wind ripping at their leaves, which whirl past, to be carried away by the water. I hate boats, husbands, and holidays, as I wait, alert for any signal from Max that we're free and I should steer to get us straight. Hand is frozen to tiller, tiller is jammed towards the left. No chance to find a waterproof, and Fee hasn't handed one out of the door.

And Max is shoving at the bank with a long pole. Then, hood off, wild black hair flying, Daze's expertly steering her boat out of the mess we made, giving a display of skilfulness in pouring rain and booming, cracking thunder. We're free again: but freezing hail hammers my back through my skimpy summer clothes.

Finally, suddenly, the storm abates, the rain stops. A wan sun seeps through parting clouds. Max appears, dark hair slicked down by the storm, board shorts clinging, trainers squelching. Though seems he's grabbed a waterproof from somewhere: could I see one within reach I could grab?

'Okay Jen: bit to the right and keep her steady? Next time, remember crew's not meant to shower when we've moving. Unless the rain pisses down on us again, that is.'

'Ha bloody ha: where'd you find that waterproof?'

'Drying,' he says, deadpan. 'On that line outside, where you left it. Look, go below, find the bairns, change, and maybe put the kettle on?'

'You?'

'I'll do for now.'

I stand for a moment, arms hugging myself, as the now-warm sun shines on my back, watching Daze's boat. Once straight, she puts on a turn of speed and chugs ahead, well out of reach of amateurs on vacation. Yeah: the things Daze can do, and the ways we find out. Last time I saw her was at her studio, near Bridget Riley's in Hackney, rented for her by my Dad. What's she up to, why's she here?

'Looks like Daze owns that boat: did you notice? *The Ironic Lady* painted in green retro-style on the side, with a cartoon portrait, obviously Daze.'

'Aye. Nothing to do with us. Go and get warm below?'

It's stuffy as hell inside, after the past hot, humid days. It smells of wellingtons and orange juice, and faintly of the onions from our salad lunch. Fee has hot, sticky Zoë balanced on her hip.

'She's far too heavy for Grandma, let me take her.' Rainwater drips from my hair.

'You're soaked, pet—'

'I'd win the wet T-shirt competition, wouldn't I?'

Fee looks puzzled: wet T-shirt competitions aren't part of her world. Then she smiles, 'I'll make a brew while you change. We'll open those chocolate Hobnobs.'

Alice pats my thigh. 'Daddy bumped the boat when the thunder came, and our drinks spilt all over the table! Grandma said better sit tight and told us a story. Jesus in a boat.'

Figures: Jesus and Fee are friends, and I'm off to find dry clothes. The rain has washed the shampoo out of my hair.

Once we're safely moored, Max, obviously cross with himself for being inept with the boat, gets out of his wet clothes, then disappears outside again with his mug of tea. Fee and I settle to teaching Alice to play Snakes and Ladders. At the Manse, they have a horrendous Victorian reproduction board, with snakes of sin and ladders of virtue. We have a nice, mild, twentieth century version.

Alice has spotted melting hail piled against the window. 'Why is hail? How does it work?'

Jenny

NEXT DAY

We drop Fee and the girls at Aristotle Lane playground, and chug the last bit to Jericho boat yard. Tim, a senior registrar at the Nuffield Orthopaedic, and Leila, who works at the lab with me, are waiting on the quay. Leila with a huge smile, and a hug, 'Jen, great news! You've done the impossible, impressed Rich with your work, and I think he'll want to present it at that conference in the States next year.'

'Oh wow: I mean, it wasn't all me was it?'

'It's a team thing, but—'

'Calls for a celebration?' Tim suggests.

Max shakes his head, 'We've my mother and the bairns.'

'Aw, did you have to?' I complain, as we drive back to collect them all, and go home. 'I know she'd disapprove but—'

'We'll have our own celebration once she's on her train.'

How can Tim and Leila enjoy family holidays in that cramped water caravan? I'm determined we'll never borrow it again. And I hope Fee will be straight off home. Last week, before boarding the boat, we took her along to Headleigh Parish Church. I blush at the memory. Walking home, Max said 'Certain keys and harmonies are known to play the emotions. That beat goes straight to the crocodile brain. That's not worship. Unless, of course, worship is crocodile-brain related. Which it may be.'

'Max—you don't mean that. The songs were beautiful, moving.' said Fee, probably terribly offended.

'Isn't it *reptilian* brain?' I murmured at Max.

'Crocodile, reptile—'

'Crocodile!' Zoë shouted and began snapping her extended arms, demonstrating its jaws. 'Crocodile!'

Alice joined in hopefully, 'Crocodiles in the canal?'

That moment, Ruth, our childminder, who's a regular, appeared, so I introduced Fee, saying, 'Ruth's my absolute saviour!' Which got me a funny look from both of them.

But now, Fee says, 'Maybe I'd better just find my train. Alisdair will be wanting me back. I would like to use your telephone, if you wouldn't mind? To see how he is?'

'Of course. And you'll have a snack before you go?'

She calls from our house phone: I can hear him from across the room, bellowing as if he's literally calling from Northumberland, querulously critiquing the care Fee's sister is giving him while she's away. 'Margaret is a good cook but she fusses about my diet. And she insists on parking my chair under the big chestnut tree so she hasna' to hurry outside every ten minutes and check I'm in the shade.'

'Well, I'll soon be back to ignore your wants, won't I?'

This teasing has developed over the time Alisdair's become increasingly disabled. I'm certain she'd otherwise feel like throwing things at him; bossy, demanding, and a stickler for women's place as helpmeets to their men.

'Och, I've missed you. Will you give my regards to Jenny and the bairns and tell Max not to leave it so long between visits?'

She's a lovely old-style mum, devoted to family and home. But stuck in a faith that restricts her talents. Hugging goodbye, a little part of me is envious of her calm approach to everything. A big part of me can't wait to get back to the problems we're solving at the lab.

'Almost forgot!' she says, fishing in her large handbag. 'A small thank-you for my holiday—Thornton's—they make such good chocolates, don't they?'

Alice dances up and down. 'Yummy!'

'Such a large box, you shouldn't!' I say.

'And,' Fee pulls out a paperback book, 'it's Alisdair's last publication, I expect. *Living with Uncertainty.*' She smiles: not meeting our eyes. Is that ironic? Not Fee. Apologetic. She must feel embarrassed, pressing Alisdair's rants on us as a goodbye present.

Max puts an arm around her shoulders, 'Mam, thank him for us? And don't forget to look after yourself. You're not missing the Carers' Group meetings, are you? Carers need plenty of breaks.' Their closeness gets to me, he cares so much about them. They depend so much on him. Even at a distance.

'Max, always the doctor,' she laughs. 'You and Jenny make sure you spend enough time together, with and without these little ones. Who are very important. And you will … read the book?'

Crouching down, she hugs Alice and Zoë. 'Grandma. I like the snake game,' Alice says.

'I hope you like the ladders too!' She stands.

Alice embraces Fee's thighs. Zoë embraces Alice. 'Bye, bye, Grandma!' Holidays over. Tomorrow Max and I go back to work, and the girls go to Ruth's. I always miss them.

Later, Max flips through his father's book. 'A changeless God in a changing world. A word to wives. Och, Dad, busy as ever, even in a wheelchair.' He snaps the book shut.

'Will you read it?'

'Maybe. Next holiday.'

'Not on a boat. So why's Daze here? London is where the action is.'

'I suppose she sold to the big guys—stuff from that London exhibition we saw—and invested in the boat? Jen: if she's staying here, we'll have to accept it.'

'My contract's up for renewal, I can't do with family interference. Though I wonder.' Max gives me a look, like, it's none of my business. 'Okay, back when I graduated, and Daze had that baby, there was an obvious mystery. I still need to be the one who untangles mysteries, even if it's organised, legal, team-player, as I said to Leila. I'm busy.'

'Yes, you do seem to be,' Max says. Drily Scottish.

'And so are you, don't forget.'

Daze

MID AUGUST

The sun dips, the shadows are lengthening. Daisy Potter strides diagonally across the University Parks towards a maze of dreary blocks varying in size and age, half hidden beyond some trees: the Oxford University Science Area. A blustery breeze agitates the trees. Something red suddenly enters her field of vision. She reaches out, catches the plastic Frisbee, and spins it expertly back towards a group of teens.

'Thanks you: you play? You like join us?'

Overseas language students. Daze waves. 'Another time!'

She circumnavigates the University cricket ground, which ripples with leisured applause as another couple of runs are added to the home team score. Passing through the wrought-iron gates she turns down Parks Road, briefly noting the intriguing architecture of the Natural

History and Pitt Rivers museums. Around the corner, she enters the Science Area. At the first grimly rationalist building, she asks for Jenny Mullins. 'Biochemistry,' the porter murmurs, consulting a list. He gives her directions.

The Biochemistry porter says, 'Wait here, Jenny will come down.' Daze waits, eyeing the notices on a board, but hardly reading them, horribly conscious of how nervous she is. It's important to appear cool. Her new project would benefit from some of Jenny's expertise. In fact, Life probably thumped them against each other on purpose.

'Daze?'

She twizzles on her heels, hands thrust deep into the pockets of her signature black jeans. Four-Eyes in work mode, lab coat, blue denims and a pink top. 'Hi, yeah, unusual visitor. I was in the Parks, and thought of you.'

Jenny doesn't take up the flip style as offered: in fact she frowns, hand to her mouth, worried. 'Is this about Max bashing your boat? It's not—you haven't come about insurance and stuff? You should've called us right away, or— You know, we're both really sorry. Max isn't usually careless.'

Jenny in a state. On edge: one to me, Daze realises. 'Oh no, I owe you an apology—for the language.' Jenny half-smiles. 'Though Max needs boat-driving lessons if he's gonna indulge in canal holidays. Oxford Canal's a narrow one and you don't want to keep cannoning into everybody's butt like a bat out of hell.'

'Bear with sore head, more like.' Jenny laughs, obviously relieved.

'Just a few questions I thought of, you might know the answers. And, that stuff you had from your aunt Val, and the printouts about my baby? You've kept it all?'

'Gosh, it's been nine years, we've moved around a bit. I may've done. I thought you didn't want to know about it.' Two to me, then, thinks Daze.

'I didn't back then. But now, I've begun a relevant project.' Her request must sound casual, and like it's part of her work, not her personal life. This public reception area's not quite the right place—as

Daze hunts for ideas where they might go, Jenny interrupts decisively, 'Look, hang about,' glancing at her watch. 'Give me ten, and I'll join you. I generally pack up around now.'

Left standing in the spacious bright lobby, Daze almost hears her heart pumping. She looks around: can't simply sit like a lemon on one of the long black leather-look sofas by the plate glass windows. Must appear nonchalant and purposeful to anyone passing by. A neat person with a briefcase enters the building, and enquires for reception. Daze points the way, then walks up to a noticeboard and mimes reading the contents.

She employs mindfulness and yoga breathing, with clock-watching slotted in. It's fifteen minutes before she hears feet on the stairs and Jenny reappears, bag on her shoulder, briefcase, rattling car keys.

'Nice place, pity about the brutalist architecture,' Daze says.

'Mm: so, how can I help—?'

'Project I'm into.'

Jenny collects a plastic carrier of shopping from the porter as they leave the building. They head out towards Parks Road. Daze rootles in her canvas tote bag, and offers Jenny 'Either or neither: choc bar or a ciggie?'

'Choc, if that's okay. I'm a bit bushed.'

Daze breaks the Snickers bar into halves, gives one to Jenny, replaces hers in her bag, and lights up. 'To update: your Dad sold the Hackney studio—with my agreement, I'll add. I was well ready to move, and I got the boat off someone I used to know. But, what I need's a warehouse, or similar.'

'For?'

'Remember Judy Chicago—feminist artist your Mum found interesting? *Womanhouse* installations? California, 1970's?'

'Maybe ... sounds like Mum.'

'Well, anyways, she—Chicago—organised a needlework enterprise—like, needlework, classic housewifely skill? Only instead of pretty flowers and birds, it was about birth, the messy side of female. Called The Birth Project.'

'Right ... so? Not Persephone again?'

'Nope: not what you think. I'm thinking from the kid's viewpoint, our very first experiences of the world. But, yes—' Daze looks around: they are alone, in a long tree-lined road opposite what must be a college. 'It's possible—actually, I'm also thinking it's about the right time to try having another baby.'

She watches Jenny's astonished face: mouth opens, about to speak. 'Don't choke on your chocolate. Don't say anything. Yet. Bio clock ticking, was told I should ask a few questions. You've got the answers.'

Jenny switches hands with the plastic carrier and the briefcase. She takes a breath. 'Okay, not for art, for real. But. That's still a big question. For me to answer. You'd do better to see a genetic counsellor.'

'And all research stuff you didn't hand over to me.'

'The research you said you weren't interested in at the time.'

Daze shrugs. 'I know: I wasn't clever was I? I was post-natal: you must know that feeling. But I'd keep things I had, specially important stuff belonging to somebody else? So—'

'Listen,' Jenny says, bossy and exasperating as ever, 'whether or not I have it all, I will explain the findings on your baby—if Max or my Dad didn't or you've forgotten. What I can't do is predict outcomes. There might be several conception options ... But if you're busy with your career, d'you really want a kid?'

Daze considers Jenny. The bag of groceries and the briefcase: how like their Mum. Even the hair, a chignon with drifting bits falling from its clasp. 'You've combined kiddies and whatever it is you do, screwing cells around?'

'Yes: and the nursery closes in half an hour. It's time I got going. Can I take you home—to the boat? Car's down the road.' She clinks her keys.

'Enjoy your holidays on the water?' Daze asks as they resume walking, hoping to take the trick.

'Huh—we took Max's mother to give her a break. Not sure we'll do it again.'

A few yards on, Jenny stops by a Land Rover Discovery.

'Yours?' Daze says, 'Four-wheel drive. Cool.'

'Four wheel drive's useful for visiting his parents, Max says. It snows a lot there.'

Inside, the car is cluttered: Jenny transfers baby wipes, board books, and one pink Wellington to the back. Daze climbs in the front. As she sits, there's a scrunch. 'Think I destroyed something.' She fishes from under her an open bag of crisps.

'Whoops—not very healthy. A treat when I collected them late.'

Daze brushes broken crisps out onto the road, 'I shan't tell,' and eats some of those left in the bag. Jenny starts the car. They turn out into the road.

'Listen,' Jenny says. 'Are you with anyone special right now? What does he think?' Daze notices the softer tones, though she resents the question.

'No, I'm doing this alone.'

'Okay. I'm not asking how you plan to get pregnant. I'm asking how you'd manage with a baby. I mean, I've got a partner and we can afford childcare … If you love your job, and your kids, and your partner, it's still hard.'

Daze takes another critical look at her stepsister. This is interesting. Max and Jen was the romance of the year, wasn't it? Whichever year that was?

'You begin to wonder where those good times went. We had a wonderful spring holiday, just me and Max. In Egypt, Sharm? We learned to dive, and we went out in a glass-bottomed boat, and we had fun. But that's not a regular thing. Watching kids on a narrowboat wasn't like, relaxing. And you couldn't get away like that—could you?'

'There are other ways to live, and raise kiddies, called choices. Some of us survive without a trip on a glass-bottomed boat.'

'Yeah, well: holidays do make life easier. Like, time to be alone? Together? So if you can't. I'm just saying—'

They're now driving down Walton Street. Daze seizes Jenny's left arm, 'Left here, look—see that building? Can you stop?'

'Don't! Bugger you, I'm driving! S'pose a child ran out?'

'One didn't.'

'I can't. It's all narrow and parked up.' But she begins to slow.

Daze knows she gave Jenny a fright. But this is important. 'Sorry, but I have to show you. This.' They leave the Discovery parked half on the pavement, and Daze propels Jenny back up the narrow street towards a small dilapidated warehouse with peeling paint and a For Sale board. 'It's got planning permission for community use. Soon as I saw it I knew: I'll sell the boat and live there.' No response. 'It was a printers', so use for art stuff wouldn't be a big change. Would it?'

'Maybe not.'

'So I think I'll get it. There's just one problem: a religious organization, or maybe a monk or a priest, I've heard rumours that's my opposition. Whatever ... I can walk down the towpath from here. Thanks for the ride.'

'Okay, I'm sure we've got Aunt Val's info. You didn't say what you're working on now.'

'Teaching art, what else? Maternity cover.'

'That's good.'

'Bloody marvellous: I so love teenagers.'

As the Land Rover turns, awkwardly, and drives away, Daze considers: Jenny Four-Eyes has let the mask drop. Can even objective Jen be unhappy when she's got all the everything a person's supposed to want? And Max, well he's a bit of a saint, for a man, so there's two sides to it.

Jenny

SAME EVENING

I sit in the car, thoughts whirling. Did Daze read me? Can do without her, gave me this creepy feeling like 'I've been here before', at a juncture in my life when Daze bounces up, clearly making some statement of her own, one that trumps what I am about to do.

Leila's guess was spot-on. Rich, our Principal Investigator, told me, in advance of everyone else: 'It's a bit of a rush: but in April, I'll be presenting your work to the world—at least, to a rather important—for us—conference in the upcoming Easter break. In California. So, what're you going to do first, Jenny?'

'Submit an abstract, three months before, that'd be—soon after Christmas?'

Hopefully, I'll have something worth submitting, results that point in the direction we're going and add a bit of certainty to progress in the field. Rich'll do the presentation, but it's basically me who's going to be writing up our work. Which is such a great chance.

I can't, shan't, let Rich down. He's bound to get me funding now, isn't he?

Isn't he? I drive to the nursery, pick up the girls, drive home. In the kitchen, I begin making them a sandwich each, and slicing apples for them. Something jazzy comes on the radio: without thinking, I swing my hips to it, then we're dancing, all of us, me with half an apple in one hand and the knife in the other.

They laugh. 'Look at Mummy dancing!'

As I pass the sink, I drop the knife into it. Then the apple on the counter, and seize their hands, pick them up and whirl them round.

We dance until the jazzy music's over, and then they won't sit at the table, they drape themselves on the sofa in the little alcove we call the family room, and flop around, eating and asking where Daddy is.

If Max was here, he'd dance.

Gives me a little pang, thinking that: and, seeing in my head me, my sister Hattie, and Mum, when we were very small. Before our Daddy went to work at Caltech. Before the era of Des and Daze.

'Bath time!' How upbeat I sound.

Finally, girls clean and in PJs, curtains drawn, evening sun trying to slither through millimetre gaps, stories read, backs rubbed, kisses and hugs done, I creep downstairs to begin chopping veg for a stir-fry.

'Daddy, Daddy!' The car in the drive, the key in the door, small feet scampering on the stairs. Sleep was let's pretend, *Dead Lions*—a game

Ruth taught them.

'Jenny? I come in and I find—' Max can't hide it, though: that grin says it all, and the smiley eyes: he's only too pleased to find his daughters awake.

'We were waiting on the land-*ing*!' Alice sing-songs, leaping up and down. Max swings Zoë up in his arms, Zoë clutching her blankie, sucking her thumb round it, thumping her other hand on Max's shoulder.

'Well, Daddy can take you right back to bed then!' I say, to family laughter.

'Daddy—' Zoë begins, nuzzling Max, and leaving the rest of her sentence hanging in the air. Their two dark heads are close as he gives her a kiss. 'Zoëy-Zo, how was your day?'

'Daddy-daddy.' She nuzzles more. Sniffing his neck. I know that smell so well: does Zoë love it too?

'Okay. Let's have story, shall we, bairns? I can talk with Mummy later.'

'All night!' Alice giggles. 'You have the big bed where you talk *all night*!'

She dances off and fetches four or five picture books. They slide precariously in her grasp. 'Off we go—had your baths? Oh dear: I like doing your baths—teeth all brushed? Bring the storybooks, Ally, we'll maybe have time for two!' Max is heading for the hallway: Alice drops the books at his feet.

I'll open some wine, and tell him my important news … getting the boring subjects out of the way first … We both yawn over dinner.

'Listen. In three weeks, Alice starts proper school. Ruth and I need to agree about the school run. Extra driving, in late afternoon traffic, will she be okay about collecting them from two different places? Ask for extra pay? We should've thought before, I know.' Max frowns. 'Now you're looking like your father.' It's not just the dark eyebrows, but how he's drawn them together. Not just the penetrating blue eyes, but their expression. 'Do I offer her more? Before she asks? Or?'

He shrugs. 'If that's what you want. I've some reservations.'

'Really?'

He takes a long breath. 'She obviously loves and empathises with children, she's kind and reliable, her home's clean and neat, the price is right. All ticks the boxes for me. But, they've maybe grown beyond her nannying skills?'

'Zoë hasn't. What's the alternative?' Max looks up as I rise and gather the plates. 'And your problem is?'

'I think you know.'

'Spell it out?'

'For example, in the street outside the surgery today, a group with banners, *Let the children come*. One of the receptionists assumed it was an anti-abortion demonstration. I looked out, Ruth was there, thoroughly involved. What a relief, I then realised they were advertising the happy-clappy Holiday Club.'

'Which Alice and Zoë will enjoy next week. It's fun, they're reliable.'

'Suppose a patient complained, *I saw Dr Mullins's little girl with one of those extreme pro-life types?*' Max says, going outside to take the rubbish to the bin.

'So it wasn't anti-abortion,' I say when he comes back, 'and how many of your patients would recognise your family? I'd tell them we're very inclusive, employing a pro-lifer.'

'Hah, bright lassie,' Max shakes his head, and the new bin-bag. 'Why didn't I think of that?'

I bat him softly, 'Blinded by prejudice?'

'Possibly. Though I'll remind you of what you said about Dad's church, *it's a horrible system. I'm sorry you were caught in it—*'

'It's not the same.'

'No? Ruthie's a smiley woman, with a bouncy attitude, and Dad's a grim, stringily built Scot with iron-grey hair.'

'You've noticed! Hey, Daze turned up at the lab today.'

'Daze? Don't tell me. About my crashing into her boat. She doesn't want money, does she?'

'Absolutely not a problem. I apologised profusely: she's cool. But she's trying to buy a place here. And as Daze usually means trouble—'

'Och, let's cross that bridge if we come to it,' he says, fishing into his medical bag. He pulls out a leaflet, and presses it into my hand. 'You know how Oxford's always hosted a shifting population of homeless people caught in the cycle of deprivation? St Hildie's are looking into providing a day centre.'

'Nice artwork.' I lay it aside, and wipe the kitchen counters. 'David's a busy little bee, then.'

'David was in touch today. They're ready to close the deal on those premises they were after. Listen: *Reverend David Robertson's experience and commitment has convinced the St Hildegard Foundation and the Council that the homeless work should be re-started, relocated further into the City, and expanded. Our aim is to set the Retreat Centre free to do what it does best, providing a superb relaxing context for times of quiet and spiritual renewal, encouraging raised awareness both of ourselves and of how we can be of service to others.*'

'Mm, *service to others* made you late,' I say.

Max follows me around, lecturing: 'Yes, sorry. David's thinking we could help by adding a clinic. Often people end up living rough because they have mental health issues. They avoid attending the surgery when they're unwell, because they discern the hostility of other patients in the waiting room.'

'So who's "we"?'

'Well, me actually.' I open my mouth: Max interrupts, 'No, listen, St Hildie's did a lot for homeless people. Until the last Director sidelined practical work, to concentrate on running spirituality weekends and writing. David's decided to revive the homeless programme in separate premises. Organising a weekly drop-in clinic might stretch my medical skills a bit further, it's very worthwhile. I want to be involved.'

This is the worst news. I need Max onside for me. 'Your work's already worthwhile. David's making absurd demands.'

'Jen, you usually support equality and inclusivity. I can't see why—'

'Because you think David needs help. He doesn't. We accept him, society accepts him. If his parents and yours can't, they're a minority.

You encouraged his application to the St Hildie's job. That's enough.'

'David's been homeless himself. He's come through some rough times, he has a lot to offer.'

'Surf bum to priest. David's the son your father wanted.'

Max laughs. 'Hardly.'

'David has to realise you haven't time to give. We don't see each other enough.'

'You're welcome to help. We're running a second hand clothes stall …'

I'm getting stressed, feeling tense. How do I introduce my news, and the need for extra time to spend on work? 'Please, I'm not the nurse type, I don't enjoy helping messy people— I'm not like Rachel …'

'No, you're not, though I recall you did well with her scrawny wee bairn when you'd never changed a nappy in your life. And you're very organized.' His eyes are dark with disappointment. And it's true: he knows I'm hopelessly squeamish in a clinical context. 'I thought you'd be—'

'I haven't changed! Or I'd be a doctor like Mum—remember you left me with your father? When he was having a relapse?'

'It's not that—'

I can't unsay mentioning saintly Rachel, this submissive woman whom Alisdair wanted as a daughter-in-law. Even though I know she realised Max wasn't interested, the thought of her can haunt me whenever he reverts to family type, and expects that unthinking, childlike loyalty in a wife. He was trained to expect it. He can assume I'll fall into role like the girls he grew up alongside. 'I'm sorry: I did charity stuff when I was a student, now I don't have that kind of time. Even for your cousin whose family behave as if he was dead.'

Max doesn't argue. He knows what he's done, and walks away, closing the kitchen door as he goes. I stand leaning against the table, arms wrapped around my body.

Then I hear the piano: Eric Satie's *Je te veux*.

How can he want me, but not who I am?

Normally we're cool about the demands of my career. I put up with his. The overlap's so much less than when we met.

I open my laptop and try to distract myself with work. I toy with sending Ruth an e-mail about the school run. Finally I creep into the living room to find Max supine on the sofa, under the *British Medical Journal*, eyes closed, watched by Zoë's teddy. Something rather unusual is playing on the radio. 'Philip Glass,' he says.

'Aren't we still soul mates?'

'Aye.'

'*Je te veux*, then? We keep Ruth and I'll pay the extra?'

He reaches out. I let him take my hand, and perch on the edge of the sofa. 'Jen, baby, I'm sorry I reacted.'

'You and me were a team. I know it sounds clichéd, but—'

Max says, 'We are. We are.'

I don't mention Daze's project. I certainly don't mention the conference. I swallow down a confused, teary sensation, and suggest a glass of wine.

Max

SEPTEMBER, A DINNER PARTY

So: Jenny's boss has thrown her a conference paper to write. Which is wonderful news, in terms of her career. 'But let's not get lost under it: work isn't the only thing that defines us.'

Jen gives me a look.

I plough on, 'Before you're too tied up with that, could we manage a team effort? Maybe an intimate dinner party, friends in for a quiet evening to celebrate David's appointment as Director of St Hildegard's Retreat Centre? And then there's Eliot, now he's a partner at the surgery, be good to celebrate that.'

'You do realise both of those are your friends, not mine?' Jenny comments, drily teasing.

'Eliot's married to Shaz, she's one of your friends. Charlie is Alice's other half.'

'Clever one,' says Jen. 'Can't argue, can I? Though Alice and Charlie aren't invited. So, Eliot's your partner: does David have one? I mean, sometimes I could think he's yours.'

'I'll take that as a bad joke, shall I?'

'Take it as you hear it. Does he?'

'No idea.'

'You'd better find out. I s'pose Shaz and Eliot aren't going to be sniffy if he has?'

'Mm. David's rather high profile as Director of St Hildegard's.'

'So publicly, he's on his own?'

'It's not me, it's—I'll leave it up to him, okay with you?'

'Have to be,' she says.

Saturday evening, bairns in bed, meal ready, table laid. Jen, almost repentant for the unpleasant remark, now rather stunning in what she calls her bodacious Boden, with clouds of what she insists is not perfume or scent but fragrance.

The bell goes: 'Max, get that?'

David, with a bulging canvas bag, Belgian chocolates, and brandy. Resplendently suave in white shirt, no collar, dog or otherwise, and tight black jeans. Kind of a blond, bespectacled version of Hamlet. I perform my *kiddies asleep upstairs* pantomime: David exaggeratedly creeps over the step.

Jenny smiles, wanly.

In our tidied-up, kitchen-family room, he plumps the brandy down on the counter. And grins. Proper crystal brandy glasses such as we somehow didn't buy or receive as wedding presents emerge from the big canvas shopping bag. 'See them as a very late wedding present?' David undoes the bubble wrap and places them carefully in two lines of three. 'So—who're your mates—the couple?'

'Eliot's a partner at the surgery: we're celebrating that he's recently got parity, that is, become part of the business. His daughter is Alice's conjoined twin. *Best mates* in the latest nursery slang. And his wife—Shaz—what's Shaz do, Jen?'

'Yoga teacher. Own studio. Used to be an occupational therapist.

Shaz is the mother of Charlie—she and Alice are practically Siamese twins.'

'So Max just said.'

'Sorry. Great minds. Shaz is not a bit like me, you'll love her.'

'Aw, Jenny—' David says, and gives her a hug.

'Jenny swears that Shaz almost fainted away when they met: *Everyone told me Max Mullins had this scary wife who works in genetics, that can't really be you?*'

'She did! Hey, the brandy's a great idea.'

'You see—I do love you.'

'Yeah, well—door?'

'I'll go.' On the step are Eliot, clutching two bottles of red wine, and a bouquet of exotic flowers, and Shaz, an exotic flower herself, knockout glamorous, wrapped up in the red shimmery folds of something soft over a black minidress. 'Max—' She envelops me in her fragrance and her strong, slim, over-tanned arms, and gives me a hug and two air kisses. All far too much to think about.

'And this is your cousin?' Shaz throws David an approving glance as she encounters him in the hall, and shakes hands. 'Jen's told me about you.'

'All good, I hope?'

'You're from Australia?'

'But Max and I grew up together in Scotland.'

Shaz beams at David, then, more a flamingo than a flower, teetering in her very high heels, adds 'It's so warm, isn't it—d'you mind if I throw off this pashmina?'

Shaz's dress is backless to the waist. Her red floaty thing's gathered up by Jenny and carried away, as we return to the kitchen, and Eliot indicates the wine: 'Shall I open this? Let it breathe?'

'Meal's ready: Max could you get everyone sitting down?'

It's not quite twilight. We start on the wine while Jenny sorts the vegetables and brings the food to the table. A draught flares the flames of the long red candles, our shadows dance on the walls. The exotic bouquet, strelitzia and lilies, mingles a heavy scent with the women's fragrances and the steaming casserole of Mexican food. Exotic and erotic. 'Max? Pass it along to David, I said?'

'Oh yes, sorry. Dave?'

'Hey, this is amazing!' Shaz beams at Jenny.

'Almost authentic Rick Bayliss recipe. Dad sent me the Mexican Kitchen cookbook.'

'You are so—God, she's been deceiving us! I've only ever eaten baked beans here before. With the kids, of course!'

Eliot is explaining to David, rationally and meticulously, his reasons for becoming a GP. Including how parity works financially. David looks intelligently interested: Shaz is rolling her eyes.

She turns to Jen, 'So, almost time for real school: are you ready for the plunge? Monday next week, bye, bye, baby.'

'Me? It's Alice's adventure. She's raring for it.'

'Charlie says I mustn't cry at the school gates. I'm the family baby, so her cousins are all older—they told her, "Don't look back when your mum cries". Isn't that knowing? Like, did we talk like that?'

'They grow up too fast,' Eliot says.

'He wants another, don't you sweetie?'

Shaz's pouting at Eliot kills conversation: how can Jen be friends with this woman? Even if they did socialise at toddler group and use the same nursery? Eliot is clearly embarrassed; David surprisingly and deftly changes the subject, turning to Shaz and asking her how long and where she trained as a yoga teacher—did she spend time in India?

Shaz smiles, and describes her guru: then says, 'It's not necessary to go there, you know. But it does have a mysterious feel, India.' She sighs. Then asks David, with a gorgeous smile, the direct question: why he became a priest.

'Well, the short answer is, one day, when I'd been working as a lifeguard for a couple of years, I came back from surfing with a fish I'd caught out there in the ocean. And you'll recall from Sunday School, if you went along to one, that Jesus said to his disciples, *Come and I'll make you fishers of men*. I took up the challenge.'

'Gosh,' Shaz says.

'After a few other less fun experiences—'

Bad move: Shaz opens her mouth to ask more, I shoot David a glance, Jenny fiddles with her fork, and Eliot glances at David and back at his food.

'—but now I'm busy learning the history of everything in Oxford: we were at the Perch the other day. I was delighted that Inspector Morse drank at the Perch, as well as C.S. Lewis. Both English heroes of mine.'

Good: he's got himself out of anything that might develop.

'So, St Hildegard's: Max mentioned you're reviving a tradition there?'

'Not exactly there. We're buying another place for the Homeless Centre. Hildie's occupies a large, leafy plot, behind huge walls, in east Oxford. The kind of place you might imagine Hildegard doing all that writing and composing. Bit of an oasis in the midst of a noisy community: student housing, immigrant families, muesli-landers. Though Hildegard was also a healer, and that location feels right to me.'

'So why invest in another property?' Shaz asks.

'Well, accessibility is essential for a day centre. Folks tend to hang out downtown, so we'll be nearby. Do you have an interest? I can let you have some information?'

Shaz seems not to want to go wherever David's leading. Instead, she says, 'Great photo of your girls,' and inclines her head towards the bookshelves, where Alice and Zoë smile from a photo frame. 'Didn't he do well?'

'Who?'

'The guy who took the pre-school pics at nursery last term ... Alice has got that Jenny look, the one that says "trust me, I'm a scientist with integrity, *and* femininity"—all blonde and English roses. Zoë— she's just the spit of Max, the black hair and blue eyes, very Scottish.' She pauses briefly, 'Only girly too, you know.'

'God, Shaz,' Eliot is murmuring. She bats him gently.

Shaz's overt sexual playfulness is a bit disturbing, I hunt about for something boring to deflect it. 'More veg anyone? Jen, pass the dish down, darling.'

'There's rice left, and mangetout. Okay, they're not Mexican, but, they are green.'

'So what happened to the worries about carbon footprints?' I tease.

Time for Jen to bat me, 'Shut up: everyone can sin sometimes, can't they?'

'I didn't mean to kill the conversation, though that question generally does,' David says, ignoring innuendos and playful remarks. 'To answer your question, Shaz, being a priest is a lot like being any other kind of professional. People call on you when they have a need, and you answer it.'

Shaz declines more veg, and gets argumentative. 'That bloke at Headleigh Parish wouldn't christen Charlie, would he?'

Jenny adds, 'Max's father wasn't keen to do Alice and Zo-zo, but Max qualifies, as a family member, don't you, babe?'

If Jenny's calling me 'babe' in public, then she, as well as Shaz, is downing the red wine too fast. I dourly add, 'Normally the children of lapsed Presbyterians are in a bit of a dubious category. Dad fudged the issue and maybe as he's a bit high-profile nobody liked to demur.'

'I think it's the parents' decision.'

'Well, it's not a human right, Shaz. It's really quite a solemn vow. No point in making a promise that's not seriously meant,' David responds, causing a very awkward silence.

'I was possibly done twice,' says Eliot, so quietly that Jenny doesn't hear, but breaks the silence by jumping to her feet, asking 'Pudding? I've made individual ones—Max, plates!'

I lean over to gather them. David turns to Eliot, 'Twice, how was that?'

Looking embarrassed, he explains, 'My adoptive parents wanted the works, apparently the vicar said "never mind if he's been done already, in the circumstances we can dunk him again."'

David shrugs, with a grin at Eliot. At the dishwasher, stacking plates,

I wonder whatever prompted me to invite this crazy combination of humanity? How did Eliot and Shaz get to be together? What'll we all discuss after the meal's over? At the Manse, games were played when we had awkward combinations of visitors, but that's neither sophisticated nor normal.

Jenny seems to be turning each perfect summer pudding out of its ramekin onto its own dish, serving it as an island in a pale sea of crème fraiche, topped off with a raspberry sauce. She's bringing them to the table on a tray when the wall phone rings.

Bummer. Out of medical habit I leap to answer it, toppling my abandoned chair, and nearly knocking wife and tray of puddings flying.

'Hell, Max, careful!' I grab the phone from its cradle. Escape from the messy talk?

A torrent of words streams down the line: little sister Kirsty has chosen Saturday evening for an intimate sibling consultation.

'I can't talk,' I say, watching the dynamics at the table. The two women have gone head to head, murmuring: both have their hair piled up tonight, their necks are long and white in the candlelight. Two swans. David looks thoughtful. Eliot looks tired. Dark marks under those penetrating brown eyes. My replies to Kirsty are anodyne and short. 'No, I don't know how Dad is at the moment. Oh, gosh, I hope not. I can discuss your career moves if we fix up a time? Will that do? No, not a word. Let me know? Yep, bye for now, bye then.'

'My sister,' I say, putting the phone back. 'Am I my sister's keeper?'

'Kirsty,' Jenny says, 'We always say, about Max's sisters, that Kirsty needs advice, Erin gives advice.'

David laughs.

Shaz says, 'Two sisters?'

'And two brothers. Too many of us, typical pastor's family.' I pick up my chair, stand it in place, and sit. The dessert's delicious. Everyone eats in silence, until Shaz waves her spoon at me, 'Must've been lively at your place.'

'Could be. In more ways than one. But, life's never perfect, is it? Jenny, this is wonderful: more raspberry sauce, anyone? Eliot? David?'

The sauce passes around the table.

Shaz says, 'Jen, I'd love the recipe. Is it', she pauses, leaning across confidentially, '*easy-peasy?*'

Eliot, where did you find her? I think. The conversation moves rapidly to childhood phrases, rhyming slang, and what was everyone's most embarrassing moment and favourite teacher, at primary school. While I castigate myself for mean thoughts..

When the front door closes on David, the last to leave, I lean against it thinking about Kirsty's message. Dad not so good, herself unsure about her future career. The boyfriend's parents are unhappy: more like devastated, and disapproving? Furious, even? How much more will ours be!

But Jenny's found Shaz's scarlet and gold pashmina, lying forgotten on the sofa, and twirls down the passage wearing it, singing the exotic tune which introduces Carmen, from Bizet's opera. *Po-pom-pom-pom...po-pom-pom*-pom. She arrives at the front door, takes hold of my tie, tilts her head back, ready to be kissed. This is then time to accept the eroticism of the evening, and end accordingly. We go with it. I slide my arms around her, stroking her behind, and kissing her soft mouth.

Jenny.

LATE SEPTEMBER

Rain beats on the windows. In the kitchen, I'm doing breakfasts, and the radio presenter breaks into the music to tell us the time. I glance across the room, and notice I've circled today on the calendar: 'Daze after school'.

I'd forgotten Daze's request. Probably because Rich Woods has now passed me something even scarier than writing up our work: a doctoral student to supervise. Proving I can do all this is going to affect that funding application. He's testing my commitment.

Max walks into the room as I'm mumbling to myself, 'Oh B, B, B—', and plopping the ingredients for two chocolate smoothies into the goblet of the mixer, a child each side of me, jumping up and down.

'B?' Max teases, making coffee.

'Ugger,' I say. 'I'm s'posed to be at Daze's after school, and I haven't dug out her stuff yet.'

'Cancel. She can't be in a hurry for it, she's in Banbury, isn't she? Until Christmas?'

'Leaving tomorrow. I wanted her to have it.'

'She wouldn't do it for you.'

'So I won't need to see her again. When she comes back. So B.'

'You *always spell things*. What's B for?'

'B? B is for—bright, beautiful, Big Girl Alice.'

'No it's not!' Alice laughs. Then Zoë laughs, and Alice says, 'B is for bug—'

'Yes! B is for Bug: we call them insects, but the Americans call them bugs. Grandpa Canada calls them bugs, doesn't he? Mummy's Daddy calls them bugs?'

'It's not, it's not!'

'Alice! Quiet, please. Or you'll be sitting on the naughty stair.'

'B must sit on the stair, Daddy.'

'Ssh!' I say, and they settle with their drinks and cereal. Max says to me, soft and conspiratorially, 'What are we in for? Curious, and precocious, like her mummy.'

I take a long, deep, breath, and butter some toast. Okay, okay: I can do it all. And the Mummy-thing. It's Friday, Ruth runs an after-school club on Fridays. I'll collect the girls myself, and we'll visit Daze. That all means leaving work early.

*

Three-fifteen, I'm outside the school, settling the kids in the car, when Shaz bounces up. 'Made a profit this year, so we're off to New York, Christmas shopping! So cool!' She does a little dance. 'And look—new Ugg boots!'

'What'll Eliot do while you browse the aisles?' I smile.

'Eliot? I'm going with my sister. You want to join us?'

'In my dreams: I have a paper to write.'

Shaz shakes her head. 'Your poor clever mummy,' she makes a long face so funny that Alice hangs out of her seat giggling, while Charlie capers on the pavement. 'Shall we go to the swings, then?'

'Oh Shaz, we can't, I made a date with *my* sister. In Jericho.'

'Mumm*eee*—'

'How about—there's swings near hers—how about we go to that playground? Before?'

'No worries,' Shaz says. 'Good playground?'

'Not bad. We found it in the holidays.'

'Hey, you never told me: how did it go with Grandma along? Wasn't the holiday on some boat you were loaned by Max's friend?'

I roll my eyes, 'Don't ask. Grandma was okay but—let's say Max has no idea how much I hated that boat.'

'Aw, Jen—'

'Mummy are we going now?'

'Yes: swings, then Aunty Daze's.'

At the canal, we both park in Aristotle Lane. Alice and Charlie rush towards the swings, jump on, and demand to be pushed higher and higher. Then the wind catches at our clothes as Shaz and I leap aboard the roundabout. Shaz pushes off with her foot, and we whirl round, Zoë sitting on my lap.

Then, because Alice and Charlie won't be parted, we all march along the towpath together, towards Daze's boat, Zoë in the buggy, Alice and Charlie charging ahead. Several narrowboats are moored, smoke curling from their chimneys, bicycles laid on their roofs.

'Look at that, a village on the water. So romantic,' says Shaz, as mud squelches under our boots. 'Careful, careful!' we mummies call to the girls.

'And your sister *lives* on one?'

'She does. For now.'

Could do without Shaz.

Daze is looking out for us. 'Hey Alice! Hey! Four-eyes! Hey, *Alice!*'

'Alice an' Charlie!' Alice replies.

'An' Charlie!'
'C'mon *all* of you!'
'All of us?'
'Yeah, all. Plenty of space.'

The boat judders as Shaz, Alice, and Charlie climb aboard. I hand the buggy over, with Zoë in it. Daze is grinning like nobody's business, probably remembering the holiday disaster. I'm looking to see if there's any marks where we collided: nothing noticeable. 'Welcome to my narrowboat!' she chirps, as I step aboard, 'mind the gap!'

Shaz looks around a bit sniffily. Though as we duck through the door into the living area, we can see it's warm, clean, nicely painted, tidy.

'She's really *Charlotte*,' Alice says to Daze, giving Charlie a sharp poke. Charlie giggles. 'And she's my *best mate!*'

'Wicked!'

Alice is scornful. 'I've been on a *marrowboat before*. On our *marrowboat holiday*, Daddy crashed into *your* boat!'

'Into my *narrowboat*. 'Cos it's long and thin? Narrow?'

'Marrowboat! Daddy grew a marrow! An' it was long and *fat!*'

'Shush.'

'And I have the kettle on, ladies.' Daze clatters mugs onto the table. 'Saw you looking to see what kind of a housekeeper I am. Sit down everyone: I've even got bikkies. From Ben's in the covered market.'

There's a fire in the stove. Lapsang souchong tea for us, and chocolate soya milk for the girls. Shaz beams, 'Snug as bugs in a rug. Hey, that's a bit nasty isn't it? Bugs in a rug?' She acts a few shivers. 'Yuck. Dunno why I said that. Anyway, this is so exciting, isn't it?'

'Tea,' says Daze, 'with or without? Soya or cows'? So, Four-Eyes, how're the stem cells, or whatever it is you're manipulating these days?'

I don't get to say, because the girls wriggle and giggle, intrigued with the idea of living full time on a boat, and soon slip off their seats, wanting to explore. We tour the living quarters, admiring the compact storage solutions. Which I well remember from Tim's *Mandalay*. Shaz spots a poster from Daze's London exhibition. 'Hey, Daisy, you're that artist who didn't get the Turner prize! You're a YBA—aren't you?'

Daze's cue to pull out some photos of her work. Installations in metal, wood, and latex. Constructions which, driven by a wind machine, play tunes made up of the voices of the viewers murmuring in the gallery, she says.

'You saw the exhibition, Jen?'

'We saw one of them.' We'd gone around with fixed smiles, trying to look like we knew why a giant condom, or pink banana, was suspended horizontally from the ceiling, or maybe that we hadn't seen it.

Daze takes the pictures back.

'So, what d'you do?'

'Yoga teacher?' Shaz says, 'and some aerobics?'

'Blimey—both?'

'Trained as an occupational therapist,' Shaz grins, shaking her head.

'Listen, guys,' Daze says, addressing me really, 'that old print shop I'm after, that's got permission for community use? It can be more than a studio and gallery: it can have kids' projects, something for pensioners, maybe for anyone who can't work?'

'What about your teaching job?'

'It's only maternity leave, till after Christmas. I'll plan a community event, get the neighbours' support, and apply. Everyone'll be used to me when I start putting up serious art, like installations. I mean, what'll a religious group do for the community that I can't?'

'But you don't have any guarantee on the place yet.'

'Hire the church hall, shan't I, for the taster? Then I'll have been making art accessible already, from the introductory event, and we can pressure the council we need that building. They don't want a block of flats. Or a homeless hostel. They don't yet know they want an arts centre, but they will.'

'Can I have a slot to advertise?' Shaz asks.

'You can have a room if you pay. Once we're up and running.'

'Big enterprise: you doing this on your own, Daze?'

'You offering to help, Jen?'

'No, just wondering about the business side.'

'I can sort it all. Schedule the event for Easter bank holiday or something?'

Alice drags on my arm for attention. She's found a photo. 'Who's this? It's got sweets all stuck round it!' Daze leans across, then crouches by Alice and Charlie, holding out her hand for the picture. 'That's my mum!'

Zoë pushes in, Daze holds up the photo so we can all see. I remember she decorated the frame, when we were kids. A young girl, Daze's mother, laughing as she clutches her daisy-chain crown with one hand and holds her skirts down with the other. Her mouth, like Daze's, is wide and her nose turns up, and she's so pretty, with her big, dark eyes. What strikes me is, she's very, very young: don't think I noticed that when I was—probably the age she is there?

'Why did you—?' Alice pokes gently at the once brightly coloured wine gums.

'Stick the sweeties round? They were *jewels* for my mum. Her name's Jewels.'

'Oh—'

'She's a princess!' Charlie breathes.

I look at Alice, and Charlie, small, eager, and defenceless, and think what a dreadful thing Jewels did, and whether she was aware. Such a contrast: this lovely young woman, Jewels, and the skinny, awkward, spitting, clawing, fighting kid who Mum brought into our family, along with our stepfather, Des, her dad. Dozy Des and Jellybean: Aunt Val's names for them.

'Yeah, my mum: the fairy princess,' she says. The phrase drips with irony.

Daze stands the photo on the table between our mugs and the remaining cookies. 'Mum disappeared: poof, like that!' She claps her hands, then blows on them. 'Dandelion clock! Poof—Poof! All gone!'

'Did you cry?' Alice asks.

'Nah,' Daze says. 'Bit of a gypsy, my mum. Fucking exotic view of life, she must've had, wandering off, leaving me an' Dad.' Shaz recoils at the f-word, or maybe at the actions, and Daze's apparent lack of feeling. Daze turns to me, "Course, that's why you're here, Aunt Val's stuff."

'Sorry, I haven't had a moment. I will—'

'Bugger.'

'Said I'm really sorry.' Hate letting her down. See myself as a can-do person. But Daze shrugs it off.

'Oh, I'll be busy in this bum of a job: no worries. An' making a few plans for that Fun Day. So—'

'Thanks. Life can get a bit fraught—with kids and stuff.'

'It's been great to see your boat,' Shaz beams. Daze opens the doors: something furry zooms past. 'Whoops—this yours?'

'Trifle!' Daze scoops it up, a tortie cat with a big dark smudge across her nose. And yes, only three legs. 'Company that came with the boat.'

'Oh sweet!' says Shaz, smiling.

After a good long kitty-stroking time, we get going. 'Your stepsister's so creative,' Shaz says, as we tramp the towpath, back to our cars.

'Yeah, Daze's full of ideas!'

'Romantic story, about her mum. Eliot's never tried to find his birth mum.'

'Even more romance, it was the first Glastonbury Festival, where Jewels abandoned her. She was five, so she remembers.'

'Ouch, awful. How can a mum do that? No surprise she's a bit—'

'Yes, sorry about the language.'

'Funny, you had that canal holiday and then—hey, Alice said something about you guys bumping Daze's boat?'

'High point of the holiday? Don't ask!'

Later I describe our visit and Daze's new home to Max. 'The boat's a huge improvement on her last place, but she needs more space. Remember when we visited her warehouse studio, with the washbasin and cooker behind a curtain in the corner? When Alice was tiny?'

'With the communal lavatory, circa 1890, down the communal hall.'

'And a skylight a mile overhead!'

We laugh: then Max remarks how strangely Daze can be a catalyst in our lives.

Max

EARLY OCTOBER

The knocker, whoever it is, doesn't enter. I know who this is, and picture her outside, hesitant. 'Come *in*.'

First the hand holding a mug of coffee, then one black-trousered leg, then Steffie herself. Her shirt, tied at her waist, is printed with fluorescent mauve flowers, the kind of exotics found mostly on curtains. 'Dr Mullins, your coffee. Where d'you want it?' She leans across, her too-sweet scent wafting over me, as I move some potentially threatened papers towards safety. She turns, as lumping the mug down she gasps 'Ooh, I forgot you have—' and a wavelet of coffee slops over the edge.

'Och—oh.' Steffie gathers my papers, stethoscope, and several brown envelopes of patients' notes, and clutches them to her ample bosom. I take a handful of tissues and mop the desk. 'Don't worry Steffie. I'll still be here if you slow down a bit—' Seventeen? Eighteen? Nervous, anxious to please, I realise, in her first job, newly graduated from a medical secretary course.

'Sorry. You've a new patient this morning—Etta Symes? She's the last. Okay?'

'Okay with me. Steffie, you're new here.'

'Started last week.'

'Yes. Just a word: I know you're a really keen worker, but, maybe slow down a bit? Might help your memory, and—'

'I am *so* sorry about the coffee. Shall I make you another?'

'No—no it's not that. Can you, could you remember to let Etta know about the med student? That I've a student with me today? In case— she'd be allowed to say no and I'll send her out—the med student.'

'Yes. I'll remember.' Steffie bustles across the room, repeating a mantra under her breath: *the med student, the med student.* She exits, closing the door very carefully. Leaving a trail of that over-sweet scent. I cross to the sink, and pour most of the pale, hot, coffee down it.

Behind me, the door opens, this time without a knock, and the med student, Suraya, enters. I turn, grinning, 'Caught in the act! Isn't it awful? Surgery coffee?'

'Ooh, sorry!' Hand over her mouth, she giggles. 'Yes, it is. Now I can admit what I do with it!'

'So ... Keep your ears and eyes peeled, and we'll go over anything interesting between cases. All right?'

'All right.'

A couple of hours later, coughing heralds the last patient into the room. Etta Symes. Her top half's swathed in shawls, scarves, and, on unwrapping a bit, two baggy jerseys. Under that is a little, wiry, middle-aged woman in a pink sweatshirt. Suntanned, probably from working outdoors. Bangles on her arms. Her rather frizzy hair was once dark, but is prematurely pepper-and-salt grey, and held back with an Indian silk printed scarf.

'That's a nasty cough you have: how long's it been like that?'

'All the time I've had it.' She laughs, and dissolves into more coughing.

'Could you—' I hesitate. The woman's a joker. '*Would* you take off your sweatshirt—so I can listen to your chest?'

'Bronchitis,' Etta says, her head inside the sweatshirt, 'I've had it since a kiddie. On and off. Mostly off,' she laughs. I reach for my stethoscope. 'Hope you'll breathe on that first, darlin'.'

I've noticed something else: on her left inner wrist and forearm, a damasky design of three pink-edged circles. I carry on with listening to her chest, which tells me this is not pneumonia—a wet kind of persistent cough—but the chesty sound of bronchitis as she'd guessed. Then I draw her attention to the marks on her arm.

'Ringworm? Ugh, nasty. I was gonna ask you—'

'Have you noticed it anywhere else?'

'On one of them poor kiddies who arrived a few weeks before I left my old work. Left it last week I did.'

'And on yourself? Anywhere?'

'Lord, no! I've kept an eye out, haven't I? Nasty rash, hideous.'

'Could you let Suraya take a look? She's an interest in child health.' Suraya looks, carefully supporting Etta's arm as she does so.

Once the examination's over, I glance at her form again: there's something about her work. 'I've got a note here: you were working in a women's refuge. Which is where the kiddies were? But you're not still there?'

'Nah. Gave me depression.' She seems to pick up on my interest in that, because before I ask more, she shakes her head, 'Not the clinical sort. It made me sad. Reminded me. All them kiddies they brought along.'

Etta re-swathing herself in her jumpers, I write her a prescription. 'Not allergic to anything? Penicillin? For the bronchitis?'

'God knows. Not penicillin.'

'I'll give you something for the skin problem as well. Can you make sure you buy both of these items, Etta?'

'Well, I don't want either of these filthy illnesses do I? Those women, too depressed to keep their kiddies properly clean. Or maybe they caught it off the stray cat we took in? Never had it myself when I was a child. An' we lived on a barge, my family. Water gypsies. Still a few left back then. An' I'm only forty-five ... Got a coupla' kiddies, I kept them clean ... gone now ...'

Etta bites her lip, and looks at the ground. Tearful? Certainly thoughtful. I glance towards Suraya. She gives a slight nod, hardly perceptible. We both heard that catch in Etta's voice.

Etta shifts on the chair. 'Son: he's with his dad, they're stonemasons. Work on restorations. Daughter: the Lord knows. She was,' Etta says, dropping her voice, 'with *her* dad. I dunno.' She looks me in the eye, then, 'I heard she did well for herself. All you need to know isn't it? Your dad and mum, they'd want to know you'd done well, wouldn't they?' she says, turning to Suraya.

Suraya's smile is professionally polite. 'They sent me to med school: yes. They want me to do well.'

Raising my hand slightly, still holding my pen, I signal to Suraya, don't get involved. 'And now?' I ask Etta, pen poised to make a note of it. Next to *Dermatophytosis, left inner forearm*. Suraya will ask, Why *dermatophytosis*, not just *tinea*? I'll explain, for greater precision: there are conditions called tinea which are not caused by dermatophytes.

Refocusing on Etta, just in time, I'm interested by her reply. 'Headleigh Parish has given me work. Nice people. I do the church—keep it clean, tidy up a bit. I went forward: God's call, you know.' Suraya's face registers nothing, of course, but I really don't like that phrase, God's call. Straight from Dad's ministry at First Truly, and laden with assumptions about divine communication with his chosen ones.

'An' then Ruth—Mrs Taylor—last week she said, how about it, we need someone to help with the kiddies' drama club—'

My stomach tightens. At HPC? With *our* Ruth Taylor? Does Ruth *know* Etta might have a contagious skin disease? Missing a beat, taking a breath, I continue, ensuring I sound detached, which I'm not. 'Right: I expect you know, seeing you think you caught it from children at the Refuge, that ringworm's very easily passed around. It'll heal up in a week or two with treatment: but, you need to be careful not to infect others. So, make sure you don't share your towel with anyone? Or anything, hairbrush? Bedding?'

'Think I would if I didn't have to? And I don't have to now. I've been homeless. In my time. Not now.'

My own inner turmoil continues as I ask routine questions, ending up stupidly asking her, 'Do we have your address?' which of course we do, seeing she filled in a form. If I'd read it before she came in, I'd have been prepared for what she says next.

'The Taylors, Keith and Ruth, they give me the spare room for a while. Till I get settled. Really nice family. She looks after kiddies, same as I did in the Refuge. Here's the address …'

My God, living at Ruth's as well? Ruth who we pay to care for Alice and Zo-zo. Ruth is a childminder … and she's taken in a lodger who has a contagious skin disease. What's she thinking about?

Jenny

SAME DAY

Such a lovely, bright, Monday. Dry, sunny, autumn-scented, and mild. Into work early: feed the cells! They'll be ready to work on by Wednesday. I've had an amazing, slightly scary, idea. I'm wondering about a fairly new IVF solution for women who have heritable chromosomal problems: it began with some thoughts about our research. It's morphed into considering whether it's something I could look into, to help Daze. To be a better sister than when we were kids.

I'm turning it over in my mind. I'm thinking I might ask our GP what he knows about it, and whether I'd be a suitable donor. And what it exactly involves. Kind of feels scary: but good scary. I'd wait until after the conference, of course.

And I haven't had time to actually look out those things Daze wanted, yet. About her mother, and anything my Aunt Val might know.

Focusing on work, I open the incubator and lift out the flasks of cells. The passaging process is second nature, now, though the timing, after adding the trypsin, is crucial. Minimum time, just long enough that they've detached. So, how experienced will that doctoral student, my postgrad, be? In doing things for herself, without prompting? Research students don't get the close supervision and teaching you have when working for a first degree. And, please, let her be a good organized worker. Who'll do what I ask, not question it all or disappear on ladette hen-nights.

And everything's ready for the next stage.

I'm finishing, and clearing up, when Rich booms behind me, 'Jenny! Felicia's here.'

My student! Small, pretty, chestnut-haired, wearing jeans and a navy hoodie, backpack twirling from her hand, running shoes on her feet. So far so good: Felicia smiles shyly. She looks like a serious, sensible type.

'Jenny'll show you around,' Rich says, all smiles and confidence, nodding at her, and then me. That's good: he trusts me.

'Hi, Felicia. We'll do a quick tour, and then have a chat over a coffee, back in the lab office, okay?' I suggest, whipping off my gloves and chucking them in the waste bin. She smiles a yes. 'Your stuff— you can leave that in the lab office?' I end slowly, catching sight of a book sticking out of her bag: John Guthrie, *A Quiverful of Arrows*— Dad's latest popular science hardback. I'm so relieved, not for the first time, that I lost the surname Guthrie while I was a postgrad. I'm Jenny Mullins in the scientific community, and nobody need know that the famous fertility guru is any relation.

Felicia's very quiet, though she has a bouncy walk. As she dumps her belongings beside my chair, I catch sight of the name of the rowing club at her previous university on the back of her hoodie. So that's her other interest. Showing her around, I try to draw her out by getting alongside. I recall my own first days as a research student. 'That first year was my biggest challenge. I know what's it like to begin doctoral research. You're all keen, with a good degree, but somehow lost in the new role. Suddenly they're expecting you to take the right initiatives, know how to find your own feet, and which papers to read around the subject. Without guidance.'

That brings another slow smile.

And, I add as a silent thought, to be a grown-up generally.

We end our tour at the coffee machine, and go back to the office with our drinks. I offer her biscuits from the group's tin, and a chocolate from a box some visitor left us.

'You were at Cambridge,' she says.

'Yep: Clare College. I didn't row. I see you did. You were at Imperial? Please—have a choc. I shall.' She selects a hazelnut praline in gold wrap. I take the first thing I see and bite into it: orange cream, not exactly my favourite.

Felicia unwraps her choc, her fingers very neat and skilful, then smooths the foil out flat. 'I row pretty seriously, and I run,' she says. A flicker of a real smile.

'I *used* to run,' I think, as smiling and animated, her voice raised beyond the nervy whisper when we first met, she leans towards me, making eye contact and grinning like she's going to confide something really special, and gets stuck into an exposition of rowing beyond anything I know about it. Her fingers are meanwhile skilfully forming the chocolate paper into a little cup, which then becomes a wine glass with a stem. She's coxed a boat and been vice president of the club, and could talk about rowing forever.

Eventually I say, 'Okay, maybe we should talk work: tell me about your research topic. It may change a bit as you settle in and get the hang of stuff—and as they see what you can do and where you fit. In the team's great scheme of things. But what's your main area?'

It is of course pretty compatible with mine.

Finally, as we prepare to strike out into town to buy baguettes for lunch from the posh deli on Woodstock Road, she smiles a bit shyly and pulls out Dad's book. 'Have you read this? He's pretty inspiring. The stem cell part's a diversion, of course, but it interests me.'

I take the book, flip the pages much as Max did with *Living with Uncertainty*, and go for being non-committal. 'It's amazing how far fertility work has come. What we can do now for infertile couples, and people with heritable conditions. When we think how each tiny bit of research adds up, and represents someone's slogging away in their little corner, it kind of makes the routine worthwhile. Guthrie, of course, is a big media guy. Most of us work in obscurity, research is all about team work.'

It came out so formal, like a pre-prepared speech, I'm surprised she doesn't rumble that I know more about Guthrie than I'm prepared to share.

'He knows how to put it over, though, doesn't he?'

'Yeah. He does. Teamwork. It's a bit like rowing, really,' I add.

Max

THAT EVENING

Ruth's lodger, Etta Symes, re-occupies my thoughts as I leave work. Irritated by my surgery running on late, so I'm unlikely to reach home for bath time and give the bairns a quick look-over to check for signs of having caught the ringworm from her. Wondering how Jenny and I should play this: we can't simply collude with Ruth telling us nothing. Tricky one, to avoid breaking patient confidentiality.

Ruth doubtless interprets it all as an act of generous, Christian, hospitality. I'd call it sloppiness. Back on our doorstep, I pause, notice my shallow breathing, and take a few slow, deep, gulps of night air. It's smokily scented with autumn, and rather pleasant. The house, as I let myself in, is dark, and quiet. Never sure whether a quiet house is a good thing. The Manse was always noisy, except when Dad was in his study, writing a sermon or counselling a sinner.

Light from the study forms an inviting path. I glance around the partly open door. 'Jen? Darling?'

The only thing moving is a pink and mauve feathery design, revolving on Jenny's computer screen. Leaving my jacket on the back of the desk chair, and my bag on the seat, I head for the kitchen. 'Jenny?'

'Sssh! Just got them both off: they were cranky as hell because— Look, there's sausages left from their tea, and then I must go in the attic and find Aunt Val's stuff for Daze.'

'Jen, because? Some reason why the girls came back from Ruth's all excitable?'

'She's taken in a lodger. I should've said.'

'I see—'

'—no, this woman's nice, actually she's funny—she was doing Ruth's ironing with enormous gusto: banging the iron up and down the board, humming along to the radio. She wears lots of rings and bracelets and she let Zoë try the bangles on. Zoë pulled her top up of course, like kiddies do, to show her belly.'

'Mm,' I say.

The microwave pings. I move towards the plate of sausages on the table, pick one up casually, and take a bite.

'Hey, keep off: the veg should be ready in a second. You should've seen Zoë dance!' Jenny gyrates, laughing, across the kitchen, takes jacket potatoes from the microwave, and humming an Arab-style tune, continues the belly-dance, a potato in each oven-gloved hand. 'We had a lot of fun till Etta—she has asthma or something and she coughed, poor thing and—'

'Etta? An unusual name. D'you know where she's appeared from? Had Ruth mentioned someone was moving in?'

'Maybe short for something? She didn't *appear*. She's the new cleaner at Ruth's church.'

'Cleaner?' Brow-furrowing, as if this is the first I'd heard. 'And she's not local?'

'She's just moved here. I thought it was nice of them. I expect it's till she finds somewhere.'

'Okay. Isn't adding to her household something Ruth should've discussed with us? I mean, we should know who our children mix with when we aren't there.'

'I was a bit surprised. Though as the children don't go in the main house proper ... Look, it's ready, there's salad in that bowl—let's eat?'

'Sure. So what've you discovered about Etta?'

'You should approve: her last job was in a women's refuge. She was working with the kids, and she is trained.'

'Mm.'

Jenny sits, chin on her hand. Evidently she is a little concerned. 'What could I do? We agreed we'd keep Ruth. It's a big career-break year ...'

I toy with the idea of explaining the whole thing, but how much can I say? Etta's my patient. Ruth might've considered not dumping her on me, when there's plenty of other GPs. Jenny presses on, 'Of course, Ruth did her silent "come here, I have something confidential to say" thing—you know, how she draws you away, "come and look at the garden"? Out of earshot, she told me how when Etta worked at the refuge, she passed all her nursery NVQ's, with distinction. She showed me craft Etta's done with the Taylor kids ... Evidently she once fell on hard times. But she's bounced back up.'

'Mmm, she's a survivor.'

'Max, please be supportive. I need extra childcare time. Rich'll take the credit, he has the internationally known name. But it's stuff I've worked on, he's given me the writing-up. They need the abstract by Christmas. We'll be repeating experiments. So please, no complaints. I'll keep an eye ...'

'Can I talk to Ruth? And, Etta?'

''Spose you must.'

'I'm only thinking about our children. And of course being a long-faced puritan.'

'Yes.' Jenny laughs.

Marriage is a minefield. I call Ruth: she hands me over to Keith. Keith is all charm, and apparently naïve, talking like an older brother about space becoming available in their spare room just when Etta needed a home—God's perfect timing. Yes, I knew they'd had Ruth's sister staying before she went off to teach overseas; we'd met her: this is completely different. Yes, I know the children are cared for in the little extension, with its own kitchen and toilet, and won't interact with Etta. But the household has changed, and we weren't told. Besides, when Jenny collected them, Etta was evidently in the same room, ironing.

Keith's attitude implies I'm suspicious, untrusting, and unpleasant—evidently I'm not up to his standard of faith. I suggest it's a basic health and safety issue. He says it's 1996, and their house is kept spotless. I end up saying that we'll leave it for now, but we'd like to be kept informed of every change, however small, from now onwards.

He does not sound happy.

I'd rather not act the over-protective father. Dermatophytosis is common and easily treatable. Enough desperate people wandered through the Manse when we were growing up, and we came to no harm. We'll see how it all pans out.

Jenny never does get into the loft, for Daze's things. Her whole focus is on her career.

Jenny

SATURDAY, THAT WEEKEND

Finally, I'm up under the roof looking at those black and white photos of Daze's baby. Shots from that day in the path lab with Max, when we took the blood and tissue samples. I'd forgotten just how the face and body were distorted, the limbs bent and scrawny, the fists clenched. Such a tiny creature. I'd called it the Thing.

Then Daze whisked what we'd called *the products of conception* out of our control by withdrawing her consent for research. She gave it a name. Persephone, the girl captured by the king of the underworld in Greek mythology. Because it was only created to be put in the ground. That grim humour's so typical Daze.

I flip through the folder of chromosome bandings and notes Dad made on the phenotype. Dad, eventually, not me. Obvious why Daze had no interest in what had fascinated me, the objective diagnosis. Only grief ... Now, my mummy hormones have kicked in. Then ... Well, has my objectivity diminished? I don't know. I didn't see the Thing tidied up and presented to Daze, only cold, and laid on a green paper towel in a metal dish, waiting to be inspected by research scientists. Max was the one Daze chose to see the dressed, tidied-up, little corpse, before it was taken away to the undertakers.

Max had this ability to understand Daze's intimate, personal, painful experience: premature labour and giving birth to an unexpectedly deformed baby. Max almost scares me: objectivity and empathy live together in him. In a way I can't begin to understand.

That hurts. It's unfair.

A sudden noise rips through the silent house: I shudder with fright.

And instantly regain perspective: only the front door bell. The metal ladder creaks as I put my foot on it, to hurry down. From the landing, I bound down the stairs, fling open the door, and Shaz, in wellies, is down by the gate. 'Hi!'

She turns back, 'Hi, you, thought you must be out!'

'No, in the loft.'

'What're you doing? I love attics.'

'You happy with ladders, then? Sorting family photos. Oh, what did you want?'

'We've got an allotment! I've been digging the weeds. Me! Could do with a loo break. And haven't seen you in a while. Since Daze's boat.'

'I'll make us a brew, you can take a look at my relatives. Max took the kids out!'

'Milky coffee'd do me. Shall I leave my boots outside?'

In the loft, I shove the Persephone pictures into their file, then bring everything down to the study. I take Aunt Val's stuff—a photographic record of life in her commune on the Western Isles—into the kitchen, make two lattes and find a few bits we can eat. Shaz appears, clearly glad of adding a snack to the hot drink.

'Hey, thanks. I was wilting. I had a little bit of garden as a kiddie, but growing veg is like real work. Eliot's idea of course. Anyhow, nice juicy carrots and fresh beans next year, if the slugs don't get them first. Let's take a look then.'

'This is Aunt Val. She's Dad's twin. She was into self-sufficiency back in the sixties. On a commune. In the Outer Hebrides. They bred sheep. Here's the whole group, in 1965. There's Daze's mum.'

'Jewels, wasn't it? Hey, your parents weren't there, were they?'

'No way. Dad was at Cambridge doing Nat Sci. And then in London, doing his doctorate on clever stuff with sperm and eggs outside the body. While Mum slogged away being a junior doctor, and pregnant.' I grin at Shaz. 'No, I don't think he ever went there. This one's Des, my stepdad, and the baby's Daze.'

'And?'

'Jewels's sister, Lucy, nicknamed Loose, and her bloke, Jack; Aunt

Val; other people I don't know. And islanders that Val maybe keeps in touch with.'

'Nice of her. Funny names, the girls have.'

'Don't they. Here's Val again—the blond guy's her partner. And she's hugely pregnant.'

'That'd be a cousin of yours then, inside.'

'Lewis. Named after an island! Computer programmer now. Look at these clothes. Hippies were so gender-specific. Barefoot and pregnant; flowing skirts, hair in braids. So that's my weird relatives.'

'Intellectuals. My family's boring. You're lucky.'

'Suppose. They seemed ordinary to me.'

Actually, the older I got, the weirder I realised my family is. The bizarre story of my parents, and how Daze came to be my sister, is an emotional maze, drawn by the older generation with no reference to how it'd affect us kids. Easier to be boring.

We're either side of the kitchen table, dipping breadsticks into a pot of hummus, when the bell goes again. 'Popular today.'

'Evidently.'

Ruth is on the doorstep, a Marks and Spencers bag in her hand. 'Is this a bad time?'

I'd like to say yes. But a polite 'No, not at all, come in,' is what I say.

Stepping in, Ruth slips off her shoes, a habit she has, and we head for the kitchen, 'Cuppa? Coffee? Afraid we're pigging it a bit, having a snack lunch.'

'I won't stop, it's only Zoë's overalls. From Thursday?' Ruth reaches into the carrier bag, out come a pair of pink overalls. 'We were at the park, she had a great time but it was muddy. I'll need something else now for spare clothing.'

'Have a seat, you didn't need to wash and iron them!' So embarrassing. 'I'll fetch you a replacement. This is Shaz, a friend from the school gates. Ruth keeps Zoë for me—'

'Hi,' Shaz smiles. As I run upstairs to the airing cupboard, I hear her add, 'My hubby works with Max. At the surgery.' And I have that awful betrayal sensation, ashamed when one contact meets another.

Ruth's so serious: while Shaz, so uncomplicated, fits the corner of my life reserved for retail therapy and girly chats.

I get back to find them leaning over a photo of Daze as a baby. 'Daze, short for Daisy. She's a conceptual artist,' Shaz is saying, 'does the kind of thing Charles Saachi buys?'

'Mmm,' Ruth responds.

'My stepsister: she's teaching out at Banbury,' I beam at Ruth, hand her the clothes, and gather up my photos. 'Daze exhibited with the Young British Artists. I'm not sure about Saachi.'

Shaz adds, 'She lives on a narrowboat, with a three-legged cat, called Trifle. Tri for three? It was so sad though: she lost a baby, the year Jen and Max got together.'

I glance at Ruth. She has on a tight, *I'm holding it together*, expression. I add, quickly, 'She lost her mother when she was five: it seriously beat her up emotionally.'

We fall silent, as if out of respect. Then Ruth says, in a cool, even, voice, 'We holiday in the Western Isles sometimes: are your relatives still sheep-farming?'

'My Aunt? She's moved to Edinburgh.'

'Ah.'

More embarrassment. Ruth has tried Changing the Subject, but hasn't gone away. It'd have been useful to run the Etta situation by Shaz, but I can't. How do I make one of them leave?

Shaz suddenly pushes back her chair, 'Just seen the time! Charlie's on a play date. I can't be late to collect her. See ya', Jen. Ruth, nice to meet you! I'll let myself out! Cheers!'

'I have to collect some dry cleaning,' I half-lie to Ruth. Hopefully it'll be ready. We leave together; Ruth has her bike, but pushes it—tick, tick, tick, tick—alongside of me.

'Ruth, Max spoke to you, about Etta? We— I'm sorry if he was brusque—he's very protective of the girls, and Etta living at yours, it was a bit—unexpected.'

'No: he was concerned. Keith reassured him. Keith would want to know who ours are with.' I turn, surprised that Keith took over that call. Unsurprised Max didn't tell me. Ruth's face is expressionless, as she speaks not to me but, staring straight ahead, to the road into town. 'Etta has good references. So your stepsister had a nasty bereavement, a baby?'

'Yes. She hopes she can have another. So much can be done now, but people expect miracles, and they don't always realise the stats on IVF. I can guide Daze through the range of techniques. There's pre-implantation diagnosis, though it's very new—we all lose embryos anyway, without even knowing we may be pregnant.'

Now Ruth turns and looks at me, 'There's adoption, children who need a home,' she says quietly, her eyebrows puckered, and her lips pursed.

Clearly trod on another sensitivity. Wish Shaz had never mentioned Daze. 'About Etta, if she wanted to use her skills and craft training there's a new centre starting up. In town. For homeless people: they want to offer art and craft, therapeutic as well as fun. Would she be interested?'

'Who would she contact?'

'David Robertson, at St Hildegard's.'

'Mmm. I'll think about it. Oh look, is that your dry cleaners?'

When Max returns, I mention Ruth's visit, and my idea about Etta. 'I suddenly thought, teaching craft's better than cleaning. And maybe she could move into St Hildegard's. But Ruth gave me a sharp look when I mentioned David.'

'She would.'

'I get the feeling maybe it's Keith who wanted Etta there. Did you?'

'His taking the responsibility from Ruth, is typical. Think Colin and Rachel.'

'Really? But Colin was violent.'

'Yes … Well, Alice, come and tell Mummy what we've been doing: we were up on Shotover.'

'People were flying kites. Great big ones!'

Jenny

EARLY MORNING, A FEW DAYS LATER

Ouch! Zoë just delivered a hard kick to my right shin. Rubbing the place, making an effort not to swear horribly, 'Mummy's got a poorly leg, now, Zo-zo. What do you say?'

'Sorry!'

Alice has disappeared. Moments later, there's a wail from downstairs, 'Mum-ee! Door won't open!'

'Which door where, sweetie?' Hurrying downstairs towards the voice, I see the handle of the downstairs cloakroom rattling agitatedly: Alice is clearly inside. 'Did you use the key, love?' Grabbing the kitchen wall phone, I extend its cord to the limit, then multitasking, 'Ally? All right, Mummy's here now—'

'I—'

'Biochemistry?'

'Ally, You're okay. I'm here—'

'This is Oxford University Department of—'

'—can you stop crying? Good—'

'—I can't hear you, caller?'

'Yes, hi, it's Jenny Mullins, from the Woods lab, my daughter's locked herself—Okay, Ally, not the handle, the little key? Can you turn it now?—in the loo, so I'm on my way but I'll be a little—'

Slowly we manage, so that by the time the lab know I'm delayed, but will materialise as soon as possible, Alice, normally so poised, escapes her prison. Tears all shiny on her cheeks. 'Mummy!' she throws her arms around me, and hides her face in my skirt.

'All okay now: you were very thoughtful, going downstairs to get ready, on your own. Just close the door, don't lock it next time? All right?'

'But now I can unlock it. You showed me. Through the door.'

*

I arrive at work to find Felicia obviously distressed.

'Oh dear, sorry I wasn't here. We had a kiddie crisis at home: what's happened here?'

Felicia's voice sounds like someone's got her by the throat. 'I was passaging my cells, like yesterday morning early ... God, I can't believe my luck. They're dead, useless.'

'Tell me, what happened?'

'Someone called me to the phone.'

I wonder why someone phoned her at work. 'Aah: was it a long call?'

'Crisis at home, same as you. I sorted it and then, well I was away too long. I hoped ... Of course they were detached when I got back, and I thought, maybe they'll survive, so it was worth adding medium ... But quite obviously the trypsin had over-digested them. I just looked at them down the microscope: nothing but horrible little floating bits of debris.'

So, I think, How many times have I impressed on her the importance of adding the trypsin for the minimum amount of time to detach the cells from the flask *and no longer?* Emphasising that longer times would soon chew up the cells—that's what trypsin naturally does in the gut, it digests food! 'Couldn't you have—wasn't it possible to phone back, when you'd finished the passaging?' Felicia often seems preoccupied, or leaves early. And my annoyance at Alice making me late is feeding my negative attitude. 'Couldn't home wait?'

Eyes cast down, she's crushed. I know I sounded sharp, but she's been careless. 'I had to check. I didn't take longer than I had to. I just ... it's my fault, and I'll have to start all over again. With new samples.'

Yes, you will, I think, and wonder why this girl who has a first from Imperial seems so uncommitted: boyfriend trouble? Certainly not worth losing you research subject for. 'I'd have had it all cleared up before you got here if I'd arrived earlier as well. But of course, I'd have needed to ask you about obtaining fresh samples,' she says, not helping her own cause.

'Mmm,' I say. Hiding her misdemeanours from her supervisor?

Maybe I should try to find out more about whatever home contains.

Surely she doesn't have a kid stashed away there? She talked about rowing, but nothing about family.

Back in the lab office, to read my e-mails, a sudden thought flashes into my brain. Why have I repressed what I really knew? I'm back in Cambridge reliving the disaster I had over Daze's baby's samples. I know I didn't do what Felicia just has. Those samples were so precious I'd have ignored all the phones in world ringing and made sure I didn't leave the trypsin on too long. And they weren't only precious because me and Max were working on them together, they were weird, and we were curious. But, when I turned up to find they'd disappeared, I swallowed Rich's peculiar explanation that 'someone turned off the incubator'. Someone would not do that unintentionally. Someone could erroneously attach a nitrogen cylinder instead of air or CO_2, but again, it'd have to be a qualified someone. Possibly, that'd be Wil du Plessis, the postdoc who taught me a few terms?

I made myself believe Rich: I was in such awe of him. Still kind of am. I went along with his off-the-wall explanations. Which has meant that I'm apparently a loyal subject, a good bet to include in his relocation here.

Wil and Max were housemates. Max wasn't upset. Max encouraged me to *move on* ...

'Jenny, are you all right?'

'Leila!' I turn, putting on a smile. She's identified tension and distress from the way I'm hunched at my computer. 'Yeah, fine. Did I look worried? Have you any ideas how to motivate a dopey doctoral student?'

'Felicia? She's very quiet, I've hardly noticed her around.'

'She's hardly *been* around. Well, she has, but she doesn't exactly radiate interest and application to her work.'

We discuss the ways supervisors can help or hinder students. I tell Leila how much I'd had to prove myself to Dr Purdey way back when I was doing my thesis.

'Because of your father being well known in the same field? Figures. But we're not like that, are we?'

'Friendly supervisors. Caring and approachable. "The best way is to encourage, and to model good practice,"' I quote Rich, imitating his voice, then realising I could've been heard.

Leila laughs. Then tells me how well her son is doing. Seven years old, and scored a hundred per cent on a maths test for the third time. I congratulate her. Friendly supervisors, proud mummies.

I regain perspective. My suspicions are crazy. Dad got the answers to that baby's phenotype from some cutting-edge DNA testing he could access, and we were all perfectly happy. Did I moan and fuss back then?

Soon after, I'm heading for the dirty lab, to prepare cultures. Felicia's in there busy preparing replacements for her lost ones. We smile: I am really sorry I was so sharp.

Home again, later, Max is all happy and bright. It's been his day for teaching at the medical school, which he always loves. 'Good day?' he asks.

'Nope. Horrible!'

'Oh dear—'

'My postgrad's proving careless: while passaging cells she took a phone call just when she'd added the trypsin. They were over-digesting while she chatted. The wuss.'

'Not your responsibility, is it? A mistake once made, always avoided in future?'

'Whatever. If I have to watch her, how I'm supposed to move my own work along? The research I'm paid to do, the research I'm actually good at? Why's she not more interested? I'm driven by curiosity, I got thoroughly trained by doing vac jobs with Dad's colleagues, I'm instinctively a tidy and a fastidious worker—'

'But not everyone is. She'll learn. That call might've been very important. Do you know much about her circumstances?'

'No. She's not exactly forthcoming. But it brought a memory back. It'd be the easiest way to make things look like a silly accident if you wanted to ruin somebody's work. As in, the Persephone project?'

'You've lost me.'

'Rich told me a tale about someone switching off the incubator by accident? More likely, someone messed with our cultures.'

'Jen, that's surely water under the bridge? Put it behind you.'

'What? Accidentally turning off an incubator, which Rich told me had happened, was rubbish. I'm saying, deep down, I always knew. Someone else was curious. Or, they were jealous. Rich protected that person with a crazy lie that implied all kinds of other work was also destroyed. If it had been a real accident, he'd have had their guts for garters, wouldn't he?'

'Whatever happened, I'd let it go.'

'Maybe. Day began badly, Zoë kicked my shin in a fight over potty or big toilet, then Alice locked herself in the downstairs loo—'

Max laughs, 'Bathroom training wars! ... Och, Jenny, here's something to laugh at. Family life! Do you not love them, and wonder why we wanted them?'

His arms are out to hug me. My shin throbs, I turn back the end of my trouser leg, 'I've a bruise to show you.'

'I don't have to kiss it better, do I?' he grins.

Max

DAWN, SOME DAYS LATER

Feathers are stroking my eyelids. 'Daddy?'

'Huh?' It's Alice. Her small fingers gently trying to open my eyes.

'Daddy: naughty dream.'

'Oh. Not good if I dream?'

'*Zo-zo had a naughty dream.*' The duvet shifts, letting in cold air.

'Don't,' I mumble. 'Ally, is Mummy awake?' I pull the pillow over my head.

Jenny proves unrousable. Though even through the pillow, I hear Zoë, bellowing. 'Okay: tell her I'll come, tell her shush, don't shout.'

Light from the hall illuminates Zoë, standing in her cot among a tangle of toys and books, one leg thrust through the bars. Apparently less scared than angry, for as I reach for the light switch, a selection of board books, soft animals, and other treasures come flying towards me. 'Steady on, baby, don't pelt the sleepy parent!'

Treading carefully between the missiles, we cross the carpet, Alice explaining, 'I gave her lots of stuff. *My* stuff she always wants. But she won't stop.'

'Maybe there's too much?'

A flying, well-chewed copy of Helen Oxenbury's *I Can* hits me on the chest. Several parts of a toughly made Fisher Price tea service (suitable from age three) follow before I finally lift Zoë out. She buries her head on my bruised front: I feel her heartbeat, and her big, shuddering breaths.

Alice pulls the curtain aside and looks out. 'Daytime. I can see the trees. Why are trees?'

On autopilot, I sort Zoë, while saying sleepily, 'Because God made there be. Let there be trees, and there were trees—'

'She goes on the pot once it's daytime,' says Alice know-all, as I reach for a nappy.

All I want is to sleep. 'Stop that wriggling, Zo-zo, you're a little eel.'

'Eels don't have legs,' observes Alice.

'And dawn isn't daytime: we're all going back to bed.'

'Story,' Zoë demands from the change mat.

'One story. Quick one.'

'*The Very Hungry Caterpillar*?'

'Etta gave us this one: *Mary meets an Angel*.'

'Really?'

'Yes: then Mummy said hurry up and we came home.'

'Etta's always at Ruth's?'

'Yes. Etta's got a bedroom.' Hum: didn't we agree that the kids should be kept away from the main house?

The book's illustrated in brightly-coloured, updated Art Nouveau. 'Does Zoë like this?'

'I like it. Mummy read it in a funny voice.' Alice quotes, almost word-perfect, in a sing-song, ironic style: *One hot day Mary went to the well to fetch some water and because it was so hot, she sat down and rested under a tree on her way home. Suddenly she heard a voice: it was an angel.'*

The voice is just right: Jenny in sceptical mood. 'Mummy read it like that?'

'Only that page. Then she read something else. You have to do the voice.'

'I'm not sure I do, pet.'

'Why are angels?'

'Why are angels?'

'Yes. Why?'

Back in our room, I get the mumbled 'Max, mm, thanks. I couldn't wake up.'

'Your lovely daughter who kicks threw her books at me.'

'Poor baby.' Jenny uncurls. Even laughs.

'Who?'

I doze. She nudges me. 'Listen? I've been thinking—about that work we couldn't complete on the Persephone cultures.'

'It's in the past. Why really are you digging it up?'

'Feel responsible. I resented Daze so much when Mum and Des got together ... Think what we have, and Daze has nothing. She won't get over Persephone till she has a healthy one.'

'Who wakes her at five thirty wanting to play. Her life is simply different. To yours.'

'No, listen. We've got our two, and I'm young and fit—'

'You are. Leave it: you've enough to think about. You said. Postgrad, conference talk?'

'This wouldn't involve me long-term.'

My heart misses a beat. 'Don't even think of surrogacy.'

'Absolutely not. This'd be far less intrusive.'

'Good.' Can breathe again.

'I—after the conference of course—I wondered, why not investigate egg donation?' she says in a rush.

'*What?*' Horrified, I sit up, the bizarre words ringing in my head.

The bedroom furniture looms at me from the gloom.

Jenny inexplicably reacts by tenting the duvet to cover us both. This only creates a draught, adding to my discomfort. 'It's no big deal, a few hormones, a bit of a clinical procedure, no pregnancy. Max, listen. Daze's life was ruined by her mother *abandoning* her. She was Alice's age. She deserves a break.'

A break? I can't speak. An alien extends an arm around me, as if I'm the one who's lost all sense of perspective. 'Max? It's all okay. I sounded out Simon. Preliminary chat, nothing more.'

Heart almost stopped. 'Simon's a partner, and our GP: how could you do this?' Mouth is dry as a desert. 'You've not started tests?'

'No. I should've told you I talked to him, yes. But, if it was no go—you'd never have needed to hear it'd crossed my mind. And it's my—'

'Your body and your choice?'

'Well, it isn't yours, is it?'

Jenny's challenge hits something so ingrained, I realise I've never thought it through. At home, at Dad's church, we were taught from Scripture, and by example, the wife's body belongs to the husband. Do I really believe that?

Thankfully John Humphrys suddenly blasts from the radio, reading the News. I rise, flip the volume dial down, and head for the shower. Can't say 'I'm wrong, aren't I' right away. Instead, 'Spare me the feminism. If it must be done, what about Harriet? She's the stepsister Daze was close to.'

'Harriet's in Australia. And if you're worried about religious scruples, your father won't know.'

'Dad isn't God.'

'God's supposed to approve of generosity,' she calls through the door. 'I'm loving my neighbour. Isn't that true, and isn't that what Ruth does? Giving Etta a home? You should be glad I've learned that from your incredible Mam—'

'Leave Mam out of it. And Etta's far closer to our children than we agreed with that slippery couple, Ruth and—her husband. Your idea has nothing to do with God.'

'Sorry, I'll speak to Ruth. I'll chuck out Etta's present. Don't junk donation. It'd be something beautiful for Daze, to misquote Mother Theresa.'

'You're twisting everything. I can't believe it of you.' I exit the shower making an effort to be equable, 'It's the shock. I'm not angry. I'm concerned from a clinical viewpoint, for your welfare. I've nothing against Daze.'

'I want to help.'

'That's very generous. It's actually rather sweet. It's maybe a bit unwise.'

I don't want her pumped full of hormones, then having her ova sucked out with invasive instruments by the fertility team. Irrational, maybe. To me, she's not merely a body, or one that's not my concern.

Downstairs, I try a last approach, as she makes the girls breakfast. 'You know the clinical procedure's painful? Never mind any side effects. How much do you really know?'

She shakes her head, *not in front of the kids*, 'Drop it. May never happen.'

'I'm relieved to hear that. Because, whatever science says, and I do believe in science, it's not nothing to have your ovaries stimulated beyond the norm.' I can't discuss it further, or calmly eat breakfast here. It's too horrible. Makes me feel ill. 'We've an early meeting. Before surgery.'

I grab my bag and keys: she grabs at me. 'Max, don't!'

I shake her off. She stumbles against the table. 'Don't you *ever* hurt me!' she spits.

''That wasn't—'

'Planned?'

Zoë starts to cry. I leave. In the surgery car park, I sit in the car, quietly breathing, thinking of Dad, and Colin and Rachel, and wonder how violent I could actually be.

Lunchtime, I call her at the lab. 'I'm so sorry. Listen, it's this: there's a part of me that feels we became one through our marriage vows. One flesh, one spirit, one entity. One flesh isn't merely a euphemism for intercourse. Though *we* create *our* children, together, with your—eggs. I'd need donation to be a joint decision. At present, I can't even imagine it.'

'You counsel patients about fertility problems.' She uses a cold, professional voice.

'I send them to the relevant department, for the relevant procedures. They aren't—*you*.' Throat tight, pathetically emotional.

'We're in the middle of something. I can't talk.'

I quietly replace the receiver, no goodbyes. And stare at my list of afternoon patients. What is on there, that isn't dancing and unreadable?

What crazy idea of God's generosity has Jenny cooked up, to get around me, using my Manse upbringing? It's an insult. Why bother to be conciliatory?

I do not want to hear more. We are both far too busy. We have children in common.

At home, days go by, we make up in a way. Evidently, neither of us wants to say more about Daze's future.

Jenny

HALF TERM, LATE OCTOBER

It's Halloween. Dad sent over costumes for Alice and Zoë, and I have a 'ghostogram' upstairs to surprise them. It rang me earlier at work, and we agreed a plan.

I've a child hanging onto each side of me, plus Charlie who's here for tea. Little squeaks and giggles escape, as our own personal ghost wafts down the stairs, rubbing its hands. 'Came through the window, straight from the graveyard, ooh, it's chilly there!'

'Ooh!' they squeal. She is rather overdoing it—hope they didn't understand?

'Who have we here?' says the ghost, leaning on the newel post, gazing about from under its shimmery grey hood.

'Go on, it is safe, I've got you.' I gently push Alice forward.

She smiles shyly, 'I'm Robin Hood, she's a witch, and she's a princess,' says Alice, pointing at Charlie and Zoë.

'And I've come to wish you a really creepy Halloween with *spiders!*' Our ghost whips from behind her back a bag of chocolate spiders with black cardboard legs. They hesitate. 'C'mon, you know who I am?'

Cautiously, Alice steps up. 'You're Auntie Daze aren't you. You're being scary!'

Daze throws her hands up in a gesture of despair 'Guilty, guilty! How did you know?'

'You talk like her!' Alice capers, then they're all laughing, grabbing their sweets.

'I'll have to do something about the voice, won't I? '

'Grandpa says you don't have to be creepy if you don't want to. Where he lives, you can be anything you like at Halloween. Mummy made pumpkin pie.'

'We'll see. *Next time!*' Daze adds, in hollow, sepulchral, tones.

'Ooooh!' the girls shriek, running down the hall.

'Okay, was I?' Daze asks. She pushes back the hood so I see her face, painted white with big grey patches around the eyes.

'You could leave out the graveyard next time,' I say drily. 'Listen, you said, pop by to change into your outfit after you'd finished showing your diploma students around the Ashmolean. You wanted to look at the Aunt Val photos and the data. But you can't take this all to the party, can you? Confidential for starters.'

'I can have a shufti, and I wouldn't mind Val's phone number if you've got it?'

'Quick cuppa then? I'm doing fish fingers for their tea. Shaz'll be round for Charlie in half an hour.'

'Wow, big envelope,' Daze says, as I hand it over. She empties everything onto the table, amongst the plates and mugs I've put for the kids. 'Okay, I'll move it …' She sorts through, dividing it into piles, her movements deft and neat.

'Hey, you made that costume, didn't you? You probably designed it. You're so—I wish I could sew like that. That shimmery floaty fabric's amazing.'

'Glad you like the weeds. And yes I did. Fucking hard to sew. Might your Aunt Val have any addresses where Jewels lived? Any idea what work she might do? Have done?' She holds out a photo of her baby self with Des and Jewels. 'Dad said she used to do folk singing—I've tried festivals ... You think Val would talk? If I went up to Edinburgh?'

'You could try. Remember Aunt Val's Dad's twin: they're quite similar.'

'Meaning she can be difficult. And evasive?'

'Got it.'

'I can manage that.'

Alice plucks at my sleeve, 'We're hungry. Can *I* see them? The pictures?'

I signal to Daze, she passes some photos of the whole commune group. 'Here's Great-aunt Val, and the baby is Auntie Daze— and there's her mum and dad?'

Alice stares with interest. 'Grandpa Des?'

'That's right,' Daze says. 'In Scotland.'

'Grandpa *Alisdair* lives in Scotland.'

'Not quite ... Aunt Val does. Anyhow, you want Val's number? Can you call her, from the college maybe?'

'I'll call from home.' Daze seizes my wrist and a pen that's lying around. It tickles as she writes a mobile number on my arm.

'That was so schoolgirl. So you've your own cell phone?'

'Could I have a landline on a boat? I need to keep in touch with people I do business with, don't I?'

'S'pose you do. Of course you do.' I rip a page from my University Diary, scribbling the numbers, circling the one I want her to use, 'Here's mine, home and mobile, not work 'cos I really am in another world when I'm there. Call my mobile, preferably?'

'Thanks. Posh busy woman.' Daze folds the paper up small and reaches under the ghost costume to tuck it in her jeans pocket.

'Don't lose that. Arts tycoon.'

'Would I?'

'Keep the info carefully, and let me know about Val? I'll call you when my term's over, and we can meet and hand over in a pub or somewhere. Okay?'

*

I call Val once the girls are in bed. As she answers, 'Jenny! It's been far too long!' the front door bangs, and Max comes into the kitchen, signalling *who?*

'Aunt Val,' I mouth.

He looks into a pan on the stove, then kisses my neck, his lips chilly from the cold outside. Aunt Val's distinctive Edinburgh lilt reminds me of her cosy flat and great welcome when I stayed there for my Roslin interview. When I mention that Daze is wanting to meet up, her voice leaps down the phone, while across the room, Max draws his eyebrows together.

'It will be marvellous to meet Daisy after all these years,' gushes Val, 'the poor wee lassie's done so well for herself. Though of course, even if she hadn't— Tell her to call me when she's coming and there'll be a bed ready. Oh, I can't wait. Though it's true I'm off to New Zealand in a week, so it looks like the New Year.'

'Better than that, I've her number here: would you like to talk with her yourself?'

'Let me find my spectacles, I'll write it down. And yourself, how are you all?'

Dear Aunt Val enjoys hearing all about the girls' antics, and my research, 'Which of course I don't understand, but it's all rather impressive. Though I hope you're not the spit of my brother!'

'So what was that about?' Max asks grimly, as I replace the phone.

'Daze was at the Ashmolean, taking a class round.' Momentarily I want to describe Daze in her Halloween disguise, and the fun we had. But maybe not. He'll have a go at me about letting Daze so far into our lives, possibly add something negative about donation. 'She came by to change for a party.'

'And? Anything else?'

That kiss: is my neck even still cold at the spot? 'Wanting to talk with Aunt Val. About the commune.'

'Talking with Val's a good idea. You've not spoken about anything else? I thought we agreed you're too busy to be involved with her life?'

'I'm not stupid. But she's family.'

'Mm. Leave her to Val, Jenny ... And what're these?'

He's spotted the spider sweet-wrappers, with the cardboard legs, which I was about to chuck in the bin. 'Chocolate spiders. She brought them.'

Slowly he reaches into his pocket, brings out something clutched in his hand, and places it on the floor. The thing sits, thinks, then, mechanism buzzing, tears across the floor and under the sofa. Wind-up spider. Max is watching me, though. His smile is still seduction.

Have I misjudged him? Why can't he see we have the power to help Daze?

*

Daze phones, over the moon. 'Val was bloomin' mysterious about Jewels. Shit, I can't go up there the dates she can do: then she's off to New Zealand, for the rest of our winter, to study the sheep! Anyhow, she *invited herself* to the Fun Day. She'll bring samples of her tweeds and do demonstrations of wool spinning. How's that for my community effort?'

'Brilliant! Go, Daisy! So you're definitely doing it? You got the premises?'

'I shall. And yes.'

Jenny

LATE NOVEMBER

I emerge, blinking like a mole, from the darkness of the microscope room into the glaring fluorescent illumination of the lab. I head straight for the lab office, pull on my jacket, while glancing at my screen before logging out.

Two parental e-mails. I'll have to skim-read these, see if I need to send them home.

'Sweetie, I'm so sorry we let the house last summer, when we visited Harriet in Oz. Of course I should've asked you first if you wanted it for an economical beach holiday. Who am I to decide whether you'd find Sennen tame? btw, can we expect you all for Christmas this year?'

Thanks, Mum. Admitting you're bossy! We're doing Hogmanay with Max's folks, so a Cornish Christmas is impossible. Sad, that. Love their all-the-village party.

'Hey, Kiddo, how about a snowy Christmas holiday in Canada? Mia's outgrown her cross-country skis. Alice ready to use them?'

Dad, his wife Karen, and my little half-sister, eight years old? And the perfect snow-scene? Yeah, right, I wish. Again.

Note to self: ask Mum and Des over for a few pre-Christmas days?

Zoë's happy, cuddly, and tired enough today to settle easily in the car with her favourite soft animal. She's dozing quietly when we arrive at Alice's school. To avoid her screams at a brutal awakening, then standing waiting in the cold for Alice, I risk leaving her in the car.

Alice bounces out of school in her lilac padded coat and wellies. 'I'm an angel.' She twirls around, arms extended, blond hair flying.

'That's lovely,' I say. Though actually it gives me a sinking feeling. 'Have you got your lunchbox? No? Shall we go and find it?'

'No, Mummy,' she pats me to get my full attention, 'I'm an *angel*. I say, Hi Mary I have good news.'

'That's nice. Lunchbox, Alice.' Fearing Zoë waking, panicking, and accusations that I'm a neglectful mummy, I seize my precocious nearly five-year-old's sticky little hand, and hurry us back into school, 'C'mon Ali, *chop chop* as Grandma says, move it.'

'Who's this who forgot her box? And with a pink princess on it? Alice!' says the smiling classroom assistant. (How can they smile after spending their whole day surrounded by other people's tinies?)

We dash back towards the car, 'Mummy, you didn't listen. I'm a very special angel. A message-er. An' I have to have wings.'

Goodness, shall I have to make them? 'What's this for, Ally?'

'When I'm a special *angel*. I *told* you. Angels are all around us, everywhere. Always.'

Are they? Does it matter she thinks so? For now, pragmatism please. We're negotiating the school gates and hoping nobody's had reason to make a judgment on my parenting.

In the car, thankfully, Zoë's slept on, furry toy cuddled against her face. I open the door for Alice: she scrambles into her seat, and grabs at the straps. Then glances at her sister. 'Mummy, Zoë's got my cat and she's dribbling on it!' Alice's arm goes out, her hand ready to grab. 'Zo, that's *mine!*'

Abruptly wakened, Zoë bursts into tears, while holding firmly to the cat. The girls struggle, Zoë screeches as if Alice is wrenching out her fingernails. Alice yells, fuelled with elder sister reason and possessive fury, 'My cat's all yucky, like you, Zoë. Mummy'll have to wash it! Mummy can we wash it? Now?'

'All around us everywhere, hey? Where's my angel gone?' I say, but am not heard. 'Now, let me help do your straps.'

'I can do them! Mummy, you *know* that's my cat: Zoë's is orange stripy. That one is *mine!*'

Checking Alice is properly strapped in, I say, 'I'm so sorry, Alice. Mummies do forget sometimes.' Then I close the door, hopefully on child and conversation.

We are ready for off, and the key's in the ignition, when Alice adds, 'Ruth doesn't forget *ever*. Daddy doesn't.'

That hits home: I'm hurt, and I snap, 'Alice, I'm driving. Settle down now.'

When Max returns, a little voice calls from upstairs that she has news for Daddy. He disappears to hear it, and returns all smiles, 'So she's to be the Angel Gabriel, she tells me?'

'Seems so. I have to make wings.'

Max chuckles.

'What's funny?'

'Your gloomy face! She's her first stage part, and you're supposed to be the doting mama.'

'Doting mama? I have to make her *wings!*'

Then I realise who could. Who is really amazing at making pretty much anything crafty?

Max

DECEMBER, A SATURDAY

'Going to Uncle David's first, then we'll buy a present for Mummy—is that all your stuff?' I pick up Alice's pink rucksack, containing the ballet shoes she's just taken off, and hand her the wide pink hairband she's left lying on the bench. Immediately she shows off to another child how she can wear the hairband as a necklace.

'Put it on properly.' Hearing my dry, exaggeratedly Scots tone, I know I've morphed into responding as Dad would've. Though would Dad ever have collected any of his children from anything, let alone a ballet class? 'I mean, do you want to wear it or shall we put it in your bag?'

'Backpack. Yes. My dancing band.'

'Coat and gloves on, it's cold. And this—is it yours?'

Alice has one foot in a Wellington boot, the other poised in the air. 'My umbrella! They match—look!' They do: Alice's umbrella has a frog face with huge eyes: her boots have frog eyes on the toes.

'Bring it with you, Ally. We're going to look at the place Uncle David's going to make into a—a day centre.'

'A what?'

'A place where people who haven't a job or a home can go and do things in the day.'

'Why don't they have a home?'

'Lots of reasons. Maybe their home wasn't very nice, so they moved out. Or maybe they can't work: grown-ups need to work to get money to have a home.'

'Oh.'

'So Uncle David—and Daddy and some other people—we're

helping them to have somewhere to be. In the day.'

'What about night? Don't they need a home to sleep?'

'That's another problem. Where they sleep.' Once in the car, to end discussion, I press the tape player button. A much-played fairy tale blares out: 'Ouch!' I turn the volume down. Politically incorrect, bought for them at the Oxfam shop by Mam, the girls love it. Certain lines we chorus aloud: *the dog with eyes like saucers, the dog with eyes like millwheels* ... Until I park the car, when the story dies with the engine. 'Here we are. Mind that puddle.'

Once out, Alice splashes into the puddle with enjoyment. I laugh. I would've done that. And been in trouble for it. 'Umbrella?'

She looks up at the sky, and shakes her head, 'Rain's stopped!'

I lock the car: Alice looks up and down the street. 'Auntie Daze has her boat here—we came with Mummy.'

'You're right. That's the canal, at the end of the road.'

David's waiting outside a dilapidated two-storey building. As he opens the door, a brown bird zooms from the eaves. 'House martin? So late in the year?'

'Good omen,' David laughs, and ushers us inside. The musty smell, the cronky metal windows, the one-tap Belfast sink stained inside with streaky colours, and speckled with dust and bits: it bleakly reminds me of being with Dad when our whole family was shown around a run-down church building by two elders in grey suits. The place that became First Truly Reformed Presbyterian Church.

I sense Alice feels the same. 'It's not a home,' she says. 'An' when you talk, what you say shouts back.' She bellows 'Hello!' to hear it happen again. We all laugh. 'Called an echo, Ally. It only does that because it's empty, no carpets or chairs.'

'We'll buy carpet and lots of chairs, maybe sofas?' David adds.

'So they can sleep?'

David and I laugh again. Alice wanders away, bored, as he unfolds some plans from a folder he's brought along, and explains them enthusiastically. 'So, breakfast bar over here, café style tables and chairs, once we've sorted the floors and fitted the kitchen.'

Dimly I'm aware of Alice, twirling her backpack and spinning around. She stumbles and sits on the floor: 'The floors's going up and down.'

'And there's a dunny, we've mains drainage all laid on, we can convert easily. Disabled included, of course,' says David. Alice staggers over, still obviously dizzy, as we inspect the tiny, cold cupboard of a room.

'A dunny, like a toilet?' The seat and lid are gone, a long chain swings from a lead cistern far up on the wall. 'It smells! Like the canal, by Auntie Daze's boat.'

David grasps the end of the chain and pulls it: 'Works, you see.'

Alice laughs as water rushes into the toilet bowl. 'So, annex a bit of the main room, and fit showers?' I suggest, now matching his mood.

'That's the idea. And you'd be—maybe here?' David indicates the area where we'd have a room for consultations.

And then he asks, 'Jenny okay if you take this on?'

'Jenny wrapped up in her career. Writing up their research.'

'Focused and committed?'

'Very.'

'I'm—sorry. You think she may come round?'

'Not to involvement here: no time … So, what's the upstairs like?'

Slightly rickety stairs lead to a large mezzanine area, where we explore the cobwebby space, and David describes plans for a library, possibly with computers, and counselling rooms. 'This'll need a stud wall of course. Several. Landing, two, three, rooms.'

Scanning the ground floor from the landing, I can't see Alice. 'Now where's my lassie gone? David, I'm away back down.' We descend, and I find Alice playing with her pink headband and a lithe black cat that's strayed in behind us.

'Is he yours?' she asks David. 'He's hunting my dancing band!'

'Never seen him before.'

'Is he homeless?'

'Maybe. Quick glance at the outside, Max?'

The tiny yard is paved with cobbles, choked with willowherb, and surrounded by several sheds containing broken furniture, cans, and an ancient press. 'Don't touch anything, Ally.'

'Dad-*dee*, can we go *home?*'

'In a moment. So: great news, and you've a builder lined up?'

'Guy I know through—'

'Uncle David,' she pats his arm for attention. 'I'm an angel. In the play, I'm an angel.'

'Now that *is* great news. Which angel?'

'The Mary-message-er.'

'That'd be Gabriel. Good part, Alice.' Then, to me, 'Yeah, builder friend through the network—Lesbian, Gay, etc?'

Lest Alice ask who these people are, I change the subject, 'You still wary of talking to your father, Dave?'

'It's kind of easier for everyone if I'm dead.'

'Bit extreme.'

'Family's extreme—How's about your father? Multiple sclerosis is a progressive disease. I suspect he may understand your settling down south as avoidance, lacking trust that he's capable of a permanent climbdown.'

'Permanent? I doubt that. Your parents certainly haven't shown any understanding of your extreme version of the same thing: moving south.' Yes, it's mean, but I throw that at him. Off travelling for a gap year, David wrote to them from Australia: I'm staying here, with the boyfriend.

Coolly, he chooses not to react. 'Your father's pride doesn't allow him to make a further move towards you.'

'Och, we're away up to the Manse for Hogmanay, whatever. You've not thought about—maybe—a visit to Hexham at Christmas?'

David replies with a friendly shove, 'Christmas?! One of my busiest times. And we always see that the homeless get a good lunch. Dad'll have to accept my continuing absence from the festivities.'

'No dutiful son stuff?'

'There's love and there's duty. The street people's needs are greater than whether my father sees me on one particular day of the year, when he's home, warm, and dry.'

'Phew: cutting and worthy of Dad, if I didn't know you better. How about your Mam?'

Alice pulls on my hand. 'You said, buy a present for Mummy?'

'I did. C'mon then—got your things? Good. David, see you soon. Give us a buzz, keep me up to date?'

Juxon Street leads neatly up to the flower shop on the corner of Walton and Adelaide Streets. 'Uncle David, why is he dead?' Trust Alice to have an awkward question ready.

'Present for Mummy: how about flowers?' I can't fathom Jenny, I don't know what it is she wants. Making up for past resentment isn't necessary: obvious that Daze's moved on.

'What is dead? Charlie's hamster was dead. Her mummy put it in a box, then she threw it in the bin.'

'Uncle David's not going in the bin, Ally. It was—what's called exaggeration, when a person—well, he's not dead and he's not going to be. He's had a bit of a quarrel—a row—with his dad, that's all.'

'Will they kiss and make up?'

'That's what we want, isn't it?'

'Why?'

'Why? Because that is what we do when—'

'Why did they have a row?'

'It was a silly family thing. Here's a flower shop: Mummy likes flowers that smell nice: these ones?'

'You and Mummy row.'

'Then we're sorry, so we make up.' Alice scuffs her foot.

'Freesias,' smiles the shop assistant. 'A lovely choice.'

They are very expensive, flown in from somewhere exotic. We buy two bunches. I am horribly like Dad: he certainly used subterfuge to avoid Mam knowing more about his dealings with the congregation than he wanted her to. As I have today, sneakily covering time spent with David with this ballet pick-up ruse, and a spot of shopping.

Daze

SAME DAY

Daze, back from Banbury and moored close to the Jericho boatyard, is making for the Londis convenience store when she spies Max and Alice, and waves. 'Hey there! Hi, Alice: oh my fave flowers! Can I have a sniff?'

'They're for Mummy, kiss and make up.'

Daze crouches, and Alice thrusts the freesias towards her, 'Smell! Daddy said freesias are in your face.'

'Oh wow, oh no, they're gorgeous, lucky mummy.' Daze gets to her feet, and nudges Max, 'Hey Max: tell Jen I'm back, and we can meet up like I said. Listen, I've had a natter with a load of locals. I enticed them with a coffee morning on the boat. They're wild about having an arts centre—they're fucking wild about the Fun Day. She's told you our plans?' Max looks vague. 'Val's coming down, maybe her sons as well, Harris and Lewis, they did fire-eating at the Edinburgh Fringe. Funky family. I am so rapt.'

'All sounds great, Daze.'

'Thinking I'll make the place available to a children's theatre group—yeah, *you* can come and do acting when I've got my arts centre!' she says, crouching down again to Alice. 'And I'll have another snifter at those freesias. Please?'

'She's already the star of the class play—'

'Beautiful *and* talented.'

'Auntie Daze, I'm an angel.'

'Really?'

'I'm Gabriel.'

'Lovely,' Daze says. 'Can I come and see you?'

Alice shakes her head. 'Mummies come. And Daddies. An' Grandmas. And I don't think anyone else.'

'Boohoo,' Daze clowns bitter sobs. Alice wriggles, and laughs. The icy wind blows down Walton Street straight from the arctic, flyers from the Phoenix Picture House take to the air.

'But, you know angels are everywhere? So actually, I can see one whenever I want—Well, gotta run: things to do!'

Grocery shopping stowed in her backpack, Daze heads for the old print shop. At present, it's forlorn and desolate, but Daze sees the future: a thriving community arts centre, with colourful banners advertising exhibitions, drama, poetry gigs. All thanks to a rather edgy sculpture she managed to sell to a celebrity. She's got heaps of contacts, and Oxford's sophisticated enough to warm to work by her London set.

She peers through the window. Floor'll be sanded and polished, there'll be a big window on the street, walls a bright white. Reception desk, no clichéd orchids or orange African bird-flowers.

Within, a shadow seems to move. There's a person in there. Not a ghost, an ordinary person. From the council? On a Saturday?

He's seen her nose pressed against the glass, he's opening the door, he looks her up and down. 'Hi, can I help?'

Bronzed and blondish, bit of an Aussie accent. Leather jacket, jeans, and little gold-rimmed specs. Natty. 'I was just leaving. But you're looking for someone? Can I help?'

'You from the council?'

'Sorry? No. You're not from—' He has a folder in his hand, opens and consults some papers. Obviously looking for a company name.

Daze finds this disturbing: what's he doing with her property? Well, her almost-property? 'I'm—I'm looking to buy this place. Studio and an arts centre. Kids' drama, local classes—'

'Oh.' Is that bewildered, or thoughtful? Hunting for words, as he rubs his chin? She now has a creepy feeling in her legs. Her hands dampen. 'You're not a—' she stops. He doesn't look religious. His body looks like he works out, and he's tanned.

'I—think it's as well we met,' he says. 'You see, I was under the impression—'

'Yes?' Suddenly she's dropping in a lift, as he says, 'I'm sorry to be the bearer of lousy news, but I've planning permission for a day centre, right here—'

'W-what?' Daze interjects, her voice high and thin.

'We understood you were pulling out—is that not right?'

'*Who are you?*'

'St Hildegard's—we thought we'd lost it, then—the first decision was reversed because—'

'Fuckinghell!' It bursts out, as one word, before Daze can moderate her reaction. 'Reversed? God in heaven. Why?'

'Council decision, no concrete details. They rang me,' he consults his watch, ''bout three hours ago. Surprised me they'd do business on a Saturday. I was right over. It's been awarded to us on grounds relating to usage and overall city planning. I'm so sorry, they should've—'

'Like hell they should.' Daze sniffs back incipient tears, and swallows a thick, lumpy feeling in her throat, as she turns away from this vile person.

'I am so sorry—looks like their reversing their decision wasn't something you expected or knew about. That's lousy behaviour. Could I buy you a drink, so we can talk?' The polite Aussie demonstrates with hand signals, a drink, alcohol, the pub, up the road. 'I'm David Robertson, by the way. You are?'

'No—no drink and chatter, I'd rather not. It's—' Daze swallows hard. When she was a kid, she'd have grasped and pulled his hair, kicked his shins. Now, she controls her instincts, as her heart pounds, her breath's shallow, her palms prickle. 'Bugger the council, you know, for ratting on me? 'Cos they couldn't fucking care about art for the people. It's bloody well discrimination. Woman artist, no clout?'

'Doubt it's that. The indication was they already wanted to do something more for homeless people. They jumped at it being done at our expense not theirs. I hear Oxford's something of a homeless magnet? Sh-aaa-m-e—'

'*What?*'

'Shit, isn't it? So *embarrassing*—'

They stand silent. Then Daze is about to speak, but he interrupts her with a final try, 'When we're up and running, we could use an artist: how about a spot of teaching—if that's not an insult—'

'Bugger teaching. Bugger you. Shit, shit, shit!' Daze turns, abruptly showing David Arsehole her back, and powering off down the street. Banging one fist into the other palm, swearing under her breath. Now and then stopping to use the backs of her hands against the tears from her eyes. Tears of rage, tears of grief: words from a Dylan song, which step-mum Caro used to play.

God, what a fool, believing in her own success. What'll the locals think now? Across the footbridge, down the towpath. Onto the *Ironic Lady*.

She drags Trifle down from the cat's favourite sunlit basking spot, and buries her face in the thick, tortoiseshell fur.

'Grrh—mrrip.'

'Okay Trifle, point taken.'

Daze drops the cat, rips off kitchen roll to blow her nose, then reaches into the fridge for milk. 'Trife? Here. I could use something stronger.' She lights a cigarette, and inhales. 'Shit. Shit, shit, shit,' she thumps her fist on the kitchen counter: cutlery left drying on a rack jumps and clangs, Trifle scutters into a corner. 'Bugger.'

This feeling of enormous emptiness is over-familiar, an unwanted friend. Abandoned. Always.

Hating herself, Daze stamps out the ciggie and rips off her clothes, flinging everything across the boat. A plate, flicked by her black jeans, flies off the table, a vase filled with brushes crashes to the floor, her sketchbook skids over the table edge and slides into a corner, her vest top is left hanging by one strap from the lamp.

Suddenly, she laughs. She laughs and laughs, gasping for breath.

The effect of creating chaos—which nobody but herself is there to clear—turns her mood. Time to tidy up later: she pulls on old leggings, and a baggy T-shirt. And finds her running shoes. In Hackney, she used to take these feelings to the gym.

Here, she heads out to Port Meadow, and she runs, runs, runs. No plans where or how far, until she's exhausted. Her prickly thoughts leap, creep, and slither away to the edges of consciousness. Her running shoes are caked with mud, her hair's a tangle, the rain, which returns, mingles with her sweat. Her clothes stick to her skin.

Back home, wrapped in a dry blanket, music on the player turned up loud, she reaches for the *Oxford Times* she bought along with her groceries. 'Cowley Road—any shops to rent or buy?' she asks Trifle.

Jenny

WEEK OF 10 DECEMBER

Sneaky Max spent time with David, pretending he was collecting Alice from ballet. Alice, deputised to give me freesias (which I love), let it out. Always knew Max's family are big on secrets, but this was horrid.

Then he admitted they'd seen Daze: she's back, moored near Jericho boatyard. And advised I'd do better not to hang out with her as I'm busy.

We threw insults. He's another Alisdair. I'm all Guthrie ambition. What's gone wrong? David. Fine to support his gay cousin in opposition to the family homophobia, but not to hang out, with promises of working for David's homeless scheme. It's really weird how David's father, Euan, gave so much preferential treatment to Max. Even if David's orientation means he's not the son Alisdair would've wanted, is Max trying to make it up to David for accepting all Euan's gifts and favours? For allowing Euan to treat him as a replacement son?

Whatever, I call Daze. Before I can speak, she bursts out, 'The fucking council changed its mind. Like I had a done deal, a commitment, then, out of nowhere, my planning permission's reversed.'

'Oh, you're not serious Daze? Did they give a reason? I am so, so sorry. Wouldn't that be illegal?'

'Jen, don't even go there! They sent a letter: but get this, I heard the gossip first. I am totally hacked off. Right?'

'Right. So—'

'So bugger, okay?'

I take a deep breath: simply say goodbye? I open my mouth, and

Daze says, 'You still there? Nothing better to do?' and cuts me off. I close it.

But I have Gabriel's wings to make. The shops only sell small, fairy-type wings: pink spangly is very not-Gabriel. Alice agrees, but is convinced that Mummy can do anything that's needed, and that if not, she herself can. Secretly, she messes with tissue paper out of a shoebox. She brings the crumpled result to me to pin on.

I want to cry: she is so game to help. Hugging her, 'Alice, these are lovely, darling, and you used so much glitter and glue! I wonder if they'll last until the Play?'

Though of course, they won't really. I long for a solution that's going to make her stand out at school in a good way.

We return from a brisk afternoon on Shotover—where the girls have tried to convince us that we absolutely must buy a dog, nobody goes out on a lovely, cold, sunny afternoon without one—to find a note taped to our door. Who but Daze? Lest we tread the note underfoot as we lump over our mat, into our house? *'Four-Eyes, sorry I was a cow on the phone: how about we go for a pie and a pint at my local? Gardener's Arms Monday around 6.30?'*

With Max fielding the kiddies, why not? Her loss has fired up my instinct to help.

In comes Max, just in time. Out I go. Into a clear frosty night, the moon shining like a silver disc, even some visible stars.

The pub, huddled and hidden down a cute side street, amongst tiny terraced houses, fits the season. I push open the door, and what's inside is magic: roaring fire, incredibly low ceiling over cosy nooks, old oak tables and chairs, shelves stacked with leathery books. A figure in a far corner, with sketchpad and pencil, a half of lager, and a packet of nuts, has to be Daze, though the curly mop's gone and she's almost had a head-shave. 'Hi, sorry I'm a bit late—hey, image change! Looks great. Are we going to eat?' I dump my bag on the round table.

'Steady on: yeah, I ordered jacket potatoes, okay for you?'

'Anything hot! How's you then?'

'Get your drink: I can wait.'

'Can I get you another?'

'Nah, I'm okay.' I go to the bar, buy a ginger beer, and rejoin her. 'Any further news from Val?'

'Like hell, Jen: she's in New Zealand, and the fun day's off, remember? An' the haircut's not mourning.'

A young guy in an apron bangs forks and knives, wrapped in paper napkins, squarely onto our tiny table. 'I was so gutted for you. What'll you do?'

'Look, the bloody new owner's a sleek male Aussie. We only met outside the building, didn't we? An' he was all happy, and then all sorry for me—I freaked, like a fool, and showed I was devastated.'

My hand goes out to touch her arm, totally spontaneously. 'Oh Daze—'

She shakes it off. 'Anyhow, hot-footed to the Council and got it out of them—their version.' Waving her fork, which she's unwrapped, at me, Daze assumes a nimity voice, *'People would prefer a homeless project to an arts centre, less noise and disruption. Another arts centre's not necessary, and they doubt I'd get funding.* God. I've lottery money promised! Crap.'

Our waiter deftly places our potatoes, overflowing with melting cheese, and side-salads with rocket and tomato, in front of us.

I murmur 'Thanks,' thinking more about Daze than the food. 'Red tape talk,' I tell her, 'I know how it feels, project kicked aside by some faceless bureaucrat with no imagination. I lost a project in Cambridge, due to rules and stuff.' Daze looks at me, like my experience has zilch relevance. I actually feel more sore at the memory than I'd expect, and surprised how that leapt out of my mouth so easily. Refocus on Daze's problem. 'Okay, sorry, hearing about other people's loss doesn't do it for you when you've been junked. But there's already one homeless centre on the cards, so why ever have they ... Can you appeal?'

She shakes her head, with a dismissive noise, 'Nah: you know what?' Plunging her fork into that delicious looking melted cheese mess in her potato, 'I'll relocate. If this town doesn't want me, I don't want it.'

Why do I feel happy as she says that? Suppressing my feelings, I exclaim, 'Great to be positive! Gosh, rocket, and balsamic vinegar. Remember pub food when we barmaided in Sennen? Don't be beaten.'

'I shan't. Half decent salad a cinch, this place is vegetarian.'

'You must've felt bad to begin with. Christmas and that.' Maybe she'll move away from Oxford? Do I want that, deeper down than I want to help?

'Christmas? I stomped home, knowing, "Shit always happens". But then pulled on some really old clothes, and went running on Port Meadow till I dropped. It was raining. Came home covered in mud, not joking. Who cares about Daze Potter? Well, Daze does! Maybe East Oxford'd be a better location. Or move on.'

'Tough though. Listen. There's something you might do for me—while you look around?'

'Shall I want to do it, d'you think?' Daze has her head on one side, eyes shining, wide mouth in a big evil grin: I wait a beat, and then, we laugh. Are we now, at last, grown up stepsisters, our animosity around her dad marrying my mum all forgotten? Has she changed? Though she wouldn't be Daze without the ire and irony. Without the *fucking* and *shit*. 'What you want then, Four-Eyes?'

'Hey, don't push your luck.' I nearly added 'Droopy-Drawers'—the horrid name we used when she first turned up, waiflike, at Sennen primary. We soon learned she could fight her corner, kicking and biting and swearing ... Bad enough for me, Four-Eyes, the intellectual doctor's kid. I stop myself, and am nice. 'Alice needs a costume.' I repeat what Alice's teacher told me, 'As the chief angel, Gabriel's outfit has to pick her out of the crowd, maybe make her look a bit bigger than she is. And very important. We'd like really special wings.'

Daze forks in a few more mouthfuls. 'Yeah, Alice said. When I met them, her and Max, buying flowers. Hope you made up nicely?'

'Should I say nunya?'

'What?'

'Dad's into internet slang in his e-mails now: trust the old trendy ... Anyhow, Yes we did, and could you—would you—design and make

Alice the most glamorous, gorgeous wings? I could run up a white tunic, or find something in a shop, but I can't even start on wings. I've already made myself unpopular by saying angels don't exist.'

'Of course angels exist. I'll consult mine to get the wing measurements right.'

The pub's filling up, a rowdy group of young men and women surround the bar, dissing each other in a friendly way.

Daze waves, 'That's the Raggedy Poets, they're not usually here on a Monday. Guess it's a Christmas outing.' She waves, catching their attention, 'Hey, you guys, hello— though I'm not here, actually. This is my biological sister.'

'Thought you only had step-family?' says a big guy.

'She's a biologist—ha ha—geddit?'

''Course! Nice one, Daze,' the big guy moves shambolically away from the bar, slopping some of his pint as he goes. A petite woman in black draperies, and another, larger, all bum and bosoms, follow along, clutching large glasses of wine.

Daze leans towards me, nudging, 'Tilly Combes and Verna Braithwaite. They're always together, but they're rivals.'

The poets settle in the opposite corner, about ten of them, and start taking turns to read out their work. Daze pulls out her ciggies, lights up and inhales. The guy comes and removes our plates, we buy another drink each. I choose a tomato juice, Daze, changing to wine, mocks me for being a responsible citizen driving my four-by-four.

I pull the folder of data on Persephone out of my bag.

'So, you remembered them, the print-out thingies.' Daze says. 'You gonna make sense of them?' I move my glass out of the way. 'Right: I'm hardly gonna try and have a baby with that fucked-up Shane again. But, would I always have a one-in-four chance of—'

'There's less chance.' I open the folder, and begin explaining how the banding shows the chromosomes' characteristics, pointing out where the breaks come, and trying to tie it all in with resulting phenotypes. 'You have a balanced translocation: the gene which has detached from where it should be has attached to a different chromosome. That means you're okay yourself. But it could detach again at fertilisation. That is, in the gametes, your ova, when fertilisation is taking place. If that happened, you'd have a problem baby again.'

'So it'd be the same?'

'No. You and Shane, who are cousins, share a genetic problem. And Shane also had damaged sperm, from recreational drug use. And we can't know anything for certain. With Down's, we can say, the fetus has three copies of chromosome 21, these are the usual range of problems. We know some chromosomal variations—say, an embryo with three copies of chromosome 16, called trisomy 16—are usually a disaster, rejected very early by the mother's body. Very rarely, they develop. Like your baby did.'

'Yeah, so what you've got to say, say it.' She's pulling on her ciggie, fiddling with the fringes of her scarf. How vividly does she remember? 'My options are better without Shane whatever,' she says, with an ironic snort.

I play straight, 'That'd cut down the chances of problems, but it remains a possibility.'

'So, to have a kid who's not buggered up, what else?'

'You could have PGD—pre-implantation genetic diagnosis. It's a delicate process, but you could give it a go. But,' and here comes my Help Daze bit, making up for being a shit stepsister way back, 'how d'you feel about something more radical, and possibly more certain to give you a baby who'd have no chance at all of carrying the mucked-up gene?'

'How?'

'You can guarantee healthy sperm using AID. There's even a group, in America, called Single Mothers by Choice.'

'Wow, they've finally realised. But cut the sperm crap: what about the ova?'

'Ova are more difficult. But the first baby born using a donated egg was in 1984, so there's a lot of experience by now. The best way to do it really is to find a willing fertile woman under thirty five.'

'Willing? To give away—'

I tingle with sweat, nervous as when I was vivaed for my doctorate.
'I could donate.'

'You?'

'Her eyes dark as cess pools, her mouth—'

Ignoring the declaiming of the guy who slopped his beer, I hurriedly return to the science of it. 'The egg's free of the problem chromosome. It has all the normal ones. They pipette them out, fertilise them, and then like normal IVF, you have an embryo—or maybe two—placed in your womb.'

Daze's eyes, round and amazed, metaphorically stick out on stalks a moment. Then she re-gathers her sense of irony and the absurd. 'God, Jen, I like it—my biological sister. My scientist adopted stepsister is its biological mother. Hey, neat. Your mum's the grandma, and my dad and yours are both the grandpas, you realise? What does Max think?'

I shiver. 'I know Dad'd be proud. And amused. I don't know about Max.'

Daze grins. 'Hey, Four-eyes, let's do it? Shake?' She extents a slender, cool hand.

Confused a moment, I realise she's offered me cooperation in a project. 'That's the first step: there's a load more to go before we've got it anything like arranged.'

But we shake, anyway. And I give her a rundown of the legal issues, emphasising that I'd make no claim at all on the baby. 'But we'll have a solicitor draw up an agreement to make sure.'

I drive home, trembling a bit with the enormity of what I've offered, and had accepted. My ova, Daze's womb. Golly.

'—her mouth's a cavern, and her womb... warm, damp, mysterious, and I, within—'

Was that poet the baby—or the lover, I wonder? But he wouldn't be in her *womb*—. Or would he?

I see him as a catheter, delivering the embryo. Or in Dad's phrase, 'We *introduce* the embryo—'

I do not tell Max. I'll wait for the right moment.

Jenny

MID-DECEMBER, THE WOODS LAB

A brisk north-east wind howls between the tall buildings of the science area and tears the remaining leaves off the trees lining South Parks Road. In the lab office, Christmas cards and tinsel are pinned up on the bulletin board, and someone's left a box of Mr Kipling Mince Pies on the long counter, with a note 'Please take one *each*'. A big bunch of mistletoe's suspended from the ceiling.

We must not adorn the microscopes with tinsel, but a couple of people work intently in the main lab wearing Santa hats, and *White Christmas* is playing on the squawky little radio.

'*Carols*, if you have to, *please!*' Rich yells, striding purposefully towards his office, arms full of files about funding applications. He disappears inside, closing the door with his foot.

Leila and I giggle quietly, exchange glances and tie tinsel in each other's hair before we get down to work. Rich leaps back out of his office, 'Jenny? A word.'

Whoops: what've I done?

'Close the door. Have a seat.' He's behind his huge desk: the chair I'm on is too low to make eye contact. 'Your contract.'

'Yes?' The tinsel rustles in my hair as I tilt my head up and smile at him. He looks quizzical. Yes, it's more suitable to an undergrad than a serious member of the lab team.

He pulls a file from the pile on his desk, and flips at it. 'Jenny,' (long pause) 'your work remains at a high standard, but that abstract, for the conference? I still haven't seen anything.'

'I'm—working on it.'

'Good to hear.' Rich's expression is hard to read. Expectation? 'Now, let's see: we need a meeting before the festivities begin and everyone disappears.'

'The whole team?'

'No: a you and me meeting. Though of course the work's a team effort ... Would—' he flips the pages of his desk diary, 'Tuesday at two-fifteen, no, two-thirty, suit?'

'That's—' I begin, but rather than 'the day and time of Alice's Play,' I end, 'fine. I'll have it done by then.'

'Good,' says Rich. I stand, ready to leave: his hand neatly spiders across the diary page, 'JLM: conference abstract.' Pen, lid firmly on, back in his top pocket, he shuts the diary and beams at me, 'And, we'll review how you see Felicia's progress. I'll be talking with her, of course. To make sure she's settled into Oxford life.'

And I'm shown the door. Back to him, I can let my face fall at last: blast that meeting, Alice will be so disappointed. And what was the point of mentioning the contract? Stick and carrot?

In every other way, I'm energised by his demand: wonderful to concentrate on encapsulating our research in appropriate form to be sent out with the conference publicity.

I'll make sure someone else does bath time and stories so I can work late, at the lab or possibly the Radcliffe Science Library, undisturbed. Max loves doing it: can he arrange somehow to be home a bit more predictably? Or Ruth keep them a bit longer? Or ... Whatever, it's only for a week.

A week in which I'll also make a real effort with Felicia. I'll be really nice, but very firm about the importance of her getting to grips with organising her time. And give her some reminders on health and safety. A biological research lab isn't the shared kitchen of a student house. Even though she intended to return to finish off, the time I found the hood open, she should not have been so careless. Close the hood, throw protective gloves in the waste. Only then buzz off to train with the crew.

*

Finding that babysitter is harder. Who can substitute for me at the Play? Not Ruth: 'Could you be mummy for me, and go to the school play?' gets the answer 'I'd love to, but I'm organising Christmas Dinner at the old folks' club.'

Max says, 'You know I'm unpredictable: och, Jenny, could you not fit this writing into your working day, it's only a sort of précis of what you're going to be—'

'It's not: but you wouldn't understand. Forget it?'

Shaz is on that shopping trip to New York just the days I need her. Daze is my last hope. She'll not only babysit: she'll make the wings and go to the play. 'Ooh, fantastic. I used to love school plays—remember the year of the Medieval Mystery Plays?'

'When you were the Serpent in the Garden of Eden?'

'I was a fucking subtle Serpent, wasn't I?'

Amazing: while I complete the abstract, making sure it's absolutely flawless, unambiguous, eye-catching, and informative, Daze, back at our house, makes the entire Angel Gabriel costume. The wings are light, but huge, curving up and over Alice's head, sweeping down almost to the ground. Daze uses very thin fabric, strengthened, stiffened, and covered with what looks like real feathers, but is actually cleverly cut fabric, adorned with glitter. And a white tunic dress, with crossover gold ribbons at the chest which cleverly help to hold the wings in place.

Daze is doing something for me that's not ironic. This hasn't happened before. I suppose it isn't ironic? I suppose none of what we're doing is ironic? Not even Max grilling steak for Daze and himself one evening when he gets home? And only mildly grumbling about my letting myself get tangled up with her?

He doesn't mention the donation thing. Neither do I. He possibly hopes I have changed my mind?

The day of the Play arrives. I hug Alice and wish her luck.

Daze

HEADLEIGH PRIMARY SCHOOL

Daze slips in at the back of the hall. Crowds of Headleigh Primary's parents are seated on quarter-sized chairs arranged in a horseshoe, their chatter like the buzzing of bees. The black blinds are pulled down, improvised curtains open, and a couple of spotlights pick out, on the platform, a bale of hay, and two large Swiss cheese plants. In lieu of palm trees, Daze thinks, amused.

'Hey, need a seat?' Someone directs her to an empty chair, mid-row. Someone asks the inevitable question, 'Who's yours?'

'Gabriel. I'm her auntie.'

She's squashed between a plump granny and a pregnant mum, and being tiny can't see over a tall mum with a halo of frizzy hair. A woman in a long knitted coat and suede boots suggests she sit on the floor at the front.

Knitted Coat has set up a video camera on a stand. Daze resettles, between the camera and a projector, mounted on a box, which throws a panoramic view of Jerusalem onto a screen behind the stage. Hoping she's got enough wriggle room to catch Alice on her Nikon E2 digital SLR.

There's much shushing, and Mary, in blue, hurries in and sits on the hay bale. Cameras flash. Alice, entering, moving her wings, gets a big intake of breath from the audience, followed by oohs and ahs. She stops, waits, and repeats her line with gusto: 'Hi Mary, I have great news. For you.'

This is greeted with spontaneous laughter, obvious pleasure, and clapping. Alice looks around, half smiling. Enjoying celebrity, thinks Daze. More clapping. Daze focuses for another shot: as she depresses the button, she could whoop with joy, for Mary sticks out her tongue, sideways.

Click! What a wow of a picture.

Alice backs off, telling Mary 'You're gonna have a baby an' call him Jesus,' and retreats, to be hugged briefly by her teacher. Daze grins. That outfit stole the show.

A promising beginning. A series of great shots. Soon, Alice-Gabriel bounces back to announce 'Tidings of great joy' to a group of solemn male and female shepherds, one wearing a proper Palestinian checked keffiyeh, who gawp at the ceiling, cuddling toy sheep, while an angel choir plays recorders and everyone sings *While Shepherds Watched*. Daze's camera catches it all.

Finally, the Three Kings, resplendent in gold paper crowns and shimmery capes, march up the aisle carrying their gifts in painted, glittery caskets. Daze cranes around to take a photo as they pass. This time, as she depresses the button, she notices, beyond the three small children, someone familiar: good looking, in a boyish way, with gold-rimmed specs. Her stomach lurches, heart pounds, hands sweat. Lowering the camera, she turns and whispers to her neighbour: 'Who's the bloke standing near the back?'

'Where?'

'Him. By that door?'

'David Robertson. The Reverend.'

'Why's he here?'

'School governor.'

'Parent?'

'No.' Neighbour makes a silent *shush!* mouth, finger on lips.

Daze has a mind to ambush David Robertson, afterwards. The rat.

On the stage, the Kings rise from their knees, everyone claps. Next there's a line-up. Three shepherds one side, three kings the other, Mary and Joseph centre-stage. Led by Alice, the Angels march in, a long line of them, every child without a speaking part. Clap, for all you're worth. They line up in front of the tableau. Angel Gabriel's dead centre, carefully placed there by a classroom assistant, waving her wings a little. To a murmur of assenting laughter. Cue another photo or two.

Someone strikes up *The First Nowell* on the piano, to accompany the group of quivering, reedy recorders. In the third verse, Mary pinches Gabriel on the behind: Gabriel swings around, tongue fully extended. A scuffle breaks out on stage. Joining in the fun, Joseph cries 'Eff off!' Classroom assistants ring down the makeshift curtain, to applause.

Everyone is asked to help return chairs to classrooms. Daze struggles through the crowd to find Alice. 'Brianna's a bully,' Alice remarks, screwing up her face like there's a bad smell, 'she only got the Mary part to stop her whingeing, our teacher said.'

'Go, Gabriel! Wonderful wings,' says a male voice with an Aussie accent.

Alice turns and grins, 'Hi,' and then, smiling enormously, she moves her arms, demonstrating again how the wings move. 'Power wings. My auntie made them.' Poking Daze's stomach, she says, 'She's my auntie.'

'Really? Beaut. What a clever auntie.' He smiles at Daze. 'I think we've met? David Robertson?'

'Possibly, I don't remember,' Daze says icily. 'C'mon Ally: Mummy'll wonder where we are.' And as they move away from David, 'Do you know that man?'

'My Daddy knows him,' Alice says. 'We were at his house.'

David who nicked the print shop: or David who received it innocently from the council? Daze lets Alice keep the tunic part of her costume on, under her coat, and carries the wings for her, as they walk home. On one level, she chatters with Alice about the performance. On another, she's stunned to bits. Furious. The guy keeps popping up in her life. Coolly in control, but he must know how much she had wanted what is now his.

What next?

Feeling someone pulling at her hand, she looks down. Alice's face, looking up, surprises her. They're stopped by the main road. 'Hold hands crossing,' says Alice.

'Of course: what a big road,' Daze responds brightly. 'Look both ways, watch for the green man.'

As they walk up the drive to her house, 'We should put my wings on me,' Alice suggests.

'Yay! We should!' Daze folds Alice's coat into her own capacious bag, and fixes the wings. They ring the bell. Her heart has slowed again. The encounter was meaningless.

'I was the star. With my power wings. Everyone clapped.'

'Lovely.' Jenny sweeps Alice into her arms.

'Mind her wings!'

Jenny gently replaces Alice on the ground. 'Daze, I am so grateful. And so looking forward to seeing the photos. Stay for dinner, why don't you?' They go through to the kitchen, 'Only spaghetti ...' says Jenny. Daze begins laying up.

Bunch of forks in hand, Daze turns and says, waving the forks, 'Play was hilarious. Wasn't meant to be. But Mary, who's a mean little bitch called Brianna, pinched Alice's butt during the curtain call. Al was like ... *blah* ...' She shoots her tongue out as far as it'll go, then pulls it in and lays cutlery as if nothing happened.

'Oh my God,' Jenny explodes, laughing.

'Can I share the joke, hey?' Nobody had heard Max's key in the door.

'Ally stuck her tongue out at the end of the play. Brought the house down.'

'She brought shame on the house of Mullins?'

'No, she defended it!'

Entering as Gabriel, waving her wings, 'Brianna is a stinky,' Alice says. 'She pinches everyone. She pinched my bottom in *First Nowell*, and everyone,' her arms go out to encompass the world, 'saw.'

Max laughs. 'How were the wings?' Crouching down to her, he hugs Alice, and she lays her head on his shoulder. 'Daddy, you smell of cold. Your face is cold!'

'Outside is getting colder.'

'Wings were a treat, according to daughter and auntie. I am so jealous.'

'Of course, it was magical. Had to be. For all those parents. To get us in the mood,' Daze adds. 'Here, shall I download my pics? Onto your computer? You'll love them ... Then see who I snapped at the play, and tell me if you know him?'

Once they're all gathered round to view Daze's pictures, Alice can relive the moment of Mary's deliberate faux pas, which she does with squeals of delight.

'Daddy, Daddy look!'

Everyone bonds over the beautiful angel line-up photo, and laughs at Brianna's naughty bottom-pinching stunt. Then, 'Okay—let's scroll back, the Kings one, tell me who that is in the background?' Daze says, 'Alice says you know him?'

'David? He was at the play?' says Max.

'Let me see?' Jenny leans forwards, staring. 'Unbelievable.'

'David? You know him? School governor and only the guy that nicked my print shop!'

'Oh no,' Max clutches his forehead. 'Not David. He's my cousin. Jenny told me you'd—'

'The bugger's a relative? He fucking well pushed forwards and tried to shake my hand. An' we'd already met once: when he let out that the Council had given *him* the print shop!'

Jenny's mouth opens—and shuts, since Max is telling Daze, 'I am so sorry. I had no idea,' as if had he known, he could've stopped David.

But Daze simply removes the lead connecting her camera to Jenny's laptop, and pockets it. 'Look, sorry—I've done what I came for—I'm off home. Okay?'

'Daze—I'm sure David didn't—shall I talk with him?'

'Max, leave it. Rich loved my abstract: every moment Daze helped me was worth it.'

Jenny

SAME EVENING

Daze stomped out, banging the door. Alice started to cry. Finally we all sat down late to tepid spaghetti, kids subdued. Max and I looked at each other in silent despair. Our two bête noirs have met. And are in conflict. Could even be funny, if it wasn't so awful.

Alice pops up again from under her duvet as I hug her goodnight, 'Mummy, where was Auntie Daze's garden-angel?'

'Her what-angel?'

'Her garden-angel?'

'Oh—guardian, I don't know.'

'She ran away. She was frightened of Uncle David's.'

Max leans around the door, 'Ally, maybe their two angels will make up, and become friends?'

Downstairs, I tell him he shouldn't give the kids the impression that religion can cure human sadness. He shrugs, 'No, of course it doesn't, but Alice needed a story to help her sleep.'

I say, 'You're laying up trouble. Life is so cruel. Look at Daze. Look at anything—your patients.'

'I know. I know what you're thinking. But, she needed an instant—you and I needed an instant stop to discussion so we can all have some peace. Agreed?'

*

Peace is something to work on a few days later. We have Mum and Des for a pre-Christmas visit. Paper over any cracks in marital harmony. Don't let the visitors cause trouble in paradise.

They've just arrived, and should be relaxing downstairs. We're piled on the bed in Zoë's room at bedtime. Both girls have their heads down, studying the pictures in the book as I read, when Mum's voice, and then her face, beaming a big Granny smile, precede her full self around the door.

'Ah, sweet!' Mum says, doing a creep-and-don't disturb pantomime.

'Granny 'way, 'way!' Zoë flaps her hands at Mum, and screws up her face.

'Oh, do let Granny stay,' I say, 'quiet as a mouse!'

'We're doing Gabriel and Mary: I was Gabriel, an' ...' Alice jumps up, heading for her room. Then standing on one foot, holding the door frame, wings on over pyjamas (though a little crooked) she announces 'I'm the Angel Gabriel. I say, Mary you're going to have a baby ...'

Bummer: though Alice can't be blamed.

'Oh what lovely wings, darling!' Mum exclaims.

'Auntie Daisy made them.' Mum glances at me. I nod, and smile. 'Look Granny! I can move them: look.' Mum looks. 'Mummy, can I show Granny my dress?'

With some misgivings, I help Alice put her costume on. 'Darling, that's lovely! And Daze made it? It's obviously inspired by that Burne-Jones painting, a whole bunch of girls coming downstairs, which he tried to pretend were angels.'

Mum then insists on staying put, and seats herself on the floor, feet curled under. Her well-remembered perfume intrudes memories of our childhood story time, as I read, *'There were no spaces left at the bed and breakfast they tried, so ...'* But I feel like a teenager caught reading erotica. Actually, Mum might've been less condemning of that than this updated version of the Bible story.

Alice piles more books on her Granny's lap. 'Grandma Fee gave me this one, and that one's Zo-zo's. From Etta. What do you like? I like Gabriel and Mary—and—this one! The man who helped the travelling man, who got robbed? And the posh people walked on by? Zo-zo likes Jesus in the boat. And Zacchaeus up a tree!'

Zoë nods, and laughs enormously. She's heard that story a million times.

Mum shakes her head, 'Very nice, Ally. What other books do you have?' she smiles, leafing through the multi-coloured pile on the rose pink carpet by the bookshelf. *'Hungry Caterpillar*—Mummy had that one—and *Where the Wild Things are*? And—what's this? *Captain Najork*? For you little princesses?'

'He's funny!' Both girls roll around, kicking their legs.

'Stop now!' I say, 'Hey, calm down. It's bedtime: and you're getting silly.'

'Silly-silly-silly.'

Once calmed, Mum gives them heaps of hugs and kisses. With a shrug and a wink to me, she nods sagely when they mention guardian angels round their beds.

Free at last, back downstairs, 'Darling, do they need so much exposure to the religious side of Christmas?' Mum says.

I reach for glasses, and open the fridge. 'How about a glass of wine?' A nice bottle of medium-priced white is cooling in there. 'Nibbles?'

I open a packet of roasted peanuts, and dump some rather special olives, 'From the deli near Daze's boat,' into a dish. 'You and Des relax with these, while I do dinner?'

Mum takes the tray, but doesn't move. 'Sweetie, we were so disappointed you aren't coming to us, you know.'

I put my arm around her: her perfume wafts over me. 'I know. But with relatives at opposite ends of the country, you do understand?'

'Of course. But Harriet's in Oz, and … Alice is so sweet and Zozo—what can I say?'

'That the terrible twos aren't over yet, though the big three is on the horizon?'

That gets a laugh. And a sigh, 'Chapel House is so cosy, a huge tree, you know how Des loves to do it all. We're having the usual party, half the village are coming. And some nice, rather interesting, people from Penzance we've been playing bridge with recently.'

'But not us, sorry.'

She dodges from my arm. 'Max always seems to draw the short straw at holiday time: can't you speak to him about being more assertive?'

Mum's question's obviously something rhetorical 'to think about', as she heads off towards the sitting room, and whatever Des has found on TV. I laid out the Radio Times on the coffee table in advance for them, snowman on the cover, touching his top hat. I know they'll say they never watch back home.

*

Later: 'Come for a top-up?' I ask, turning from the oven and seeing her standing in the kitchen doorway. She looks weary. 'Long drive: I hope Des took his turn.'

'Des drove all the way, my darling. Can I do anything? Peel potatoes, lay up?'

'Veg are on, everything's nearly ready. Grab a chair. Okay, if you must, fold laundry!'

Mum smooths and folds. Even though, at home, she has a woman from the village who does it all for her. She didn't react when I mentioned Daze's mooring, so I try again: 'Speaking of Des, Daze hasn't stopped searching for her mum: is he aware?'

'Daze doesn't keep in touch with us.' Hard to read Mum's face, if you hadn't begun as I have to see through the mask.

'She worked someone's maternity leave at Banbury College, and she's here now, moored on the canal. So, if you went to see her, maybe she could talk with Des. He should get involved, and come clean if he knows more than he's told her.'

'Oh, I don't think he'd be any use on that. Des doesn't do nostalgia.'

More like, he doesn't want to. 'Daze is so talented. You saw Alice's wonderful wings. I would've called him to see them, but he'd gone to buy the wine. We'll get her to do another performance.' For a moment, I think I could share with Mum what I want to do for Daze. I begin to say, 'Glastonbury—', meaning that her abandonment there has screwed up Daze so that she can't trust or relate normally, and needs another child to heal the loss of her first. But my brain tells me wrong time, wrong person, and I stumble into 'Glass empty?—oh not yet—You could see her while you're here? Boat's cosy.'

'Possibly. Now, *while I'm here*, tell me honestly, how's your work going?'

The moment's passed. 'I'm always honest! Right: a rundown. My project's pretty important, but I can't give you details yet. It's getting exposure in early April next year, in California. I'm writing it up for Rich—my boss, Dr Woods, you remember—it might even make *Nature*.'

'Yes!' Mum punches the air. How embarrassing she can be, picking up gestures like that. 'Oh sweetie, you deserve it,' she adds. My face must've betrayed my disapproval.

I don't need Mum to ask anything more personal. Back in Rich's favour, I chat happily about the social side of international academic events, even adding a touch of cynicism, 'Yeah, well: it's a smallish conference, bit oddly timed in the midst of the academic year. But Rich explained it's important as our rivals will be there, in fact they've put the thing together. Sponsored by guess who—Dad's commercial outfit. The faceless ones behind his private lab?' I do the eye-rolling thing.

She makes a face. 'Guthrie promotions!'

'I'm strictly a Mullins. Anyhow, this event's been put together by the spin-off company, but, hah, I know the background. Knowing Dad, he'll lurk on this occasion rather than advertising that fact. He'll charm his way around, getting out of people what they are really up to, how far their work has gone successfully. They'll maybe tell him a bit of a story to sound further on than they are.'

'How well you read him.' Mum pats the completed, neatly piled laundry, and turns to sip more of her wine.

'Also glad it isn't me who's presenting our work. Don't want Dad targeting me with questions. Or—remember Wil du Plessis? Max's housemate? Taught me a bit? He's gone to the rivals, drawn by the pay and the place. He'd enjoy putting me on the spot. Dad, of course, will be busy getting in on the new karyotyping process for financial gain. All in the apparent cause of giving women what they want: healthy babies.'

'You'll be fine.' Evidently Mum hasn't been listening properly.

I remove the lid of my new fish kettle, where a salmon is cooking, and take a knife from the drawer. The blade slides into the fish like a dream, between pink flesh and backbone. Mum holds out the warmed plate, we slide the salmon on.

'Talking of babies, remind me, that person you met at the baby group? Who you employed as a nanny?'

'Ruth? Hey, could you wash this parsley for me?' I wave the bunch.

Mum picks up her wine again, takes a big gulp, 'Yes, Ruth—' she emphasises with her now empty wine glass, 'how is she? I s'pose you still use her?'

'I hope not. I pay her. She enjoys it.' Inwardly I cringe at that defence. 'Shall I do that parsley?'

'No—no of course—you've plenty to do—' Mum stands her glass on the draining board, grabs the parsley, runs the cold tap severely over the leaves, and shakes it sharply. 'Ruth. She reminded me a bit of

Fiona—Fee—when we met. A bit of a home-body.'

'I expect staying at home was entirely her own decision. She loves caring for other people's children, and enjoys being her own boss.'

'I hope it was. Some religious groups—I don't want you to ever think you can be pushed around by Max.' Shaking the parsley for emphasis. 'In fact I do begin to wonder about you two. Can you honestly say you're living the life you wanted? The babies are adorable, but don't get blown off course and end up like his mother. With five of them.'

'Mum, I do know how not to.'

'And your Max can be very persuasive. As, I'm sure, his rather awful father is.'

'The congregation eat out of his hand: he charms them. And controls them. Can we talk about something else?' I chop the parsley and make a sauce. Why must Mum poke at our relationship?

'Only I remember how Alisdair mentioned the "natural order", in his sermon at your wedding. Really, he was *so* offensive, to at least half the congregation. "Man the head of the family"?'

'Mum! That was years ago! Now, Zoë and Ally—'

'We could never understand why you perpetuated that name in your first child—Alice, Alisdair—?'

'Clever, wasn't it? She's named and not named for him. Ruth's hubby calls Ally and Zo-zo the Alpha and Omega Kids: top and bottom of the alphabet. We never even thought when we were naming them. I think dinner's ready: can you raise Des? Or is he glued to the TV News? We won't wait for Max: it makes him cross to have people hanging on his being present as if he were, well, the head of the family,' I throw a smile at Mum: she grins back.

Halfway through dinner, Max returns. He then tries to suggest a family outing to the Candlelit Carols at David's church the coming weekend. 'So we can all share a bit of Christmas together.'

'Sorry Max, lovely thought,' Mum says quickly. 'But we have to head home before then. My mother's insisted on joining us, and she's arriving by train in time for our pre-Christmas party.'

Poor Mum: my ancient Granny remains indomitable: charming, albeit wrinkly, she'll steal the limelight. And me: I don't want to even see David, after what happened to Daze.

Jenny

SUNDAY 22 DECEMBER

Our tough, feminist Granny taught me and Harriet that to be fair and clear-thinking was part of what good science was about. People who don't think are her total bête noirs. Okay, she's an intellectual snob, but there's something to her beliefs that's right. Prejudice is what people who don't think suffer from. Rationally, condemning David for the council's decision is unreasonable. It wasn't David's fault. So, I'm going to his carols.

Zoë's in bed, and the babysitter expected. The phone rings. Max tears upstairs two at a time, 'I'll take it in the bedroom.' Bedroom door slams shut. Will I end up taking Alice on my own?

'No my *other one, Mummy.*'

'Your pink hat, Alice?'

She nods. I sigh. A pre-Christmas present. 'Only one tiny pressie each, to help them wait for the main parcels.' Mum is an indulgent grandma: where's she got this idea of presents to help you wait?

'Sit tight, I'll bring it when I come down.' Leaving Alice on the bottom step, I arrive upstairs in time to hear Max: '—at her age. Meanwhile, if her chest's no better in the morning—' I open the bedroom door, and stick my head round. He's replacing the receiver, then he falls back on the bed, eyes closed.

'Max. You're not on call and you know we're going out, as a family. Alice's treat. You know what they say, *Don't give out your home number: there's an out of hours co-op, they should use that. You deserve family time without interruptions.*'

His eyes open, his serious gaze takes in the sight of anxious wife in coat and boots. 'She's a worrier. Her mother's over ninety.' He sits up, stretching, yawning, running his hands through his hair. 'You're right. Sadly Uncle Euan's traditional round-the-clock care for his patients rubbed off on me well before med school.' He swings his legs off the bed. 'Time to leave?'

The bell rings: fetch Alice's hat and let the babysitter in.

'Hi. Yes, leave your coat there. You know where coffee and chocolate live, make yourself a hot drink and we shan't be late—If Zo-zo wakes, one story and don't let her come downstairs, okay?'

It's another starry night, bitterly cold, a north-east wind blasting through our clothes. We pile into the car.

St Hildie's porch is warm and welcoming. A black-robed person is handing out tapers. Another shows us through the double doors. Inside, crowds of tiny candles, multiplied by their own reflections in the dark arched shapes of the windows, form a band of flickering flames around the walls. Their light picks out shimmery things on the huge Christmas tree. The warmth, the smell, candles everywhere: on shelves, in racks, in candelabra hanging from the lofty ceiling. Bemused by some alien emotion, I grasp at Max.

'You okay?'

'Yeah: yep.' Breathless, actually. Jolted into somewhere I don't want to go, while a distant voice requests, 'Could you light your tapers from your neighbours' ones, please? Then pass the light on?'

Max leans down to help Alice: I snap, caught by overprotectiveness, 'She'll burn herself. What if she drops it?'

'I'll not let her. Will you not fuss?' he hisses, then turns away, guiding Alice (holding her taper, beautifully careful and confident) up the church. They're whispering together: Alice looks back, smiles, and hands me the taper. My eyes are full of confused tears, as we're borne along by the crowd.

Alice stops again. 'Daddy, is this the stable? With the baby?' A huge Christmas crib occupies a side chapel. The coloured plaster figures are set in straw, surrounded with holly and ivy and branches of pine. Beside it stands a complicated wrought-iron candelabra, filled with blazing candles.

Max crouches, one arm around Alice, 'It's the stable, yes.'

'Oooh.'

Breathless again, I catch the moment. Alice, eyes wide with pleasure and curiosity, is me in Cambridge when I'd also had my first experience of candlelit Christmas, with carols. Up for interview, and with the man I fell in love with.

I can't do this. He gives her all his attention: he loves her, and makes the magic work again. She stands in the crook of his arm, her mouth half-open, seduced. Did Dad care like that for the five-year-old me? I turn away.

'Jenny? We need to move on.' A traffic jam has formed. A robed helper, holding a sheaf of service papers, tries to herd us all into the chancel. Reluctant to leave the stable, Alice won't budge. 'Where's the baby?'

A woman in a tweed coat leans over, 'Oh, the baby's not here yet, is he? We put him in at the Midnight Mass.' She addresses Max, 'Do you come to the Midnight?'

'Sorry, no. Just for the carols.'

Alice's eyes shine with tears: 'I won't see him!'

'Oh dear, oh what can we do?' the tweedy woman says.

'Nothing. Alice, the baby will be here at Christmas. We'll come and look,' says Max. Alice's lower lip trembles.

'Now we've started something.' Emotionally walloped by my feelings about Dad, I hate myself for blaming Max, Alice, or anyone.

He says, 'Delayed gratification: it's something we all have to learn.'

'That is so Scottish of you.'

'It is not.'

'That's right: move along up and fill the choir stalls, the choir will be standing around the Tree.' When we find a couple of spare seats, Max pulls Alice onto his lap. 'You come and sit up here. So you can see the choir and the Tree? Jenny, can we have that taper please?'

Thankfully, she's mollified, and sits almost completely still. Until she notices that the opposite choir stall is painted with Bible stories. Noah's Ark, Moses and the Burning Bush, and, importantly, as she points out, 'There's Gabriel and Mary, look!'

'Yes: ssh now.'

The church is packed with expectant Christmas visitors, each with a lighted taper. The organist is noodling quietly. The choir's assembled down by the main door. We all stand. It has to be *Once in Royal David's City*, it must: once I discovered the Carols from Kings, the huge college right next to mine, that carol had to herald Christmas.

Max holds Alice up to see. The procession's led by a teenage girl with a ponytail, carrying a tall, silver cross, then the choir, then David, robed, solemn, but also smiling, his hands folded.

It's partly to try and be generous towards him that I'm here at all. Other times, David's just ordinary; here, he's a priest. This is all about a baby. Does David know any of Daze's story? Her losing her arts centre to him is heart-wrenching. Would he care?

Glancing at Max, does he feel this frisson? About David in God-mode? About … about the day we met and he worked magic to persuade a sceptic to experience the spiritual side of Christmas?

He leans across as the choir assembles round the Tree, and whispers, 'I can almost hear Dad's voice, *A pagan travesty around a pagan symbol.*'

Not thinking magic. We're totally out of synch.

'Oh don't spoil it! Remember Cambridge 1984?'

'Mm.' He lowers our daughter to her feet on the ground. She leans forward to watch the choir. Will she remember this?

Jenny

CHRISTMAS MORNING

'Okay: short, upbeat, and child friendly.'

'Oho: God before self, worship before presents.'

'Dragging in the irony?'

'Nope. Approving the plan.'

We arrive early at Headleigh Parish: it's already crowded, and the porch is decorated with balloons. I smile at Max, drawing his attention to a monitor which beams *Welcome to HPC's Christmas Celebrations! Jesus is Born!*, then collect our name badges from the welcome stand. There's a bowl of spare plain ones for visitors. Standard conference type: about eight by three centimetres. As I write *Max Mullins, Alice and Zoë*, he leans over and says into my ear, 'Is that necessary?'

'It's practical: parents always have their kids' names on their badge.'

'And shouldn't that screen say *Happy Birthday Jesus?*'

'Please behave: or I shan't.' I'd like to laugh at it all, but instead shove the label into its clear plastic covering, and pin it onto Max's coat. Yes, he's beginning to hate being here before we even pass through into what's called the worship area. 'Please don't embarrass me by whispering ironic things all the way through. Please don't make me laugh by drawing a cartoon on the service sheet.'

'When have I ever done that?'

'Hox Genes lecture, soon after we met? Dad gave us tickets?'

'Oh *that*,' he grins. Then, flicking at the name badge: 'Bizarre to wear one of these in church.'

'Darling, we are a friendly bunch, as they say. You're here to find out what it is the kids enjoy. We made a bargain.'

'What's my end of it, what do I get?'

'I came for carols at David's? *And* I'm coming to Hogmanay. *And* we're staying over at David's parents'.'

It's upbeat and kiddie-centred: well-known carols, an action song by the Sunday School, stories, audience participation, and a big birthday cake with *Jesus* on it in blue icing. Half to three-quarters of an hour at most. As we leave, the worship band plays a medley of carols, the sound man's seated at the sound box, twiddling knobs, and the welcome team (with red and white Santa hats) are on duty in the porch.

Even Santa's there, with a huge bunch of helium-filled balloons. 'Well, his proper place used to be in the department store's fairy grotto,' murmurs my husband, as each child is handed a balloon.

'Hang onto those!' I say, and give Santa a big smile back.

'Or you'll float away like Mary Poppins. Happy Christmas, Ally and Zoë, the alpha and omega girls.' Oh my God, it's Keith, Ruth's husband. His unmistakable voice, and his toothy grin, discernible through the white beard. 'It's Max, isn't it?' he adds.

'Very festive.' Max's words are almost drowned by Keith's Happy Christmases to a large family behind us.

'Move along there, Zo-zo.' Max swings her up onto his shoulders. Alice, trailing behind, is caught up with the other family. One of the girls is showing her something pink and spangly. 'Did you have a stocking? This was in mine.'

The merry crowd seems reluctant to leave. 'Oh—sorry, traffic jam!' cries the Vicar, AFP, complete with mock reindeer antlers, and props open the door. I spot Ruth, and drag Max round to face her, not the antlered Vicar.

'Max, there's Ruth. Ruth, St Hildie's carol service was awesome. You should've come.'

She takes a second before smiling, 'Yes, the music at David Robertson's church is lovely.'

'I didn't see you there,' Max says. Wickedly.

'No, but plenty of people have told me.'

'We enjoyed it. Happy Christmas, Ruthie,' he beams. 'Have a lovely day. We must go: big parcels from Grandma to unwrap.' With Zoë on his shoulders, Alice's small hand firmly grasped in his, and a determined stride, he deftly escapes the crowd.

I feel he's been rude, and give Ruth a big hug, 'Thanks for everything you do for us. Sorry hubby's so dour today.'

In the crisp cold outside, I ask him why. 'It's vapid.' He hums *Rudolph the Red-nosed Reindeer*. 'Was the Reverend Field-Plowright acting something out of Narnia?'

'It was nice.'

Masses of people I superficially know greet us with *Happy Christmas* like we're old friends. Including Simon, our GP, one of Max's partners. That's a surprise.

Once we've moved away from everyone, Max turns to me, 'I'm sorry, my mind went blank back there when I saw Santa. What should you say to an accountant who's dressed as a mythical cultural figure, and hands you a balloon because the long-promised Messiah's birth, two thousand years ago, is being celebrated? I wanted to brightly comment, "So you read the name badge!"'

'They make an effort to be family-friendly.'

'Effort was obvious. Ruth's remark about St Hildie's music reminded me of my great-aunt Jean. She'd say *"You don't want to do that"* about anything remotely connected with the arts.'

Max says this so deadpan that I know he's laughing under the apparently dour mood.

And I'm right. He laughs. 'As for the reindeer!'

A few tiny snowflakes are falling. 'Wouldn't it be perfect if it was a white Christmas?' I say.

'That's really why we're going North. To find one.'

A few days later, we're heading for Northumberland. I've made a nice, fruity, whisky-soaked cake as a gift for David's parents, Euan and Margaret. With a red ribbon tied around it like a cake frill, and packed in a new tin. Max knows the route like the back of his hand, and does the protective male thing, driving the whole way. I play wee wifie and Mummy: chief CD-changer, distributor of bickies, chocolate, and answers to 'are we nearly there yet?'

It will be nice seeing Fee. She's calm and good: most of us human beings are fairly horrible.

Max

AT UNCLE EUAN'S

After a Northern tea, Margaret supplies a Disney cartoon for the girls, and hustles me off to relax with them. Jen's fallen into role, helping Margaret clear up, and my eyes are closing, but then Euan appears, sent along with a cup of tea. In a stage whisper, sat close on the couch, he states his reason. 'D'you ever feel the Lord might be calling you to serve him where the need is greater? Before the wee bairns need secondary education. Now'd be your time to go.'

'Mm ... Talking of moves, have you thought about David? Would you not consider—some tentative steps towards a reconciliation?'

'Och, the move's for David to make.' He looks thoughtful, though. As if he'd like things to be resolved. 'The two of you were so close as bairns—do you recall when you were first home from Cyprus?'

'And do you not see the need that we all be a family again?'

'Your father—' Euan shakes his head.

'My father'll not change his mind. The Lord has spoken through the Scriptures, and, whatever my father feels for his nephew,' the thought makes me pause, with a demonstrative sigh, 'he believes he must obey his Lord. It hurts, but he sticks to his guns.'

'*His* Lord?' Euan emphasises.

'His interpretation of what's in the scriptures.'

Euan doesn't wince, as Dad would. 'Aye. Well, I leave you the tea. And Margaret's shortbread. It was a long drive.'

Euan departs, Zoë drops off to sleep, half on my lap, her legs sprawled on the couch. Jenny removes Alice with the promise of a bath in the new whirlpool tub upstairs. I take out my cell phone to call the Manse. Waiting for someone to pick up, I watch Zoë's quiet breathing. My girls are marvellous, amazing. Intelligent, bright, and, even this one, usually good. Mam's forever saying, children are a gift from the Lord. So what has their arrival done to us?

'Hello? First Truly Reformed—'

'Mam—'

'Max, pet—now you're not stuck in the snow?'

'Absolutely not. Just a quick call to let you know we've arrived. Will be with you suitably equipped the day after tomorrow. Is he up to it?'

'I've not promised when, but he's on tenterhooks to see you. It distresses him, being so restricted by the illness.'

'I know. I hope he's not giving you grief.'

'I'm fine.' Mentally I see her, mouth tight closed against complaint, followed by a struggling smile. 'How're the little ones?'

'They're fine. More than that: they're great.'

'Children are a blessing ... and Jenny?'

'Glad to be on holiday. So, see you soon, Mam?'

So here we safely are, me, Zo-zo, and the cooling tea, the comfy couch, the less than professional shortbread. The good son's hat is firmly on. That antique grandfather clock which Euan so loves chimes nine. Sounds above of scurrying feet, running water, hushed voices, exclamations. Someone drags a piece of furniture across the floor. Jenny and Aunt Margaret, it's taking two to put Alice to bed.

Children are a mixed blessing: soft, beautiful, loud and very determined. I stroke Zoë's hair off her face, which is streaky from crying—her usual ritual on arrival. Where would Jenny rather be? Doing what?

Christmas night, we talked about the time I took her to candlelit carols in Cambridge. I said, taking Alice to St Hildie's carols was us passing on the magic. 'I know,' she said. 'But I want it for me.'

'It's what parents do, pass the best things on.'

'Mine—Forget it. Your family tries to eat you up.'

'No. We hardly ever see them.'

'David?'

'David will not come between us. Just make sure that nothing else does?'

She slapped me. We fought, which turned to making up, and making love on the couch, while the fire burned low. It's awakened an uneasiness in me, about who she is, who I am.

She calls down the stairs, 'Max! Bring her up can you, now? And the pot from the car? It's in a Waitrose bag under the back seat?'

Daze

OXFORD, NEW YEAR'S EVE

Jenny's Aunt Val could at least answer, and divulge more of her secrets. 'Hello, you're through to Valerie McGregor's phone: if you're interested in weaving or spinning classes, please phone after Hogmanay. Otherwise, please leave your message ...'

Blah.

The boat is cold, smells of damp; the stove takes hours to light, then more hours to warm the place. Daze tries another number.

'Jenny, Max, Alice and Zoë are busy: please leave your message or call later.'

Humph. May as well wish Dad and Caro a Happy New Year. 'Hi, it's Des and Caroline's place: we're out celebrating but will be pleased to hear your message. Ours is Have a Happy New Year.' Dad: how utterly typical. What a lightweight.

Blah. Blah. Blah. Busy. 'Bastards!'

And Val's in New Zealand: I forgot.

Celebrating the Solstice with her London friends had been great. Somebody found a fallen tree on Hackney Marsh, and sawed off a large piece, probably illegally, to form a Yule Log. There was sweet, spicy mulled wine, a vegan roast, games and storytelling. There was getting pissed, or rather, merry, and there was even a spot of sex.

'*It was, you may say, satisfactory*,' as T. S. Eliot wrote in that Magi poem her dad always read aloud beside the fire on New Year's Eve in Sennen. Yule's emphasis on renewal, the meditations on moving out of darkness into light, and turning away from the past towards the future, were disturbing. Past rules future. Can't escape that.

So, what now? Maybe that was an old message: maybe Max, Four Eyes, and the cute kids are back? A walk would burn up her aggressive energy.

Wrapped in her black coat, a big scarf someone gave her as a present, Doc Marten boots, and woolly hat, she marches across town, over Magdalen Bridge to the Plain, down St Clements and all up Headington Hill. By now, snow is falling. She breathes in gulps of icy air, and stamps her feet. Reaching the house, she feels almost able to behave well. Hot buttered toast, soup, mulled wine, and maybe a silly game.

House is dark: Discovery is gone.

She watches the snowflakes. Such silent beauty, mocking. Evening setting in, it's late, everyone's celebrating: I'm not wanted. Jen might've had the decency, the inspiration, the festive spirit to throw a New Year's Eve party: or at least be at home.

Images dance into her brain: that smile, the soft hippy clothes. Daze feels the loss all over: brain, eyes, arms, feet. The pain of that day, those succeeding days, that went on, and on, till night dawned (she once wrote a poem, *The Day Night Dawned*): Mumma wasn't coming back. Dad didn't know where she was.

Or, did he?

Daze tramps back, all the way down Headington Hill, passing South Park as the snow thickens, falling like feathers from a ripped pillow. It doesn't lie thickly enough to kick. The roads are silent and still. Darkness wraps Oxford.

The tracks of one car lead over Magdalen Bridge. Daze follows them, then marches up the High Street through increasingly slithery conditions. Snowflakes are still falling, but as they fall they melt, and touching the ground, they freeze.

The print shop was almost hers. What evil act of Fate—if there is Fate—wrested it away? Why is loss built into some lives? Put your hand out, grasp—the object of desire melts. Who hasn't disappeared? John Guthrie paid the rent on her Hackney studio. Until he needed the cash for something else. She'd a partner, until the guy got mean. And another, until the woman decided maybe she wasn't lesbian after all, and went back to her husband. Why do people go? That one, because shacking up with a girl, Daze, wasn't about love, or desire, but about making some point.

The print shop was almost hers: what evil grabbed it? The Rev David Robertson. Like God was having a tease, giving it to a priest.

She swings past St Mary's, and rounds the corner, taking the Brasenose side, slipping and sliding on the cobbles, towards the Radcliffe Camera. People are hurrying with care: party people, carrying bottles, shouting to one another, groups, couples: happy. Somewhere a clock strikes, and a bell tolls. Daze counts the beats: nine. Two couples, older, pass her, the men discussing some cultural work in loud voices. 'The viscerality is what draws the viewer in ...'

'Well, as language is basically unable to convey any semblance of the real—that is the external—world, verbal communication is of course more conflict than expression of meaning.'

'And hence the visceral is more real?'

'That, and of course the ironic self-regard—'

'God,' Daze breathes.

Her breath hangs in the freezing air. The couples move on, the women's voices drifting back on the wind, 'Everyone knows Rupert is a windbag, his students—'

'Amelia's trip to Thailand—'

'Ironic self-regard,' Daze breathes to herself, mockingly. Imagining Amelia—daughter? Most likely. Newly graduated, or taking a gap year, funded by Mum and Dad. She idly follows them to the corner of Brasenose Lane. Here, her feet abruptly describe an un-bidden dance on the freezing, slithery cobbles, and the ground rushes up to meet her. Her face doesn't quite touch the stones, but pain shoots through both knees, one more than the other. 'Shit!' she pulls herself up to sitting, getting her breath back. Her hands sting.

Struggling to stand, her feet slide and slide. 'Oh, bugger.'

When Life's against her, she always fights back. She must pull herself out of this. Feels like when I fell in the playground, she thinks, as she hobbles back towards Brasenose like an old bagwoman, collapses onto the step, and leans back against the immense carved entrance doors. 'Bugger New Year's. And I've not even had a drink.'

Leaning her head on the cold stone surround of the huge gates, some inner despair suggests, 'Why not stay here, abandoned'?

People pass. More groups, more couples. Laughing. Daze closes her eyes.

'Hey, you okay there?'

''Course. Great place to be.'

'Maybe. Don't think I'd choose it.'

She has a horrible feeling she knows this Aussie voice. Him again? She opens her eyes, 'God: it can't be you, can it?'

The figure crouches. The face smiles. The gold-rimmed glasses steam up: he removes his gloves, then his glasses, and wipes the lenses using the end of the long scarf wound several times around his neck. Replaces the specs, then his gloves. 'Not the first time I've been called God.'

'Bastard.'

'Bad joke, yes. Stupid. You're sitting on the step in the freezing cold: are you hurt, or—?'

'Nah. Maybe yes. My knees. Stupid cobbles: stupid to walk on bloody icy frozen cobbles.'

'Only your knees? Mind if I look?'

'Nothing to see.'

'If they weren't like that before, you've torn your jeans. Nasty grazes.'

'So?'

'How's about we find a hot drink and maybe you can wash those cuts? See if somewhere's open?'

'An' if it's not?'

'Look, we kind of know each other. We could go to my place. St Hildie's guest house. I've a few people staying over for a New Year's programme. I'm not alone.'

'Would I mind if you were? You don't half fancy yourself.'

'It's not that: I'm a clergyman, I have to cover my back. Max told me you're Jenny's stepsister? Daisy?'

'Hah. Yeah. Daze, actually.' He's holding out his hand to her. 'Leather glove,' she thinks. 'And a leather coat.'

She risks standing: her knees feel very playground, sore and unwilling to straighten.

Reminds her of her first day at Sennen village school. When the teacher tried to help, Daze had told her 'Bugger off!' Caro, criticised by the teacher for Daze's language, made it worse by saying she was adopted. Does she have to take charity yet again from some stuck-up person?

'Okay, Daze: let's hold onto each other and get over these old stones. My car's not far away.'

'You expect me to jump at the opportunity, don't you?' David Robertson doesn't respond. 'Well, you're in luck: I could do with being somewhere better.'

'Great. Let's go.'

Daze hobbles in silence beside Aussie Dave. With each step, her knees sting. Why this third encounter? The car, parked in Broad Street, is her next target. 'I thought a person like you might drive a Ford Ka.'

David laughs. 'Sorry, Volkswagen Golf MK3—European Car of the Year 1992. It's nearly 1997 now—are you disappointed?'

'I couldn't care.' He opens the passenger door: Daze slides onto the seat, and pulls the door shut. She's still flummoxed by the situation: why the hell did he turn up, where from, and what can she do with this?

At least something's happening. David: how very funny, how utterly ironic. What a tale to tell. Rescued from a dreary New Year's Eve by the enemy.

Jenny

NEW YEAR'S EVE

Perfect weather for tobogganing: we give the girls rides on the beautiful wooden sledge Des made for them. Our second evening, there's a ceilidh in a local hall, to celebrate Euan and Margaret's daughter Chrissie's eighteenth birthday, a whole year late. The frightful thing is, I'm enjoying my stay. Euan and Margaret are cheerfully hospitable in a Horlicks-and-shortbread kind of way, with board games, and a dram before bed for the guys. I'm selfishly glad they're still not speaking to David. Imagine what it'd be like if he were here.

OMG: of course, Chrissie's his little sister, born when he was a mid-teenager. How's she feel about him not being here? How's she feel about him, period? Are they alike? Do they see each other?

In bed, warm and cosy, I have to ask Max. 'They do,' he says, laconically, ending with a silence.

'And?'

'Chrissie's away studying law in London: her attitude towards David's orientation is her own choice, she keeps details of her life to herself, and nobody asks. Up here, she'll be the dutiful daughter. You get my meaning?'

'You mean they collude: Euan and Margaret know Chrissie sees David, but they don't want to know more? Because of your Dad?'

'Possibly because of him.'

He then tells me Euan's suggested a period of work overseas. Waved an advert for a doctor at a rural clinic somewhere. 'No worries, I shan't apply,' he ends, evidently knowing I'd not be enthusiastic.

Breathing again, I suspect he'd like to hear me say, 'And I shan't donate my eggs.' I just need to find the right time, and persuade Max to accept my pact with Daze.

Today, we'll move over to the Manse: the Mullins siblings are already there. We've been lying low, so that the old Hogmanay custom can 'surprise' Alisdair. It's as if the Mullins family express some undiscovered gene for secretiveness. Ironic, since it's me who's keeping a secret from them this time.

Anyhow, twenty to midnight, we're all here, wrapped warmly, packed and ready to go. Snow has been falling all afternoon. Now, the moon's out, and stars sprinkle the sky. 'Your vehicle or mine?' Euan asks.

'Ours: we've the seats for the bairns,' says Max.

Daze

ST HILDEGARD'S

'Here we are.' David turns the car, the headlights illuminate a signboard, *St Hildegard's Church and Retreat Centre*, and looming bushes, lining a short gravel drive. The drive widens out and ends in front of a dark hulk, randomly set with lighted windows. Daze momentarily imagines Northanger Abbey-type adventures, mad scientists at work, or even poor women of the night, forcibly brought here to learn virtue by washing laundry.

David parks the car to one side of the arched front door.

'You thought I was a homeless person, didn't you? To pick up and be sorry for?'

'I didn't know who you were. I could see something must've gone wrong, possibly with your celebrating the end of 1996.'

'Where were you going, or coming from, then?'

David turns off the ignition. 'I had half a plan, but then, we met up.'

'Sorry.'

'No probs. Think of yourself as the other half. Of the plan.'

Daze opens her door and looks properly at where she's going to have her hot drink and wash her sore, throbbing knees. The main building, with leaded windows, a low-slung roof like a hat pulled well down, and bulging bays, is in Arts and Crafts style. The wings are crass extensions, obvious modernisations, added at random over a period of years. One, glass to the ground, is better designed.

David unlocks the arched main door. As they enter, Daze is dazzled by bright lights, white paint, and a shining floor. She smells polish, cooking, and, bizarrely, incense. There's a Christmas tree, an antique table, pigeonholes with labels, and a statue of Mary. Daze sniffs the wonderful pine scent of the tree, as David hunts through a pigeonhole marked 'Director', then sticks his head around a door marked 'Lounge' and murmurs to the people within. A woman laughs loudly: for a moment, Daze feels the laughter's directed at her. David tells someone named Eta (like the Basque separatists?) he'll not need a chaperone. More laughter. Then he leads off towards his part of the place, swinging himself out of his leather coat and long, Charlie Brown woolly scarf, as he walks.

He waves towards a door. 'Bathroom. You'll find TCP in the cupboard. Tea, coffee, chocolate?'

Daze likes that: no sentiment, no offers of help. 'Hot milk, plain. You got that?' Why choose hot milk? A memory?

The spacious bathroom is predictably cold. She finds the TCP and some cotton wool pads in the cabinet, and pokes around a little to see if there's anything more she can learn. High protection suncream (back of the cabinet) is just in date. Toothpaste is the whitening kind, which probably doesn't work anyhow. Shower gel claims to be good for after swimming in a chlorinated pool. Shampoo and conditioner are the same matching brand.

She looks at her jeans: more badly torn than she thought. Her knees are a mess: there are cuts, and bits of ripped, grazed skin. The grazes are dotted all over with granular dirt, a blue bruise is coming out on each knee. She gets to work with TCP, which stings mightily.

Oh shit, it's all too complicated. The guy's heating up a kiddie's drink for her in his kitchen. What next? He ought to be an ogre: he isn't her type, he's religious rather than spiritual, he's part of some hateful plot. He's clean and seems to look after himself; he's sexy in a kind of a neat, precise, organised way.

Clean-up completed, she lets herself out and looks up and down the corridor. The hallway's floored with quarry tiles. Doors to left and right. A hallstand: his coat, a jacket, a big dark cape, and lots of hats. A tall earthenware pot, inside it two umbrellas and a professional-looking alpine walking stick. A set of golf clubs in a tartan holder. Very neat and organised.

She hears a door opening. 'Kitchen. In here!'

Limping round the corner towards the voice, Daze is gobsmacked. A huge, bright yellow, finned surfboard is mounted longways on the whitewashed stone wall. Crikey: unexpected.

She heads into the large, warm kitchen. 'Yours? The board?'

He hands over her drink. 'You're a surfer?'

'You?'

'Best beaches, in Oz. Spot of whisky in that hot milk?'

'Cornwall, me. God, you're a surfer.' Daze holds out her mug.

'Two seconds.' David pauses, finding the whisky in a cupboard, dotting a dram into both their mugs. Daze blows on her drink, thinking about this new side of David. The blowing makes waves. 'Some people find it unexpected. Milk okay?'

'Sorry, diverted by surfing. Yeah, milk's good. Ta, as they used to say.'

Amicable silence is disturbing: she isn't sure enough of what a religious guy might or might not want. Whatever else, if not for David, she would definitely not have slipped on the icy cobbles, and been found sitting on that step like a prize wuss. She'd have been planning the Fun Day, arranging building works at the print shop, and looking forward to pumping Jen's Aunt Val about Jewels's whereabouts.

She refocuses, pulls out a chair, and sits at the round pine table. He responds by seating himself half-on the table. Close enough that she's wafted with the scent of his aftershave. 'What did you do before? How far did you get? Teaching kids on gap years? Competitive stuff?'

'A bit of instruction, surf school for kids, and yes, gap year students. Quite a bit of competition work. I belong to ASP—Association of Surfing Professionals?'

'Hell.'

'Sometimes.'

'Got the awards to prove it? Why the dog collar then? Why the bloody homeless?' David shrugs. Daze comments, 'Nice board. Great lifestyle. Sun and sea. Paid well? Perks?'

She may or may not be being ironic. Her emotions are tangled: David could be a challenge, a conquest, but the priest part might get in the way. She's already noticed his neat bum, hooked on the table edge, and his swinging foot, in the black leather ankle boot. Mentally, she undresses him. Bronzed body, fit and firm. Don't even go there—he's the enemy. Also, perfect body might be twinned with a complicated mind.

Max

NEW YEAR'S EVE

As we park, the Manse looks dark and silent. I turn off the ignition, and swivel round in the driving seat, addressing Euan. 'Mam is aware we're doing this?'

'They'll be in the family room, at the back so he doesn't hear anything.'

Very quietly, I open the door, and step down into the snow. Jenny hands down the basket of traditional gifts: Margaret fusses, 'Do you have it all there?'

'He'll have the whisky, it's a double malt.'

'You've the coal and the shortbread?'

'I've it all in this basket. And the fruit cake.'

'The one I made,' Jenny adds. She made it for Euan and Margaret, but they assumed it was for the first footing.

It's for me to approach the house alone, first: a light goes on in the hall, Mam flings the door wide after a deal of unlocking, 'Oh, Max—pet—Happy New Year!' She extends her arms to include us all. 'Perfect.'

And here's Dad, still in command of everything from his wheelchair. 'He's the colouring and the build for it, aye.'

'As you had.'

As Mam steps around him, and we actually hug, most unusual but maybe less rare than when we were bairns, I have this odd feeling she's thinking not of me, but of him. As he was. And I am feeling how small, how slim, Mam is.

'This is a surprise!' Dad bellows. Sounding utterly taken in. 'And you've brought the family!'

'Of course they have. Now, you'll have to move so everyone can come in and we don't all freeze on the doorstep.'

Margaret steps up, with Zoë in her arms, Euan arrives with the parcels, everyone greets Dad. 'Father Christmas,' Zoë says, rubbing her eyes.

'That's Grandpa.'

'*I* knew it was,' Alice pronounces.

With the basket of symbolic gifts on his lap, and a tartan rug over his knees, he really looks the part.

'They've been with us,' Margaret is explaining as we're bundled into the family room. 'To make this a proper surprise.'

And under the bright light in here, Euan is opening the whisky, and Erin is organising her children: Cameron at the piano, Chloe with her clarinet. Mam and Margaret are laying out shortbread and slicing fruitcake. But I suddenly see Dad as old, tired, and fragile, surrounded by his family, yes, his fussing, celebrating family, who're putting on a show for him. But worn down by his illness, and possibly not got long to go: any infection could grab him away from all this.

It's painful.

All this stuff we're doing is nonsense: we're hardly close to him are we? To where he is? To where he and I are?

I turn away from them all, and pretend I'm busy with my violin, taking it from its case, tuning it up. An angry frustration is churning my emotions: deliberate defiance, marriage to Jenny, working in the south, avoiding contact as much as possible. Acts of quiet aggression against his control. Against his vision of God. While he … He took the responsibility when things went wrong in his church. He accepted it when he was wrong.

He is my father. We used to know each other. How would I feel, if Alice …

'Max! Glad you made it!' Alex wumps me on the shoulder. So irritating, inappropriate. Ian and his enormously pregnant wife chatter something at me about Jenny's Dundee cake being 'Mam's recipe and almost perfect'. The phone rings. Margaret answers, and announces 'Kirsty can't get away but love to everybody and happy 1997'.

We play music, sing carols, and of course we sing *Auld Lang Syne*.

Daze

ST HILDEGARD'S, A LITTLE EARLIER

'So, why not go back, and get on with your beach bum life? Why give your heart to God, or whatever it was you did? What else did you do, for work, then, down there?'

She tries to ignore that his expression changes: real pain for a second, like she hit home and hurt.

David's cool. 'In my mid twenties, a few things went wrong. I began to think, surfing has been fine for a while, but now it's time for real life.'

'And looking after a retreat centre is more real than whatever you did before?'

Does he look pained again? He's silent, anyhow. She's curious, but knows not to push further. And then, David says, 'Daisy: about the print shop.'

'Yeah. Well. Listen, I've been living in Jericho a while. I've talked to people. The locals didn't want a homeless shelter. They're afraid of druggies. Drinking, pissing, and noise. They want to keep their kiddies innocent. I had better plans: an arts centre.' Hands around her mug, Daze begins rubbing her ire into David. 'Drama and kids' fun, experimental work, exhibitions. But fucking council gets what it wants whatever.'

Another inscrutable, silent negative: like his eyes go inside to a place she isn't gonna hear about.

'If you want to know, a person like you, with everything, isn't going to get something out of doing stuff for people who have nothing. It doesn't work that way. An', I don't mean me. I mean the street people. It's something you don't know about. You should leave it alone.'

David focuses on the council's behaviour. 'I was as surprised as you about that deal. I've no idea how the council made its decision. Only that I was contacted and told that if I was prepared with plans and funds for the homeless centre, we could go ahead. It's a great down-town location, and the centre would be carrying on the work of the women who founded St Hildegard's.'

'Do-gooders?'

'Is it bad to feel you have so much you should contribute something?'

Daze leans her elbows on the table. 'I've no argument with that, 'cept I'm fucking left without a location. Small thing. Like hope you get the irony.'

'I get it. Life is full of irony. Like finding that pile of clothing on the step was you. Of course I feel bad about where this leaves you.' Daze grins briefly. 'You told me not to interfere with what I don't know about. Have you been homeless?'

'Mum dumped me, don't let that bother you. I don't.'

But David gives her a look like he sees through the bravado. 'As I hinted, the beach bum life isn't all bright and breezy. How're those knees? Were you actually on your way anywhere?'

'Goin' for a walk. In the dark. Went to see my stepsister and I guess they've gone to celebrate Hogmanay with Max's dad: who, as you know, is in your game ... Yep, being dumped is as bad as being homeless.'

'Any clues? Have you been looking long?'

'Jenny's aunt knew her. Without the project and the Fun Day, I've lost the reason for seeing that aunt. She was going to do weaving demos. I was gonna pump her for clues.'

'No other clues?'

'Nah. She walked off at Glastonbury Festival. 1971. I was five.'

'Right. Maybe *she's* homeless. People who are homeless are very difficult to find. Obviously.'

'God—don't start on the message of Christmas and Jesus being born homeless.'

David ignores that, and repeats his question. 'Have you ever been homeless?'

'Not really. I've always had somewhere. I was at Greenham for a while. But you, if you weren't homeless, what were you?'

'Without a home: beach bum literally. Sleeping rough.'

'Crikey. Sorry. Girlfriend kick you out?'

'I'm not unfamiliar with being dumped,' says David. 'But—by a girlfriend, no. I'm also familiar with being an outsider, you get the drift?' Another pause: she nods. Yeah. So finding him attractive would've been a waste of time. Shame though. 'So: let's cut a deal, Daisy. There's something I want, and I can't do for myself. You might—'

'Be interested? Old one.' But the enjoyment of creating a fight is blighted. She apparently can't outdo David on experience of the world.

'You might know that labyrinth in the floor at Chartres cathedral?'

'Yeah. Pre-christian mystical symbol.'

'Right … Well here at Hildie's we've been thinking we could use something like that. A large labyrinth on the floor for people to walk. Suppose you were to design and make us one? With attitude—something a little different?'

'Hang about: you nicked my venue. I don't owe you a thing!'

It's very late, they have talked for hours. David not only nicked something she wanted. He rescued her from a really stupid situation. Daze feels she's shot all her bolts. Maybe a quirky friendship is beginning. Also, some steady work in unusual surroundings.

'Yeah,' she says slowly. 'Actually—*you* owe *me*.'

'You're interested?'

'The flattened spiral?'

'The flattened spiral. That's a good description.'

'It's an archetype. A journey to our own centre and out again.'

'It can be a journey of prayer.'

'Or meditation.'

'About a century after those highly religious bluestocking women founded Hildie's, someone who'd visited generously left us a bequest. The Grace Griggs Memorial Fund.'

'And?' she smiles at the name.

'It's a restricted fund: to be used to provide aids to prayer and contemplation. Maybe a garden or work of art. In creating a labyrinth, you'd be making a version of an ancient symbol of wholeness, a sacred space. And the important bit, being paid. It's a commission.'

Her brain tingles, and then, her emotions dance.

'Now, you could doss down here for what's left of tonight. In a guest room. And if you feel the same in the morning, New Year's Day of course, we'll be having a communal lunch with wine and chocs, and a quiz afternoon. Are you vegetarian? There's a nut roast.'

'Yeah, nice.'

'You're invited.' She gives him a look that could kill, narrowing her eyes. 'Shit, girl, none of this is charity!'

'What, then?'

'The hand of friendship, it's an apology.'

She breathes deeply. 'Yeah. Accepted.' A beat passes. David glances at that expensive, surfer-type watch. 'I make it pretty much midnight: Happy New Year, Daisy, whatever it brings you and me, let's toast 1997.' Daze raises her eyebrows. David steps across the kitchen to fetch the whisky bottle. 'Another *wee dram* in that?'

Clever guy, she thinks. Always one jump ahead. 'Why not?' She holds out her mug: a small amount of now-cold milk is left: and they toast the new year in a slightly milky good malt.

Okay, he's apologised, offered her work, and she has to admit he's actually rather sweet. New Year's with a gay priest: what's become of you, Daisy? She's ironically amused.

'I'll need to go back first thing to feed my cat. Then, yes, thanks, the New Year's Day lunch you talked about?'

Jenny

3 JANUARY

Soon as the Scottish holidays are over, we set off for home. With hugs from Fee, and one of her amazing travel picnics. Hugs, so very un-Scottish, are worth all the more from Max's Mam.

It's a beautiful morning, the snow glittering with frost. Max, still in head-of-the-family mode, is driving. Zoë waves 'Bye-bye Snowman', out of the window. The dazzling sun casts the snowman's long blue shadow across our path as we scrunch down the drive.

'That's over,' says Max, once we're on the A1M south of Newcastle.

'With our last couple of nights sleeping in the attic on a blow-up bed!'

'I liked your blow-up bed, Mummy,' Alice says. 'It went wibble-wobble when I rolled on it!'

'And when we slept on it,' Max adds. He grins at me. Heart stops a moment: then I think of that vision in the carol service, when I so envied Alice being her dad's total focus. Though that smile is seductive, and the shades, necessary in this mid-winter sun, put a sexy spin on my thoughts.

After dreading it, we've had a great few days, even a romantic few days, despite the more religious relatives.

'What did you like best?' Max asks Alice, 'As well as our bed?'

'I liked Uncle Euan's *Kay-Lee*, and I liked the party when we stayed up all night!'

We both smile at Alice's pronunciation, like it's a girl's name, then Max says 'Not quite all night.'

'Nearly nearly.'

'Making the snowman!' says Zoë.

'You didn't make it: it was Uncle Euan and Cameron and Chloe and *me*.'

'And me!'

'Let's not quarrel, has Mummy brought a story?'

'Story tape, story tape!'

They argue which one. 'Shush, shush,' Max says, 'if you can't decide, it'll have to be me, and I shall choose a long, sad, opera. You know what that is? They sing everything?'

'No! Not you! You mustn't! Let Zoë have her story!'

And so, Alice learns to practice compromise, and we have peace. Kids perceive who's a child-person, I think, like animals know an animal-person. She'll cooperate with Max.

We have a long stop for the delicious packed lunch. Then I need to be doing something, not slumping in a seat, carried along like a parcel. 'I'll drive now. Back to work tomorrow, isn't it.'

'No, you relax. I'm okay.' The sun blazes between gathering clouds, reddening the sky with a glorious, wild sunset, as it drops towards the horizon.

Radio Three is playing a Vienna waltz. The light's fading fast, and the kids begin to whine, 'Are we nearly home?' Small feet drum on the back seats. Then very slowly, they stop ... Silence, only the swishing of car wheels on wet tarmac in a grey, gloomy twilight, as snowflakes land quietly on the windscreen.

Two lorries screech past, hooting, apparently in competition. Max curses.

'Don't stress,' I say, 'I said I would drive.'

Max says, 'It's not me, it's them. Louts.'

'The ceilidh was wonderful.'

'A pity David wasn't there to celebrate his sister's eighteenth.'

'A year late. But fun. Glad we were there.'

'Humph. Euan didna' think to book in time for last year. Anyway, she didna' mind.'

'They're quite easy-going, your Uncle's family. I can't see why there's this huge issue about David.'

'Belonging to somewhere like First Truly, you must conform. Anyone who disagrees with the teaching is out. Same culture for Ruth—you know that. The miscreant is edged out, the rest keep on—as David calls it—line-dancing their way into heaven.' Max laughs.

'I suppose that's funny? Why have a go at Ruth?'

'Sorry. Only she's quite a line-dancer isn't she? Follow the leader, keep in time, face the front, all stamping away to the same tune? It's about the safety of the group, isn't it? Ruth's certainly like that.'

I don't like that side of Max: like his father, only inside-out. 'You sound so arrogant. I used to love the rebel in you.'

He's not responding to my comment. He concentrates on driving. Then 'Oh no, illuminated signs. That'll be lane closures.'

As we all slow and halt, I crane around, trying to identify the hold-up. While blinking back the pricking in my eyes, and angry for stirring up that reaction. Ahead, the line of brake lights stretches away forever. Outside, the snow flurries thicken.

Squinting across the lane next to ours, I notice what looks like a large family squashed into another four-wheel drive, their car untidily stuffed with duvets covered in cartoon figures. A mop-haired girl in there stares back at me, and draws a face on the partly steamed-up window. 'Daze would've enjoyed Hogmanay: I wonder what she did for Christmas?'

'Let's not go there,' he says.

'Pardon? I only said—'

He gives me a dark look, eyebrows together. What've I said now? 'The first footing was fun, wasn't it? Your Mam loved how we all kept the secret and—New Year's is so much bigger in the North, maybe because of the extreme weather—'

'They do it in Edinburgh with fireworks ... What is this jam about?'

'God knows. At least the girls are sleeping.'

'If they've arranged to do roadworks over Christmas and New Year's, in the dreich weather, they're mad. But bureaucracy is mad ... I hope that's not—an accident down there ... Did I tell you how once I was—'

'Yes. It's typical of bureaucracy that the council was crass enough to reverse their decision, and use St Hildegard's to do a job they should do themselves. Another of Daze's dreams snatched away.'

'You've lost me.'

'Daze. Everything she tries goes pear-shaped.'

'Really? She's a pretty successful artist. Whatever someone paid for one of her pieces meant she could buy that boat, and even consider selling it on to finance that studio idea. It wasna' unusual to lose out on the first property deal she ever got started on.'

'Yes, but ... Persephone? Discovering she has a translocated gene?'

'Life's never perfect. How long've we been here?'

Why's he like this today? Irritable. Impatient. Gloomy like the weather?

'But when it isn't, we can do a lot more to—you were interested in genetic research once—if your father—'

'Jenny, let's not discuss Dad, will we? Let's think about getting home?'

'It's no different to Euan and David: you don't line-dance, though, do you. You're needlessly worrying about your own identity.'

'I am *what*? That is certainly not it. This is beyond belief, Jenny. Donation is something you can't and won't do to our family.'

My stomach tenses, my coat's suddenly far too warm. Sweat sticks my clothes to my back. 'Where's this come from?'

'You said it. You led us into this. Your obvious guilt about Daze.'

'*God*,' I say. Max winces. 'We had the best holiday. It was even romantic.'

'You think that was about sex?'

'No.' There is no way to explain my remark.

'I can't discuss it. Not now.'

What is eating him? 'Is that movement up ahead?'

Max says nothing. He's somewhere else, apparently. Someone hoots behind us. I lay a hand on his arm. 'Traffic's moving,' I say in a small, gravelly voice. 'And you needn't be horrid about me and Daze. God isn't watching.'

Max puts the car in gear, his mouth closed like a line. We slide forwards, gathering speed. Then there's a wail from the back. Unusually, it's Alice. 'Mummy, my ear hurts. My ear hurts *a lot*, Mummy.'

Max murmurs, 'Hardly surprising, with what she's had to listen to.'

'Sorry?'

'I said, I'll take a look at it when we're home. Maybe an antibiotic's needed.'

So he'll use his professional skills to comfort our child. While I'm criticised for using my initiative to give my stepsister what she wants. This has all ended up wrong.

Jenny

4 JANUARY

Alice is tight asleep, dosed with antibiotics and painkillers, after a restless night. I'm yawning over an early lunch. Shaz has arrived to play substitute Mummy.

'Right: how was yours, then? And have another.' Topped-up mug of latte in her hand, she indicates the box of iced ring doughnuts.

'Of course they're fake from Sainsbury's, but near as not American. Especially that choc with sprinkles.'

I shake my head. 'I did guess, you know. But I'll keep one for Ally. Chocolate? So, tell me all abut Christmas. And first, New York.'

She describes the shops, snow, carriage rides, all the glitz, and the presents she bought. 'And back to Christmas UK-style: with the frightful in-laws. Jos and Gussie don't get any better.'

'Alisdair doesn't either. Hogmanay was nice, though. We had fun: sledging, making a snowman. Euan and Margaret organised a ceilidh for their youngest's eighteenth. All flying kilts, breathless reels, and nostalgic nonsense. We stayed at theirs, cosy, not at all like the Manse.' I sigh suggestively. 'They've a lovely pink flowery spare room with a huge bed.' Shaz giggles. I add, 'Slept late. Two days slept late. Almost like before we had the kids.'

'Ooh. Well, Jos and Gussie have a fearful futon. Romance struck dead by the thing smashing your fingers as you wrestle it into the bed pose.'

'Bed pose. Love it, Shaz.' I turn my laptop to face her: 'Here's the photos. And by the way, at the Manse, we had to sleep on an inflatable. A blow-up bed. It slowly deflated during the night.'

I look at Shaz: she looks at me. We laugh.

Then, Shaz concentrates on my photos, admiring everything. 'Can see you had a good time. Except for the blow-up. Ooh, sledge topples over! And the swinging kilts ... And the grim father in law ... Wow, Jen, you're such a good photographer. Hey, this one—did Max take it? You and Alice are so alike.'

'Yeah, well—coming home, we had a nasty spat at a service station. Max had a headache and was buying painkillers, Alice was cooking up her ear infection and needed Calpol. In the car park, I was sat in the back, spooning it into her, and he took the opportunity to insist, "You stay there with her and give her a cuddle". I said, "Let me drive if you're migrainy", and he said, tight-lipped, "It's only stress". So of course I worried. And then home to find Katerina, my wonderful help, has had to return to care for an ailing relative.'

'Aw, Jenny!'

'Yeah. Aw, me.'

'"So," he says, "we'll have to manage", examines Alice properly, spoons in more Calpol, and jam with the antibiotic powder mixed into it, and I tuck her up in bed.' I yawn. 'And we spend the night sponging her to bring the fever down. Then the foul lab demand that I show my face whatever: so you, brilliantly, are here.'

'Glad to help. No classes this week, and glad to leave Charlie with Mum: the two of them cosying up to DVDs I've seen a hundred times. What about the spat?'

My hand moves towards a pink iced Dunkin' Donut manqué. I give in. Salivating, take a huge bite. 'Men: why do we fall for them?' says Shaz, rolling her eyes.

'I know. I was so sorry for poor Alice, with her painful ear, and her daddy shouting at her mummy. Like he'd morphed into his father. Gloom and control and—he's not the rebellious guy I met. He's lost his sparkle and turned moralistic. Like, suddenly?'

'Moralistic over—?' Shaz asks, inspecting her nails. 'At least you had long hours in the comfy bed.'

'Yeah, right: sleeping the hours we needed to catch up! Moralistic over something I want to do for my stepsister. What price altruism, hey?'

'Never pays off.' Shaz sighs, and again inspects her neatly polished nails. 'Mum and Dad's was all right, though. And you'd already had your mum before.'

'Mum wasn't exactly into Alice's angel phase, and she flirts with Max to his face, then badmouths him behind his back.'

'She's jealous.' Shaz has her nail file out. She waves it at me, 'I bought this at Macy's: travel thousands of miles and buy a nail file!'

'Of us?' I laugh, and rise from the table, gathering our mugs and plates. 'She may be, of us not being divorced. Yet.' I roll my eyes, lest Shaz thinks I'm even half-seriously concerned. Shaz grins.

'What's Des like, then, your stepdad?'

I run water into the sink. 'Great when we were little. Taught me photography, developing, printing, all that. But now— When he and Mum were leaving, Des backed the car down the drive *whizz*, sending gravel flying everywhere, not looking one bit. The girls were out there. Didn't think about their safety. Des made Ally and Zoë those sledges for Christmas presents–'

'Amazing.'

I turn back to face Shaz, 'There's things you don't notice till you're a parent yourself, aren't there?'

'You're so right. Rioting with the kiddies, then leaving us to calm them down.'

'And he didn't make time to visit Daze when she was just down the road, here. I'd have done, wouldn't you?'

The doorbell rings. ''Scuse me: Ruth suggested her help might come over and do some cleaning.'

'It's only me!' Etta's voice sings out from behind the door.

I open it. 'You're a star.'

'Come twinkling along to save you. Where shall I begin?'

'First come and meet my friend who's here to look after Alice?'

Shaz settles in the study, with some work to do with the tax on her business. I warn her, quietly, 'One small drawback to Etta, she sings while she works. And she has a powerful voice.' Shaz grins. I look in again on Alice, who remains very asleep, and fix up the baby alarm so Shaz will hear if she wakes.

Pulling on my coat and boots, finding my bag, I hear Etta downstairs, 'Excuse me while I clean this handle. I was ironing this morning. With the radio. Well not *with* the radio, but you know. They was saying how viruses can be passed around on people's hands. So you see, that's why the little ones are all coughing and burning up. Door handles.'

Etta's style puts a smile on my face as I gently close the front door.

Although I didn't mention it to Shaz, I've begun to compare my parents unfavourably to Max's mother. I wouldn't want her life, especially *submitting* to her husband. But, there's something about her. I wish I had her grit. Whatever her family does, she's got this way to keep loving people. Why can some people hack what ought to be misery-making? She's happy and generous, while being exploited and overworked.

My car doesn't want to start. It takes three goes till the engine coughs into life. What's Max's problem, why doesn't he share it?

Daze

ST HILDEGARD'S

The New Year's Day feast with the St Hildie's community and visitors was beguiling. Good food, undemanding company. The bloody boat's chilly and damp whenever the stove's not lit. Daze was already almost tempted to give up on the *Ironic Lady*. Even if she'd got the arts centre going, would the baby thing have worked? But the labyrinth idea's wicked.

Oxford is bone-chilling and grey, under a white sky, the snow gone. She cycles her ancient bike to St Hildegard's. Hard work, heart pumping like crazy. She's reduced to pushing the bike up Headington Hill. Her healing knees remain stiff and painful.

When David answers her knock, she mimics a salute, 'Artist in residence reporting for duty. Lead on: where's this artwork gonna be?'

'Great to see you. Leave the bike here, I'll take you over the whole complex. That'll give you a feel for what kind of labyrinth might suit. You can think about style and materials. How's the knees?'

'How d'you think? You know a bit about design?'

'I'd a friend who was an architect once.'

Partner? Daze wonders.

David indicates the arched door, the steeply gabled roof, the shape of the windows, 'The original red brick building is Arts and Crafts, of course you'd know that.'

'Voysey.'

David nods. He briefly describes how the Retreat House was extended and modernised.

Daze feels rather taken with the place, and amused. Looking across the grounds, she spots what must be the chapel. 'Can I take a shufti at your church?'

The door creaks as David opens it, and ushers her inside. In the porch, she's weirdly compelled, stretches out her hand to dip in the stoup of holy water, and crosses herself. 'It's what you do. Isn't it.'

'Go ahead.'

In the nave, she breathes in the scents of incense and damp stone. There's light enough coming in from outside, despite a deepening January gloom, to make out the odd church furniture as her eyes adapt. Hyper-traditional, everything ornate. 'Wow, it's so Goth! *St Agnes Eve, ah, bitter chill it was! The owl for all his feathers was a-cold!* Keats, A-level—or didn't you do English?'

'Physics, maths, chemistry—very badly. Dad intended me to be a doctor.'

'Control freak,' Daze says. 'Mine didn't do intend.'

She gazes around, loving the painted ceiling and choir stalls. And, 'I like the triptych window. That's St Hildegard? Writing at her desk, and composing music with the angel whispering in her ear, and conducting her choir of nuns?'

'She was quite a woman, for medieval times. She headed up a convent and wrote about philosophy, and medical herbalism, as well as the music. We've a book in the library: read it.'

'Kind of early feminist. I like that. Though you'd not want the labyrinth here, would you?'

'Absolutely not. The church, as you said, is terribly Goth. We want our labyrinth to be a timeless sacred space for today. Library's in the main building,' David says. 'We'll go in via the Livingstone Lounge, added in the 1970's.'

'That's the room with glass to the ground, is it? That'd be great, loads of natural light.'

Despite its floor-to-ceiling windows, the Livingstone Lounge is dreary and ripe for an update. 'God, closing my eyes, I could be back in the school gym,' Daze bursts out. 'Can we take the green lino up?

Get rid of that rubbery smell? What about those stacking chairs, the mats and the piano? Have to go, if you want a decent Labyrinth.'

Slightly apologetic, though grinning, David admits, 'You're right. We let out the space for a number of groups to use. So we need to store yoga and gym mats.'

'Mm: but you also need a labyrinth.'

Touring the simply-furnished bedrooms for weekend visitors, 'It's like a monastery!' Daze comments. 'My guest room was a bit more—'

'Got it. A monastery.' He twinkles at her. 'Yes, we put you in the only room that was free. Usually that's reserved for the Bishop. Now, the library?' Mounting the stylish oak staircase, 'Have you heard of the Venerable Bede?'

'Bead?' Daze laughs. 'He'd do all right on a rosary.'

'Have you visited the site of Bede's monastery? After Scotland, my family lived in the North East, so we visited Holy Island a bit. Have you been?'

'Yeah, Lindisfarne. An' Whitby, for Goth stuff.'

'And I hope read *The Name of the Rose*, or seen the movie?'

'About those anti-religious monks?'

'Umberto Eco is a postmodernist.'

'Aren't we all? Maybe not ...'

'Here we are: anyone studying?' A woman a few years older than Daze, wearing a black shirt and dog collar with jeans and a pale blue fleece waistcoat, is the only occupier. A computer with a bulky monitor hums to itself, but she's busy sorting some books. 'Tamsin? This is Daze, she's an artist. She's looking for what we have on labyrinths: okay with you?'

The woman smiles. 'No probs. I'm the librarian, so ask me for anything you need. And do use the computer: sorry it's so loud, it's a bit elderly.'

'I'll leave you three together.' Oh-ho, joke, Daze thinks, as David and Tamsin laugh.

New things are always interesting. Daze hasn't met a woman priest before, though when she camped at Greenham she met a couple of women who wanted to be.

'Making a labyrinth for that space downstairs. The Grace Griggs foundation?'

'And you're interested in Hildegard's story?'

'I thought I'd read it up. For background?'

Daze spends the morning browsing and making notes. Design and make a labyrinth for people whose lives are disciplined, organised, and centred on the Christian God. Does it have to differ from pagan use? Will it still be a metaphor for the journey to the centre of your deepest self? How can this labyrinth say anything new?

After a while, Tamsin disappears to see to some guests. She returns with two mugs of instant coffee and a plate of digestive biscuits. They chat about what they studied at college: surprisingly, Tamsin did physics and is interested in astronomy. 'Me, I'm more like, astrology, alchemy, all that,' Daze says, 'but my sister's a biologist. Genetics.'

As she spends time at St Hildie's, Daze, amused, begins to imagine telling Jenny Four-Eyes that now she's also working in a lab. Maybe not: feeble joke. And, since it's for David, this whole thing's a big irony. Though she becomes aware that her deepest self is feeling relaxed and warm. They're not her sort, but they're liveable with. The cook makes cup cakes and gingerbread and there's tea at four every afternoon for those guests who inhabit the cell-like bedrooms. None of that is ironic.

She draws and redraws the labyrinth, experiments with colour, considers materials.

'You wouldn't consider outdoors, with the path edged with herbs? Use an all-weather surface. Imagine: walking it in a storm?' she says.

'Great idea. But not disabled – or elderly-friendly.'

'Have to be the Livingstone Lounge. Why Livingstone?'

'Built with Edith Livingstone's bequest. A regular retreatant until the mid-seventies.'

'And no more yoga mats. How about mosaic? Undulating fish, boats rocked by the storms of life?'

David is half convinced. The expense would be in getting the floor up and concreting it.

'But you agreed to get rid of the green lino!'

A few days later, Daze is taking photos in the Livingstone Lounge. David sidles up to her looking pleased with himself. 'I'm afraid I've got another project for you. I thought we might reinstate the Fun Day, and …'

'Hey, cool!' She interrupts whatever else he's saying, utterly amazed, then, 'Why'd you think of that?'

'It'd raise awareness of the homeless project amongst the neighbours. And we'd have a ball ourselves.'

'Listen, my stepsister Jen has cousins who eat fire. Not their day job: they're in IT. But fire-eat on the side. How fun is that?'

'Great stuff.' They high-five.

Then pause, slightly embarrassed.

Daze, to get over it, says, 'Their mother, Valerie McGregor, is my patron's twin sister. My patron—John Guthrie, fertility guy?'

David grins. 'Talented family, what does the twin sister do?'

'Spins and weaves. She does demos. And sells shawls and tartans. I told you, she was gonna do that at my Fun Day.'

'Ask them all. So Guthrie's your patron. What does that entail in today's world? I do mean the printable version.'

'He understands conceptual art. Get it?'

'I think so.'

Jenny

SOME DAYS LATER

I'm walking down Parks Road, it's a bright cold morning, and Daze zooms past on her bike. She waves, slows, and screeches to a halt. 'You okay?' I shout.

'Yeah. New project. You?'

'Mum and Des were here, before Christmas. I told them where you're living.'

'I can't think why you bothered.' Doing the watch-glance thing, Daze adds, 'Actually, gotta go, late. By the way, Fun Day's on again. See ya!'

Fun Day? The council surely couldn't have changed its mind again. Where does this leave me, and our pact?

As I arrive at the department, Rich is tethering his bicycle outside. We enter the building together, and there's no subtle way to avoid sharing the lift with the boss. 'Trying to take more exercise, now Danielle's school runs its own bus. I'd forgotten how good it feels to ride in on a sunny morning. Now, I'm glad we met, because, I've been thinking about you.'

Stepping out of the lift, Rich makes a 'walk with me' gesture. I fall in, he says 'No worries, this could be a great opportunity,' sweeping me to the lab, and straight into his office. 'Have a seat.'

I sit, curious and hopeful. And undo my coat.

He goes behind his desk, unwraps his scarf, removes his windproof jacket, and hangs them on the coat stand. 'About the conference. A problem has arisen: Danni's been needing a foot op for a while. They've finally scheduled for early April. Down's syndrome, especially the heart problems, makes her having a general anaesthetic a bit worrisome. So I want to be here for her.'

'Of course. So would I.' Could hardly get that out. *The conference? What a great career move if ...?*

Rich is cool. 'Slight change of plan. The work's chiefly in your special area, how about you going to California after Easter?'

Really? Did I stop breathing a second or two? I can't speak.

So he gets reassuring, in his terms. 'I'm giving you a chance to shine. So let's see if you can do it?'

Oh, wow. Me. Present the work. Without him, the head of lab, being there.

'Jenny? Got plenty to do today, then?'

I feel the smile on my face, and the quivering of my insides, as I stand to leave. 'Yes—yes I have. I am—amazed.'

'And you're going to be preparing to field those awkward questions, and represent us to the opposition.' He grins. I am then dismissed, the door held open for me, by our Principal Investigator, who closes it quietly behind me.

Leila looks up from her work, like there's a big question mark over her head, 'All okay?'

I do the thumbs-up, 'Oh. My. God. He wants me to go to present our work!' Leila and I hug: she is so sweet about it being me, not her.

*

Though how to explain to Max that I shall after all be the one going to the USA to present the Woods' lab contribution? After assuring him I wouldn't? Best to beguile him. I call the surgery and leave a message for him to come over to the lab after work.

He turns up a bit bewildered. 'Thought you might like to see what I do all day, what it all looks like. Come in the microscope room, you can take a look at some cells we've marked with the green fluorescent protein I was so excited about.'

To end with, I demonstrate on one of the computers, with graphs and tables, our very small but possibly important advance, the research I'm writing up.

'So is this where I say, Why the big grin?' he asks. With a big grin, of course.

'It was a total surprise,' I say, and explain Rich giving me the great news this morning, and why he won't be going. Max leans back against the desk, where we've been concentrating on the computer screen. 'This was the only way I could think of telling you. You don't mind? I can hardly believe the opportunity's been thrown at me.'

'Mmm. How d'you feel about it?' His hands are in his pockets, and he studies his shoes: I'd prefer he looked me in the eye, or gave me a hug.

'Point is, how do you feel? How do we manage it?'

'Oh, me: I'm totally in favour.'

'Right. Me, the *oh, wow* is mixed in with the *how the hell do I field those inevitable tricksy questions from scientists experienced in the field, the big names, the jealous ones?* They'll all be there. Wanting to grill me alive.'

Now he does give me a reassuring hug. 'You'll be fine. Take it slowly.'

'Rich said, it'll give me a chance to shine?'

'Jenny, you're a star. Already. Don't worry.'

'That's not ironic, is it?'

'Why should it be?'

I shake my head. 'It shouldn't.' I relax. And let the excitement take over.

Though Max has performed his old trick: turned the spotlight onto the other person. What're his real thoughts and feelings?

In bed I toss around, dreaming of fluorescent cells and jeering scientists. My voice is croaky, my throat is sore. In the morning I struggle to the lab. And come home with a streaming cold and a cough.

'Doorhandle-itis,' says Etta, who's cleaning.

'Pardon?'

'That's not flippin' nonsense, it's what research has shown.' When Ruth delivers the girls home, Etta insists, 'Go to bed: I can manage their tea.'

She grills some bacon. 'Done you sandwiches like my nan made 'em,' I hear, followed by a familiar tune. Alice and Zoë are teaching Etta to sing *I belong to Glasgow* …

Max laughs when I tell him this. I say, 'Saw Daze yesterday. Seems she's got some exciting work too.'

'Good. She's occupied. Did she also tell you she and David made up?'

'When? David told you?'

'He left a terse message asking if I would play for Scottish country dancing at the reinstated Fun Day. Apparently a special request from Daisy.'

'So that's what she was mysterious about. She's got David on board. Our bête noirs are working together. On what?'

'She's doing him a piece of art.'
'Weird.'
'Miracles happen. It appears.'

Jenny

11 FEBRUARY, SHROVE TUESDAY

I kneel on the bathmat, my sleeves rolled up beyond the elbow. I'm happier since Rich told me we'd have a rehearsal of my conference presentation, where I can experience in advance the hideous question session by having my lab colleagues fire the worst they can think at me. Yes. It'll be nasty, but it'll give me a dry run. I'm looking forward to the real thing: more excitedly nervous than I've been in a long time … But at present, I'm playing the mummy role … I soap Zoë. Alice, using a sponge, says 'Look. Mummy, a lace body suit with leggings.'

'Lovely.' I blink, pushing away my imaginings about being on that conference platform.

'Done everything, done my bottom, and my *belly button!*' Alice says.

'Belly button, belly button!' Zoë shrieks. They both dissolve into squeals of laughter, water comes over the side, soaking my jeans, as they giggle, squirm, and splash.

'Damn!' I seize a towel, as we hear a noise downstairs. 'Calm down, now—isn't that —listen—'

'Daddy!'

We hear Max close the front door, and go into the study, dumping his bag. We hear his feet on the stairs. 'All my wee girls in one room!'

'Daddy, Daddy!'

'All my three beautiful lassies,' he says, exaggerating his soft, almost imperceptible accent.

'You're back early.'

'Oh, you want me to leave again?' he teases.

'No—it's nice.'

'Good. We're going out, remember? Pancake Day, David's place?' Pancake Day: I'd forgotten. So that was why my postgrad student went shopping for lemons in her lunch hour.

'You did book the babysitter?'

'Yikes, Max, I forgot. I'll try Daze,' reaching into my pocket for my phone.

'I'll dry them off. C'mon you wee lassies, out of the bath.' Max begins rolling up the sleeves of his work shirt. Seizing Zoë's pink hooded towel from the rail, he holds it out to Alice, 'Time to come out. Rub a dub dub!'

'That's mine Daddy!' But Alice is already plucked from the foamy water and half covered by the hooded, baby-style, towel. From underneath, she continues, her voice now very serious, 'Daddy, my teacher Miss Roberts is having a baby. Her belly button's sticking out: you can see it. Through her stretchy top. Will the button—undo?'

'Undo?'

'Is that where babies come out of? To get out of their mummy's tummy?'

Max and I exchange glances, trying not to laugh with a kind of pleasure at her idea. A caught-on-the-hop moment. 'Not quite, Ally. Nothing undoes. We'll talk about it later, shall we?'

'Your job or mine?'

'You're their mam, Jenny.'

'You're the specialist. I only look at embryos.'

Max clutches his forehead mock-dramatically. 'Och, I forgot.'

I leave them to it, and step out into the hallway, to call Daze's cell phone. '*Daze is Pottering at her lab: please call later.*'

What? Weird. I try Shaz.

'Ooh, please: Charlie's driven me nuts today. I mean, you love them to bits, but they can act up can't they? Eliot's welcome to do some daddy-time with that young lady! When d'you need me?'

'In an hour: we're going for pancake supper at Max's cousin David's retreat house.'

'So you won't be late?'

'No. Alice's latest interest is where babies come from,' I add. 'Be warned.'

David's pancake do is the *cordon bleu* version: there are bowls of whipped cream and jugs of maple syrup on the tables. Some of the guests have dressed up in costume, 'Proper mardi gras. And a pancake race,' someone says, as masks are handed out. 'After that, we'll be fasting for over a month.'

Why didn't the invitation indicate this was an evening with potential? 'You should've warned me,' I hiss at Max.

'I've never been before: I'd no idea.'

Wearing our masks, we line up outside. Looking around, I see there are about twenty of us. Though no Daze. I remove my high heeled boots ready to race, and am handed a small frying pan with a hot pancake in it.

Arrows on sticks mark the route, which goes once around the buildings, and the idea is to toss your pancake at each turning. As we all tear down the drive towards the church, then back up past a glass-walled extension with a small skip outside, we lose the people who've dropped their pancakes and are bending to retrieve them from the gravel. We lose more by the wheelie bin store, and finally nearing the main door, I'm well ahead of everyone except Max and David. Breathing hard, my chest aching, I put on a great spurt of speed, and end up the winner, hair trailing out of its elegant chignon, tights laddered to shreds, laughing.

My prize is the privilege of reading out the Lent Prayer, which asks God to help us, thinking of his great compassion, to glory in his forgiveness, and to forgive others. To make a good Lent, and be ready for Easter. I feel such a freak, a lapsed secular humanist who can't get her head around any of the faith options.

Though I could thank God that we don't have to eat the pancakes we tossed as we raced: the chef's been preparing a pile of lovely, fresh, hot, crepes. On goes the cream, the maple syrup, a scattering of chocolate powder, a nip of brandy. Scrumptious.

'Glad you came?' David asks, fork in one hand, plate of half-eaten pancake in the other, as we all stand about, shovelling in fattening food. 'You see, Jenny, we're not all like Uncle Alisdair.'

'Great evening,' I smile, 'good thing we walked over. But now, we must really rescue the babysitter.'

Max

SAME TIME

'Phew, quite a spread.' Yep, and David's idea of kicking off Lent, the season of self-denial, characterised by the not-eating of chocolate or the not-drinking of wine, in light imitation of Jesus's temptations in a hot, dry, Palestinian desert.

'I was a big fraud,' Jenny responds.

Yes: but then, the whole thing is. How far from the reality of what it draws our attention to. 'It's the church take on new year's resolutions, what did you expect?' I say.

We reach the end of the drive, and turn down the quiet street. I'm covering my real feelings with cynical humour, an easy way out of sharing them. Part of me enjoyed the silly race, the luxurious food. But the other part, the deeply buried part, has been probed by the rather misplaced prayer. Compassion, forgiveness, and Easter.

Reaching into my inner self, I pull out what seems the best introduction to attempting to share with Jenny something important, that she won't necessarily like. It has to do with Dad. Whatever becoming a bigshot pastor and preacher made him into, the person I'd known, that person disappeared long ago. The awe I felt as he showed me around his plane, or as I watched the planes on manoeuvres over the Mediterranean, knowing my Dad was responsible for one of those speeding, deafeningly noisy, ear-popping powerful jets. Memories that made me too angry and sad to think about, while growing up in the Manse. Which I've avoided sharing with her. Obvious stuff, but meaningful to me at Alice's age.

Memories shoved aside I need to deal with. Under the pastor's disguise, Dad is still that person.

'I'd a patient this morning, guy with Parkinson's. Mainly he was depressed, but what struck me was, how very fragile he looked. Like his skin was as rumpled over his body as his clothes. Did you not notice Dad, at Hogmanay, this guy had a look—we've not talked about it, but, did you not—'

A poke in the ribs, and Jenny's saying 'Thinking of our cholesterol levels! What do they normally eat at that place?'

I shrug. 'It was David's idea of Mardi Gras.'

She's not been listening.

There's a convenient stone on the path: I give it a kick.

'What's up with you? I mean, isn't Lent about giving up stuff?' she complains. 'Giving up stuffing ourselves? Another feast like that one, and we'd be totally on the way to the obesity clinic!'

'Mmm.' If, as I suspect, Dad needs a visit, I'll go alone. To be honest, it's me who's realised I should visit him. And to re-connect, we'll prefer to be without distractions. I'll not say it, I'll just … turn up to visit and that'll be without being asked, that'll make him know … that I care?

Of course, Jen can't be blamed: she's not a mind-reader, though she's used enough to my brand of humour. I seize her hand, and draw her arm around my back. 'Och, you won the race: streaking around the course, after two babies and working all hours,' I say. 'D'you miss how we used to go running before breakfast back in Cambridge?'

'I miss a lot of things we did,' she says.

'Yes … family life takes up time …' We begin to walk in step, thigh to thigh. I wish it were symbolic. I wish she'd see into Dad. His behaviour towards her's forced her to live in her own locked castle and leave him locked inside his. So much for teaching by example.

As we enter a gloomy part of the road, where a neglected house stands behind a tangle of overgrown hedge and trees, 'He knows how to run a good party,' Jen says, suddenly breaking the silence.

'Who? David?'

'Didn't expect that.'

'Oh. No. His family's—not like mine, of course, as you know.'

'Full of surprises ... Odd Daze wasn't there, now they're friends. She loves a party. Nobody even mentioned her.'

'Friends? He's given her a commission. Friendship—I don't think that's what it's about.'

I can't think about Daze. I ponder about David's take on Shrove Tuesday. His faith is clearly multi-cultural, extroverted, and slanted in an all-creation-is-good-so-let's-enjoy-it direction. I've no problem with that, he's honest about it. Not for David a mask of puritanical solemnity: ironic that we wore masks tonight ... A squeeze on my arm: I'd forgotten there's two of us here, walking home ... 'Max, are *you* listening? I said, I only wondered why she wasn't there. I'd kind of expected he'd have included his artist in residence, that's all.'

Letting go of Jen, I drop my arm by my side.

'What's wrong?' she says, 'what did I do?'

'Nothing. It's not you, it's me, okay? Let's not get into discussing Daze, and her needs.'

'What you always say. The "it's me not you" thing. You throw the blame where we can't work it out. You do see that?'

'Och, I didnae mean to do that.'

'Pity you said it, then. So, why you've gone moody?'

I've stopped moving, so she's stopped moving. We lean our behinds on the low brick wall of the dreary, overgrown garden outside the apparently deserted house. Our arms hugging our own bodies. Our eyes on the ground. The pavement's humped and broken by the strong, thrusting roots of a sycamore tree.

'Jen? Sorry, miles away. Not your fault.' (A lie, actually.) 'Of course you'd have thought we might bump into Daze.' Jenny would refuse to understand anything I could say about her optimistic attitude that Daze needs cutting-edge fertility treatment to solve her problems. Or this bother over what I need to do for Dad.

'It's only that I worry about Daze. Even if she's a nuisance, popping up wherever I am. How could her mother walk away? The girls can drive me nuts, but I could never dump them. She was dumped into my childhood by circumstances, she's damaged, and I want to help.'

'Your father walked away. All loss is like a kind of death. We move on, we get over it.' Bitterly, I kick at a sycamore root.

'God, that's unfeeling! Dad never totally disappeared.'

'It's the only way—'

'No, it's not. I maybe got it wrong when I assumed Daze'd be a hopeless mum. I changed my mind. She can do it, she's enormously resourceful, her boat's beautiful, neat, organised.'

'But not—not by you getting physically involved.'

'Oh, don't be moralistic. Your father isn't going to know.'

'This has nothing to do with him.' The world rocks about. The moral boundaries are clouded. It's not about Dad's preaching. It's something else. 'Jenny, it's a good thing to want for Daze, but it mayn't be the best thing for you … Look, it *is* all me. It's here, in my heart,' I say, pounding my chest, 'it's part of who I am. It's—it intrudes on our family. It makes you and Daze part of something outside of us. It *joins* you two.'

'That's crazy. And not true.'

'Have it your way, that's how I see it … Okay, I met you and thought you were—whatever your background was—the best thing I'd ever found in Cambridge …' I pause, trying to discern her expression. It's too dark under these intrusive bushes to see. 'Bar the medical school of course,' I add, as if for humour. 'It's that I care about you, and your health, and how far anyone should go for another person.'

'Isn't it the Mother Theresa thing, *you should lay down your life for your friends?* You should know. And it's only laying down a few eggs I wouldn't have used.'

'Laying eggs?' That makes me snort a laugh. 'Okay, not funny. Seriously, it's no' the same. Have you not read Dawkins on altruism?'

'Can't we—Shaz'll need to go home. I said a short babysit. Can't we shelve this, lighten up and say we enjoyed the party, or whatever it was, more than I expected? I really did. I thought it'd be dreary, being a retreat house.'

I make myself change tack. 'Jen, can we look after ourselves, each other, the bairns? Spend some family time. We'll take a cottage or something and be the four of us over Easter.'

'You don't have to work?'

'Good Friday: we'll leave midday Saturday?'

'Brill. Centre Parcs. Shaz and Eliot go there. Holiday in a forest, cliché, but easy. And then, I do my conference thing. And if that's what's bothering you, when I get back maybe you go and visit your father?'

'I may well visit him, yes. I'll arrange something for May, in the better weather. I'd better give them a buzz, make sure he's doing okay for now, though.'

'Baby, don't stress,' she says, and tucks her arm around me. 'Life is for living an' all that?'

Living with Uncertainty?

I should read it before I visit Dad. Where'd I put it?

Jenny

NEXT SUNDAY, AT SHAZ'S YOGA STUDIO

'Hey Jenny: chat after?' Shaz says as I lay out my mat in the bright, airy space. 'Eliot's picking up Charlie for ice cream at a new place in town: he could take yours?'

'Please.'

It's so peaceful, affirming, alone (in a room full of others, but basically alone), concentrating only on my breath. And stretching my body. I listen to my body, the gentle exercise doing me good. *Let everything else float away.*

The girls are at the children's class. Shaz rents two large rooms here; upstairs two attic ones are let out to counsellors, there's a tiny massage room, and there's a beauty therapist downstairs, and a hot tub. When she first mentioned it, Shaz gave me the idea the whole place was hers: but it's actually shared. At the back, there's a garden: plants in pots, a stone Buddha, and a pond full of goldfish. Koi carp, actually.

I'm feeling so much better. I'd got so tense, I'd forgotten to breathe properly. I'm following Shaz's voice as she says, 'on the in breath, peel your back off the floor vertebra by vertebra ... stay there for a few quiet breaths ... on an out breath, come down vertebra by vertebra, bringing your arms to touch the floor at the same time as your buttocks ...'

Oh, wonderful moving meditation. Thinking only about tucking in my tail bone, using my belly muscles, getting into child pose to stretch my back the other way. And consider: Max said his Mam was 'convinced he wasna' ailing more than usual.' Which I just hope is true.

And then, it's not a joke, Shaz has us all try a headstand against the wall before we end the session.

At last, relaxing on our mats, we listen to her read from Thich Nhat Hanh. It's about what a real miracle is: and he says it's not walking on water, or in the air, but is all around us, in the everyday. '*In the sky and the leaves and the eyes of a child. All is a miracle.*'

While the last stragglers leave, Shaz and I tidy the room. Goodbyes, thank yous, and have a good week. Shaz, stowing the last cheque away in her bag, says, 'Coffee? Or yoghurt smoothie? At my place?'

Smoothies, we decide. In her bright sunny kitchen, Shaz demonstrates her new machine, which masticates imported strawberries into Greek yoghurt, and whirs them together into smooth, cool, sweetness. If only Max and I were as mixed as that. We sit at her kitchen table with our drinks, and she says, 'So, how's you? How's Max?'

'The same. I made a promise to Daze. He doesn't like it.'

'It's not his business,' Shaz says, straight away. 'I'd not let Eliot get between me and my family.'

'Not exactly between. What you read just now: *the sky and the leaves* bit. That's me, wide-eyed, into all kinds of nature, I mean, I was almost a kid, when we met, before I started Cambridge. We'd both grown up away from city life. We were curious about living things. It seemed simple and it seemed to fit. We both had well-known parents who bugged us, though other people idolised them. Know what I mean?' I feel myself blushing and smiling, as I re-experience our walk on the cliff tops towards Lands End, our erotic episode, and how Max said I was too young. For sex, or maybe, for a serious relationship. I don't spell it out. I want Shaz to perceive intuitively.

'Yeah, lots in common,' she says, unsatisfactorily. 'But he meant, see, experience, wonder. Not analytically.'

'I thought I could wrench him away from clinical medicine and into research. We'd be a partnership. Naïve or what?'

'What I said. Really see the simple stuff. Together?'

'I've been so committed to our project. Made me think, do me and Max still want the same things? He pretty much says, *Once you're a family, everyone's lives are woven together. It's not about my situation, my future, my plans, my ideas, any more. It becomes the future plans and the present moment of the group.*'

Shaz rolls her eyes.

'Which group, I want to know. Us, or his birth family? We're going away for three nights at Easter. Three nights. And Max will be gone for the third one, to be at work on the Tuesday.'

'If he's stopping you—'

'His father's not well. I'm off to the US in a few weeks. I don't need anything to happen. You get the picture?'

'It won't. And if it does, it won't stop you. I know you, building your career's important.'

'Well, Max really pulled himself out of that family and the dour religious stuff. It's not anything like over. Look, he's still a great guy, he can be very funny, we're good together …'

I'm groping for how to put this, knowing that I'm talking to the wrong person. Shaz is great for a laugh, or when you're buying shoes. 'Look, it's just I can't see into his mind. It's about that Scottish reserve. Or seeing things from the same angle. I thought we did. Forget it.'

Shaz waves her spoon, and shrugs. 'Maybe. Are you suited? Think about it.'

'I haven't managed to make him give up the idea that he's the person to run a clinic at David's homeless centre.'

'You're the one who's being over-generous. If he's not given up anything for you.'

'Living in the North? Ciggies? His svelte car, when we had the kids?'

'North and ciggies both unhealthy. Car old, and a male fantasy? You were good news to that guy. Sparky, intelligent, beautiful and interesting.'

'Shaz, he gave me a lot too.'

'You gave him those girls. What's he giving you?'

'Grief.'

'Well then.'

'Well what? I have a promise to keep to Daze. I can't hurt her to please Max. Can I?'

'Thich Nhat Hanh has something to say about that.' Shaz flips through her book. 'It's this. *When another person makes you suffer, it is because he suffers deeply within himself, and his suffering is spilling over.*'

'Max isn't exactly *suffering*,' I say.

COMMITMENTS

Jenny

SATURDAY 5 APRIL, LATE

I am in bed. I have done something I'm not proud of: it wasn't quite a lie. Fee called earlier, while Max was out. Could hardly believe it: the worst has begun to happen. I told Fee I'd give Max her message. But I haven't. Because, I *know his feelings about duty.*

Palms sweaty. But, I shall pretend she never called.

Phone goes. Max is in the en-suite shower. 'Jenny can you get that?'

It rings and rings. Max shouts at me, *'Jenny will you get that for God's sake?'*

He's so obviously tired, overstretched by having a partner on maternity leave, and can't quite deal with the ritual significance of my accumulating luggage. I shan't get up. I cower beneath the duvet, eyes like slits watching him from under my hair.

'Jenny!'

My eyes blink shut: I shan't react.

'Max Mullins?' The gentleness glides into his voice as he speaks … Let this please be some patient who's got his home number. I open one eye. Naked, holding the receiver, Max leans across the room, stretching the cord to its limits, to grab at a towel, any towel, from the bathroom. He grabs at a striped pink one. Mine. 'Mam?'

Oh my God: she's called back. I stretch my ears to hear her voice. 'Oh—did I wake you, pet? I rang earlier.'

Please, please can't you leave us alone till I'm on that plane? I want to seize the phone: 'Won't another of your brood do? Must it be Max? I fly midday on Tuesday ...'

But then, her voice is high and anxious, I can hear everything, and begin to feel terribly for her, as she quavers a bit, telling Max, 'Dad's—Dad's not at all well. I think maybe, maybe you should ... know?'

Oh no: I knew Alisdair was now catheterised, and susceptible to infections. But, please ... Don't give in to one now ... There is no one else who could go. To keep abreast of other research scientists we must be represented. Our work must be presented.

It'd be crazy to give up a career break for the sake of a sick relative. Wouldn't it? They *can't* expect me to do the Mother Theresa thing!

'*Mam* ...' Okay, he's annoyed too.

Now he puts his clinical voice on, 'Mam ... how unwell?' He cradles the phone between shoulder and chin, and makes a sarong of my towel.

He sits, on my side of the bed. In order that I can hear properly?

'Not well at all, pet. Our new GP's got him on—' (a pause, I can visualise this: she'll be glancing at the prescription drugs, adjusting her specs). She names the antibiotics. 'It began ... It's turned to pneumonia now—'

'Okay: listen. What's going on medically is what I'd do: don't worry about the treatment. But, I will try, *try,* to find some cover.'

Not what I want to hear.

'And grab a bit of my annual leave and come up and see him. And you.'

Hey, but you *can't*, you *mustn't*. Not this week, or next. I can't take the kids with me, can I? I'm often the sole parent while he gives himself to the community of the sick. Baths, tea, going to school: okay, it's all routine. He should put them first.

'All right? Try to keep everyone away—that assistant Pastor, Dad finds him difficult. Keep him quiet: can Margaret pop by and help you a wee bit?'

'She's terribly busy with Euan.'

'Euan's retired. Like any sensible GP he's seized the moment at sixty to have some life of his own.'

'Yes, so they like to get out a bit.'

I so agree with the comment, '*balls*', which Max breathes almost silently. Maybe time to wake up, and put my side of this. I toss around, and surface, hair still over my face.

'I know you, you're simply soldiering on, as you'd put it, not asking for help when you need it. Margaret'll no' mind. Now, I have to go, I'll call you in the morning and I will *try* to come up. Don't tell Dad: in case I don't. All right?'

Heaving up onto my elbow, 'Your mam?' I say, sleepily.

'Bless you, pet. I know that—' Max has begun to replace the receiver. 'We always pray for Jenny and the wee ones. When he's better—'

'Yes, Mam, I know. Try to sleep now, won't you?'

Max replaces the receiver. It clicks softly in its cradle. He pulls on grey tracksuit style pyjama bottoms, and towels his damp hair.

'I'm sorry: she rang earlier, I was busy packing: but she didn't really say much—I forgot to ask you to phone back.' So there's my lie again, intentional, underlined.

'Dad's very unwell. I'm sorry: I shall have to go up there, if I can.'

'You know I can't cancel going to the conference? Rich handed it to me. What'd we, I, look like? No chance. Danielle, his Downs kid, has surgery in two day's time. When I should be on my way.'

'I'm not asking you to. You should be there. Presenting your work.'

That makes me feel it'd be easier having a big shouting match than have Max giving stuff up for me. His father might die. What then, if I'd stopped him going to the Manse? 'I don't know.' My head's a storyboard of *what ifs*. And people really do tear their hair in extreme stress. I'm clutching at mine, pulling it back, letting it go. 'Maybe I—'

'What?' Max chucks the towel towards the en suite: it catches on the washbasin, then slowly slides to the floor in a heap. 'There's nothing you can do.'

'Zo-zo and Ally. Who'll field them now? You could take them along?'

'House of sickness, no. They're too young, Mam's too bothered.'

His back kind of droops, as he goes to hang the towel properly. Returns and sits on the bed.

'No—unworkable, isn't it. God, your father! *Max*, you can sit there, head in your hands, but what do we *do*? He would do this! Do I leave my children with whoever I can grab at, or let your dad stop me at my greatest career break yet?'

'Whoever you can grab at?' He looks at me: his eyes are dark pools. Contempt? Or pain? My career: his father. An old problem. 'You did give the obvious person, Ruth, a hint of this possibility? Now that eventuality has happened.'

'No, no, sorry, sorry, it isn't his fault. Your Mam had them when we went to Egypt. She can't this time. Okay, Okay, I'll crawl to Ruth.'

'It isna' his fault, but he knows when to move centre stage.'

Jenny

SUNDAY 6 APRIL–MONDAY 7 APRIL

Alice has a ballet exam rehearsal. Home again, as Alice and I walk through the door, Zoë trailing behind, Max comes from the study, with that grin which says he's pleased to've accomplished something. I feel wary.

'If I don't arrive, he'll take a turn for the worse. If I go, he may rally: and I'll be back before you've been away a couple of days.'

'Oh.' Alice drops her coat on the floor: I let it lie, as Alice hurries through to the kitchen—'Where's my drink and biscuit, Mummy?'—and I grab Max by the arm, 'So, you've arranged something?'

'All organised.' He turns to face me, and his other arm, the one I'm not holding, goes around my back, drawing me close. 'Jenny, the locum's a guy I knew at med school who's been working overseas. They're back so the family can go to school here ... It's perfect timing, since they're already renting a house, living on his wife's salary.'

'Hang on,' abruptly removing myself from this patronising embrace, 'What about childcare? For *ours*?'

'You spoke to Ruth—'

'I warned her. I hoped she'd agree because she believes in your duty to your father.'

'Well, then.'

'Well what?'

'Daddy, Daddy?' Zoë stands on Max's feet, gazing upwards, expectant. 'Up your legs?'

'All done while you were out,' Max says, taking Zoë's hands, and her weight, letting her climb her feet up his shins. 'You'll like this: Dad would've said God's timing.'

'Don't tease.'

'No, I'm not. Dad would appreciate it though. I went to the morning service at Hildie's, and a very strange thing, Ruth and Keith were there. So, caught as they were, where they never go, when I mentioned our predicament, Ruth smiled very understandingly, and agreed to help. She's going to move in, using the spare room.'

'Here?' What? Without asking me? Takes my breath away. Half astounded how Max continues to be secretive, acting like he's the boss around here, half almost grateful the thing's sorted, I use picking up Alice's coat to take time to control my thoughts.

Then I brush it down and hang it on its hook. 'Okay. But you've done it again like you always do.'

'Enough, Zo-zo, down now. Mummy and I are talking.' He turns to me, 'It'll only be maybe for a couple of nights.'

'I'd like to've been consulted. Involved. It's like when you arranged for Daze's baby's funeral!'

'So she could see her baby, and for it to have a decent—coffin.'

'All very Mullins. P'raps your family don't realise, or maybe that's all part of the headship of husbands and submission of wives?'

'I hope our house is up to her requirements.'

'Don't. You're dissing me now.'

'No: I'm mortally afraid of that woman's standards.'

'You asked her to stay here ... If you're back before me, don't try any of your irony on Ruth, will you?'

Max packs a bag. I make him realise it's far better not to drive overnight in a rush. Start in the morning, say goodbye to the girls properly. We all talk a lot about how Daddy, as well as Mummy, has to be away a bit, and how Ruth will be living here all the time and do everything we usually do. I'd made a calendar already, for them to cross off the days: though will Ruth decide that's actually a bad idea?

Max

MONDAY 7 APRIL, LATE AFTERNOON

My stomach's in my boots, as I turn off the ignition, and sit a while in the car, staring at the grey granite Manse. Yellow daffs and primroses Mam's planted amongst her rose bushes at least add a splash of colour. A woman in a pale anorak, obviously one of Dad's congregation, comes around from the back with a load of laundry in a bright blue bag. A thought lurches into my consciousness: how much I'd've liked Jenny with me here.

Here I am, anyway. Dutiful son. Slowly getting out, and removing my holdall from the back, locking my car, finding my house key.

'Max! No Jenny?' It's Aunt Margaret hurrying up the drive, a cake tin in her arms. 'He's no' well at all and I've been doing some meals for them. Though this is only a pizza, it's home-made.'

'Can I take that?'

'No, you've your bag to carry. If you could do the door?'

Before my key's in the lock there's a scrabbling behind it, and the door opens, 'Max! You've made good time, pet.' I drop my bag. Margaret bustles past towards the kitchen as I hug Mam. Then Mam's smile fades a little, 'Oh, all on your own?'

'Jenny's away with her work. In the US of A. And Ruthie'll take care of the bairns, it's no' a place for them now.'

'No. I suppose not. Well, come in with you.'

Mam doesn't present as she usually does, the ever-coping Pastor's wife. Her limp hair, creased blouse and skirt, less than brisk walk, say it all. Summing up the situation, clinical mode is the easiest way to go. 'You've not been sleeping in the chair beside him, have you?'

'Oh no, only the once.'

'Mam, I've not come to sit and watch you work: I'll take a look at him, and you put your feet up.'

'I can't, pet: I've things to do.'

'Washing? Baking? I met them in the drive: Margaret with your tea, someone from the Church taking Dad's stuff to launder …'

'I had to let her do it: though he mustn't know.'

'He'll not know.'

'They're all being very kind. The ones who really know your father.'

'Of course they are. He's their Pastor.'

'He *was—*' I draw her along, protesting, to the family room. 'No, really, pet: I wanted to look at something in one of those books in his study.'

'Tell me which book: I'll bring it you.'

'You're all very naughty to me. But let me make a pot of tea, you've driven all this way.'

In the downstairs cloakroom, the cross-stitched text, *I can do all things through Christ who strengthens me* is still there. Encouraging all who enter to carry on serving others. Though, shaking my head at it, I realise there's something different: she's moved the text to the side and this mirror's new. We have one at last! Jenny'd say 'about time!'

I'm here for Dad: I climb the stairs and leave my overnight bag outside the door of the main bedroom. Knock gently. Half hope he's sleeping. 'Dad?'

'James Maxwell, I thought I heard your Explorer on the gravel.'

'Discovery, Dad. How are you?'

'Is this a house visit?'

I grin, and sit on the bed, touching the hand that clutches at the bedcover. Hot, and dry. 'That's for Euan—or your proper GP. Mam said you'd not mind if I came up for a day or two. D'you need a sip of water, Dad? Can I get you anything?'

He moves his hand away. 'Nothing.'

'I see Mam left you this in case of need.' I pick up the small hand bell from the bedside table. 'We all used to have this when we were ill.'

'You didn't need to come.' Dad then closes his eyes, and lies still, breathing noisily.

I replace the bell, and survey the sickroom: drugs, medical equipment, the patient. Dad's nose seems more aquiline than ever, his eyes (they open a moment, regard me curiously, then close) blazing with fever—rather than fervour. I walk about a bit, and look out of the window at the dim, Northern, late afternoon. A family passes: two bairns running ahead, mum in tight jeans and a fur-edged jacket, a baby in a buggy. I'd like to've arrived with my family, head of my brood. At least with a supportive wife beside me. I turn back to Dad.

He opens his eyes and keeps them open. 'No. It's good to see you.'

A winged armchair is by the bed, draped with a blanket. So obvious, where Mam has been spending her nights. I fold the blanket up and sit.

His cautious, papery, hand claws at the air outside the duvet, I take it and fold my fingers over it. His grip is a fraction of the old bone-crushing grasp.

'Mam's making tea downstairs.'

'Not tea. Maybe I'll have some of that orange juice she buys … In a while.'

Jenny

THE WOODS LAB, SAME TIME

'They're so young, I felt so mother hen,' I tell Leila, who pops by late afternoon as I clear my work space. Rich, also tetchy with nerves, is on the phone in his office, evidently discussing Danni's admission for surgery with someone on the children's ward. I look at my watch: is Rich's family involvement going to make me late to collect mine?

'So how is he, your father-in-law?' Leila asks.

'Not good. I know Max is right to go.' Yes: I'm sounding nicer to

Leila than my thoughts when Fee rang and I was so deceitful. 'But, what a time to choose. Everything has to happen at once!'

'I know. But they can't, can they? Jenny, it's harder for us women.' She sighs, and perches herself on my desk. 'I would've had your girls, but, like you, I am out such irregular hours, and Tim, he's so busy, and—'

'That's a dear thought, Leila. But, I understand. Max managed to persuade our child minder to move into the house with them. Difficult, but he did it. I feel awful.'

'You shouldn't. Your big break, Jenny. You should be excited. Nervous, but all tingly with looking forwards.'

'I am. I am. Tingly's right. You know who my father is, so you appreciate the spin on everything. And Rich has dropped me in it at a conference where our subjects touch just enough for Dad to be there. Dad'll devise some fearful questions to ask, needling me, trying to get as near to the truth as he can.'

'Max appreciates the situation?'

'Oh yeah. We share famous father syndrome.' I roll my eyes. 'Then, there's Wil du Plessis, a doctoral student who Max shared a house with briefly, at Cambridge. I got rather good at enucleating cells, and one day Max let out that Wil had this name for me. The Princess of Micromanipulation.'

'Oh my goodness!'

'Yes, groan. Wil's gonna be at that Conference. At least now we're equals.'

'And perhaps—the funny nickname, maybe he found you attractive?'

'I hope not.'

She waggles her index finger at me. 'You be careful!'

'Dad's arranged that we tag on a couple of days' hiking together in Yosemite before I go home, and Max insisted I accept.'

'Yosemite is amazing. You must go. Don't worry so much!'

'Talking of Max, it's not like Alisdair snaps his fingers and Max jumps. Though Alisdair thinks of the Manse as his children's real home, however established they are. But the fact is, his mother is right to be worried, and it is serious. God, why does life do this?'

Leila shrugs and laughs again, 'Jenny, if we really believed in God, we'd have an answer. From some ancient text we'd rework to fit.'

Leila must see I look a bit shocked. OK, she doesn't wear a hijab, but I thought she honoured her traditions a bit more. 'That's what my husband would say,' she adds. 'I—I don't know. How does religion fit the modern world? Does it ever fit women?'

'It's exciting that the schedule's all been planned around a group of affected families who're attending. I should've told Max more about that development. Why's there never time to talk? We used to be so engaged with each other's work. Now we hardly ever—are you two the same?'

'Probably. Though our son's older.' Leila smiles. 'You pushed the envelope, having two, right now when you're building your career.'

'I know. And we planned. S'pose we thought we were different, we'd manage what other people can't.'

'You do. I've seen you together.'

I let that go. But, 'Well, you know: cross-cultural, same as you. Not that different. His father being a fundamentalist pastor, and me from a secular family.'

'Our families are both secular, only from different religions.'

'Does it make a difference?'

Leila shrugs. 'You are okay, in your relationship?'

'As much as anyone.' Leila has empathy. Same as us, research scientist and clinical medic. 'We're far too tired at the end of the day for those lovely deep chats. Our work's pulling us apart. I don't want to end up with only the kids in common.'

Leila nods, looking down at her shoes, navy pumps with small heels. Her clothes are always smart and neat under her lab coat. 'Over-educated women!' she exclaims. 'And my mother, taught at Cairo University!'

'She'd understand then. When Rich called me in and explained why he needed to be with Danni, I could totally relate. If that was Alice or Zoë, I'd need to be there. And be the first person she sees as she wakes up. Or if anything—unthinkable—happened.'

We fall silent. In our work, you can feel so aware, and so grateful, that you have perfect children.

'All packed, anyhow. Just waiting for a final chat with Rich, agree again on the emphases and how I'll field questions. Wish he'd finish on that phone, it's his second call.' I notice my breathing's shallow, and my mouth dry. 'It's scary. How'm I going to come over, as a serious substitute for an Oxford professor?'

'Like one in the making?'

'I'd like to think that—oh relief, that door's opening ... here's Rich at last ...'

*

At home, early evening, Daze calls, and offers some childcare at the weekend.

Then Max, with an update of Alisdair's condition. 'Not well at all,' medispeak for seriously ill. But not in hospital. Our plans won't change: Max will remain at the Manse.

'You didna' expect otherwise?'

'No, not really.'

'Och, how're you then?'

'Seriously excited, seriously scared. What an opportunity to wave our flag and pick up on where the competitors actually are, if they're open enough about it! And show my face in the scientific community as more than one of Dr Woods's sidekicks. Or to flop horribly and make a fool of myself.'

'There's no need—'

'Forget it. Heaps of love to your mam. Alice and Zoë send hugs and kisses.'

'Jenny, I meant ...'

'Yes?'

'No need to either worry or—no need to worry. You'll do fine.'

So he really cares about my work? A lumpy feeling in my throat, as I replace the receiver. Zoë comes and hugs my legs. What was that quality I wanted, that Max's mother has?

Ruth arrives after tea, with a big smile, her overnight bag, and a tin of homemade cookies. Keith's brought her over. Isn't this a bit odd? He stands in the hall, apparently looking around at our décor, and follows us into the kitchen where I write down Daze's number, and explain where she's moored. Ruth's face changes. First a tight mouth, then a quick rearrangement to a smile. But I notice. 'Mm, the stepsister?' she says.

'Is that a problem?'

Ruth looks thoughtfully again at what I've written. 'No—no—Daisy Potter—'

'Yes. You saw some photos of Daze's birth family?'

'Right. Well, that's all then.'

'Mmm,' Keith says. Moving away from where he's been studying the bookshelf at the family room end, over the toy chest and the rumpled sofa. His hands are clasped behind his back. 'Mm.'

'Would you like to see the spare room where Ruth'll be?'

'I'm sure it's very comfy,' says Keith.

'Do use the phone to keep in touch,' I say.

Max

THE MANSE

'Max, read to me? I can't seem to see these days, my glasses—'

'What shall I read?'

'Psalm. Fifty-one. Bible's on the side there.'

Psalm fifty-one's a very penitential reading. Now why does he want that? Reaching for his Bible, on the lower shelf of the bedside table, where he's always kept one, I'm surprised it's a new copy. The spine says *Contemporary English Version*. American Bible Society translation, published two years back. An easier read for him? An interest in updated attitudes? Reassuringly, notes, as usual, have been stuffed inside it, Dad's scrawl on them sparse and irregular. I find the place, and begin to read. The translation's almost colloquial. And the words are discomforting: *'Please wipe away my sins. Wash me clean from all of my sin and guilt … You are really the one I have sinned against; I have disobeyed you and have done wrong …'* Is Dad making some kind of statement—if so, to whom? Or about whom? Me? *'Whose voice is reading this?'* my Calvinist upbringing whispers in my ear.

'Tea?'

Mam's face in the doorway. Shaking my head, I indicate: No, not yet. From the bed Dad says, 'The fear of the Lord is the beginning of wisdom.' Mam nods. I smile. Maybe that phrase, torn from another part of the Bible, is the reason Dad chose that psalm? Whatever he means, does it imply an angry God? Or a pastor who now feels that he's done wrong and hurt his family, and his congregation, with his controlling ways? When his intentions were to bring us into whatever heaven, or God's kingdom, is meant to be.

My eyes are damp, blurring the words on the page. Mam treks away downstairs. The stair before the last squeaks, as it's always done.

'Okay. Dad, anything more?'

'Sleep, I think.'

'Right. The bell's here if you need it.'

I shall take over. Changing his catheter is a small task. Reading to him. Holding a cup so he can sip water. Mam's grateful. 'A nurse could do these things: but he doesn't want a nurse around him.'

'Nope. Family always. I'll sleep in his room tonight. You've that blow-up mattress, I'll fetch it.'

Jenny

TUESDAY 8 APRIL, 08.00

The taxi driver stows my bags. I'm kissing and hugging Alice and Zoë. 'Mummy will call you, Ruth will be here all the time, and do baths and bedtime, and read stories … Daddy will call you too.'

'I can help Ruthie put Zoë's PJs on,' Alice adds, 'so's she won't cry.'

My fear is that Zoë won't understand how long I'm going away for: and, that Alice will think it's forever. It's hardly bearable. At last I extract myself from the little plump arms and legs, with more kisses and hugs and promises. Get in the cab, pull the door closed, and we chug off. If I have a qualm or two about not leaving the girls with Daze, who is family, I can rationalise: with her zany lifestyle?

Midday, seat belted ready to rise into the stratosphere, my face must be a silly grin, because my neighbour asks what's funny. 'Oh sorry: the Oozlum Bird. You've heard of it?'

Now my neighbour grins. As we tear down the runway, and whoosh into the sky, I add, 'My father worked at Caltech, and when he first flew over there he told us that he was now the family Oozlum Bird, because you go backwards in time, flying to California. You know, the Oozlum Bird flies up its own backside.'

He laughs politely.

Now for almost eleven hours of boredom. My neighbour's about my age, geeky specs and a rucksack he's stowed in the overhead luggage place. He pulls a book out of his pocket and opens it. I slide my eyes sideways. Looks like a novel. I open my *New Scientist*. When food arrives, he lays his book aside. It's Stephen Fry's *Making History*. We begin chatting: he explains the plot. I have this feeling he's going to the same place I am: but, something stops me and I don't ask. My head's too full of what I'm about to do, and what I've left behind.

Max

TUESDAY 8 APRIL, THE MANSE

Mam's able to rest a bit, while I field the callers who come with casseroles, bags of clean laundry, inquiries about the patient, and assurances of prayers being said.

I also discern guilt that they've been ignoring Dad's increasing disability over the past few months, about which I have learnt from Mam's remark, 'No, he's not been using the stair lift recently: he's preferred to remain up in our room. You'll see I moved him a wee table in there, for a desk. Mine is too small for him to use from his chair.'

'The stair lift hasn't broken down, then?'

'Oh no. It would take more than a few surreptitious trips up and down, during half term—while Erin was in charge, and I was shopping—to destroy that thing.'

I catch her eye, 'Erin brought Cameron and Chloe up to see Grandad?'

'He didna' approve at all, but he couldna' stop them playing on it. Erin apparently sounded very disapproving as she told them off.' We clutch each other, laughing. Mam, though tired, has merry dancing eyes.

Mam's small walnut desk is now in the spare room, a pile of books and proofs beside it. Curious, I scan the proofs. The title page: *Living with Uncertainty*. Dad's book that she gave us. Och, I've not read it yet. So, did she proof-read it, then?

She's also made a few changes to the house: downstairs, that large TV which the congregation bought them, and which he'd set behind the couch as 'not necessary', has been moved out to where it can be watched. And when I slip into his study, to fax a short encouraging note to Jenny, there's a pile of books on women's ministry, stacked on the big desk. Strange.

Mam calls out that tea is ready. No time to dig into that pile of books; I quickly scribble the note, and fax it off to Jenny's hotel.

After we eat, I call Erin, Kirsty, Alex and Ian. 'I'm visiting Dad: I'd suggest you find a way to arrive here as soon as you can manage?'

I watch the news, then insist, 'I'll sleep in with Dad, again. The least I can do.'

Jenny

CALIFORNIA, USA

We arrive in San Francisco after lunch, their time. Geek is nice enough to help me take down my hand luggage (though I could've done it myself), laugh again about the Oozlum Bird, and say goodbye.

Loneliness and isolation kick in as I approach the car hire desk, where I'm now supposed to collect the car Rich Woods ordered, and drive it to the hotel he booked. The hotel's been alerted to assign me his room. I can't expect to be pampered: he booked with economy in mind ... I hope it's clean, reasonably comfortable, with a decent-sized en suite. 'Dr Jenny Mullins? There's a message for you here,' says the woman at the desk.

A car with a driver will take me to the Ahwahnee. I'll be staying where the prestigious delegates and people with massive funding or huge resources will be? The hotel where the posh guys are staying?

Yay! Dad's style, must be his doing. How I love him. I shouldn't give in, but it's so good to ditch independent conference delegate mode, and admit to myself my fear of American freeways and lonely, less than luxury, hotels. Feeling so much better now.

When the car turns off the freeway and into the park, I have my first views of the amazing Yosemite. Yes, I'm gonna have a wonderful time, any thought that I'd change my plans and leave immediately the conference ends have dissolved into nothing. Standing outside, surrounded by my luggage, I can take a really good look at the weird 1920s architecture, and notice how cleverly the hotel merges with its surroundings. Then, I'm calculating time differences: here it's early evening Tuesday, but it's about 1.30am Wednesday at the Manse. Too late to call them: I'll fax a message later about my changed accommodation.

'Hi, Kiddo!' Dad descends like a huge but friendly raptor, arms outstretched. Using my baby name despite my doctorate and my kids. His hair's a little bit greyer than last time we met, and his face is one huge grin below the trendy specs. I'm crushed in a bear hug, stifled by his familiar cologne. 'Hi Kiddo, hey isn't this just amazing? You and me, together?' Hotel, father, and scenery, certainly all amazing.

'Yeah, thanks Dad. Though, wait till you've heard my talk.' He has to hold me at arm's length, looking to see if I've grown up more. Like I'm back from my first term at college. 'Hey, are we related here? I don't want to go around being, you know, the daughter of the famous father. It's Dr Mullins from Oxford. Okay?'

He changes to thoughtful mode. Scratching an eyebrow. Drawing his forehead into a frown. 'Well, it's either the daughter or the mysterious yummy mummy isn't it?' Yummy mummy: that's what his now-wife Karen called me when she thanked us for some photos of Zoë's christening.

'They all know I'm married with kids, do they? How's that?' I yawn, and stretch my cramped limbs.

He gulps at the implication that he's spread the news of my arrival ahead of me. 'Will do, when they spot you buying soft animals in the gift store and calculating the hour over there so you can call at bedtime.'

'Oh yeah,' I laugh. 'Stop it right there. Where's my room? Next to yours? Had I better check in, and,' I yawn again, 'get some rest after those horrible hours in the flying toothpaste tube?'

'Hey, over here?' He hails someone to carry up my things. Pointing out that they should take care of it all. Then, 'You need to keep awake to beat the jetlag.'

'Whatever, Dad!' He rides the elevator with me, and insists on giving a guided tour of the scenery from my window. It's glorious. Mountain peaks, forested and just beginning to look properly like spring is arriving.

'Okay: see you *later*?'

Off he goes bright and bouncy, down the passage. That alone-feeling again, like being sucked out by the responsibility of my situation. Longing for it to be time to call home. What they'd say, what I'd say, is so small, and means so much and so little, in that tiny scrap of time we're connected. Eight thousand kilometres is a long way away.

Did Dad ever feel like this? What about me and Max? Lately, it's like we're in different parts of a maze, and can't find each other. Why'm I focusing on that, now, in this distant alien place? Fear? Could we end up, like my parents … Living apart? Breathing deeply, now. I must return to the present. Excitement and hard work shouldn't morph into a sensation of inadequacy. Action is what's needed. I'll peel off my travel clothes, and shower away the journey.

Then, I pull the conference paper out of my briefcase: good sound research which must stand up to scrutiny. An antidote to morbid marriage speculations.

'Room service!' A loud knocking at my door, and then, the trolley appears. Behind it, Dad.

'Hi again, Jenny-Wren! Thought you might prefer a light supper here than dinner in the restaurant.' Club sandwiches, OJ, and a basket of fruit.

'You not indulging down there either?'

'Nah: how often do I see my bright bodacious daughter these days?'

'Your work sometimes takes you to Australia? Monash University, kind of your scene, isn't it? And then an internal flight?' I tease him. I know I'm jealous of my real sister, Harriet, a sporty physio, who's not driven by ambition, and loves just being a mum. He never pushed her academically like he did me.

Dad shakes his head. 'I mean you, Kiddo,' he says, and takes a beer and a packet of crisps from my bar. He sits down to munch, nodding at the printed pages in my hand.

I shake my head, still teasing. 'Not sharing anything with you in advance. Wouldn't be fair, would it? So, how's Karen—and Mia? My little half-sister growing up fast?'

'Have a chip.' He proffers the bag, shaking it to entice. 'They're fine. Bright kid, Mia. You should come over more often and let Alice see something of her—auntie?'

'Mmm.'

He's happy to be diverted. We begin telling each other stories about our daughters. Alice, Zoë and Mia ... How strange is this? But maybe, probably, second-family people chat this way with their first families all the time? I'm now on a level with Dad, as a parent and as a delegate, and it catches at my throat to think of all the growing-up years when I rarely saw him. Gradually, through that time, the fact that he was famous, and controversial, penetrated my schoolgirl mind.

Twilight's fading into night, as Dad adds, grinning, 'You'll spend some time with Mia later. On our hiking trip. Doing all the best sights. So much to see, I've booked us a guide. Sound good?'

'I—Yes, lovely,' I smile at him. I need Dad to go, and me to be alone. 'Okay: great to update our news, thanks so much for all this—' I wave my hand at my surroundings, 'the room, the snack ... Need a bit of me-time now ... See you around?'

'That's okay, I got stuff to do,' Dad says. Had he nothing to do, he'd hang out with me whatever I had on my own to-do list. He slides far enough back around the door, holding its handle, to give his parting shot, 'You know Wil du P's here, don't you?'

'Yep, I know. Not under this roof, is he?'

Dad winks. 'Should I find out for you?'

'Married woman, me, don't stir. Hey but, listen, Max had to go north to see his father. Alisdair's pretty unwell. I'd better send a fax, let him know I'm not where I thought I'd be.'

'My secretary can do that for you. Remind me of your number?'

'His parent's number, which is—' I write it down for him. 'That's the Manse office number, okay? That's where the fax should go.'

'Gotcha.'

'Look, here's what I want to say.' I write that for him too, sending loads of love and concern to the Mullins family. I'll let Max, and them, know I care.

'Right, Kiddo. Hint: place is crawling with delegates now.'

'Well I'm gonna lurk here, read through my work, get some rest.' I pick up my conference paper, and wave it at him.

Dad very quietly closes the door. How he loves organising us.

Max

TUESDAY 8 APRIL, EVENING–
WEDNESDAY 9 APRIL MORNING, THE MANSE

So now, here I am again, biting back any complaints which try to rise to the surface as he criticises how I'm not as deft as the district nurse at changing his catheter. Or as Mam when he drinks, coughs, splutters, and dribbles the water back. I mop him up. Neither of us refers directly to this messiness. His strategy is to comment that the women make better nurses. 'Especially your grandmother, Max, a grand woman, soft as a bird she was, and tiny hands. Rough skin mind. On her hands.'

Mam's single-size inflatable mattress, presumably bought for one of Erin's bairns, is so narrow that I keep rolling off it onto the floor. And when that wakes me, I'm puzzling whether he intended Psalm 51 as a message? Pastoring even as he slips away? The flesh may be weak, but there's a powerful spirit within my father.

Moonlight sneaks through a gap in the curtains, silvering Dad's face. His mouth is slightly open as he breathes with effort. I look at my watch: half midnight. Later I'm woken again, by a kerfuffle downstairs. Two more of us have arrived: Erin, from London, and Alex, from Jedburgh. They'd arranged to meet and arrive together. They visit Dad briefly: he doesn't speak, but he clearly knows who they are. It's awful to watch: he looks at us all, and then, his eyes close. And they flicker open, briefly, as he takes another look.

'You've been here a while: shall I take over?' Alex asks.

'I'm fine.'

'I'll stay with Mam,' Erin says. 'She insists on remaining on the couch, though the spare bed's made up.'

I check his vital signs. It won't be long now. What'll his Lord say? *Well done good and faithful servant*?

'Max? Is that you again? Could you read to me—I canna' see—Psalm 23?'

Reading by the light of a torch, the book balanced on my knees, I hold Dad's hand. He thrashes and worries and interrupts, which tells me we're passing over a bridge as I read, half as his oldest son, half in professional mode. I check him again: his hands and feet have turned colder, his agitation slows, his breathing becomes erratic. I loosen my hold on his hand, and step across the room, open the bedroom door a crack, 'Mam—.' They're all together downstairs. Erin has evidently made them tea. Mam comes hurrying from the family room.

'It's me, Al.' She clasps her dressing gown around herself, and sits on the bed. She takes his hand. A tiny movement confirms his consciousness of her. I clasp his other hand. 'Erin's driven all that way,' she says, 'Alex has to teach school in the morning. Where's Kirsty?'

'On call for emergencies. I left a message.'

'Oh dear. He's so proud of her. He almost got over his prejudices.'

Prejudices, were they? She admitted it: Dad's opposition to Kirsty's entering med school. Amazing, twenty years after the equal opportunities act.

It takes another half hour. It feels longer, and it feels odd. Right, but odd, until I, in professional mode, check the vital signs again, and confirm it to Mam, who, of course, knew already. Time of death: 2.47am. Swallow down my personal feelings. My hand on Mam's arm, I ask her very gently, 'You want to sit here a little longer, Mam? I don't have to call anyone straight away.'

She nods. One hand over her mouth, as if she mustn't speak. Or sob.

Oh, how hard we extreme Presby families make our lives by this cultural need to remain tidy and organised whatever befalls us. My throat constricts, I can't speak either. The sensation is—a profound emptiness. I expected numbness. I fear the tears which nudge the back of my eyes … uninvited. Loss, as when me and Erin were hauled away from the only home we'd known, the military base in Cyprus, and dumped in bitterly cold alien Scotland. So he could become a full-time pastor.

Mam will sit with him: I head for my old bedroom, under the eaves. This dreadful emptiness is unexpected: I'm more unwilling to tell the others downstairs about a death than—than if they were a person—and family—I didn't know … I placed enough between myself and him to keep us apart. Was I cruel to him?

What's this? The room's crowded with boxes: floor, desk, even on the bed. Hard to see it as it was at Hogmanay, when we four were crowded in here, Jenny and me on that other blow-up mattress, the one Alice loved. Cuddling together in silence while the bairns slept. These boxes, full of our childhood stuff, filed away by Mam, silently witness to her preparations to leave the Manse. She's known she'd be homeless sooner rather than later, and begun to pack. How awful …

The window, where he threw my antique microscope crashing to destruction in the garden, is a dark rectangle, the night has clouded over, the moon obscured.

To sit on the bed I must move some boxes aside. Mullins family life stares from the neatly stacked, neatly labelled, plastic containers of our childhoods, and the worn green rug … I was supposed to carry on the torch, to pastor First Truly … His disappointment … My guilt, anguish, loneliness … My disappearance into a career that could take up all my time, my own family … I kept away, I put off giving him my time in his last illness.

Mam's bulletins played down his decline. Why had Ian and Alex not called me? Or Erin, here at half term? … *Max and his marriage with an unbeliever* …

The ironic, unexpectedly genuine grief wells up, takes over, and tears me apart.

Daze

WEDNESDAY 9 APRIL, ST HILDIE'S

Breakfast at St Hildie's: there's a wonderful scent of food: fresh hot rolls, coffee, tea. Bacon, if you want it. Daze has given in to lodging at the Retreat Centre in one of their cell-like bedrooms. The cat, Trifle, is being fed by a neighbour moored near the *Ironic Lady,* which also means somebody gets to make sure squatters don't invade her boat.

Breakfast, unlike lunch which is always silent, is a cheerful, noisy meal. You never know who may've arrived since yesterday: a writer needing quiet to meet a deadline, a group of churchy teenagers on pilgrimage, a priest with a faith crisis, a person who won't speak to you because they're here to escape from some dire, traumatising, personal event, and today, well, Daze joins a table of women which includes one in a nun's brown habit.

What'll she be like? Dour, like the habit, and plain-speaking? 'Hi, I'm Daze Potter.'

'And I'm Sister Monica Mary.'

The voice surprises Daze with its strong northern accent: Manchester, perhaps? 'I've—never—' Her only brush with nuns was dressing up as one for a nuns and priests party, which she blushes to remember, sitting next to a real one. Pretending proper behaviour, she changes 'met a real one before' to '—seen such lovely brown rolls as these.'

'Marmalade?' the nun smiles, 'The butter's recently gone down the table, it'll come back.'

'Thank you so much.' Gosh, now I sound prissy, Daze thinks. She studies the wimple-framed face next to her. Hard to guess her age: her skin looks very scrubbed, with of course no hint of make-up or anything to enhance or improve its earnest, plain features. With her hair entirely hidden, no help there either. So what do nuns do all day?

'Are you here on retreat?'

'Artist in residence,' Daze replies, 'I'm making a labyrinth.'

'Ah, the Grace Griggs foundation.'

'You've heard of it?'

'One of our Sisters was involved with cleaning that stained glass recently. The life of St Hildegard.'

'I love those windows,' Daze smiles. 'Wicked, wasn't she? Or rather—'

'I think I know just what you mean. She was. An example of women's equality before her time.'

'You don't expect—'

'No, people don't know much about convent life or indeed about how it could liberate women in an age when marriage was probably as much of a prison as living in community.'

'I s'pose not. I mean, we kind of don't need—we've so many options now.'

'Yes.' Sister Monica Mary says no more, though she exudes a quality of stillness. Daze finds this unnerving, and after anxiously searching for an appropriate subject, remembers the last religious festival, which she had spent away from St Hildie's since the solemnity of the Holy Week retreats gave the whole thing a depressing run-up.

'Did you—I mean, have a nice Easter?'

'Wonderful. It was lovely to keep the festival here. You?'

'Trekking around looking at labyrinths for inspiration. Okay, this is one kind of religious place, but I want the labyrinth to be universal?'

'All religions and none?' the brown-habited Sister suggests.

'Yes—something like that—yes...' The nun seems totally composed. 'So, what's your convent like?' Suppose they should be interested in a labyrinth, or some other artwork?

'Oh, our convent's been closed because we're only six sisters, so while I wait to be sent wherever I shall be, I'm at St Hildie's. And here comes the butter at last!'

Daze butters her roll, wondering how it feels to be told not only how but where to live your life. Or are nuns so used to being sent wherever the order says that they lose the quality of wishing things were other than they are?

'Do you mind being sent around like that? No choices?'

The nun laughs. 'I don't think it's for me to mind. How much can we really choose? And even God put up with restrictions when he was on this earth. I can't complain.'

Max

THE MANSE, SAME TIME

Bugger: I must've dropped off. A raw grey light has replaced the utter darkness. I am a mess, damp with tears, rumpled with sleeping rough among those boxes. Cold. Stiff. I stretch my limbs, turn over and see that window. What crazy father would throw an antique precision instrument through a window because ... Why be obsessed with that?

Stuff from the bed has fallen to the floor: that double inflatable mattress, deflated and packed neatly into a square, awaiting our next visit as a family. Catch myself, almost break down again: that time's over, the old family home went with the job. Dad goes, Mam's homeless, we'll not be here again, or only for … saying goodbye to what he was … Gather myself together again … At least my unexpected racking sobs last night could not have been heard downstairs.

So, today. Birds are singing outside. My watch says eight-twenty. Strange to be surrounded by the rubbish of our childhoods. Can't ignore it, must take a look through. Boxes of toys, board games, and books: even that skateboard tidy with shelves and hooks for helmets and pads. Dad made it for the twins … Everything's old and weary. Why keep it?

Running my hands through my hair doesn't do a lot: better grab the overnight bag, make myself presentable, take charge. Of the family, of myself. Gather up the threads of what I'm meant to do: oldest son and all that.

The family bathroom's chilly (what's new?) and from downstairs drifts the combined aroma of coffee and toast.

God nudges: *Teach me your way, Lord, lead me in a straight path.* A text for every occasion, responds my cynical side.

I pause in shaving, for a moment seeing David's face in the mirror, and know what is necessary. David *must not* continue to shun his father even if Euan's beliefs do embrace homophobic interpretations of obscure Biblical texts. He can't let Euan die with no reconciliation. What exactly are Margaret's feelings? She's so brusque and private. Despite their comfy home.

I find a familiar scene in the kitchen: each one of us in role. Mam and Aunt Margaret making breakfast. Erin and Alex talking into phones: Erin on the wall phone to her family, Alex on his cell to his employer. Both explaining they're here because Dad is not—while Mam is saying, 'He's gone, and I am so—relieved. For him, you understand.' She and Margaret clasp together a moment, Margaret holding a full toast rack. Mam nods, very slightly, and takes off her specs. With the back of one hand, she brushes her eyes. I have seen this before: typical gesture, when she and Margaret had been talking, heads together. Then they snap apart, as the door is heard opening. Only this time, it's not the door of Dad's study, and it's me not him.

'Max,' (a little nervous start) 'you're awake.'

'I really shouldn't have—'

'Oh no pet, you've been up with him both nights since you arrived. But you could phone Kirsty? Before she leaves for work?'

'Of course. And his GP.'

Euan appears in the doorway. He doesn't exactly push me aside. But he announces 'Oh, I've dealt with the details. Death certificate on the mantelpiece in the lounge. You'll deal with registration?' I open my mouth to speak as he adds, 'Inquest, as died at home, yes. Ring the Coroner's office.'

'I am a doctor, Euan. I was with him.'

'Rules, Max.'

Margaret, speaking to Mam, cuts across Euan, 'It's not wrong to be relieved. For him. And for you the burden's lifted.'

Mam quotes, *'With Christ, which is much better.'*

'Well done, good and faithful servant.' Margaret responds.

Erin frowns across them at me.

I slip into the lounge, and taking the certificate, read what Euan wrote, *'Urinary infection. Pneumonia.'* I tuck it into my wallet. Safe along with photos of my wife and bairns. Will Jenny understand my grief and anger and—anything?

Back in the kitchen, Margaret hands me a coffee. 'Will I make you fresh toast? They've demolished what was in the rack.'

Reading that brief clinical description of what I witnessed last night was the oddest feeling. Euan hands me the phone. 'Kirsty,' he says.

'Yes.'

I swallow some of the coffee before dialling Kirsty's number. 'She'll have left for work,' Erin says. 'She's living somewhere on the tube line to St Mary's.'

'I hope it's a decent area?' Margaret asks.

'Nice flat,' says Erin.

'And don't ask about the area,' I think, as the phone rings and rings. I begin leaving her a message: someone picks up. The voice, male, deeply sleepy, answers, 'Yes?'

I say, 'Could you get a message to Kirsty: I'm her brother, Max. I called yesterday: she was working? She needs to phone me. Soon as she gets home?'

'Kirsty spent the night in theatre, anaesthetist for emergency appendectomy. I give you her cell?'

'No: she should call mine, from home. Okay?'

'I will give her your message.'

*

Late morning, and Mam has decided we'll hold a thanksgiving prayer meeting after lunch. Erin and I escape the family and walk into the garden, mugs of coffee in our hands. I say, 'All of us in there, I almost expected him to appear from his study, tell us off for making a kerfuffle, and demand what the fuss was about.'

'Yes. Like "why are you telling everyone I'm gone, eh?"' Erin smiles a moment. Then as I smile, she turns serious. 'Gosh, it's weird. His being the pastor made the family into a congregation. His personal one. D'you think that too?' We're silent, missing a beat, then she says, 'Mum's free. We're free.' I can't speak of the sensation. Though I partly agree. 'He was—a kind of bully—it was all meant to be good for us.'

'It's too much to take in.'

'You were there.'

I have maybe begun to achieve numbness. 'I should call the undertaker. And the assistant pastor.'

Erin makes a face. 'Nicholas in waiting?'

'Waiting?'

'He's hoping for the appointment, yes. And he's got his eye on Kirsty, Mam thinks. He was visiting before you arrived. "Pity Kirsty couldn't be here", that kind of thing. So, *in waiting*.'

'Och, nasty. It'd be bad taste to make a move right now.'

'Yes, very … So … Jenny's away: what is it she's doing?'

'Jenny's presenting their work at a conference. Big career break, or so I'm told.'

Erin slips her arm around my shoulders. I back away from contact, fearing I'll break down again. 'Here's the undertaker,' I say, indicating the arrival of the shiny black car, and relieved to have to resume a professional attitude. 'Euan must've phoned.'

Behind it, Ian's red VW Golf, which screeches to a halt in the drive. Ian, wife and eight week old baby, with piles of baby stuff, extract themselves, yawning.

'Euan rang around six: we organised ourselves right away.'

'Eleven thirty now.' I raise my eyebrows at Ian, 'You made good time.'

'Didn't hang about, no,' he grins. His wife looks relieved to be in one piece, and gently rocks from one foot to the other, soothing the baby. Erin looks at me meaningfully, then turns to admire the little one.

Meanwhile, Ian starts straight in with plans. 'Okay: Dad outlined his wishes, no probs, Alex and I have it all planned.'

'The funeral? Alex didna' say.'

'Quiet family service. Then, we all thought—us and Nick—we all decided on a memorial service later. It'll be early summer.'

Erin and I exchange more glances. Does she think, as I do, that Dad got together with them, leaving us out, and told them what he wanted? 'Right. No consultation, with—for example—Erin, Kirsty, me?'

'We thought you'd be too busy to have time for arranging it. Besides, it's all part of the ministerial training.'

'Indeed. Part of the training.'

Too busy to arrange our father's funeral? *We all decided.*

Only thing to do: turn away. Swallow down my instinctive desire to punch Ian's complacent face. 'So, it looks as if you don't need me. You could let me know when it's to be. You may have to wait. For the Crem.' Hope that level, calm, professional tone, did it instead.

'Ouch,' Erin says. 'Will they not use First Truly?'

I shake my head. 'Just a brotherly—' I end by kicking wordlessly at the gravel. Erin appears to understand.

Mam bustles from the house, her smile ready to greet the new arrivals. Erin bustles the other way, 'Max, let's—let's do anything, get away. Mam'll need shopping.'

'Let's go and—register the—this …'

'Yes.'

I tap Ian's shoulder, and hand him our mugs. 'You'll not mind taking these indoors for us, will you? All part of the pastoral ministry?'

Erin and I walk down the gravel drive, close as conspirators. 'Was that collusion, or submission, letting the twins take over?'

'Who cares?'

'The twins are so much younger. We're like two families. They didna' experience life as bairns in the forces. First Truly was their world. Did you call Jen?'

'Later. Today's her big presentation day.'

Jenny

WEDNESDAY 9 APRIL, 07.30 US TIME, THE AHWAHNEE HOTEL

My alarm is going off, and the phone's ringing. Max?

'This is your wake-up call …'

'Oh—thanks—'

Dad arranged that, of course. Hasn't Max got the message Dad's secretary sent? Maybe she didn't send it yet? Maybe he rang the wrong hotel … We're disconnected. He doesn't know where I am.

I know where I'm going: to the biggest challenge of my life so far. Presentation, then fielding the questions. Look like you know who you are, I think, dressing for the occasion. Fuchsia pink vest top, with a black shirt. Trousers of the grey trouser suit bought for the occasion. I put my hair up, step into my low-heeled court shoes, and study my profile: the hair's good, and shows my pearl stud earrings. Undo a few buttons of the shirt, more casual, nice to see the fuchsia pink. Feminine, but not ditsy, as Shaz agreed when we went shopping. Not sure about the jacket's length but can't change it now. Cardigan coat too casual.

It's all *my work*. With the team of course. All I have to do now is describe it. It's written and printed out and the slides are in order. It's my special subject and I'll put over our work as if I'm introducing the delegates to my lovely children, wanting them to admire not me but Alice and Zoë. There's no need for nerves.

Only about the delegates who'll enjoy interrogating me. With those wretched questions.

In the dining room, I decide to leave eggs, hash browns, and all that for another day. As I look around, there's the geek from the plane! I guessed right, he's a delegate too. So who does he work for? We grin and wave. I even smile over a cup of tea and a slice of toast with jam from a tiny individual pot.

In the lecture theatre, after an introductory address, enduring the first session feels a bit like waiting in the wings at the school play for my entrance. When I finally get to my feet, it's almost worse. The older scientists stare. They came to hear Dr Rich Woods, whose name was on the advance information, but on the podium, there's this unknown, me, being introduced. They're disappointed he's sent a minion.

They shuffle their conference papers, until called to attention. They murmur as I briefly refer to Rich's reason for not attending. 'She's too young, too female. *What does she know?*' they'll be thinking. Though as we're a group of people working on chromosomal abnormalities, they can hardly not relate to his concern for Danielle.

Scanning the audience, *imagine them all naked*, I find that geek looking right at me, and I smile back: I'll talk as if just to him.

And I enter another world, where there's only the information, my voice, and the almost imperceptible sound of the air conditioning. No mistakes, no stumbling over words or frightful blunders. The slides were indeed rightly sorted. All goes well.

As I end, there's a silent moment, then a slight buzz. They're almost certainly consulting on what questions they'll ask. Yes, they think up some horrible ones. It's a thousand times worse than my viva. People ask, *Dad* asks, Did we try this, or that? They argue amongst themselves. Then they remember me, and ask another tricksy question. My specs steam up, so I can't see the geeky guy any more, but, as I take slow breaths, my brain stays clear, I seem to do okay.

As we leave the conference hall, Dad sidles up. 'Nerves stopped doing a lambada now?'

I double-take, then laugh it off, 'Dirty dancing? Dirty interrogation, yours!'

'Touché,' he laughs.

We high-five, as I admit, 'Well, lambada could actually describe it, during question time.' My legs feel trembly and weak, as if I've danced all night. He wants to take me for a drink, he'd like an intelligent blonde on his arm as he networks, especially one who shares his genes. 'Could I take a rain check? I need to let the adrenalin settle.'

I lock myself in a cubicle in the women's room, and let my brain slow down. Free to relax and enjoy other people's contributions, and my own bit of networking. Far from Dad, who'll doubtless be making sure he wanders into the path of the TV crew covering the conference.

Max

WEDNESDAY 9 APRIL, 14.45 UK TIME

If I'm not required, I'll go home and care for my children and do a few days' work until the funeral's date is firmed up. Ian's made it clear he imagines himself, the minister in training, as Dad's successor in every area.

Packed and ready to leave, I hesitate around the next event: the family prayer gathering, giving thanks for Dad's life and ministry. Followed in Mullins style by tea or whisky, and a choice of several cakes.

'Can't you see it?' Erin says, as she arranges the table: best china, paper napkins. 'Aunt Margaret anticipated this, and had her cakes ready, in the freezer?'

'At least Mam didn't have to make the cakes this time.'

But there's David's little sister, Chrissie, outside the door of the lounge. Mam's already disappeared inside, carrying her Bible.

'Max—I drove like the clappers to be here. I'd rather this than attend the memorial service, or the funeral. So when Dad phoned, I took a couple of days off right away. To see everyone.'

'I doubt you can stay away from the service.'

'I s'pose Dad was with him when he—?'

'No: I was.'

'*Max.* Gosh. How was it?'

'Peaceful.'

'Good. I mean, everyone deserves that don't they?'

'Mmm—Chrissie, listen, before we go in. You see David don't you?'

'Yeah. Though sixteen years makes David and me different generations. 'Cept, now he's back from Aussie-land, I'm all grown up, we kind of relate.'

'David and your father should make up their differences. Losing one's dad is complicated: dying is a time when people realise too late what's important. Sorry, but it's true. If you and he ... What I'm asking is, I'll try to make sure David does something about reconciliation—any likelihood you could help?'

She's evasive. Holding the doorknob, but not opening the door of the lounge, she says, 'You know what I'll always remember? You and me and Jenny discovering marital violence in your Dad's congregation. I was nine, maybe? I've really thought about that. It's why I want to do family law.'

'Is that an answer?'

'Maybe. Can see where you're coming from. I probably know more about David's life in Australia than Mum and Dad ever will. Or want to. Really, they're all a bit naïve, aren't they? First Truly people?'

'Och, no they're not. They know the score. They're set in their ways. We need to open their minds.' Chrissie looks at me a bit lip-trembly. 'It's not that they're innocent. It's just their way of behaving as if their God doesn't want to know the ways of human beings. He does. They wish it were different. That's the problem.'

'You think?'

'I know. So should you. Same as the Rachel business opened your eyes when you were a wee lassie of nine.'

'Okay. Okay. You're not my teacher.'

'Sorry. I wasn't thinking. But please, think about David and your Dad.'

'Yep. Maybe. Are we going in? Do we have an alternative?'

'I'm only staying on for Mam: she needs protection from the pious.'

Chrissie smiles. 'I need that too: let's brave them together.'

'Right, we'll pray? With the relatives? And you will come to the memorial service?'

'If I can hack their terrible style.' Chrissie rolls her eyes (why have women begun to do that so much?) as a gesture of appalled amusement. And then, those brown eyes dance wickedly as she meets my gaze.

Euan calls from beyond the door, 'Who's that I can hear standing outside?'

'Me, and Max—how are you Dad?' Hauling me along, she sweeps into the room, grasps Euan's hand with her free one, leans over and gives him a big kiss. 'Mm—Daddy, sorry I've not phoned in a while.'

'Aye.' Euan smiles, and I notice he squeezes her hand. 'It's right that you're here now.'

Her other hand lets go of me. I look around for a seat: they're all occupied but one—Dad's pretty much sacred armchair: the one nobody would dare plant themselves in. I cross the room, and firmly settle into it. Then trump my brothers by pulling a New Testament from my pocket.

Taking a breath, looking around at the whole family, I announce, 'We're gathered here to give thanks for my father's peaceful passing after a frustratingly disabling illness which ended his ministry at First Truly. I'm sure you'll all agree that we should begin with reading together the twenty-third psalm. We'll follow that with a short silence to remember Dad as he was, and a few minutes' extempore prayer. We'll then sing one verse of Dad's favourite hymn, *Great is thy Faithfulness,* and we'll close with the Our Father. And then, Margaret has prepared afternoon tea, with a dram for those who wish to partake of it.'

My eye remains fixed upon Ian. He's lost out on leading the proceedings, like a carpet's been pulled from under him. Tension crackles across the room.

Soon as I can after tea, I slip into the study to fax the news to Jenny. She'll have done her session and be free to take it in. The family haven't yet recovered enough to have a go at me: though Chrissie winked during the Psalm, Erin gave a discreet thumbs-up while manning the teapot, and Mam's hug says it all as I leave for home. Interesting.

On the way, around midnight, I realise I've put my foot right in it: over in the US, it'd have been breakfast time when she got my news. Breakfast time on her special day.

Jenny

13.00 US TIME, THE AHWAHNEE

Dad and his promises! I'm assuming my message about the change of hotel didn't reach Max, so I've sent another to the Manse. Giving my new address, and adding *Wow, I did it! They liked it!*

There's time now to mingle with the families. One mother lets me hold her tiny, frail-looking baby. Does she realise I'm not the world's best with precious infants? At nine months, the little boy, pale and so delicately formed, is only alive because he's fed through a tube into his tummy. Two other rather intense-looking delegates close by hang around us as I try to hold him safely and talk with the mum. The two women turn out to be in an area very close to our work in the Woods lab.

That reminds me, be very wary. They may want to probe into what I might've left out of my presentation. I hand the baby back to his mum, 'Thank you for letting me hold him,' and join a family with a little girl, who've tried to catch my eye. Oh gosh, she reminds me of Serafina, a child who Max introduced me to, the day after we met. So cheerful despite her disability. Serafina was a little fighter, but she didn't survive her eye surgery …

And so, I've avoided both the intense women researchers and my Dad. That geek from the plane is waving across the crowd, indicating a group of young delegates heading for the buffet lunch. He's more talkative now. His name is Matt, he's a neonatal paediatrician, comes from New Zealand and works in London. Like several of us, he's had personal experience of dysmorphic kids, first through delivering an Edwards Syndrome baby when he was a med student. I look at him with different eyes, then learn he's got a partner he obviously adores, and a year-old daughter. Behave yourself, Jenny, I think, as the conversation moves on, and we all share, rather solemnly, how heart-rending it's been to meet the families. It's awful how they want answers, and treatments, faster than we can deliver, or promise, or speculate. It's the hardest thing when the parents ask if we've children of our own. Most of us have: so far they're all healthy.

So, apart from a silly thought about a fling, everything today's making me feel more than ever that I should give Daze a chance of a healthy baby. And that Max's attitude is incredibly mean and selfish.

In the coffee queue, Wil du Plessis shoves past the others towards me. The Persephone cultures! If he knows anything about their destruction, he might just be persuaded to spill. 'Jen, excellent presentation, and far more decorative than from your esteemed PI.'

'Mm,' I say, reading on his label the name of the rival lab he works for. Commercial like Dad's. But no worries, I accept his invitation, 'How about a catch-up drink after dinner tonight?'

*

To please Wil's eye for a nice-looking female, I take care with my appearance. Low-backed black dress, pearl studs, court shoes, shimmery pashmina. A bit Shaz, really. We're meeting at the Ahwahnee, since I don't want to disappear off Max's radar, and I need to call the girls. Time thing's a real pest: before the session, I was too nervous. After, it was too late. I so want to speak with them, I promised, and anyhow, I miss them terribly.

Wil arrives in the bar all cashmere and loafers, casually suave. 'Yes, your piece this morning, very interesting.' That intense look could be a giveaway: he's another one hoping to probe into my brain for more information than I put into the presentation. I've listened out to the others for anything useful, so will he have done, so do we all at a conference like this. Just because he was once my teacher, I shan't let him know more. We'll simply spend an evening in the bar chatting about the old days. Hopefully, including that piece of original research I embarked on just after my finals. Which mysteriously met with a sad end.

I smile sweetly at him, 'Thank you. And thanks for thinking of this evening: I'd hate to be spending it watching TV.'

'What're you into? A white wine or something more exciting?' I accept a wine. Wil almost but not quite takes my elbow, to guide me towards a quiet nook. 'Before I forget to say, I have to make a phone call later, around ten-thirty, eleven, maybe?'

'Sure.' We chat about Cambridge. I try to steer the conversation towards the Persephone research. Not surprisingly, like me, Wil won't be drawn, beyond, 'Yep, I do remember something …' He shakes his head. I study his face: I think he does know more. 'Everything's been tightened up since we were there. No more messing with stuff without ethics committees and red tape.'

'Sure has. I even left a few bits and pieces in preservative: better make sure I don't get associated with them.'

'Or you'll make the headlines.'

We've both heard rumours about people who are going to be investigated for keeping tissues, and worse, stashed away for years without permission. 'All those controversies, suddenly the public's got to know some of what happens behind closed doors,' Wil says, looking at me like he's assessing what my attitude is.

'We never thought it was stealing, did we? Actually, did anyone talk about the ethics of it? Saving tissue from the incinerator in order to advance knowledge?'

'Need to be complete for the resurrection,' Wil says, with a sardonic smile.

I decide it's time to dig deeper. 'Back then, Max had no problems with me asking for—a neonate body. You remember that?'

He gives a little start: obviously he does. I press on. 'We took some samples. It'd only have been incinerated, so—' Yes, if we hadn't hung onto Persephone that couple of days, the body wouldn't have been around for Daze to grab back the way she did. To arrange a funeral. We did do something for her. Accidentally. And Max went with it.

'Yep, times have changed.'

Wil underlines change of subject by extending an arm along the back of my chair, and suggesting another drink. So has he shut the door on more information, at least for now? 'Probably, for the better. Students can rush into things, not realising the implications ... I've come to agree that the rules are necessary.' That sounded easy to say. Though I'd found Max's comment on our work as *something we could do as students but life moves on* had been crushing.

'Pity, though, isn't it?' Wil responds. Is he fishing now?

'Whatever: rules is rules,' I say, 'and I'll have a tomato juice, please.'

'Nothing more exciting, Princess?'

'Nothing more exciting.'

While he's at the bar I miss that warm, cuddly arm, keeping my back cosy. And notice he is rather less fit and trim than he was: an ex-rugby player who doesn't keep up enough exercise. On the plus side, as he returns, can't deny I'm here with one of the best-looking men in the room, and one of the youngest, Matt the geek having disappeared. His hair is still blond, his tan is still in place, and he smells wonderful when he leans across and places my glass in my hand, his fingers lightly brushing mine.

In fact that brings on tugs of desire I haven't felt in a while. Wil in place again, back goes the arm, I sip my drink, then put the glass down and riffle in my bag. 'Us, my family.' Smiling, I show Wil the pictures. 'Alice is five. Zoë's just climbed out of the terrible twos. And Max: here's us on holiday in Egypt, Sharm el Sheikh. Superb for diving. Have you been?'

'One to keep on the list,' Wil says. His eyes are slightly hooded, slightly bloodshot.

'So, your work is going well. How about—dare I ask—are you and Patty—?'

'Nope. She was quite right, not the one. I have a son,' he moves to take out his wallet, and our thighs touch. Wil keeps his leg there, showing me a photo, a boy about five.

'He looks bright. So, you and his mum?' I shift my thigh a little, and he gives me a look like this is a game.

'Wrong again. She lives in Ireland, I don't see my kid as much as I'd like. Her choice.'

'I'm sorry.'

'But here we are, here I am with the Princess of Micromanipulation. Both of us away from home. I knew you were a bright girl. A star among the brights. And here you are, standing in for your boss.'

'Mm. Here I am.' Enclosed in Wil's aroma, and his enfolding presence.

Back comes the adrenalin rush of success, and the satisfaction of connecting with Wil about our work. Now Max and I can't. 'Max hasn't the time to keep up with developments in my field. He teaches a bit at the medical school, but he's almost totally a clinician.'

'Time, or the inclination?'

'Probably inclination.'

'The world of the general practitioner isn't cutting-edge.'

'You are so right.'

A romantic song comes on the piped music. I nuzzle up to Wil's side and let him muss my hair a bit. Now, I notice how he smells of beer, and wonder how much he had before we met up? But, he's warm and male and I was the star of the day. I breathe his cashmere jumper and it tickles my nose. Being appreciated is so nice.

Jenny

22.30, THE AHWAHNEE

'Dad gone—returning home until funeral arranged—Love and don't worry. Mx.'

Oh. My. God. I've forgotten everything, and now this fax, launching huge guilt feelings, is brought into our nook by an invasive bar waiter. My skin prickles: my romantic illusions skid to a halt.

'Bad news?'

'Gotta go: sorry.' Untangling myself, pulling my dress straight, finding my purse, 'Here, for my drinks?' I plump down what I think might be the right money.

'Hey, Jenny—no goodbyes?' Wil pulls me off-balance: I bump back into my seat.

And grab my pashmina, which had fallen and slid under our table. 'Let me—' I shake myself free of him, '—look, I'm sorry, it's serious, okay? I have to go.'

'Aw, Princess—you have to?'

'Yeah, I do. Family stuff.' I see his hesitation: he doesn't want to know what's happened and get involved. He's drunk too much: so possibly have I, since that careful tomato juice. 'Wil, I am sorry, this was nice, you were nice and—' I make myself kiss him properly, 'there, and we can't do this again. Right?'

I don't look back. Any tears, in the elevator, are about my own confusion. Must call Max. Who's going to be there? Who'll pick up? Erin? Euan? The awful twins?

My room engulfs me. That message didn't come from the Pastor, but it's still made me feel dirty. I wash my face, and then, I look properly at the paper in my hand. Why send a fax? Hey, it was sent to the other hotel, it's been forwarded. He wrote it hours ago—damn, damn: it'll look as if I didn't bother earlier. I can't face the Manse family.

Rationalise: the Manse phone'll be in constant use.

The photo on the bureau smiles at me. I never called the girls! Oh, terrible, uncaring, hormonal Mummy.

I'll need to get an outside line, dial our home number, apologise to Ruth that it's such an unsocial hour…whatever hour is it? Nearly six, no seven? Oh my sweeties, how are you?

I can't. I have failed everyone I love. I'm not together enough to talk to my girls. Especially not Ruth, to get to them. Guilt, resentment, misery. Shall have to endure a dark, lonely night, before I can sort it all.

I strip off, fall into bed, cry a bit more. Want to crawl along to Dad's room and borrow a sleeping pill. But resist.

Max

9 APRIL, WEDNESDAY, ABOUT 17.00

Passing a sign to Leicester Services, I remember Ruth.

She'll not be best pleased to wake and find an unrelated male sleeping in the house, albeit his own house. Her moral code says we can't sleep under the same roof. Indeed, my car and hers mustn't be seen in our drive together. All I can do is turn off at the service area, pull out my cell phone, and call the house. 'Ruth: I'm on my way back. Dad … I'm not needed there any more, and—'

'Of course. I'll pack my bag, and be ready when you arrive.'

She is so efficient. And compliant. Chilly, even. Gives me a frisson, reminds me of Rachel.

At home, the hall light is blazing. In the porch I pause, key in the lock, to figure out what to say: the door opens a second before I've settled on the right expression. 'All done. Little ones fast asleep,' says Ruth.

'You have been wonderful …' I would like to say more, but as Ruth stands, packed bag in hand, ready to leave, I know that less is better. She says, 'Oh it was nothing. Max, if there's anything—' and looks curiously at me, eyes narrowed a bit.

'Dad—he went—' How do I put this to her? Even to myself? '— last night—I was with him—'

Ruth shuffles her feet, and fastens her raincoat. 'That must've been hard.'

'It was—peaceful, all the family were there.' Actually, they weren't: the phrase rolled off my tongue, and I forgot Kirsty, and Ian …

There's a pause: we stand on the step, me just outside, Ruth just inside. 'Well, mustn't hold you up,' I say, horribly hoping she'll move off soon, since this is very awkward. Her faith, and attitude towards my perceived lack of it, hangs between us.

'Yes: and if I can help again, in any way …'

We change places.

'Yes … We're very grateful, and, you mayn't be off the hook. I may need to call you back … For the … funeral, if it's before Jenny gets back. Would that be okay?'

'Oh …' Do I see her swallow? And hesitate a second? 'I should think so. I'll check with Keith, of course. Yes.' A tight smile. 'Your father will be missed. His writings have been an inspiration.'

I think of the book upstairs, and those proofs in the spare room at the Manse. 'I have his latest: would you like a copy?'

Her face changes, 'I loved those first two: I have them both,' she says. 'Well, must be off.'

The kitchen, where I go to make a hot drink, smells disturbingly of some cleaning product we don't use. The house is shinier, tidier and slightly less like home than usual. Mounting the stairs, I realise Ruth's coded message was, Dad's last book deviated in some way from his others. I feel more inclined to read it.

I fall into bed: our bed. Jenny's put clean sheets on before she left: or did Ruth? Did Ruth interfere with our bedroom?

Now that is a mean, evil thought. It would've been seen as kindness, not spying. Wouldn't it?

Max

10 APRIL, THURSDAY, 07.00

I'm woken by the sun, and Alice and Zoë, peering around the door. 'Daddy, Daddy!' They jump on me, and bounce on the bed. No time to spend on the memories, that Dad's left a gaping hole of inner loneliness and incomprehension as his legacy. I swallow it down, and talk about breakfast. Realising I have to take Zoë to nursery, and find something Alice and I can do all day.

Back from delivering Zoë, Alice and I each look to the other for inspiration. Suddenly the phone rings. Erin. 'There's a fax come for you, from Jenny. Shall I read it?'

'Go ahead.'

She reads Jen's message, and adds, 'You were so right yesterday. Sat in Dad's chair. Ian couldn't say a thing, but you made a great point there.'

'As long as Mam—'

'Mam's well aware who each of us are. You okay?'

'Easter holidays: I've got Alice to look after me.'

The Ahwahnee: John Guthrie: own goal, Jenny, I think, as I put the phone back.

Then I begin stacking the dishwasher. Behind me, Alice asks 'What did Grandpa say?'

I turn around. 'When?'

She shrugs. 'When you said goodbye?'

She can't, mustn't, know what the words do to me. I'm back in that dim bedroom, his last slow, ragged, struggling breaths; his now cold hand lessening its grip on mine; how I slowed my second reading of his favourite psalm, *the Lord's my shepherd*; reaching out for a tissue to wipe a dribble of saliva from his mouth, knowing it wouldn't be long.

'When you said goodbye and came home.'

'Oh, then. Grandpa was all right about it. He didn't need me anymore.'

'Is he better?'

'Ally, come here.' I sit on the sofa, and pull her onto my lap, 'Ally, Grandpa was going away. On a journey.'

'Oh. And Granny? On—holiday?'

'No, Granny's not gone with him. But they're all right about that. Grandpa has gone to see Jesus, and one day,' I almost break down here, 'one day Granny will go and they'll be together.'

'And us? Jesus lives—at Hildie's?'

'That's where Uncle David lives. Jesus lives—' I hesitate. Where should I say? Heaven? All around us everywhere, as Alice thinks angels do? In our hearts, as Ruth might say? 'Jesus, Ally, lives in, a place which is very near to us, but we can't see him.'

'So how does Grandpa?'

'Hard question. I think Grandpa can see him—can see everyone who comes to live there—with special eyes—but we can't see Grandpa any more right now.'

'So when?'

'When we go there. And we don't know when that will be. So, we live here and we can look at photos of Grandpa, and one day—one day we'll all be together, all the family. Is that okay?'

'With Jesus?'

'With Jesus.'

Momentarily, Alice goes very quiet and still. I feel her heart beating. And mine. Then suddenly she flings herself at my chest, arms out wide, in a huge, powerful hug. 'I want to be with *you!*'

My eyes fill with tears, and I bury my face in her back, the pink sweatshirt smelling of clean laundry and her hair sweetly of clean child. 'Daddy?'

'Ally: I want to be with you, too.'

She untangles herself and slides to the floor. Looks at me as I cross the room, heading for the kitchen paper, then blowing my nose. 'Why are you sad?'

'I—miss Grandpa …' It is a peculiar sensation.

Jenny

THURSDAY 07.30, US TIME, THE AHWAHNEE

Aaiee! Woken, by my alarm, from a very deep sleep. See first my little black dress with the low, low, back, thrown over the top of my suitcase. And then, as I reach for my specs on the bedside table, Max's message. Disgusted by remembering self last night, entwined with Wil. Why the heck—?

I slipped into that dress last night, thinking, *How wonderful, I've made another significant career step. Wow, I'm on top of the world. And Dad's jealous, I can tell ...*

But Max was in the house of death, while I nearly consented to a one-night stand. That is so horrible. Ironic that this trip's reminded me of Dad's silly comments about the stupid Oozlum Bird. Wish *I* could disappear. From myself, and Wil.

The dress reeks of stale perfume, as I scrunch it up and zip it away in my suitcase. I hadn't really meant to sleep with the guy, had I? No. Dressed in my smart grey trousers and a nice pale blue cashmere jumper, I re-read Max's message, and calculate it's mid-afternoon, UK time.

Why didn't I notice before? Max was going home. Relief: no worries about the Manse phone. Sitting on the bed, photos of my family smiling at me, I dial for an outside line, then our home number. Pick up, Max, pick up. Please. There's my conference papers, lying on the coffee table, and on top of them a silly little evening bag, and Wil's business card, where I scribbled down stuff about his work.

'Jenny? You got my message?'

'Too late. Sorry. I was stupid enough to trust Dad to fax over my change of hotel, and obviously that never happened. Then they were ages finding where I'd gone.' Max waits silently for more. 'Listen, how was it? How are you, baby?' How will Alisdair's death impact on his family? Do I sound warm and caring?

'Peaceful in the end: I was with him.'

What should I do? Go home? I can't deal with it. Nobody in my family's died, yet. 'Do you—should I—come home early? You know Dad made hiking arrangements to—' To die for, I nearly said. '—that I can hardly reject. I'll cancel if you want.'

'No, take the holiday. You should. You're owed time off, they gave it you to extend your stay.'

'You're home till when?'

'Don't know. I'm on compassionate leave, so I'm fielding the girls, and Mam'll let me know about the funeral. Family only. There'll be a memorial service in the summer.'

He sounds so cool and organised. I'm needing to beat myself up over almost-adultery with a probably seasoned seducer. 'But your mam—she must want me there.'

'You're not to come back till you've seen Yosemite. Chance of a lifetime.'

'If you really want that.'

'I really do.' My holiday mood, though, is spoilt by a foggy gloom: Pastor Mullins has managed to die while I was not only high on my own success but behaving badly.

'Jenny—'

'Yes?' Silence. 'You still there?'

'Jen, I realise that message—it's as well I sent it to the wrong hotel. Or you'd have read it immediately before standing up in front of all those delegates.'

'Well, fate intervened! Love you, Max,' I say, though it feels wrong, like I'm being strangled.

'Love you, baby. Dr Mullins. Who gave a brilliant performance.'

'Who could've told you?'

'Not a wee bird. I just know your style.' Max believes in me. This makes everything worse. 'Have to go, I've to collect Zoë from nursery. Stay cool about the trip, remember to take lots of photos.'

'What about the—' I begin, but he's gone. Daze's Fun Day: will he play for the dancing?

I re-read his message. Is 'Mx' a shortening, or 'M, kiss'? It was nice he apologised.

Can I eat breakfast?

Well, yes I can, since hunger tells me that food will replace sleep and give me energy for the interesting day ahead.

And in the dining room, there's someone waiting for me.

Max

THURSDAY 16.00, OXFORD

Daisy's left a haranguing phone message. About: *Will I remember the Scottish Dancing at the Fun Day this weekend?* Well, at least it'll occupy us all. So Alice, Zoë, and I are off to see Daze.

I park the car in Canal Street, and encumbered with a doll in a buggy, and two violins, we cross the bridge to the towpath, and begin marching towards the *Ironic Lady*. My instrument is in a clever case on my back, but Alice carries hers, carefully not running. She tells Zoë that violins are very expensive and mustn't be dropped. 'It's not a toy, it's the real thing.'

Zoë hurries to keep up, bumping her pink doll's buggy along the stony path. At each pothole, the doll bounces and almost falls from the buggy. Zoë sorts it, refusing help. 'Not a toy, Daddy.' Birds sing. The willows in new leaf dip across the path, forming arches. A swan family paddles by. A narrowboat full of holidaymakers passes. They wave. We smile and wave back.

I find myself happy, I've not done enough of this.

Or spent enough time with Dad. Especially when his guard was down, after that Rachel episode. When he apologized about Jenny, when Jenny was even a little on his side. Missed my opportunity. We concentrated on our careers, thankful he was leaving us alone. The famously piercing notes of the Allegri *Miserere*–Psalm 51–don't even do justice to the meaning, the utter sadness and regret, encapsulated by the psalm-writer so long ago. Dad, dominant, controlling pastor that he was—I don't know. It haunts me. Must it pursue me, and catch up when we are happy?

'Daddy?'

Zoë pushes the doll into my hand, breaking my negative thoughts.

'She falls out. All the time. Naughty!'

'Okay—' On autopilot I can reassure Zoë, but then where's Alice? Could I be so stupid, thinking about myself when I'm in charge of our bairns? On the canal path? *Jenny's bairns?*

'Alice? Alice!' I scan the path. It curves gently, in both directions. The wretched lacy curtain of new willow leaves obscures everything. Frantic, I hardly hear Zoë: 'Daddy, look.'

She points. Not far behind, a flash of shocking pink, half hidden by umbelliferous white-flowered vegetation. Alice, crouching, concentrating on something on the far side from the water. My relief is sudden and wonderful. As we hurry up, she shushes us. She is utterly still, her eyes focused, watching something moving among the leaves. Slowly, she extends both hands. Closes them together. She stands. 'Daddy, Zo-zo, it's a mouse!'

'Can you open your hands very slowly, a wee bit?'

'Look.' Between Alice's half-opened hands, a tiny sharp nose quivers, and beady black eyes stare.

'It's a field mouse.'

'Can we keep it?'

'Would it want to live in a cage?'

'We could keep it in the garden?'

'Ally, that mouse has a home somewhere.' (I am inspired.) 'You take a good look at it, and then, we'll let it go home to its family. Its brothers and sisters.'

I crouch beside Alice, Zoë leaning against my side. 'Look, Zo-zo, see Alice caught a little mouse?'

She paws at me. 'Wee-wee.' Heartsink moment.

Alice turns, her mouth twisted in disappointment and contempt. 'You are *so* boring! Look. I caught it. It's a mouse.'

Zoë wriggles. I make the effort to calm Alice's older-sister feelings.

'Let it go, Ally. We're nearly at Daze's boat. Zo-zo will grow up and be less boring.'

Alice, still crouching, opens her hands: 'Go, mousy, go home now!' and turns to Zoë, as the mouse scuttles away, 'You'd better not wet yourself. You just better not.' She wipes her hands on her jeans, and picks up her violin case. She's all of five years old and knows her own mind. Is she, like me, intolerant, or is it merely a child's fear of others behaving embarrassingly?

Daze, as we arrive at the boat, is attaching a banner to two long poles. *'Fun Day for the Homeless Centre! Fun Day for all the Family!'*

'Hey, my fave nieces! Max—I thought you were away?'

'Daddy was sad. We came to cheer him up.'

'Och, Alice. We came about the Fun Day, Daze. But first this one needs the bathroom.' I hand Zoë across to Daze, then help Alice onto the boat. 'No pot here: you'll need to perch on the loo. Can you do that?'

''Course.' Daze takes Zoë's hand, and hurries the doll's buggy into a safe corner.

'Don't go and fall in an'—well don't fall in,' Alice giggles.

Daze laughs. I try to frown at Alice. 'She caught a mouse on the towpath: Alice, better go with Auntie Daisy and wash your hands.'

'You caught a mouse? A real one?'

Jenny

THURSDAY, 08.00 US TIME, THE AHWAHNEE

First the grin, then 'Hi Kiddo—what're you having for breakfast? Don't say OJ and coffee. Fried bacon, egg and—hash browns do you?'

I'd like to mumble 'whatever' like a teenager: instead, I mention Alisdair's passing. Immediately, Dad gets annoying, 'Well, it comes to us all,' and starts on about Max's odd family.

'Please, can't you accept they're different and I want to do the right thing by them? If they need me at the funeral, I can't do the hike. Though Max says no need.'

'He's right. You'd be passing up a wonderful experience: Yosemite in springtime. Terrific photo opportunities. Snowy mountain peaks and superb waterfalls. Great time to get to know your half-sister. The giant sequoias ... trees a thousand years old? Besides, funerals take a while to fix up. You'll have time.'

I sip orange juice and try to focus my mind. Wil was trying it on. I really knew he only wanted a romp in the bedroom with someone he imagined he fancied way back. I should pay for my stupidity by flying home for Alisdair's funeral. Why'd I have that crazy idea I could maybe manage pillow talk around the destruction of the cells from Daze's deformed baby?

Out loud, I say to Dad, 'It's a family thing. Families are important. Did you, have you, taken time to talk with some of the families here?'

'The ones with the syndrome? I'd love to—but you know, it's not my specialty. Any work we at Vangenics could do would be to try to find a way to knock out the faulty gene. Can that be done? Over to you?'

They'd pay us for information, would they? I register nothing as he continues, 'Of course, I can make sure, with other techniques, that they have a healthy baby. Pre-implantation diagnosis, egg donation, GIFT, that kind of thing. But—' he spreads his hands, 'not my area, coping with a disabled child.'

'You remember Daze's dysmorphic baby?'

'Oh that, ten years ago?'

'Almost. If Daze wants a child—'

'Egg donation. I can do that for her.'

'You can?' I tease him.

'I can find her a donor and fix it all.'

'I—think she may find it hard to pay that kind of money.'

It could help to have him on my side. He talks a bit more about the range of treatments on offer at his clinic. He even mentions a few celebrities who've had other women carry their fertilised embryos, so they can get on with their lives without being pregnant. 'Essential if you need to preserve your position in the company, or your figure,' he winks. His suit jacket's on the back of his chair; he swivels around, reaches into an inner pocket, and pulls out a small folder. 'Let me show you, the perfect kiddies I've enabled some families with faulty genetics to have. Using the latest methods in our catalogue.'

The coloured photos, varying in size and quality, have been sent by grateful patients. 'Read the backs,' Dad tells me.

Dutifully, I do. Most of them have dedications scrawled, or neatly written, on the back. 'Nice. Good feeling, to have your work affirmed.' How much irony I put into that, I hope Dad doesn't realise. Why my feelings about his work are always so mixed, I'm not sure. 'Well, I spent some time with the families who are our target group. For them, it was like, *This is urgent. Okay, we know it's a genetic mistake, but how does it work?* They find it hard to understand we can know the what, but it may take ages to know the why. Or prevent it.'

'So they have pre-implantation diagnosis. Or you produce a test.'

'Mm, some of them wouldn't want to terminate. Those ones went ahead and had the baby even though they knew there were negative signs during the pregnancy.' Dad gives me a look. 'It's so awful, they care so much. The amount some of them read up and understand is awesome. Though others are just, well, enormously depressed and downhearted.'

'Try not to be too involved, Jenny. You'll ruin your objectivity.'

'I know—I know. Actually, involvement can be good. It spurs us on. My work can feel like endless careful routines. Running computer checks. Fiddling about with cells,' I say, almost as if it bores me, which it mostly doesn't.

'You have an easier time than when I was first in the game. You have,' (he waves his hands demonstrating masses of information to choose from) 'ready mixed feeder layers for your cultures, and—and the confocal microscope and—'

'You saw my images. Most of those parents were fascinated by what we showed and that's the beauty of fluorescence *in situ* hybridisation. It's easy to see what we're talking about. Even easy to explain the problem at the chromosomal level to people who haven't the background. The slides are pretty, you heard how everyone aah-ed at the way they look like sweeties. Then comes the irony. They were almost in tears.' He's silent. Yeah, I planned it that way, dramatic style learned from him. 'But when I met the families, then it really hit home. It's not just cells *in vitro*, it's people. Kids.'

He clears his throat.

'Dad, I think I ought to go, don't you? Support Max?'

'What? Oh, well now: it's a few hours, a religious ceremony, a traditional way to mark a life event. What Max'll need is, you back home refreshed. You may need to see his mother—what was her name?—Fiona?—more often?'

'Yes. Fee. But this part may mean a lot to them.'

'Them, Kiddo.' He reaches for the sizeable glass jug on our table, poising it over my cup, 'More coffee?'

'Half. Fee's gonna miss Alisdair. And it's not like only a life event, it's more like their faith is their life. Or their life is their faith.'

Dad sighs audibly. I push the last of my egg and hash browns to the side of my plate, and break my roll in half. Reaching for the jam, to counteract the cloying fried food.

'Don't get me wrong. I'd never engage in the debate against religion. That's pointless. Max's family, nice traditional people, pity about the religion. Beats me why, now we can scientifically explain the mysteries that led our early ancestors to cook up their myths, some otherwise intelligent individuals waste their time on it! Your Alisdair Mullins—'

'He's not mine—'

'Your hubby's dad spent his life keeping unnecessary myths on life support. His son has more sense. Though I believe he's not protecting my grandkids from a spot of indoctrination—' Hey, who's told Dad we're indoctrinating our kids? Mum?

Swallow hard, then smile over my coffee cup. 'Alice was an angel, school nativity play. She was so proud to have a part, and a costume.'

'Your mother mentioned it. Sent a photo. Lovely girl.'

'Yeah, well, that's not indoctrination.' Apparently she didn't say anything more. 'And you invited us for Christmas—an unnecessary myth, so you're as inconsistent as we are.'

Dad grins. 'Maybe it's genetic? Religion.' He sighs, 'I've always said, we need a strong secular state to move forward in science.'

'So why'd you choose North America?'

'My research unit in Vancouver is safe. Canada hasn't a Bible Belt, unlike the U.S. All I'm saying is, everyone has a right to their point of view, but some people think they have a right to force others to agree. Time the faithful stood back.'

Dad is onto his hobby horse. He's masterful at deflecting conversations. And maintaining his dislike of discussing ethics.

'Jenny?'

'Huh? Sorry, lost you for a moment.'

'I was saying I know a guy who's writing a book you should read. Kind of reverse-Bible, a secular "how to be the good society". Full of wisdom. And a charming man. Erudite. You should read it. You should meet him. You'd like him.'

'Maybe.'

He glances at his watch, 'Time to freshen up and then, first morning session? And I also have another thought that might grab you ...'

'Yes?'

'Colleague of mine runs a facility similar to the place I ran in Cambridge. Not far from here. If you want to see egg donation, start to finish, we could take a couple of days out of the Yosemite trip? Help with talking to Daze, and help with counselling those parents you met?'

'Can I—think about that one?'

The thought of visiting that clinic excites me more than I let on. I'm very up for gaining a more than theoretical knowledge of the donation process, *and* it's arguably work-related. It would totally justify my staying on. Max would understand.

Max

THURSDAY, 16.30, AT DAZE'S BOAT

When Daze returns with the girls, she opens some under-seat cupboards, sticking her head into each in turn, 'Paper and crayons for young artists, draw me something while we talk!' She sets the things on the table, then begins hunting in the galley kitchen, 'So, hey, Max, how you doin'? Okay?' I hesitate. 'Well I'm on a great project, did David explain? Your cousin is something else—I've some cookies in a tin—Oh, shit,' turning and shaking her head, 'Alice said something—Jenny's okay, isn't she?'

'Jen? Gave a fantastic presentation. I'm on leave because, well I went North to see my father—'

'He's not—'

Alice interrupts, holding up her drawing: a brown creature, pointed nose and whiskers. 'Look: it's a field mouse. They dribble their wee all the time, did you know that?'

'Yuck. Who told you?'

'Guilty. Actually what I said was, they dribble their piddle, didn't I, Ally?' Alice rolls about giggling, 'Dribble their piddle!' I think she mainly laughs because it rhymes.

Daze says, 'Blimey, you medics love it don't you—your Daddy's worse than me! Dribble their piddle!'

Zoë, unmoved, waves her artwork, 'An' mine! An' mine!': a smiley face, with long yellow hair, and stick arms and legs. 'Mummy!'

'It's deliberate, to mark their territory—och, lovely pictures, but enough zoology. It's only so they'll know to wash after playing with—. Sorry, Daze.'

'It's interesting. And lovely art. But you were saying, your dad?'

'He—died,' I say, softly, thinking of small ears, though both girls are busy again.

'Oh, God, sorry. I was yacking on, while you—' In no time, she's leapt the narrow space between us, the breath's knocked out of me as I'm suddenly encompassed in a hug. 'You were going through hell. Max, I am so sorry. Are you gutted? Jenny's away, how can I help?'

Even without her fond, crushing, obviously caring embrace, I'd be stunned wordless. It's strangely comforting as I gasp for breath, and inhale her musky perfume. Daze's reaction and real concern practically melts me into breakdown. Even though, or maybe because, her hair and signature black clothing are also highly nicotine positive.

It is so different from what Jenny offered. Or Ruth.

'It's awful, losing someone. Need to talk?'

We finally break apart. 'Och, I'm—coping.' Bereft, I slump onto the long padded bench and stare through the porthole at the dark, greasy, water outside. 'I think no talk, if that's all right.'

'Tea and brandy's a lot better than tea and sympathy—or how about brandy without tea?'

'It wasna' unexpected. But—' I nod towards the girls, 'Life must go on. He loved a good ceilidh.' My voice wobbles. Daze with her enormous capacity for depicting painful emotions in art has tapped into my desire to explain that it's impossible to put Dad's death and my grief into words. Why the hell does Jenny obsess that Daze needs a baby to complete her life? Can't she let it go? This is her mam, Caroline, over again. If only she saw that ...

Daze interrupts my thoughts, she's on her knees, rootling in a cupboard 'Right. But you gotta have the brandy anyway. You need it.' She pulls out a half bottle half full, and glasses. 'I'll have one with you. And with Jen away you guys could do with feeding?'

'You're very kind. We didna' come to be given our tea.'

'No worries. Baked beans on toast? With eggs? And—mashed bananas?' All far too much kindness. From an unexpected source. 'It's shit losing someone. We'll eat, then we'll do what you came for.'

Daze's words fit perfectly: it is indeed utter shit. Under the violent language and strange clothes beats a warm heart. Love, supposed to drive the household of faith, shames us by popping up where it will. Caring is also known among pagans and secularists. Dad with his knowledge of the scriptures should've made more of that to his congregation. Which stories might he've used?

'Max?'

'Sorry: thoughts drifted. We came about—I'm happy to do the Scottish dance music.'

'Okay.'

'I'm not the best by a long way. Not enough time to practice.'

'I'll cover my ears. Certain you've no thoughts to share?' She gets busy with saucepans and egg beating, and carving up a rustic wholemeal loaf.

I shake my head. 'Complicated. Raised in a pastor's family, which skews your view of the world. You never quite adjust.'

'My dad said, living on a commune was like that. You began to imagine the world outside's hostile, only you have true vision. Fact is, it's also hostile inside. All worlds are hostile. All worlds are this one.'

'And?'

'There's the *be true to yourself* rubbish. What the hell does that mean?'

'It's a get-out clause.' We laugh. Then I feel teary, and very warm towards her. It's seeing a side of Daze that's not often on show.

After we eat, Alice and I take out our fiddles, and I tune both instruments. 'Saturday I'll have a couple of friends along. We'll be a proper band with real musicians. Meanwhile, is this the kind of thing?' I stand, carefully avoiding the hanging bunches of sage and lavender, and play a couple of reels and a Strathspey. Daze applauds.

Alice plays her pieces, slowly and with concentration, and explains that she won't be playing on Saturday. Watching her, I've a sense of Jenny: serious, totally absorbed by what she's doing. Zoë, famous for her ability to fall asleep anywhere, is flopped out on the bench, eyes closed, breathing peacefully.

Alice ends her performance with some plucked notes. Zoë then stirs, and wakes.

'Better take these home: Dad less responsible than the childminder, otherwise. Daze, thank you.' We gather our things.

''S'okay. Take care. Hey, call if you need me?'

'Ally, Zoë, say goodbye. We're off.'

Hugs all round, then we tramp down the towpath, with a certain amount of raucous singing of *I Belong to Glasgow* and *They're Changing Guard at Buckingham Palace* to combat any silliness and complaining. The strange, outdated, songs remind me of Manse family walks: Dad with his *keep the team together* attitude looking to me and Erin to control the wee ones. Compassionate leave is a bummer for introspection. Alice will be at Charlie's tomorrow ... I'm thankful that's arranged, and I'll be catching up on paperwork.

Max

SATURDAY 12 APRIL, OXFORD

My mind struggles between preparations for the Fun Day, and Alice's needs for the beginning of term. Mam phones. I refocus: 'How're you doing?'

'Max, we have a date for the service. It'll be Wednesday. Ian wanted to ring you but I—'

'I'm glad to hear it from you. He's still with you, Ian?'

'He's very efficient. I feel I should be doing more, but they won't let me.'

'You need the rest.'

'I need to keep busy. I'll make the cakes for the tea. Only it's to be a lunch, Ian says, so I'll make quiches, and sausage rolls, and fruit salad. Family only. You did tell David?'

'He knows. Whether he'll feel it's right to attend the funeral, I can't say.'

'Oh, dear.'

'I'll do what I can about the Memorial Service. Really you know what I think about this rift continuing.'

'I do—'

Does Mam perhaps have other ideas than Dad's strict interpretation of a few ambiguous scriptures? Her tone, and the half-said sentence might indicate she does? She's left the subject open, and now, as we talk, we keep any emotions carefully in check. 'I'll arrive on Tuesday, and I'll have to get off immediately after as I can't leave the girls longer. And—we'll all see you soon.'

Outside, it's another wonderful mild spring day, bright and sunny. A day to blow the cobwebs away. Leaving the whole miserable business of Dad's demise on one side.

St Hildie's grounds are a grand venue. As we performers and stallholders gather, an ancient Volvo bumps over the field to the car park. It's Jenny's Aunt Val from Edinburgh, come to do spinning and weaving demonstrations. She's brought a carload of capes and throws in heathery colours. As I show her to the marquee earmarked for her use, Val, in long tweed skirt, homemade soft woolly cardigan and straw hat, comments, 'So it's a cross between a music festival and an Edwardian church fete! I'll fit in here fine.'

The celebrations begin. I've had no chance to speak with David, and now's not the time. He circulates the crowds in priestly black suit and dog collar, efficient, welcoming, and in charge. We meet up briefly, watching Val's sons Harris and Lewis do just what was promised: eat fire, to the enormous excitement of crowds of children.

Meanwhile, a large straggly collection of keen but mostly untutored revellers has gathered for Scottish Dancing. As I approach, it's forming itself into rough lines ready to gallop around to our tunes. We, the band, are kept busy for some time, until the caller signals a break. Val uses this to catch me, in the beer tent. She's exchanged the straw hat for a knitted tam-o'-shanter. Her long, chestnut hair, streaked with grey, hangs loose about her face. 'And where is Daisy? I've to sleep on her boat tonight, so you'd better introduce us.'

We find her painting tiger stripes on a boy's face. 'Shit! That Etta, that David said would help, is worse than useless! I dunno why, but she took one look in the spinning and weaving tent, and then she's off, *Sorry I'm not feeling too good*. Leaving me a pile of animal masks to sell, or whatever. I'm supposed to do face painting: I can't do everything!'

'Daze: Aunt Val to see you.'

'An' she had her effing animal mask on. Bloody badger, or something. Which is okay, but all the time, so's I couldn't see her eyes or anything.'

'Daisy—Aunt Val—'

Daze grins at Val, then lays aside her paint stick and extends a hand, 'God, so sorry. Yeah. Great. To meet you.'

'Well now, Daisy, your mum and dad's life together is quite a story.

Are you prepared for it, d'you think?'

'I'll finish here, then you try me.' The little boy's tiger transformation completed, and Val's plump arm around her, Daze is almost bowled along towards the food tent, 'So you knew Mum well? But you wouldn't tell me more on the phone! You must have some idea why she did a runner, from me and Dad?'

'We'll talk over a cup of tea, I saw some wonderful cakes on offer.'

Glad to unite those two, I return to the second dancing session. We complete our act with a wordless version of an old song, which Annie Marie, my girlfriend in my teens, used to sing when we had a folk group. Annie was a looker, lively, and fun. But she'd put a real sorrowful longing into that song. We were seventeen. It's a really bad idea for me to tack it on the end here: though the crowds like it …

*

We had a great day. That odd combination, Daze and David, have run a very successful event.

Home, once the girls are asleep, is too silent. I find myself thinking of Des, raising Daisy alone. The trick is to keep gloom at bay: hunt down necessary tasks. Housework. The clean laundry, including Alice's school shoe bag and painting overall, has spent the day sitting damply inside the washing machine. I shove it in the drier, and switch on.

I wish Jen would phone.

Wouldn't mind visiting Yosemite myself.

What scam is her dad up to, what temptations has he pulled out of his back pocket, in a break between trekking the trails and snapping the scenery?

Her half sister Mia, she told me, is 'a lot like Alice but heavier and definitely more sassy.' Like their Dad?

I capitulate and switch on the TV. The main news concentrates on the upcoming general election, underlining Labour's win at the Staffordshire by-election, and leading into a discussion of *Can Blair's New Labour win and govern?* How might Tony Blair meddle with the Health Service?

Comparing the world we live in with the strange walled world of my narrow religious upbringing, surely it's time to seriously tackle Dad's last book. I've a new, painful, ambiguous, compulsion to look into his mind. An angry kind of—affection? And, curiosity about Mam reading the proofs.

It's still upstairs, under the bedside phone. I retrieve it, a slim paperback, the cover photo conventional, a road leading through wooded countryside. The back is yellow, with positive recommendations. *Living with Uncertainty*: an odd title for him, or his publisher, to choose. Standing by the bed, I cautiously open it, almost as if the book might bite.

His previous writings are Calvinism reinvented for the modern reader. My eye catches some chapter headings: *Uncertainty and the Word of God, God's Map in the Wilderness, Can Rules bring Certainty?* Hum: where's the expected Pastor Mullins's style here? Where's the *Jesus our Certainty (in an Uncertain World)*? Gradually, I sink down to sitting on the bed, as I skim-read some fairly untypical thoughts my father's made public in a book.

Even some thoughts I'd not believe he'd have: *you can't make an omelette without breaking eggs.*

Changing world, changing lifestyle? Whatever is this all about? Yes, it's a fast-changing society, post-Freud, post-Jung, post-Nietzsche, post-modern. People need logical, workable answers. But Dad's message has always been: *Never mind all those, we have an unchanging God!*

Dusk falls and I can hardly see the words, as I read on, Dad's *Message* surprising and intriguing me. For the first time.

Jenny

SATURDAY 12 APRIL, THE AHWAHNEE

Now, in Reception, I'm watching the delegates gather with their luggage ready to depart. I've regained perspective. That episode in the bar meant nothing. Last night's conference dinner wasn't a problem.

After the meal, I danced with Dad, and Matt the paediatric surgeon, and even Wil. I didn't make an issue about the night before, he didn't try it on. It was good to clear the air about the fax though, to tell him Alisdair had died. He looked suitably shocked. We're sorted.

How easy it is to be silly, how little flirting means. Thankful I didn't take it further with Wil though.

A group of delegates who were waiting for an airport minibus surge out of the foyer, and at the same time, on a burst of fresh, cool, outdoors air, Karen and Mia arrive. We hug, and air kiss, and that gorgeous smell of the forest gets my adrenalin flowing: wow, how good to be outside a couple of days after being stuck in the fusty indoors sat down using only our brains and our ears. Then, 'Could you watch our bags, Jenny? And catch John for us? We'll just go and freshen up after the long drive.'

They've backpacks and bags and Mia leaves me her minidisc Walkman and earphones. Something's playing in there, but as I try to listen, I'm called to the desk to collect another fax. It's in Daze's beautiful, almost unreadable, italic script: *'Jen, I absolutely had to rush to the newsagent's fax machine to tell someone— you—your Aunt Val says my mum could be Romany! How cool is that?'*

Uh? Of course, the Fun Day, it slipped my mind. Did Max play for the dancing? Aunt Val would've done her weaving demos. Romany? I can see Daze, small, dark, wiry and strong, as a Romany: but can I believe it? Val's description of Daze's mother, on the commune back in the 1960's, sounded more like a weekend hippy on a very long weekend.

'More from the loving hubby?' Dad's arrived in the foyer. He leans over, full of curiosity.

'No.'

'Kids okay?'

'Mm. Just family stuff. Sorry. Anyhow,' as I fold the paper and zip it into my bag, 'I'm all ready. Right clothing, right boots, camera, all prepared. Karen and Mia in the loo: you ready? And I've thought about your invitation. I'd like to visit your colleague's clinic: it'd be useful background.'

'Great,' he says, clapping me on the back. Karen and Mia appear, I hand back the Walkman with its tinny music still playing.

First, out into those mountains we've seen from our windows. Dad introduces Bradley, our guide, suntanned and fit with a grin and a very bright woolly beanie. Karen's obviously at home with trekking and a good deal more fit than me. Mia can be a tad whiny. Yosemite is awesome. Bright in the sunshine, and the very cool, clear air.

The highest peaks, which are still glittery with lying snow, contrast with the blue of the sky. We're not climbing that high though. The waterfalls tumble so beautifully that I keep stopping to take photos, while Dad stands there, stamping his feet. Karen carries a guidebook, and a flower book, and stops to point things out, especially the wild flowers on the valley floor. 'Here in the lower elevations we should see tufted poppies, spider lupines, fiddlenecks, popcorn flowers, owl's clover and redbuds,' she reads. More foot-stamping from Dad, and whining from Mia, 'Mom, d'you have to read all of that?'

Karen bats her away, then gathers her back, arm around her shoulders, 'I'm sorry, hon, why don't you point them out to Jenny, huh?'

I snap everything and scribble notes to help me remember the names. I take so many shots on the trip that I have to buy another card for my camera. Mia wants to try photography: she finds the digital SLR heavy and cumbersome. And when I try to teach her how to focus, she complains, 'You're my sister: you can't boss me like a teacher.'

'It's a skill, Mia. If you do it properly, you'll have a great picture.'

The picture she tries for is Upper Yosemite Fall. We go back after nightfall to see the Moonbow over the Lower Fall. 'It's fairyland,' Mia breathes.

Dad doesn't miss the opportunity to woo me. 'You want Alice to see this: come work at Vangenic Solutions and bring them over. We can match your income, maybe give you a little more. We can certainly use your skills. Vancouver is a wonderful area to raise kids. Great climate. Best of everything.'

'The scenery could tempt me.' Dad grins, mouth wide as a happy frog, then takes a breath to speak. I almost instinctively hold up my hand like a stop sign, 'But you're forgetting something. I've a life in England I'm not prepared to give up.'

'No—no, not forgotten anything. But think, if you lived in Vancouver, you could bring the kids here more than once. See it in all the seasons. C'mon, Kiddo: Max could fly over for every vacation. You and I are broadly in the same field. All kinds of advantages.'

I slow, stop, look up and point at the sky, where fortunately something large and raptor-like is hovering, 'What bird is that? Could I borrow your binocs a moment?'

Could I do that? Live apart from Max and his devotion to his work? Dad pampering me. Giving me chances I mayn't get in the academic research world. Oh, I am so tempted: it'd be great to spend proper holiday time with Max, but be free of the dreary bits of relating. Such a guilty dream. Reminds me of all the dire stuff that'll be waiting back home. Duties and compromises. Disagreements. Distractions.

Bugger gloomy thoughts: I'm here to have fun. It's all amazing: the snow-capped mountains, and flowers and plants I've not seen before, the unbelievable giant sequoias, which we're lucky enough that conditions are okay for access. By effort and hiking! All too soon, Dad and I say goodbye to Karen and Mia, who're spending a couple more days here. And drive to that clinic, with attached labs, which advertises the whole range of possible fertility treatments.

'Unregulated,' he says, as we leave the car and walk towards the impressive buildings, sparkling in the sunshine. 'over here, we can really push ahead.'

'You don't find it difficult to recruit egg donors?' I ask the lab operator a few minutes later, mounting the stairs from the airy atrium.

'College kids. Who'd you want as the bio mom of your baby?' he replies.

'Med student? Grad school lawyer? Athletics coach?'

'On the money. And what they earn helps them through school, so everyone's happy.'

I smile, cynically, I certainly knew that one. And Dad would want no less. His two older daughters' mom was a newly qualified doctor, and a pretty splendid tennis and hockey player too. His second wife is a research biotech scientist and triathlete who plays the oboe.

'This way—you'll see we select the stunners, they're all cool chicks. Blondes, Hispanics, all on our books.'

I meet two egg donors, a college senior and a grad student. 'Doing this for my cousin,' the leggy blond grad student says, 'I was a biology major, anyway, so it's interesting. I'll be glad when it's over, I've been feeling nauseous with all these hormones circulating.'

I sympathise, smile, tell her good luck for her cousin, and explain I'm in genetic research. We discuss the hormonal drug routine, me taking notes as if my interest is totally objective. These donors supply the inside knowledge to supplement what Dad and the clinic staff tell me: they actually name the drugs and the way it feels as they work. Donation sounds quite a commitment. Pretty scary, to have to inject myself daily. With my distaste for clinical stuff. I ask them about how they managed and whether they got very sore. 'By now, I feel kind of like a bloated pincushion? But it's like before your period, isn't it? Like I get that feeling anyhow? There's actually a lot of stuff to go through first. Counselling. Scans.'

Does this worry me?

Dad says, as we discuss the effects of these massive hormone doses on the donors, 'Well, if we didn't do it this way, we'd be restricted to a small number of possible sources. Women being sterilized or having hysterectomies are usually over forty, their eggs are getting too old. Failing fertility is almost totally the egg's fault, but aging doesn't seem to affect the efficiency of the uterus to nurture a child. And there are other factors.'

'Those are?'

'If we're not overstimulating the ovaries, the hormones to prepare the uterus for the embryo are more effective. Did you realise that egg donation works best in menopausal women, whose own hormones aren't interfering by working on the ovaries?'

I do a double take: our hormones 'interfere with our ovaries', do they? Don't they simply work to produce a mature ovum ready to become a fetus in the prepared womb? Dad's way, the fertility industry's way, of looking at the cycle: take it apart and pump one set of drugs into a young woman, so she over-produces eggs. Meanwhile, use other drugs on the uterus of an older woman, to prepare it to receive an embryo. Makes scientific sense. Even so, Dad's attitudes are disturbing. As is the clinical side of this work. I wish I'd read it up in advance of talking with Daze. What exactly do those hormonal drugs do? *Preparing the womb to be out of sync with the ovaries?*

Whatever! Time to watch the college senior's scan. Wearing borrowed white surgical clogs, I clomp down the corridor and knock on the door. It opens, 'Hi, Jenny, isn't it? We're about to start,' smiles a nurse.

The scan shows possibly twelve follicles developing in the ovaries. The drug regime and any side effects are discussed. 'And $10,000 for my efforts!' the donor tells me, with a grin. Another question in my mind has been whether they were paid reasonably. I shan't ask for money: but if I lost work time, and it looks as if I might, my donation to Daze wouldn't be free for me, it'd be expensive.

Later, I gown up, and witness the grad student's eggs being harvested. She's produced fifteen, supposedly the upper average number, which are carefully sucked out through a long pipette, a very delicate procedure. My brain is recording everything, from drug regimes to surgical procedures, how they've been explained to the women, and what they are like in reality. After we're back at our lodgings (Dad expected his colleague to offer us hospitality, but no) I consult my notes, and consider the level of ovarian stimulation. 'How safe is this for the donors?'

'Not my department,' Dad says, 'I haven't done clinical medical work in a long while. You could talk to the team tomorrow.'

Tomorrow comes, and I watch the fertilisation process. There's something very special going on here, and it reminds me of a lecture Dad gave years ago. He talked of *Introducing the sperm to the egg*. 'Sperm, meet Ovum. Ovum, have you two met before? No? I'll leave you together...' Can't resist a smile, as I 'meet' the guy's sperm, and re-meet four of those harvested eggs. Though it rather trivialises an amazing occurrence, one that, for us, took place inside me. Here, they mix human gametes as if they're making a cake.

Of course, I don't meet the couple who'll be parents.

All very illuminating: how a woman who carries a heritable genetic disease can have a baby to call her own. She can at least carry and give birth to a baby which is fifty-fifty her partner's and a stranger's. Very neat. And how much of the research that led towards this did my father actually engage in? 'We were a team,' he smiles, 'just as your lab are.'

'And like us, you were in constant competition with a number of other teams. So the first baby conceived after egg donation was born in 1984, the year I started Uni. How long before that were you all working to get there?'

He tells me about an article, 'Look it up. *The use of donor eggs and embryos in the management of human infertility.* Australian Journal of Obstetrics and Gynaecology, if I remember right?'

*

Back at the Ahwahnee for one more night, I find an A4 envelope outside my door. Ah, obviously a copy of a scientific paper. Who'd leave me that? Anyway, I'll read it on the plane.

Jenny

WEDNESDAY 16 APRIL, 19.00,
ON THE FLIGHT FROM SAN FRANCISCO

Travelling back with some of the other European delegates would've kept my mind focused. As it is, my brain buzzes with too many thoughts. Soon as we're airborne, the man behind snorts his catarrhal cold and orders a brandy, and my neighbour pulls out her knitting. Sky-blue wool flows steadily from the yarn ball in her bag to be transformed into a sleeve.

I reach for that journal article someone mysteriously left me. The content is surprisingly relevant: *Egg donation: an enquiry into long term health issues.* But the abstract's more disturbing than I expect. I read the rest at high speed, my hands increasingly tense and clammy. I finish it in a whirl of anxiety and of frustration at not being able to check the facts.

'It's a cardie for my granddaughter.'

'Sorry—say again? Was miles away.'

'Just, it's a cardie for my granddaughter. She'll be five.'

I make myself smile. I'm actually thankful for the change of subject.

'You got kids?' she asks.

'Girls, five and just three.' Okay, nice to have my mind taken off that subject. Until I can access more research, there's no point dwelling on it. Let's refocus, with effort, on the present moment. Pulling out my family photos, I show her Alice, Zoe, and Max. She admires them all, and pulls out hers. 'And these: my American family. They've three little boys. That's where I've been.'

Let's not mention scientific gatherings. 'I was visiting with my Dad. We hiked in Yosemite.'

It was good to spend time with Dad, I muse, as our conversation ends. He's positive, ambitious, and curious. Like me. He's continued making a bid to prise me away from the Woods lab. He'd adore to have his grandkids around. I could cope with the mummy-thing out there. He'd help with affording a nanny ...

How'd it really be to work for him? He's in it for the kudos and the money ... He represents everything I began to question when I met Max ... Max must be relieved, in a way, that his father's no longer around to control everyone like some tribal leader? Like, actually, my dad also behaves?

Snuffle, snuffle, and worse, comes from the guy behind. Clickety-click go those knitting needles. The worst thing about flying is being up close and personal with so many strangers for such a long time. The lights dim, knitting granny neatly sticks the needles into the yarn ball, and rolls up her work. The movie is boring. We nod goodnight, she snuggles under her airline blanket. I do the same, with headphones on. The classical music choice is *Dido's Lament,* Ravel's interminable *Bolero,* and the Allegri *Miserere* on a loop. They think it's relaxing? That article bugs me, and the slow, sad music underlines the doubts and worries it's raised.

Think rationally. Think of something nice. I shut my eyes. Images of beautiful, wild, Yosemite excite my brain. Conflict tears me in pieces. Eyes fly open: remembering how Max described the clinical procedure around donation: now, I can't refute what he said. It *is* painful, it is *far worse when you've witnessed it.*

They may be right about the health hazards … Everything's a mess, my mess I've made … I don't know how to tell Daze I can't do it, I don't want to admit to Max he was right … I don't know how to talk with Max about his father …

Max

THURSDAY 17 APRIL, 13.00, HEATHROW

She swings towards me, waving, 'Hi, family!' A big hug; then, as she turns, my kiss lands on her neck.

'Oh—no kiddies?'

I'm not enough, she wanted her children. 'Jen, flight okay?'

''Course. Where're the girls?'

'School. Nursery. I thought you'd be tired.'

'Yeah. A bit.' A silent beat passes. Then, 'How're *you*? I thought you might still be away.'

'Och, the Manse spat me out after the initial day dealing with official stuff. Mam swung into practical mode, the congregation is looking after everything. Alex and Ian—'

'Are they relevant?'

I grab the luggage trolley, pushing it one-handedly at speed towards the exit, she accepting my arm around her, till she squawks, 'Max—careful!' as we almost run down a couple of women in bright saris, tucking a baby into a buggy. 'Near one!' she says, and I flinch. Rude, clumsy, inattentive.

'They made it clear Mam would—do better with fewer of us hanging about.'

'Oh no: how could they? And when's the—'

'So Erin and I scarpered. And when we knew the day, dashed back for the funeral. Yesterday. You'd not have wanted to be there. You couldn't have been back in time.'

'What did your Mam want?'

'There's a memorial service. That's when everyone turns up.'

'Am I everyone?'

In silence, we reach the car: I load in her luggage, Jen trying to do it for herself. What was it Eliot boasted about? Taking Shaz to a hotel for the night when she returned from New York? We, Jen and I, shouldn't need some false, honeymoon-style, night in a huge, hotel-owned bedroom. Should we? Though at least Shaz allowed him to demonstrate his form of caring. If that's what it was.

'Of course you aren't. But funerals can be dire. The memorial will be positive, celebrating his life.'

'Maybe.'

'And you didna' get along with Dad.'

'He chose not to get along with me. I'd've been there for you, and your Mam.'

Being together is no comfort. She clearly doesn't understand anything. Fastening her seatbelt, 'I'm sorry I had such a good time,' she says, almost in tears. Like me.

'Och.'

'What d'you mean? I am really sorry I was away when—'

'Let's drop the subject.' We wait in a queue to exit the car park. My eyes are moist. I glance at her: clenched hands, closed eyes, her face pale and hair limp. Is *should Mummies try to be top-flight scientists* the only question? Maybe the answer lies in Dad's book. Or rather, in what I discern was the mysterious conception of that book, my parents' last mutual creation. 'You did so well: tell me about it, the conference, the hike? Was Yosemite unbelievable?'

'Later.' Jenny goes silent. Probably drowsy. But as we arrive home, she says more cheerfully: 'I'll be okay once I see the girls. It's been strange, just me.'

They bounce all over her and the couch: hugs, cuddles, and squeals. She takes her laptop, opens her photo album of the trip. 'Want to see where Mummy's been?' The girls are too physically busy to give more than a glance. Eventually, calmed down, Alice stares at Mia staring as water bounces and glistens its way from rocks high above. Jenny's angled the picture so Mia's face, mouth half open, bright woolly hat on her head, is in the foreground, with the huge waterfall as a backdrop. 'She's my little sister,' says Jenny. 'Grandpa Canada's baby girl?'

'Grandpa Canada is her *Daddy*?' Alice sounds incredulous, then leans her head on Jenny's knees.

Jenny yawns, closes the laptop and lays it aside. She pulls Alice onto to her lap instead. 'Hey, did you go to Auntie Daze's Fun Day?'

'Yes! Yes!' Shoving at Alice, Zoë tries to climb aboard. Alice slides off Jen, and demonstrating excitedly says 'Daddy played his fiddle and everyone danced!'

'There was fire-eaters!' Zoë jumps up and down.

'We made animal masks!' Alice drags at Zoë, they scurry off upstairs. Jenny covers her ears.

Carefully, gently, I seat myself next to her on the couch. Touch her hair, sweep it off her face. 'Please,' Jenny says.

'Sorry. We missed you. We're happy you're back.'

'Yeah.' She exhales.

Inside, I'm screaming; outwardly, I say, moderately, 'You're a wee bit abstracted? Everything okay? When we spoke you were on a high—'

''Course I'm okay. You look wiped out.'

'I'm fine.'

'No you're not … Come here, I am so sorry—how's your Mam taking it?' And she instigates the arm-around, kissing, cuddling.

I am wary: what is wrong? 'You know Mam. She soldiers on. Even if his RAF career was long gone, the pastor's wife's role hasn't been much different. From the military one.'

'So she's—released from—all that dutifulness.'

'The funeral, Alex and Ian had it all organised, you ken the type of interference. Same with the memorial service.'

'They were closer to him.'

'Och, were they?'

'Well I thought—'

'Never mind.' I untangle myself from her, and move off to fill the kettle. 'Tea—or something stronger?'

'Whatever ... Tea?'

'What's eating you? Listen, Jen, it's me who's—or did something happen between your wonderful success at the conference and your getting on that plane? What's your father done this time?'

'Nothing more than usual. Hey, in the plane just now, the woman next to me was knitting. A little jersey for her granddaughter. Watching her reminded me of when I explained my interests to your Mam, and her apposite description of chromosomal abnormalities, "a knitting pattern gone awry". The families we met at the Conference would've got that straight away.'

'Aye, Mam's a talent for how to speak to people.' I begin to wonder if this exposure to the clinical side of her work has hit Jenny hard, and that's the cause of her mood. 'Has that conference shifted your perspectives on something?'

'No. Well, yes, in a way. Then, you know Dad, he's cautioned me, "Don't be drawn down that subjective route". But, maybe like when we nicked Daze's baby, she got her back and named her Persephone, and it ended up with a funeral. Does scientific objectivity have to mean sitting on your human feelings? It would, if I worked for Dad. It would ... I don't know ... What about your Mam, will what's happened mean she won't have to—'

'*Who's the king of the jungle ...*' The stripy face of a zebra, the honey-coloured face of a lion, as Alice and Zoë chant from behind their Fun Day masks. Jenny's attention flies to her children. 'A zebra with sparkles, and a lion with feathers?'

'He's a lion-bird!' Alice giggles, Zoë imitates.

'Let me see them properly, they're lovely.' She makes the girls stand still, admires the masks, then turns to me, grey eyes stabbing mine, mischievously, with what feels like love. 'I am so jealous, Daddy. You had a wonderful Fun Day. And I only had a boring conference and went hiking in the mountains. But guess what I saw there? I saw a bear.'

'A bear?' we chorus.

'A *very small one*,' says Jen, indicating a cub-sized animal. 'They take food scraps from the rubbish bins if people don't lock the lids on.' She pauses, shakes her head, 'Grandpa Guthrie was very naughty, keeping Mummy away so long. I'm glad I'm back now.'

*

Later: 'Photos? The bairns were too excited, but I'd like to see them?'

'Now? Okay. From the beginning. I was putting them on my laptop as I went along, so … Imagine: I've arrived and this was the amazing hotel Dad booked me into. The façade's real 1920s.'

'Your father—'

'You know Dad. And the conference was taking place there. I couldn't refuse a car with driver for the last three and half hours of my journey, could I?'

Silence for the length of a heartbeat, while I think about this. And look at Jenny. 'Should I have?' she asks.

'Mmm. So you were right inside the Yosemite parklands the whole time, were you?' I say, hoping she can work this out herself. 'I wonder if that was, altogether, a good idea?'

'Why? The families and a few underfunded delegates stayed in different accommodation. But we were all there. Dad's generosity meant we could socialise without hanging out together in full view of everybody in the public rooms. What's the problem?'

'Rich Woods, your boss, he'd maybe be a wee bit fashed about you being treated, entertained, by the commercial sector, possibly?'

'Max, it was my dad!'

'And he used to head up a private clinic, with research labs, down the road when you were at Cambridge. Now he's doing it all again, in Vancouver.'

'You are so picky!'

Jenny

FRIDAY 18 APRIL

'Wowuu wowuu!' The bellowing hurts my ears. I ought to go to her. Before something happens that nobody wants.

After that clinic visit, I'd begun to worry about egg donation. And then, the article. The authors suggest that the hormone treatment given to donors may increase their risk of ovarian cancer. Well, there is far more drug treatment than I expected. It's really painful, that student said, to have fifteen ripe ova inside you. Admittedly these researchers used a small sample, but—must I go ahead and keep my promise, despite it could ruin my health, or take my life away?

I go cold and shivery. What if I do this, and what if I don't? I promised Daze. I believed in what I was offering.

'Wowuu wowuu! Mumma Mumma!'

My neck's stiff, and my arm, caught half under Max's body, is like a dead thing. I want to curl up tight and cry: none of this has been the homecoming I imagined. Or that Max needed. I know that. But, I manoeuvre myself free. And Max grunts, 'Thank God.'

I shuffle to Zoë's room, putting on my specs. In the doorway stands a scarlet-faced horror, eyes screwed up tight, little fists gripping the gate we put across at night. She jumps up and down, her pyjama trousers now fallen round her feet. 'Oh baby, what's the matter?'

'Wowuu Mumma *you didn' come!*'

Is this any better than waking at the Ahwahnee, after that misspent evening? I swing my legs over the gate, and pick up my wailing toddler. The noise abruptly changes to juddering hiccups. 'I'm here now.' She nuzzles my neck with her wet face. You are both Max and me, I think, holding her close. It's you who've been howling for us.

'Is it morning?' Alice, who can climb over the baby gate into Zoë's room, tugs at my PJs. 'Is it tomorrow?'

'I expect so.'

The *Today* programme booms from our room, a persistent interviewer haranguing some public figure hauled early from his bed to be interrogated about the general election. Whoever it is throws back the usual off-centre answers. Sounds like us. A tear runs down my face and drops onto Zoë's hair.

Oh what a contrast. From my luxury hotel room, everything provided, stunning scenery and a stimulating environment. Whiny kids, belligerent radio, and gloomy husband … Rich will now want a more than half decent report on all that I did, and learned, on my trip, in less time than it takes to write it up.

Max evidently can't wait to get to the surgery. He passes me outside the kitchen, a quick kiss as he hurries by.

'Hang on—'

'Compassionate leave over: back to the mill with slaves.'

'What?'

'Milton, long poem about Samson—never mind.'

'It's Friday.'

'Yes: but I—'

'I'll take Alice to school. Least I can do …' I call at the departing car.

Alice to school, Zoë to nursery, me to Ruth's with payment for her stay, and a small, floppy parcel wrapped in brightly patterned paper.

'We're enormously grateful,' I say. She looks at me: and then at her shoes. 'Ruth: you've been amazing. It was horribly short notice, and you—rallied round,' I say, grasping for words to convey everything in terms that express just how much she saved my career and my reputation with Max's family. 'Here's what we owe you, and—this. I'm sorry it's so small.'

Ruth, who'd been staring beyond my left shoulder at the flowering tree in her front garden refocuses, and beams at the small parcel. She takes it carefully. 'Shall I? Open it?'

'Go on.' She doesn't rip the wrapping. She carefully peels the sticky tape away from the paper, and unfolds it, revealing the soft woollen scarf I chose for her at the hotel shop. She shakes it out to its full size. It's printed with native American designs.

Obviously disappointed a second, she rearranges her smile, 'I love these shawl-type scarves: thank you, you shouldn't have.'

'They had gorgeous pottery, but—'

Rolling her eyes, 'I know, the suitcase, and the baggage handlers. But, this is really useful and it's my colours,' she says, holding onto the side of her front door.

It is. A very pale blue, and white, and green. I almost mention that the colours have meanings, and that blue is for women, sky, the moon, sadness. Green is earth, and rain. But stop myself. This is Ruth, not Daze. 'I hope they behaved for you.'

'Oh yes! We kept their routine. And they did some new things. They played croquet. After church at St Hildegard's. Did I know Max and David Robertson are cousins?' Ruth's head is on one side, like an inquiring bird, eyes bright with curiosity.

'I expect not.'

Ruth smiles, but sounds brusque, 'I think Max took Alice and Zoë, because they do a church lunch. Mainly for overseas postgrads.' So Max went for the lunch, and Ruth thought that wasn't quite right. A game of croquet would've helped occupy Sunday afternoon … He didn't mention it to me though.

'I'm so grateful you were able to take over again while he went to the funeral. He really should've insisted I came back. But the conference was wonderful, and I had a chance to spend time with my father. His field overlaps with mine, so he was there … Today I'm writing up my trip for the boss.'

'Mmm,' says Ruth, 'Well, hope the writing-up goes well.' Her mouth, as it closes, is a tight smile, I sense a signal she wants to close her door as well. Pity she can't discuss the subject she used to work in herself.

'Right: must dash, yes. Here's Zo-zo's jersey if it turns colder later. I'll swing by about six for them? Would that be okay?'

Ruth nods, affirms, takes the jumper, hugging it against her chest like it's Zoë herself. And retreats into her hall. 'Yes: gotta slog on,' I say brightly, and hurry down the path to my car.

At home, the sun pours through the windows. Even though it's Oxford, not Yosemite, a seductive spring has arrived, with little bursts of birdsong. I reread the article. I think about the data. Can I back out now, to save my own health, on the basis of this slim study? Who the hell would pass this to me? Wil? Matt the paediatrician? And why?

Must work: Rich will want to know everything I've done, witnessed, heard. Trawling through notes I carefully made about other people's papers, the questions, and my networking, it's cheerful, affirming, to reconnect with my success. The daffs nod and dance in the breeze, and our robin perches on Alice's scooter, abandoned beside the swing.

I begin typing my summary. By the time I have to collect the kids the printer's clacking away, spewing out pages.

Life ought to be good, it ought to be great. Work is going smoothly. It's just the other bits.

Max

SUNDAY 21 APRIL

Sunday morning: a hard-going week. Etta's been mysteriously unavailable, and Jenny's now morosely catching up on the ironing, not best pleased. Good time to escape the house: taking Alice and her chatter away is the best plan. Alice is a great companion: enthusiasm and cheerfulness embodied. Wee bit like her Mam used to be.

We're off to find David, I've a copy of *Living with Uncertainty*, signed, incongruously, by Dad. '*To my nephew David, with my very good wishes, Alisdair M.*' Signature firm, no excessive signs of weakness: a long-term plan to reconnect? Written last summer, before those last months downhill?

A dead man to a dead man. Dad had, on principle, considered David dead for ten or more years. But, he'd fixed me with his eyes, handing it over, '*You be sure to give that to him, will you?*' Euan mustn't die without getting his son back, and knowing what a remarkable son he has. David mustn't remain cut off from his father as I did, and then blame himself. It is urgent that we talk. Before the memorial service if possible, then he can attend.

We arrive at St Hildegard's slightly before Mass is over. A hymn is being sung, or rather, belted out, in the chapel. How else to sing *Amazing Grace?* Behind the Livingstone Lounge, I'm locking our bikes together when there's a sudden screeching of machinery that drowns out everything else. And clouds of dust.

Alice darts towards the source of this, to investigate, me dashing behind, 'Wait. I don't think you—' I catch up, as she skids to a halt at the entrance. A figure emerges from the settling dust, ripping off goggles and a mask.

'Auntie Daisy!' Alice takes a cautious step into the building. She stands at the very edge of a bare, rough, concrete circle, marked out with pegs and string. 'The floor's gone!'

'Hey Alice! Don't move. I'm coming to you.' Daze lays aside the protective stuff, and wipes her hands down her jeans. 'Yeah, it's me again, ruining the building. If you came to see David, he's busy performing the rites.'

'So this is what you're working on!' Down on my haunches, I've an arm around Alice, showing her what Daze is making. 'Tell us about it?'

'It's a labyrinth. You know the one in Chartres?'

'Saw it once. Under all the chairs.'

Alice looks up at Daze. 'What's a labby-rinse? What's it for?'

'A lab*yrinth*, Ally.'

'A lab*yrinth*. Like Mummy's work?'

'Your mummy works in a lab*oratory*, I work in a lab*yrinth*. How fun is that?'

Alice stares at Daze like she's gone mad. Daze crosses the room, and fetches some large pieces of cartridge paper. She kneels, and spreads out the paper.

'This is the one I'm doing. The circular one.'

Alice kneels to look. 'It's a maze-thing.'

'Not quite. It's a squashed spiral.' Great way to describe it: just how it looks in Daze's working drawing here, quartered with faint pencil lines, scribbled over with measurements, notes and calculations. Daze sits back on her heels, and looks intently at me. 'Hey Max, how are you now? How's it going?'

'Not so bad. We're getting the memorial service sorted out. Mam's realised how exhausting the last few months have been. And you were very kind, exactly what we needed that evening.'

'Glad to help.' Since Jen's been back I've experienced how impossible she finds it to cope with grief in another person. Somehow Daze has picked up the skills, though obviously not at home from Des and Caro. Whatever else, she understands how to comfort, and show concern.

She interrupts my thoughts, 'It was David's idea. Though I've known about labyrinths for a long while.'

'So making this maze is what brought the two of you together?'

'Not a bloody maze! People hear labyrinth, and fucking think maze. Sorry, but they are *totally different*. That's the first thing to learn. A maze is a puzzle, twists and turns and blind alleys. It demands logical, sequential, analytical thinking to get in or out. Labyrinths are right-brain, *friendly*, and creative.'

'I stand humbly corrected! Interesting working drawings.'

'What's sick-wentchel?' says Alice, who we've almost forgotten.

'Ask Daddy later.' Daze moves another sheet on top of the first one, 'Here's the other style, the one where the Minotaur lived. Not in the flat-on-the-floor model, of course,' she grins.

'That one reminds me a little of a diagram of a sliced-through human brain.'

'Brain is another mystery,' Daze says.

'What's a Minotaur?' Alice asks.

'Mythical beast. Like a bull.'

'What did he do?'

'Forget the Minotaur, Daddy'll tell you the story later. My labyrinth is nothing like that. And, Max, these tiles I'm using are rather special, the guys at the business park ordered them from Provence. I've had to cut a lot of them to shape. Almost at the exciting bit now, but had to cut a few more of the boring ones, which was the godawful noise and dust as you arrived.'

'Mm.'

'A labyrinth's an ancient symbol for wholeness, and a metaphor for the journey of life. So you walk it. Make sense to you, Max?'

Alice walks her fingers around the labyrinth drawings. 'It works, doesn't it? You can't get lost. Look: the path goes all the way in, and back to the entrance. And when it's all done, we'll walk it properly, on our feet.' Daze seems to've forgotten me, and to be addressing Alice.

'Why?'

'It's a spiritual thing. And it's fun. It helps you think. About God and stuff.'

'Oh. Grandpa went to see God. Or maybe,' she looks to me for confirmation, 'Jesus?'

I nod.

Daze continues the lesson, addressing me, 'Yeah, David's lot would hope to meet God in it. Whatever, it's a symbol that creates a sacred space and place, and takes us out of our ego to That Which Is Within.'

'Mm. I see.' Has the morning service ended, can we escape to see David? 'I thought that which was within the labyrinth was only the Minotaur,' I add wickedly. 'Obviously at school they didn't know everything.'

'Not your thing,' Daze sighs.

Alice is rootling in a cardboard box. 'Hey, what're you doing, pet?'

'It's full of tessa-ray.'

'Tessa Ray?'

'Tessarae, tiny tiles,' Daze laughs.

'I can do this: we had paper ones at school. Can I do some, pleeese?'

'That's for Auntie Daisy—'

'No probs. Though she may get bored. C'mon Alice: this is how the Romans did it, one tiny stone and then another—careful! Then I grout them—using that stuff there—then I very carefully wipe them over. Just like tiling a wall, but much, much more skilful. Alice, show me you mean business, I want three tessarae laid here, look, following this curvy line.' Daze carefully lays out the tiny, glowingly azure, mosaics.

'Max, you should come to the opening. We'll have candles all round the edge and David'll do a blessing. Wicked, hey?' She winks.

'If you're happy to watch her, I'm away to find him. You're sure, about her doing the labouring job?'

Daze twizzles her left wrist, looking at her man-size watch. 'He'll be with the after-Mass coffee-drinkers by now. Alice, remember it's not a wall, to keep the Minotaur inside. We're creating sacred space together. Then you can decide, whether or not to walk a spiritual path.'

Was that more irony, I wonder, heading for the main building. Or does the labyrinth have something to it? Keep the Minotaur within. The choice to walk or not to walk a spiritual path?

A crowd of Anglo-Catholic coffee-drinkers mills about in the refectory. I push through to David, wondering: 'did Dad know—yet deny to himself—that Euan's son now wears the pastoral mantle intended for me?' They had it all worked out, but the two of us swapped places.

Noticing me, David's excusing himself from a group. 'Max, how are you? Did you—'

'Nope, avoided Mass. Doing okay. Good to have the bairns around.' He appears to understand my underlying meaning, and, hand on my shoulder, asks, 'Coffee?' and nods towards the hatch. We step that way, me holding out *Living with Uncertainty*.

'David: Dad signed a copy of his book for you. Take it—he won't do it again.'

David ignores the black humour. 'That was kind. I'm grateful. Your coffee, black? Sugar?'

'Milk today, and I'll have one of those biscuits, the blood sugar's a bit low.'

'Busy week?'

'Dad's funeral, keeping the bairns, collecting Jen from her travels, work: standard week.'

'Hah. Yes. Her travels.'

'I was glad she was away. Easier. With the family.' The blessing of talking with someone who understands our laconic family language. He knows that *what we are silent about, of that we cannot talk*. Or not yet. 'So: you have the book. And, just checking, you need me at your congregation's annual general meeting, to speak about plans for a clinic at the Centre?'

'Yeah, yeah, five minutes and back to what you were doing before.'

'Tuesday week, evening. In the church?'

David grins. 'Under the eye of the Blessed Virgin, yes.' And rubs his hands. 'You know, I believe she approves.'

'Enjoy your book, mate. I must away and rescue your artist in residence from Alice.' I dump my half-finished coffee, and raise one hand, as if in salute, a habit learned for waving departing patients from my consulting room.

Striding back down that long, cool corridor towards the exit, I mentally kick myself for treating my cousin like an acquaintance. Because we are restrained, ex-Calvinist, Robertson-Mullinses. Because we met in public.

What I want and don't get, what I miss and ache for, is Jenny's understanding. All she sees is me escaping to spend time with David. Where's the insight in that?

Jenny

SAME MORNING

Katerina, please come back! I long for your wonderful accent and your cheerful smile over a basket of ten shirts!

The phone rings: I lean over and grab the receiver off the wall. Fee. Not at First Truly on a Sunday morning? 'I'm sorry, Max isn't here. And that I missed the funeral. Max told me not to change my plans. I hope that was—was it?'

'Yes. No. You shouldn't have worried. It was very small and quiet. Afterwards—' She seems to need to talk, I switch off the iron. 'When it was over, I went to Lindisfarne with a friend. We were at the St Cuthbert's centre and then—well, I'm back and I should thank you for the card, and the e-mails.'

'I feel I should've done more—'

'No, pet, I understand. It's difficult when someone's—'

'Yes.' Please don't say it.

'—bereaved. But it's a blessing because he didn't have to—' Her voice trembles, 'manage hiding all that frustration at his disabilities any more. Which he very much resented, and fought against. The disabilities—'

Fee struggles to control her voice. I smile across at Zoë, down on the floor with paper and crayons. 'Grandma,' I say, my hand over the receiver. When I take my hand away, Fee says firmly, 'Of course I'm tired, but I keep busy, there's so much to do. The few days away have set me up. How was your trip? And how's Alice, pet? And wee Zoë?'

'Zoë's right here. Zo-zo?'

'Hi, Gram'ma.' She twitters and giggles, hands the phone back, Fee and I say our goodbyes. Of course they didn't expect me at the funeral: the Mullinses close up around tragedies, and they'd want everything cool, and organised, no untidy family hangers-on rushing in at the last minute. I don't fit.

Life here's hardly like that. I'm hardly finished with ironing when Max and Alice come banging through the front door. Alice's voice moves down the hall ahead of her, 'Mummy! I saw Auntie Daze's laby-rinse she's making!'

'What's Auntie Daze making?'

'A laby-rinse, a big round, round, thing,' Alice extends her arms, stretching them out as if to encompass the world. 'On the floor. Like hopscotch.'

'Okay. A labyrinth. Like a maze.'

'Not a *maze*.'

'Ssh, Alice. How was Daze—Max? What's this thing for? Must be alluring—she was totally involved with a sort of homage to Judy Chicago, feminist statement, that kind of stuff. When she moved here.'

'Sacred space, apparently. She was busy tiling a floor. In their big meeting room.'

'Weird. All of it.'

'They've taken up the floor in what they call the Livingstone Lounge. A seventies extension meeting-room with floor-to-ceiling windows. Daze is redoing the floor as some kind of spiritual aid, a mosaic tiled labyrinth. Financed by a benefactor's restricted fund. She kept Alice for me while I spoke with David. Arranging mosaics.'

Alice is pulling on the end of my shirt, 'Mummy, it's tessellated, like we made in school. With tiny-tiny stones. She let me help. She said because the tessa-ray are small, they feel different, so if you can't see, you know through your feet where you are. You take your shoes off. It's a mosaic, like the Romans made, in a story we had at school.'

'Lovely. Did I know you learned about the Romans?' I turn back to Max, 'So, they made up, David offered her a commission, and she said yes and this piece of art's a kind of installation at St Hildegard's?' I'm confused. And then I'm cross. 'She's never shared any of this directly with me. Does she think I'm not interested?'

Max throws me one of his grins, the ones I used to be so easily seduced by. 'I happened to be there, so she showed me the thing. I suppose she didn't think—'

'And David's your cousin. Why'd neither of them tell us?'

'People are peculiar. They've found a mutual interest in religious things. Pagans use these labyrinths too, Daze seems to know a lot about them. I took David a copy of Dad's book.'

'That'll hardly be a Daze-friendly object.'

'Mummy!'

'Quiet. Haven't you something to do?'

Max walks across the room, and picks up a drawing Zoë made. He turns it round, as if looking to make sense of it. Deliberately dropping our conversation. I'm near to furious, quivering inside at how let down I am by his ability to tolerate the most annoying people.

'Mummy I *told* you! About the Romans. *Listen*, Mummy!'

'In a minute. Amazing Daze's now *completely okay* about David. Even though she was mega-upset by the betrayal of how he got that property.'

'Solves a lot of problems,' says Max, shrugging his shoulders and laying Zoë's drawing back on the kitchen counter. 'David wasn't the one who decided: it was the council. What d'you use to stick their pictures up with? This is rather splendid.'

'In the drawer,' I hiss, 'if you have to. Where the string lives.'

Yes: I'm really jealous of these easy lives. Max, Daze, David, even *my* Aunt Val, enjoying the Fun Day together, bonding over Scottish Dancing, cakes and ale in a marquee, kiddies' face painting. I was so focused on the conference, but now I see: Daze's traded her feminist idea, and her right to those premises, for making David a kind of spiritual aid. Why's she acted all complacent and yielding? And I'm left with our pact: what's she expecting me to do?

The egg donation article's awful, but can I pull out? She's no right to expect me to do it now, has she? She's got something better, has she? David's work. David's friendship. And, Alice's admiration. Wings, and now this labyrinth.

While I'm screwing up everywhere. Even resisting Wil's overtures, I still made some mistakes at that conference: Max is probably right that I shouldn't have accepted accommodation from Dad. Though so far Rich hasn't made an issue of it.

Jenny

THE WOODS LAB, A FEW DAYS LATER

The whole team's gathered in the lab office, talking about the upcoming general election. After the Government and public reaction to Dolly the cloned sheep, is it possible that Tony Blair's New Labour would be more open and positive towards embryonic stem cell research?

Rich, visibly more relaxed now Danielle's op is over and she's recovering well, leans back in his chair, stretching his arms out behind his head with a sigh. 'Basically,' he says, 'a more go-ahead, adventurous government must mean better funding for our kind of science. Though don't hold your breath. Everyone's after money for stem cell work. And the religious lobby'll howl and campaign every step of the way.'

As the group disperses, he turns to me. 'You did well fielding those tough questions at the conference.'

Rich is pleased: even if I'm not totally pleased with myself. But I am definitely disquieted. My brain buzzes, thoughts won't stay quiet about how to end my offer to Daze. Without looking stupid in front of Max.

I glance at Leila: I've lent her that article, has she read it yet? Suppose other stats on associated ovarian cancer have been suppressed? Those women at Dad's friend's clinic hadn't been given any warnings about long term health risks.

As if she could read my mind, she's at my side, 'I've read the article. I know we've all had an extended coffee break, but could you and I meet over lunch? How does your schedule look today?'

'Tomorrow's better for me.'

'Tomorrow then.'

I'll not mention Daze. Much better to centre my concerns objectively, on options for couples who have a known genetic problem, and want a family. We settle with our salads in a nice café up the road from the science area, and I begin by referring to the families I met in America. 'Maybe I'm over obsessive, but I saw how deeply wounded women can feel if they've conceived a baby with disabilities. Some of the parents I met in California told us how cruelly some people label a family who have a malformed baby. Like "Don't go out with her, have you seen her sister's child? You don't want to marry into a family where there's bad blood."'

Leila argues that egg donation is a bridge too far, since IVF with pre-implantation diagnosis is available.

'Not sure about the religious families. They don't allow interference with an embryo.'

'In Islam, we encourage all procedures which are for the well-being of the child. Of course, we must balance the interest of the family, and don't permit testing to choose a boy or a girl.'

'The beauty of egg donation is, there's no interference with the fertilised ovum. It looks like it would solve genetic problems or female infertility. Of course with a genetic heritable condition, you'd obviously choose a donor who's not related to the affected parent. But if these are the facts ...' I pause. It begins to seem like slavery, once you factor in that it's harmful to the donors. Or could be. 'Those of us who think we're involved with something harmless should be told.'

Leila takes a sip of her mineral water, and looks intently at me, her dark eyes searching my face. She puts down her glass. 'I think I need to ask you, is this a personal thing, Jenny? Have you promised to give your eggs to someone, possibly a cousin or a sister?'

Lying would be pointless, and lose Leila's respect. 'Okay, it's not theoretical. I've a stepsister who's already had a severely dysmorphic child. I want to help her. She's not conventionally religious, but she's very conservationist. When she was pregnant, she refused to have further tests when they said the baby might have problems. So I know she'd not want PGD, she'd never put an embryo at risk of being accidentally killed by a procedure.'

'Which is unlikely.'

'Yep. But suppose the person won't accept the risk—'

'Or maybe you have some other reason for wanting to make a genetic link?'

'To the baby? I'd never want to do that.'

'How about we do an online search at the Science Library? We'll tell Rich we had to use the databases if he wonders where we've been.'

We hurry past Keble College and along Parks Road. Not sure whether I'm full of dread about the negative findings being confirmed, or attracted to the possibility of release from the unpleasant procedures. But, though the data seems thin and the studies inconclusive, Leila's adamant I simply pull out of any commitment. 'Surely,' she says, 'If your stepsister isn't religious, she will accept genetic diagnosis of a portion of the embryo, one blastomere or its nucleus for a specific genetic defect?'

'The facts about the baby are smudgy because the guy who was the father has a translocated gene and was a recreational drug user. We tested Daze's DNA, she also has a translocation. And she's definitely not going to change her mind about testing a fertilised egg.'

'But you—you mustn't donate. Explain you've read some negative research. Or tell her you're too busy, which is true? I can tell you're anxious about this. And you have no obligation.'

I know she's right. It's shocking that they haven't put this treatment on hold until they know more about the risks. Aren't they profiting from women's generosity? 'You're right about that. Thanks for listening.'

I'm beginning to hope that Daze has become so involved with this work for David that it's replaced her need for a baby.

Mum phones during the evening. I'm sat on the bed for half an hour while we chat, me pretending everything's fine, and as she talks on about her yearning for a cultural life beyond Cornwall, I notice a slim paperback lying under the phone. I can read its spine. *Living with Uncertainty*, Alisdair's last publication, which Fee gave us after the narrowboat holiday.

Uncertainty's a feeling you may be stepping out onto ice, or quicksand, or solid ground, and there's no way to tell which. It's familiar, but I don't want to live with it. I don't want to live with feeling so divided, between what I want to do, and what I think I should do, and whether ought and should are relevant in today's world. I gently pick up the phone's base, and still holding the receiver to my ear as Mum continues—'*but sweetie, the occasional really professional concert, not just waiting around for the Endellion Festival or the right weather for the Minack*'—I draw out the paperback, and read the recommendations on the back.

Then I flip it open. A quote in the front claims to be from Einstein. '*The most beautiful thing we can experience is the mysterious. It is the source of all true art and science. He to whom this emotion is a stranger, who can no longer pause to wonder and stand wrapped in awe, is as good as dead.*' Intriguing. Did Alisdair agree? Is uncertainty necessary, to protect mystery? I suppose so: I suppose it actually creates mystery. It's a mystery that Alisdair didn't just write one sentence on this: it would be, *Uncertainty is unknown to the believer: d'you no' ken all the rules to be followed are there in Scripture?'*

'Darling, are you still there?'

Max

ST HILDEGARD'S CHURCH, TUESDAY 29 APRIL

I've crept in at the back, as the Annual Meeting draws to a close. David said that I didn't need to sit through the whole thing, and indeed, not being a signed-up member of St Hildegard's congregation, I'm not supposed to. My eyes gradually adapt to the gloom, and I'm surprised to see the place is packed. Had no idea his regular congregation was so large. From the altar step at the front, David's summing up the past year as a success, with an increase in the numbers of guests, a couple of large legacies, and most recently, the redevelopment of the Livingstone Lounge as a quiet space (with labyrinth, I think). I slip into a space in a pew about halfway down the church, as David finishes, and announces the item I've come to contribute to: the Day Centre for the Homeless.

Suddenly the place is filled with murmurous talk. People shuffle the papers they've been circulated about the project. They swivel round to speak to those sitting behind. A few even get up and walk over to consult with others sitting further away. Oddly, a fair number are familiar. Patients of mine, and not only that, people who've told me they've read Dad's books or been to hear him give what they refer to as his 'inspirational addresses' at those large conventions that take place in holiday camps. People who then smile broadly, and somehow knowingly, at me in the surgery, and ask after him, and mention how helpful the books are.

How strange that people like them should have joined St Hildegard's. Or maybe not? Something's bringing them here: I've a bad feeling about it. I hope I'm wrong. And while I'm puzzling about this, David's signalled for the movement and buzz to cease, and they're hurrying back to their seats. As I go up to the front, there's Ruth, in her signature blue anorak, and Keith beside her. Ruth turns, smiling. Keith stares ahead.

'I'd like to introduce Dr Max Mullins, whom some of you know: Max has agreed to head up our clinical work. Max.'

Giving my brief outline on why and how the Centre plans to offer a free surgery for the drop-ins, I keep noticing those upturned faces, the intense interest they seem to have in everything I say, the little jottings they make on their papers.

They must have an agenda. St Hildegard's, strongly scented with incense, the statue of Mary gazing down on this meeting from behind her votive candles, the stained glass windows depicting various saints, is no more their culture than it's Dad's. All this flashes through my mind, as I start to field the questions. They have carefully thought these out. *Why the necessity of this Centre offering a clinic to the homeless? Is there a reason they can't sign on at a local practice?*

Heads shake as I put over rational arguments. 'They're nervous about having no address to write on the necessary forms. If they haven't seen a doctor in a long while the consultation may be protracted. We can offer services, through the nurse, such as advice on overall personal care in their situation, make referrals—often we may need to talk to the psychiatric services and—'

'It's a day centre, not an assessment centre,' somebody protests.

'You are right. But all this is now part of caring, since the Care in the Community Acts put large numbers of vulnerable people into the wider community.'

The climax seems to be Keith's question: everyone looks up expectantly, 'Do we know where the funds for all this are coming from? Presumably the clinic is part of the NHS?'

'On that one, I refer you to the Project Director.'

I smile at Keith, and resume my seat.

David, who's discussed all this with me and the Trustees of St Hildie's, patiently explains the details about funding. 'We're now on a firm financial footing thanks to a couple of very generous legacies. We're also launching the Friends of St Hildie's scheme—everyone in the scheme, which involves a pledge or a donation of four hundred pounds, will have their name on the wall plaque—and everyone will be kept in touch with developments. This will include details of funding for the clinic.'

Mm: I notice David doesn't go into details of the negotiations with our regional NHS Providers. And wonder if David suspects Keith is asking this on his own behalf or as a kind of leader of the group of migrants from HPC, since after a couple of questions from others, he accepts another from Keith.

Keith rises to his feet, pauses, and smiles. 'We've heard about the art group, the possible computer training group, and of course how the daily hot meal will be organised and funded. Including a call for volunteers to make nourishing soup. Dr Mullins has explained the reasoning behind providing a surgery where vulnerable people can consult an NHS doctor in the privacy of the Centre. I'm sure that those of us who've recently joined St Hildegard's would like to know that the Centre is committed to care for the *whole person*, soul as well as body, or perhaps I should rather say, *your* commitment to this?'

The meeting shifts about, murmurs, and becomes even more attentive. I've a good idea now of the meaning of this sudden influx of HPC members. Yes: and I recall that quite a few of them attended the Fun Day, and joined in the Scottish dancing.

Full membership of the church electoral roll is necessary for attending this meeting: they must've all signed up. So is Anthony Field Plowright aware of his flock migrating to David's fold; or even, in favour of it?

By now, I've a sinking feeling in my stomach, and a sense of dread. The beginning will have been when someone researched David's background. Another reason for a serious chat with David. I'll not bother Jenny with it for now. She doesn't need another reason to see me as having a negative attitude to Ruth and grim doubts about our children getting too much happy-clappy religion.

*

At home, bedroom light's on. Jenny looks asleep, but she stirs as I begin to undress. 'Did I wake you?'

'Wassa time?'

'Half past ten.'

'Mum rang: she talked forever about my trip. I dropped off once I was in bed.'

'Nice of her to be interested.'

'Yes. She's insanely proud. It'll be round West Cornwall whether they want to hear it or not. Then she had a long moan about the lack of culture down there ... I took a look at your Dad's book.'

'Did you—read much?'

'Too weary. Odd quote at the front.'

'I'd like you to read it. Before the Memorial Service? You'll find it interesting.' In the old days, that would've been enough to catch Jenny's curiosity. We'll see.

Jenny

EARLY MAY, A SATURDAY SHOPPING EXPEDITION

We have a new, young, socialist PM. But in our own small lives, Shaz needs a 'pedi-conference' day to buy some carpet, and I need a day out to forget the tangle I'm in over donation, and the fall-out from Alisdair's death.

Shaz and I take Charlie and Alice, and head by train to Reading. In the carpet department at John Lewis's, the girls seat themselves on a pile of rugs, drumming their feet. Shaz flips carpet samples, which give off a wonderful, slightly salty, woolly, scent of newness. 'Eliot won't, absolutely won't, attend my new Sunday morning family yoga class.

My sister brings her two, and hubby—he's in IT. Yoga's important after all that hunching over a desk. Don't you agree, Jen, a GP's life is so stressful, they ought to do something to promote their own health?'

I pretend to listen, while leafing through fat, heavy binders full of samples. Eliot worries Shaz because he won't do yoga? Her domestic concerns contrast with my crushing sense of guilt. It's all gone wrong because I was drunk on my own success. How can a person be so self-satisfied and hormone-driven they'd consider flippant adultery while their partner's watching his father die? Then find observing the work in a fertility clinic more of a pressing need than going home to show support?

'Jenny? Jenny! I mean, they tell their patients to exercise, and yoga's not only muscle stretching. It's ancient wisdom.'

'Yep—maybe Eliot feels general practice stretches him enough?'

Shaz misses a beat, then giggles, 'Oh God Jen, you ever serious?'

'All the time,' I say, deadpan, thinking *if only you knew*. I hold the carpet book open at a powder blue sample, 'How about this? Blue's relaxing.' I read the label to her, 'A hundred per cent wool twist—'

'Sweet. Suitable for heavy use, hallways and stairs—I don't know … Maybe it's something to do with being adopted. Jealous of me having asked my sister along?'

'Max would run a mile from a yoga class. I s'pose that would count as exercise.'

'He's even bought a ride-on mower to do the lawn.'

'Max plays squash. With David, or Tim from the Nuffield, the knee specialist.'

'That's violent. How good for the knees is it? Exercise doesn't have to be vigorous. With yoga, you learn to discipline your movements. Here: I like this one. I could get away with keeping the same curtains—'

'Max is obsessed with doing a clinic at the homeless centre. Has Eliot volunteered?'

'For what?'

'Homeless clinic, David's. Didn't he talk about it when you came to dinner?'

'Gosh, maybe. I forget what I hear at parties. Where's the kids?' She grabs my sleeve, shaking my arm. 'Jen—Where did they go? They've disappeared—Charlie!'

'We only turned round—they'll be somewhere—obvious—?'

'People do terrible things to children—Jenny, where are you this morning? Brain left behind in the lab?'

I wish.

My heart thumps wildly. I scan the third floor of John Lewis's, I dart amongst the piled-up rugs and the bedroom furniture. Only one reason anyone would go off with two pretty five-year-olds while their mummies gossip … This vast space is empty of humanity, except a woman talking with the one visible assistant while fingering a huge, wall-hung, oriental rug, and a couple inspecting the drawers of a white-painted Regency chest.

Suddenly Alice exits the matching white Regency wardrobe. Carrying her sandals. Relief!

She has an evil grin: my heart now pounds with fury at their naughtiness, giving us a fright. 'Ally! Where's Charlie?'

'I don't know.'

'You really don't, or you're playing you don't?'

'I'm—playing,' Alice says, slowly and quietly, into my coat. 'Mummy, we're bored.'

'So where's Charlie?'

'Underneath.'

'Underneath what?' Shaz snaps, bending from the height of her spike-heeled boots.

Alice quails. 'Underneath the bed. Hiding. So her mummy would worry.'

The furniture area stretches away towards Toys. 'Which bed? Alice! Which bed is Charlie under?' Shaz speaks sharply.

Alice's eyes tear up, 'I don't know! I was in the wardrobe.'

'Hide and seek?'

'I was in Narnia that Ruth told us about.'

'Right. And Charlie was—'

Across the furniture floor, the lone assistant leads Charlie towards us, pushing her shoulders gently so she keeps moving. 'Is this what you're looking for?' Charlie's eyes are lowered, gazing modestly at the ground, but her mouth is quivering with the need to smile, or even, to laugh.

Shamed by our five-year-olds, we retreat to Children's Clothes. I hear myself, strict-nanny-style, 'We're not here to buy pink things. Your school has a colour code: we need another navy gingham summer dress. And put your sandals back on, Ally. You could undo them: can you do them up?'

"Course. In here—and out here— velcro's easy-peasy-lemon-squeezy.'

Oh the awful wave of mummy-love and pride, she's so good at everything she does. Having not lost my Ally to an abductor, I indulge her, buying a pink glittery sweatshirt she doesn't need. Charlie has three carrier bags by now, and Shaz is being forced to carry them.

Then off to Shaz's favourite veggie café, an elegantly bohemian dive, serving fried plantains, wild rice, and salad.

'So, seen your cool stepsister recently?'

I shake my head, 'When I was away, Daze got stuck into a new project. Shaz ...'

'Yeah?'

'The other thing was, Max's father, the famous fundamentalist preacher, died ...' Shaz's face rearranges into a sympathy frown. 'Yeah. Not easy for me. Alisdair accepted me with oh-such-obvious pain and reluctance. And now I discover they were really close deep down, and, well, Max won't talk to me about that.'

'But when they go, people remember the good bits. When my Nan died—Mum never got on with her mother—' Shaz's stories about her Nan don't help.

'It's different. This is me, Shaz, and he's my partner, not my mum... We need to share this.' What I want to confide is that I can't begin to approach the subject myself. I've never seen death. Max's relationship with his father hasn't demonstrated much fondness on either side.

'Oh I do see what you mean ...' she says, leaning over to halve a big sticky vegan flapjack the girls are supposed to share. She nicks a little bit off the side and pops it into her own mouth. 'You need to find a way in. What did they share, Max and his dad?'

I sigh. 'Bloody-mindedness? There's no path into empathy from where we are. I feel relieved the old guy's out of his life, and out of my lovely ma-in-law's. I know that's not going to help, don't I.'

'Jen,' Shaz says, with an earnest look, 'you're gonna have to ride it out. He's not gonna share with you, he'll bury it all in his work and then he'll get some perspective again and move on. What's Daze doing for David—who's a sweet dish, such a shame he's—or maybe not, he'll make some guy a lovely wife one day.'

'She's putting a mosaic labyrinth on the floor at the retreat house. I haven't seen it.'

'Wow. A-*maz*-ing!'

Alice has evidently been listening: she taps Shaz's arm, and says seriously, 'It's not a *bloody maze*, it's a *squashed spiral*. That's different. You can't get lost.'

Daze

A FRIDAY, MID-MAY

Daze, who has been in the craft section of the art shop in Broad Street, buying gold thread and matching colours to embroidery silks, steps out, straight into Jenny.

'Wotcha! Caught! I heard you've been hiding out in a nunnery,' Jenny says.

'God, it's you.' Daze finds Jenny's greeting annoying: such an unwitty, stupid, statement, based on some poem or whatever they read at school. A couple of backpackers, eating baguettes from the paper bag, almost stumble into them. After the 'sorry, sorry', and as they begin crossing the road away from the tourists gathering around a sandwich place, Daze finds Jenny still at her side. 'So where've *you* been?' she says. 'Since you touched down? How was the US of A?'

'Brilliant. And Yosemite is out of this world.'

Hum ... But Jen looks stressed, Daze thinks. Face a bit pinched, ponytail a bit tight, plant that's been kept out of the sunshine?

'Hey, Max said you're well sorted with David, and you're making a labyrinth.'

So Max told her, and she's changing the subject from her conference to my work. 'Yeah. You could come up to Hildie's anytime, and take a look at it. Since now we both work in a lab. Hah, hah.'

Jenny groans. 'Heard it before, answer message on your phone. How come you took David's commission?'

'I needed the work. He needed me. Hildie's couldn't have got half the people I did to whack in their talent and raise money at their Fun Day.'

'Bit disingenuous, getting your idea implemented by David?'

'Nah. Why? He was cool. The publicity was good for both of us. I've a whole new client base, as your Dad would say.'

'And have you been researching your Romany side?'

Here's another put-down, discomfiting statement. Why needle me? Why resort to bossy-sister mode because you can't take it that David and I made friends? 'Think. I don't have her surname do I? I mean, were they ever married? And Jewels is a nickname ...'

'You could find out. About marriage. Didn't Aunt Val tell you?' Jenny looks away, fishing around in her bag. 'Bought this in Oxfam: Fair Trade organic. Want some?' She breaks some squares off the bar of chocolate she's holding. 'Max told me Val and the guys were brilliant. Why was Etta helping? How d'you know her? She's my cleaner ...'

'Ta. You've got a lot of questions. Etta invited herself.'

'I've seen her looking at our photos, the ones of our wedding with you and Kirsty playing bridesmaids.'

'So she likes your wedding photo. Listen, I'm going this way.' Jenny is of course going the same way, past Blackwell's bookshop and round the corner into Parks Road towards the science area. 'How I know Etta: a load of people turned up at St Hildegard's. For the Sunday church stuff. Don't ask me why. Etta was one. I think she lives at Ruth's or something?'

'She does. That's how I got her as my cleaner.'

'Be careful she doesn't start telling you how to run your life. She said Trifle shouldn't live on the boat. Humans and animals don't mix their living quarters. She loves cats, but she's like, fastidious.'

'She won't use the same bowl for washing up and soaking clothes.'

'Sounds like her. Anyhow, she was soon gone on David, hung out a lot around Hildie's, not for the church stuff. She loved it that there was an artist in residence and volunteered to help with kids' stuff on the Fun Day. I was stupid enough to say okay, yeah, do it.'

'The masks the girls made with her were amazing.'

'She's got flair. I've seen other work she's done. She's actually a fucking good artist. But she's a maniac, and she's been a right pest. You don't need a volunteer who drops out just when you're at your busiest. Don't you find her unreliable?'

'Not until recently. You know she's worked in women's refuges?'

'Yeah, she mentioned that.'

'So maybe these new people want to be part of the homeless project—the one that deprived you of—'

'The one that brought me quite a well-paid commission. They're all from that church, HPC, where Ruth hangs out. Etta comes round the boat and suggests we go for fish and chips, then she's forgotten her purse, or lost it, and I end up paying. She likes to sit on the roof and chat, with a cuppa, and feed the ducks all my bread. She's a right pain. She's onto some romantic kick about living on water, with no water laid on. She'd move onto my boat tomorrow, if I left the keys anywhere she could find them, an' make herself a copy. She wants to stop living with the nutters, as she calls them.'

'Why?'

'She's heard stuff, like the way they talk about David, and some of their books. Ones about healing. Which include things like being gay is sort of a disease. I mean, she thinks that Ruth your child minder's homophobic—you should act on that.'

'How could Ruth know David's gay?'

'No idea. Maybe she just looks at him, and she knows ... They're a nosy bunch, asking questions, and thinking they're better than the rest of us. But it's discrimination. Your kids'll learn it off her.'

'Do you think? Seriously?'

'Up to you, in'it? Listen, Jen, how's Max?'

'Busy.'

'I'd say he was well cut up about his dad.' Daze watches Jenny's face. Jenny looks puzzled, uncomprehending. Daze adds, 'They must've been close.'

'You know how Alisdair dominated and controlled the family. Max should be relieved.'

'But he isn't. I'd be careful, he may look like he's okay, but he's hiding a lot of grief.'

'Is that what you think?'

'Etta let me down, but Max didn't. He came by before the Fun Day, about the dance music, even though his dad had just died. I could see he was *acting* cool. Doesn't mean he isn't falling apart inside. You should look after him.'

'Right. Okay. Thanks.'

'Just thought I'd put in a word for him.'

Jenny does look taken aback a moment. Then rearranges her face to be a blank canvas. 'I've gotta get back to work.' She heads off, brusquely, into the science area.

Daze watches Jenny march across the tarmac, and disappear round the corner of a brick building, her leather shoulder bag bouncing against her side. She's almost thankful that she has more insight into emotional pain than Jen does. Being knocked about by life may even have some benefits.

Jenny

THE WOODS LAB

Leila is pulling on a pair of bulky protective gloves, which she does very elegantly, almost as if she were an Edwardian lady preparing to attend the opera in evening dress. We're by the cell storage tank, and I'm slowly lowering a rack of cells into liquid nitrogen.

'You know you're procrastinating: don't. It's not good for you. Or for your sister, because while you say nothing she hopes,' says Leila, in a soft, determined, voice.

How did she guess I walked into Daze on my lunch break? Because I am not feeling elegant, or poised, or in any state to engage with our intricate work, unless I can control my strange desire to throw everything in sight out of the window, including myself. And it shows.

'So deal with it. Like a nasty medical appointment, like a cervical smear test.'

I take a long breath. 'Okay. How's this: I tell her how someone at the conference mentioned that a link's been found between the overstimulation of the ovary in egg donors, and ovarian cancer. Ovarian cancer's seriously life-threatening. So maybe the Universe, which is Daze's way of saying God, is trying to tell us something? Like I have to, very sadly, withdraw my offer? And I'll explain how pre-implantation genetic diagnosis would be a good alternative.'

Leila makes a very dubious face, puckering her forehead and her lips. 'Why blame the Universe?'

I carefully close the lid of the cryopreserver. 'Because Daze is an awkward person to disappoint, and I'm, well, feeling guilty.'

'Don't accept the guilt. She should realise your offer was more than generous in the first place.' Furious with the whole world, knowing she's right, I pull off the thick gloves I'm wearing against the intense cold of the liquid nitrogen, and lay them aside.

*

Etta's on our doorstep, bag on her shoulder, locking the door as I arrive with the kids. 'I did a hoover all round. Cleaned both bathrooms. I brought in the washing. You seen them mare's tails clouds up there? They mean rain's on its way.'

'Thank you. But aren't they beautiful against the blue? Cirrus clouds, the highest clouds there are.'

'I saw your Max up at St Hildie's: he's good on that fiddle. You should go there sometime, they've got an artist in residence. She's done a beautiful piece of work, a labyrinth, takes up the whole floor of the meeting room.'

'Sounds lovely,' I smile.

'It is. Down on the floor, but colour of the sky. Well I'll be off now. See you Monday.'

Yes. What a simple life Etta has. I need to deal with that problem I gave myself: I've decided to ask Dad. In his roundabout way, he'll reveal his clinic's view on donors. It's probably the baseline standard.

I could email, but I want to hear his voice, gauge his reaction. After dinner here means lunchtime in Vancouver. Max is busy outside, cutting the lawn under an increasingly greyed-over sky. As Dad picks up the phone, he's lunching at his desk, gnawing on a submarine or a wrap or something. 'Yes?' he says, through his food.

'That article I mentioned, that was left outside my room at the Ahwahnee, in a brown envelope. Addressed to me. I read it on the plane.'

'It's some research on the outcomes for egg donors?'

'Dad, I've explained my interest.'

'I'm intrigued who you shared it with, and they cared enough to—'

I do a big sigh, 'Yes, okay, I spent some time with Wil. I mentioned the effect of meeting the kinds of families who could be helped by our research. Mine. At my lab, like here in Oxford? Point is, how seriously do we take this work? I've done a literature search. Not much is coming out yet. Do you know more?

'Kiddo, why bother with the egg donors?'

'Perhaps because they might like to know what outcome their generosity could have? Before they donate?'

'Okay. And you aren't thinking of doing that yourself?'

He's almost caught me unawares. 'Well—Dad, I always like to know as much as I can about stuff on the edge—the edge of my work. What might impact on it, and what other solutions are out there. This is about the safety of clinical applications.'

'Jenny, I'd not bother. If a young woman's completed her family, and wants to donate eggs, that's great. With a completed family, she doesn't need those ovaries any more. We can remove them, after donation, seeing they're surplus to requirements. Then she doesn't need to worry.'

'What about?'

'HRT,' he says, quick as he can. 'Avoiding premature menopause. And any health risks.'

'Yeah, well, I wouldn't want to do that. At under thirty-five. But as I said, I'm not thinking of donating.'

'Leave it to the experts, Kiddo. A professional opinion.' Silence follows: he's chewing his snack lunch. Then, 'Now, how're my grandkids? Bright and bodaciously beautiful as ever?'

'When did you last see them?'

*

Hum: after I've put the phone down I go away to think. Upstairs in Zoë's room I part the curtains a tiny crack, slip through and lean my elbows on the windowsill, watching Max on the lawn with the Flymo. It's a Ladybird Book scene, from times when egg donation wasn't an issue. But the sky's dark with clouds: Etta was right about the mare's tails and the rain.

If Max is breaking up over his father's death, why doesn't he talk to me? He talked to *Daze*. How do men work? My Dad couldn't have appalled me more with his arrogant attitude: solve the problem by cutting out the ovaries? That's so calculatingly pragmatic it'd take a sci-fi mind to think of it.

My hands are clenched as if I'm threatened with it myself. Taking a few slow, calming breaths, I tell myself a lot of what we do is just as coldly pragmatic: we see differently only because we aren't personally involved. If I worked with him … could I change his attitudes?

The options for donation look increasingly bleak. A stiff breeze gets up outside, blowing the first few drops against the glass.

Max

SAME EVENING

I wander through from the garden, damp with sweat and the rain, inadequately towelling my hair with the T-shirt I peeled off in the laundry room. Jenny's in the kitchen, back against the counter, a bowl of three strawberries in her hand. 'Talked to Dad.'

'He's okay?'

'I had a question for him—'

'Jen, are *you* okay?' I've seen that article she left in the study, about egg donation. Probably left so I'd see it?

'Why wouldn't I be?'

'Really okay?' I flip the hair out of my eyes, pull on a dry top I found in the clean stuff waiting to be ironed, and take a proper look at her. Her shoulders are hunched. Could we talk? Is she up for serious communication? Two steps towards the kettle, then change my mind. And open the cupboard where we keep the alcohol, 'Do we have any Pimms left?' Crouching to peer into the cupboard's dark depths, I add, 'That invasive mint Mam gave us made me think of it.'

'Actually—'

'Yes?'

'Max, listen! And say nothing—*I'm not going to donate for Daze.*' I swivel round, clutching the bottle. The best words I've heard in months. I must be gaping like a frog, sat on my haunches, Pimms in hand, because 'Well, aren't you pleased?' she asks with enormous emphasis.

'Och, Jenny. Oh, definitely.' And I laugh a bit. 'I am so—relieved.'

It's as if the wall between us is down at last. A long hug is necessary. From within it, Jen says 'I—spoke to Dad—about research which I wasn't happy about, on the long-term health effects of donation. I'll have to tell Daze—I'll say I had a message from the Universe.'

'If that's what she'll accept,' I laugh.

We break apart, she adds, 'It does seem mean though. And people won't stop donating.'

'It's not mean, it's sensible. Explain how you hadn't known about the risks, and research is always moving forwards—and—will we drink to your decision? Can I use these leftover strawberries? Bit of sliced apple?'

'Yeah, yeah please. Women must be aware of the risks, and make informed decisions.'

'Of course. Once the research is—'

'To be honest, I feel there's evidence to stop donating until more is known. Otherwise egg donation is exploitation.'

'But you're not being exploited. It was hard—but you've done the right thing.'

'I care more about myself than her.'

'If we're honest, don't we all? Let's take these somewhere more comfortable. Listen to that rain: I was removing most of that invasive mint, but the storm was too intense …' I guide Jen towards the couch, well aware now of how living with unnecessary guilt has affected her. 'Altruism isn't false or non-existent, but it does carry risks, which we must face up to. It's not your job to solve Daze's problems,' I say, my arm around her back. 'She'll understand it was an offer, a generous offer.' I pause to think, then the desire to share beats the bred-in reticence. 'I've a problem with the eulogy for Dad's memorial service. It's not only not enough time to write it, everything's far too ambiguous to think about or I'd have been at the desk, not messing about in the garden.'

'Babe, I'm sorry. I've been tangled up in my own stuff. Your dad was a complex, ambiguous person. Like mine is an ambitious, amoral bastard who doles out the hope of babies to make people happy.'

'I might use a few anecdotes about growing up in his family. People see what they want to see, his powerful preaching, his charismatic personality.' More to draw Jenny on side than to find a solution to what I can reasonably say in public about Dad, I add, 'You understood him over the Rachel business. And maybe—look, please, try and finish reading *Living with Uncertainty* before the Service?'

Max

THE MANSE, NORTHUMBERLAND, MONDAY 16 JUNE

We arrive at the Manse late afternoon. Under a cool, grey sky. In the drive, something's not quite right. 'See that?'

'What?'

'Cars, parked at all angles. Dad'd go nuts.' I carefully line up the Discovery alongside Erin's Volvo estate. It just fits in the space. 'No need for everyone to symbolically defy his military precision parking.'

Jenny smiles. Are we back—in Dad's phrase—keeping the team together?

Indoors, a scent of lamb roasting in the oven. Always a roast dinner on arrival! The kitchen table's laden with baked goods for the after-service tea. Fruitcake, chocolate cake, scones, quiches. Mam, in role, bustles up. Unbearably like old times. I kiss her cheek: soft, dry, cool, sweet scented. 'Mam: all this, did anyone help you?'

She lays her hand on mine, 'Of course pet. Now, your father's reflections on his ministry. You have read it, haven't you?'

'All through. *Living with Uncertainty*'s a strange title, for him—'

Before I can share more about it with Mam, Alice interrupts. Blue eyes wide, staring at her Granny, 'Where's Grandpa? Where's his chair?'

'We have talked it through,' I murmur, but Mam's already quietly dealing with this. 'He doesn't need his chair any more, pet. Grandpa's with Jesus and the angels.'

'Oh. I forgot.'

'Alice, here's Chloe, shall we let Granny get on here, and you play with your cousins?' I steer all the bairns away before further discussion can upset Mam. Though I'm with Alice on this one, it *is* as if Dad is here. It is as if he is about to walk into the room, rubbing his hands together, declaiming 'Max! Wonderful! Now we've got enough for a game of cricket before tea. And afterwards I've a wee question for you—.' Which would be, whether I've reconsidered taking over

Euan's practice, or read his piece on the evils of assisted suicide.

Aunt Margaret's been busy packing all those cakes, scones, quiches, into tins and Tupperware. She spies me, apparently hanging about, doing nothing.

'Max,' she indicates the pile with a wave of her hand, 'this all needs to go down to the church. Could you—?'

'Of course. Mam didn't—'

'We all helped. Erin's somewhere. Max, pet, David's not been in touch. Did you speak with him?'

'I gave him the date.' This is very awkward. Margaret looks hopefully questioning. 'He understood my meaning. I'm so sorry he didn't follow it up.'

'Och, you did all you could.'

'Mm. I am sorry …' Aunt Margaret seldom drops the brisk manner, but now for a moment, staring down at the cake tin she's holding, she visibly wilts. Then, 'Oh, can't be helped. We've things to do.'

'Should we take these down now? Or—'

'Uncle Max! I made the girls' under-ten football team, did Mum say? It's inter-schools, it's well serious and we train every—' Erin's girl, football clasped to her as yet undeveloped bosom, T-shirt, jeans, long blond hair, is the spit of my big sister.

'Chloe, Chloe—,' she has to be grabbed and held. I meet her eyes, blue as harebells, 'Auntie Margaret's talking—then I'll—'

'Sorry sorry *sorry*—' Chloe escapes, and bounces her black and white ball.

'After tea, pet,' Margaret says, indicating the boxes and tins again. 'We'll eat first. Please, Chloe, stop that.'

'Uncle Max—' she drags on my arm, 'Cam thinks he can *bend it like Beckham,* but I'm better.'

Jenny appears. 'Max, where were you? I took the bags up. We're in the green bedroom. Your Mam's put the girls with Cam and Chloe in the attic. Ours one each end of your old bed.'

And here's Zoë, clutching two dolls, one upside down. 'Zo-zo!' I lift her up.

Together, we escape to the family room and the piano. What to play? After picking out a few notes, we're in the right key for a hymn tune. *Thine be the Glory.*

Which is too much, since we last sang it at the Crem, as Dad's coffin slid down the hatch. So let's do something about that. Soup it up to a honky-tonk style. Zoë bounces in time.

'What're you doing, murdering *Judas Maccabeus?*' says Jenny, slipping into the room, and perching on a chair arm. 'Remember that performance at Cambridge? I was pregnant, and desperate that Rich would be taking me over to Oxford when the lab moved?'

I try to recapture our happiness, the extraordinarily wonderful timing of Rich Woods's lab move, which meant for us that Jen and I could again live in the same city. I play a few more celebratory bars, and Ian puts his head around the door. 'Hey, man, is that cacophony necessary?' He's got his baby in a sling on his front.

'You find my playing bothersome?'

'Does it feel right to you?'

'Today isna' tomorrow, and tomorrow is to celebrate Dad's life.'

'There's still respect.'

I swivel round on the piano stool. Zoë stares at Ian, then points at the baby. 'Yes, he's your littlest cousin.' She slides off my lap, and re-tucks her dolls under her arm.

'There's time for respect tomorrow, Ian.' I say. 'I see you've had the service sheets printed, *decently and in order*, with a photo of Dad on the cover.'

With a very old photo of Dad, as RAF pilot in the early 1960's, as I knew him and Ian never did. It's indicative that the old pastor's already been sidelined. Don't tell me things are different if your work is serving God.

'I have.'

He leaves, without referring to my mocking use of the Presby phrase, and meaning to close the door very quietly—but Zoë tries to slip out behind him, dolls under her arm, and gets a bit tangled in his legs. 'B—other,' Ian hisses under his breath. 'Ankle-biter!' he exclaims. 'Which way're you going?'

I watch as Zoë stares up, round-eyed, at Ian, then decides crying would be wimpish, and says 'Out dere!' with determination.

'Okay with Mummy?' Ian, modulated voice now, addresses Jenny.

'Yeah, yeah—go ahead.'

They leave, Ian softly closing the door on Jen and me. We laugh, sotto voce.

'It's like you described family Sundays,' Jenny says then. 'Them all over at Euan and Margaret's for tea and cake, you back here playing ragtime. Very sexy, but I'd disapprove because you'd be smoking.'

'I'd leave the window wide open to let out the nicotine, and rush to the evening praise service, arriving late. Afterwards, I had to help kick the under-fifteens into shape at First Truly youth club.'

'That'd be around the time when, you told me, David was pretending he was interested in girls.'

'Sixth form. He was worried about fancying a boy who'd recently joined our school.'

'Did David make a move?'

'He was scared to death. We'd not heard of this, and wondered whether it was sin or a developmental stage. I read up some research in an encyclopedia, at the library. Maybe it'll go away, he suggested, if we pray about it?' I shake my head. 'Young, well-indoctrinated fundamentalists that we were.'

'Granny Ianthe indoctrinated us with the *Well of Loneliness*, and Vita, Violet, and Virginia, and how the war was a great time for lesbians to meet, driving ambulances,' Jenny grins. 'Can't you see it? Granny went on and on. Like maybe she hoped one of us might fancy women.'

The sounds of table-laying come from the kitchen. I get up from the piano stool, and stash the music carefully away under its liftable seat. 'Billiards and Bible Study. You never forget home: where there's nowhere you're allowed to be alone. Except for piano practice.' All Dad's grandchildren are now outside, playing noisily, with no inhibitions. 'Will we drag the bairns from their game out there?'

'I'll see if your Mam needs help,' Jenny says.

I go to the garden, where Zoë's running about kicking at the ball and waving her arms, abandoned dolls forlornly lying under a bush.

I'll burst into that mêlée, demonstrating some deft footwork for Chloe to admire. I rush towards the flying ball, but my Beckham imitation merely sends it bashing into Mam's peonies. A huge pink flower bursts into a thousand shimmering pieces, petals scattered across the lawn.

'Ooh, Grandma'll get you!'

'Possibly. Where's Alice?'

'Here!' She looks around the end pole of the runner beans: 'We're picking lettuces.'

'I like to hear Max at the piano: I don't suppose he has much time for that in the ordinary way?' says Mam's voice. Home is where you're discussed for ever like the child you were. This time by Mam and Jenny, who answers 'Sometimes. He's terribly busy though.'

'Everything all right?' Mam asks, seeing me.

'Margaret's laying up. It's great you have her to help you.'

Alice is carefully reaching among the leaves of a lettuce. She holds up a lime green caterpillar. It arches itself: all fat and ready to pupate. Alice grins at us, and drops the caterpillar into a patch of radishes. We go in for tea.

Jenny

SAME EVENING

Everyone's crowded around the table, and mostly, everyone's noisy. This visit could be fun, except for why we're here. Ian's a pain, but everyone else is more relaxed than I've seen them.

Max calls them all to attention, and begins a short prayer: Ian's forced to bite back his effort to thank God for the roast lamb, God's goodness, and being together. He scowls a bit. I am horribly pleased Max is grabbing the upper hand over dreary Ian. Does Ian remember me doing a sort of hockey tackle in this kitchen, to catch his pet rabbit? And how he and Alex marvelled that I could do it?'

When we're settling the girls in the attic room, Max looks down at the garden. It's begun to rain. 'See there, Alex restored the tree house. Wrong kind of ladder, before. Health and safety,' he says deadpan, then smiles.

'Remember the angel cake?' I say. 'Alex and Ian stole one your Mam had made the first weekend I came to stay, ate it all up in the old tree house, and she sent you off to sort them out?'

'I told them to learn a psalm or two and have it word perfect for me in the morning. I told them which ones. They'd not want to be reminded of that now.'

'Or the frog they put on your pillow.'

'Toad. You corrected my lazy description of it. A toad. Och, we'll do the service and we'll be away home again, and not think about them by this time tomorrow. You doing all right?'

We're creeping away after the goodnights, when Max stops at the top of the stairs. 'Ian's not really what was getting you. You aren't really bothered by him,' I say. 'You came up here after—'

'Yes. I've a sense of that night.'

'I can't imagine—'

'It's not about Dad—it's when—after … I'd not been up here, I'd slept in his room. After he … it was maybe three a.m., I came up to my old room. Opened the door and—all our childhood, packed and labelled—Mam had already begun sorting and preparing—very practical, she knew she'd have to give the house up. But, it hits you— the past is over, it'll never come back.'

This, I do understand. 'Oh, Max. I was ripped away from London when my dad left us.'

'This house was full of falsehood. All the pastor's family bit was a cage. We were dumped here without any choice, as you were in Cornwall. But when the time comes, the old home's destroyed … I remembered how it began. Being Alice's age, maybe a year older, when we arrived. First in Edinburgh: we were billeted at Euan's old place.

Icy streets, melting snow piled on the kerbside, not white, mostly black. Mam saying, "You two need warm clothes, with this gale straight from the Arctic. And Wellingtons." And then here. Our own place. Northumberland wasna' any warmer, and Dad had become the pastor. But, I didna' want to lose it all, when it came to it, did I? No more chances to visit and talk with him, nothing left of where we all were as a family. Nowhere left where the team had lived together.'

The desolation of what Max felt sinks in. It's not the same as leaving London, because apart from Dad, who was often somewhere else anyway, our family is all still potentially together. Chapel House, Sennen, has a strong sense of home when I think about it. I'm not quite gone from there: I sometimes call it home. Neither is Harriet, even: her things are there, in her old room. 'I know what you mean.' But, I don't. It hurts to wish I'd been here that night. And to kind of fear whether it'd have made a difference.

'Right,' Max says, shaking his head, and putting an arm around my shoulders. 'Now we have a mission to deliver cakes and scones to the venue.'

So, he's brushed the subject away before it really began. Like a crumb from his suit, or something. Why?

*

First Truly Reformed Presbyterian Church, that dim Gothicky pile from which Alisdair ruled his congregation, smells like a flower shop this evening. The heavy oak doors are propped open, as we arrive: Max, Erin, and me, all carrying tins and plastic cake boxes. Two women in flowery frocks are working on triangular fans of pink, white, and blue roses, stocks, delphiniums, sticking flowers into oasis, snipping off the untidy bits and shortening stalks. We step carefully over green tarpaulins, scattered with rejects. There's a frisson in my innards as we enter the main church. I remember Max leading me right up that carpet to the Mullins family's pew below the pulpit, my first visit. Alisdair freaked me, with his sermon about God demanding our all and our everything.

Today, the organist is noodling away, hidden in his organ loft, and a guy around our age, crinkly hair, beige chinos and boat shoes, hurries towards us, grinning.

Erin leans over to speak into my ear. 'O.M.G.'

'Who is he?'

He reaches our group, picks out Max, grasps his hand and pumps it. 'Max. Good to see you. These are for the feast?'

Erin murmurs, as they move away together, 'The assistant pastor. Nick Noble. Notice how he ignored you and me. And look what he's been fixing up.'

She hauls me along, still carrying my share of cake boxes, to where a huge flat TV screen's been set up, right where, in my college chapel at Cambridge, there's a vast painting of Gabriel swooping down towards Mary. It's way more huge than HPC's *welcome* screen. We're in Orwell's *1984*, this thing dominating all activity. Nick's obviously switched it on remotely, and maybe for us: a message appears in blue against pale mauve: *Today we honour the memory of our first Pastor, Revd Alisdair Mullins.*

Erin does an illustrative gulp, clutching her throat. 'How yuck is that?'

'Your mother allowed it?'

'Mam hasn't any say-so here now.'

'She's his widow: she's the person they should listen to. At least about tomorrow.'

Erin silently shakes her head.

'I see you're admiring the screen.' Nick's crept up behind us, silent in those boat shoes. He grins enormously. 'It's our newest acquisition. Put anything up on that—song words, prayer words, Powerpoint photos and charts, Bible passages. Going to make the worship a real wow.'

'Mm,' says Erin, like Ruth when I mention Daze or David. She pauses, then smiles, 'The flowers are gorgeous. Mum loves scented flowers. Dad used to buy her them. Though he never knew their names, and they gave him hay fever.'

'Mm,' Nick's turn. 'I left Max having a browse. Is Kirsty with you? Ian's brought the service sheets, has he?'

'Kirsty's back with Mam. The service sheets are in that box, over there. I can answer any questions. Or ask Max?'

He draws Erin away. Her straight back and purposeful stride look ready to cope with him. Left standing in the middle of the sanctuary, I survey the serried ranks of pews: tomorrow, they'll be filled with Alisdair's loyal followers. Or as Erin hinted, the followers will be there, but loyalty may be mixed. Might Rachel come?

'Now it's our turn. The men have the tables set up ready,' says a woman beside me, gesturing towards the long gloomy room where I first met Rachel, and then witnessed how hubby Colin hauled her away from our conversation. And I made one terrible gaffe after another, talking with Max's earnest friends, or rather, the earnest young people of First Truly who he was forced to be nice to, seeing his dad was their pastor.

Preparations are gathering momentum: women shake out huge white tablecloths, and smooth them over the tabletops, like efficient nurses making up beds. Erin and I lay out groups of forks and knives, wrapped in paper napkins, and pale green cups and saucers, and piles of plates. We put the tins and Tupperware ready for plating up the contents tomorrow. We promise to bring the quiches over last thing before the service. We discuss the salads everyone will make. Erin goes into the kitchen, and drags large teapots out of a cupboard, while deflecting questions about her children. Doing well at school? Made a commitment to Christ? I know which they'll think more important.

Finally everyone begins to leave. Where's Max?

Coming in from the porch. He doesn't see me, but turns to the bookstall just inside the main door.

He picks up and flips through three or four books, then runs a hand through his hair and begins searching through a rack of brightly-coloured leaflets as I approach.

'Groups for everything,' he says, and waves them at me. 'Mums and toddlers, pre-schoolers, Pat-a-Cake for EYU, Bakers and Homemakers, Men's Breakfasts.'

'Soul Food for Teens,' I say, taking one. It's a list of meetings, every Thursday evening in term time.

Max is making notes on one of the Men's Breakfasts leaflets, using a stub of pencil attached to a clipboard for listing anything you want to buy. He looks briefly at all the stock: paperbacks, bookmarks, ballpoint pens, spangly pencils, notebooks, cards. Each with its biblical text.

'You worried about tomorrow?'

'No, not about tomorrow.'

In the porch, a flowery-frock woman is carefully topping up the water in her arrangement using a long-nosed watering can. Her face is lined; she has a pert smile. 'Max: a lovely photo on the service sheet. So handsome in his uniform.'

Max remembers her name, Myra, and tells her: 'Ian's responsible. He's very competent.'

'Nick's not much like your father,' I say, once we've escaped. 'And he's doing the new broom thing a bit fast.'

'Mm.'

'Weird idea of Ian's to chose an old photo: what's wrong with something more recent?'

'Why do people do things, Jen?'

'To express themselves? Maybe it's a good thing?'

Max slings an arm around my shoulders, so that we walk closely, in step, back to the Manse.

*

The evening ends with northern supper, hot drinks and slices of homemade Bakewell tart left from tea, which I'd call dinner. The atmosphere's cool and respectful. The awful twins are in one camp; Erin, her husband Gary, Max and I definitely make up the other. Fee's given us the beautifully appointed green spare room. Erin and Gary are in Erin's old one, which she used to share with Kirsty. 'Status for the oldest son, at least.'

What exactly did I mean? Max gives a short acknowledging laugh, adding 'I've put the alarm on for five. Don't get up when I do. I've some things I need to change in the speech.'

Jenny

FIRST TRULY REFORMED CHURCH, 17 JUNE, 14.00

We sit in the family pew. Fee looks anxious. 'I left Max helping Zoë with her shoes,' I say, reassuringly, 'She was in such a Daddy mood. He'll drop her off at the crèche, and be right over.'

'I hoped he'd still persuade David,' Fee whispers. 'I thought when he was in Alisdair's study early this morning—'

'Finalising his speech. I don't know about David.' Swivelling around, I see hovering at the back, looking very out of place, a tall woman in capri pants, a baseball cap, and shades. As I watch, she turns and moves towards the doors. Euan, Margaret, and Chrissie (in a very smart suit), arrive and sit behind us. No David. Wickedly, I briefly imagine David leading this service. Instead of Nick. Impossible.

The screen wakes up, giving us a slide show of Pastor Mullins's years of ministry. Alisdair is beaming, as he holds up keys of the navy blue Audi, his wonderful ten-years-at-First-Truly present from his congregation. And looking so like Max.

Where *is* Max? I feel Fee's worry.

Knock, knock, knock. Alice, pretty in her silky tartan dress, swings her feet. So hard that her patent leather Mary Janes knock on the pew in front. I lay a hand on her knees, and lean down to speak into her ear: 'Shh! Darling, can you ask your legs to be very still?'

She grins, but stops. Fee and I exchange glances. The organist strikes up. They've a frightful organ, the tune is funereally slow and dignified but it sounds like a fairground.

As the terrible organ segues into *Great is thy Faithfulness*, a hymn from my very first visit, every line speaking First Truly, Max slides into the pew beside me, smart suit, white shirt, dark tie, grasping his notes. 'Where've you *been*?'

He dumps a huge floppy black Bible on the seat. 'I'm here now.'

'Nick of time.'

Squeezing my hand, 'Interloper.'

'Who?'

'Nick.'

Then his arm goes around my back as we continue singing his father's signature hymn, and he kisses my neck quickly. Alice looks up at us, her face a big question mark. Unusual for Max to be demonstrative in public. Signalling our togetherness to them all?

Great is thy Faithfulness, Oh God my father—how often it's happened: the phone rings in the middle of dinner: Max goes, 'Oh God, my father!' Here, now, it can't be funny. Alisdair *was* God. Enthroned in his wheelchair the past few years.

'You did read it, the book?' Max whispers under cover of the hymn.

'I—began.'

'*There is no shadow of turning with thee: Thou changest not ... As thou hast been, thou for ever wilt be.*'

We sit. Bible readings. Prayers, led by Nick. Really, he is a bit of a cartoon clergyman, young, with trendy clothes, but his prayers ... Dire, slang from the 1970's, eighties at best. Why use colloquial language, if you don't know what's current? The Cambridge chaplains wisely stuck to the Prayer Book, formal and mostly unembarrassing. He's got a trio of instrumentalists and a couple of young women in long skirts up there with him, and they sing: *Wisdom unsearchable, God the invisible, Love indestructible ...*

Then Max is gone, into the pulpit. High above us. On the podium at the conference I was too nervous to appreciate the possibilities of crowd manipulation, but I can understand it: I did enjoy having all those people looking to me for information. How about Max?

'*I have fought the good fight, I have finished the race, I have kept the faith. Two Timothy four, verse seven.* My father,' he says, and pauses. 'We are gathered here to remember Dad. My father, our Pastor and

Minister. But first let's bow our heads to our Father in heaven, the author of our life.'

Hearing Max say that, holding that large leathery Bible balanced on his outstretched palm, stunningly Pastor Mullins style, my throat goes tight. I have a goosebumpy, hand-sweaty, feeling.

Alice wriggles. 'Daddy looks funny up there.'

'Ssh, he's going to talk to us about Grandpa. Soon we'll be done with this, and we can go back and have a big tea.'

'Chocolate cake? Can I sit on you?' I smooth down my skirt, she climbs aboard. She leans her head on my chest, her small arms embrace me.

'The picture which we—which Mam and my brothers—chose, typifies one aspect of Dad—'

Max swings into a short bio of Alisdair's RAF career and the temporary blindness which he'd interpreted as a call to serve his God twenty-four seven. Fair enough: and fighter planes weren't designed to spread life and peace across the world.

He moves on to the family relocating first to Edinburgh, then to Northumberland and the failing church which Alisdair revived and which became the First Truly we know today.

'My father. A father to all of us gathered here. A great evangelist, a great man. The phrase "larger than life" was used of Alisdair Mullins more than once. It was appropriate—'

Alice pouts and wriggles her nose. She opens and shuts her fingers, dark with melting chocolate. 'S'all squidgy, yuckety-boo.'

'Where's it from?'

'Granny. She gave it me. Before.'

'Maybe I'd better have it?'

We're whispering: people stare. Alice gives me the squidged remains of a dark chocolate mini Easter egg, in gold foil paper. I reach into my bag for a tissue, and without baby wipes, resort to a smidgen of *Obsession*, by Calvin Klein, to dampen it. 'Too not-sweet,' Alice whispers, wiping her palm, as Max, so much more the proper inheritor of Alisdair's pulpit than Nick, eulogises on. He's in charge, direct, no slime.

I pull another tissue from my bag, and glance at Fee: she's also fished out tissue for Alice. No, she's dabbing her eyes, as Max describes First Truly when his Dad arrived, his own memories supplemented by those of members of the congregation he's talked with. He describes how he now sees, from the bookstall and the extensive programme of events, as well as the numbers gathered here, how greatly the little flock of almost thirty years ago has grown under Pastor Alisdair.

'*Go to the fields and hedgerows and compel them to come in!*' Evidently a quote. '*A really miraculous draught of fishes. What kind of fish are you?*' apparently another one, gets a laugh.

I feel them, all around me, relaxing.

He leads into listing their activities. All those gender-specific breakfasts and coffee times and the age-related stuff from birth to over-seventies. And their own school. They sit up tall and straight, proud of themselves. But then, like the organist segueing from introit to first hymn, Max changes the tone as he quotes from that hymn, *Pardon for sin and a peace that endureth; Thine own dear presence to cheer and to guide,* and begins to pick the lines to pieces.

This give me a sensation like insects on my back. What's he up to? Carefully swivel my head as far as I dare: there are some nods in the congregation, some people staring hard at their laps, as Max connects those words to Alisdair's acknowledgment of being wrong in some crucial areas. Yes, his father's work was the public face of the Mullins ministry, but what about the immeasurable input from Fee? Alisdair without Fee would be bacon without eggs, Lennon without McCartney.

'Never so much as in these last nine or ten years of ministry, when Dad was battling with increasing disability, was that *dear presence* a force behind the preacher.' The congregation murmurs. They seem a bit shocked. Possibly, I think, because what he's said twists the words of the hymn. He's put Fee into the line which talks about the presence of God. They can't like that, but it is undeniably true.

Carefully, I glance at Fee. Her gaze is on her hands, folded in her lap, her face is pink.

Max pauses, then assures them of what he means. I stop holding my breath.

But he goes all autobiographical. 'Whatever details I haven't taken into adult life, I hold onto the core values learned from my parents and their ministry: values that are ultimately more important than the petty, divisive, attitudes we find lurking in some churches.'

He exchanges the Bible for a paperback book: he waves it at them. Its yellow back is familiar, the book I'm supposed to've read. 'And if we don't know what those are, we have this, *Living with Uncertainty*, Dad's last published book, to consult. He realised the importance of listening to, and having compassion for, others. Demonstrating unconditional love in practical ways. Opening ourselves to those rejected by society, and those who are not of our household of faith. Over the past ten years, my parents were not afraid to think deeply about societal problems, and prayerfully accept that God's ways are mysterious and some of our traditions are of our own making.'

He looks upset. He actually sweeps his hand across his eyes. Whatever he's driving at, it means a lot to him, and the congregation must've seen.

'I had time to browse your bookstall last evening: singleness, married life and sexual behaviour, Healing for Homosexuals, pro-life, raising children, God's Design for Women, Manage your Money for God. This insightful book, by contrast, was conspicuous by its absence from the bookstall. I am wondering why!'

Please, don't *rant*. It means a lot to you: you mean a lot to me, and I can't take you behaving like this. In public. Please: you've already embarrassed your mother. What about the religious extremists, what about Alex and Ian? Euan, who whatever he believes, is actually nice to us!

'Faithfulness to the truth; honesty; respect; and above all the ability to repent and change one's mind. Ten—no, nine—years ago Pastor Alisdair was blinded—spiritually, not physically—by prejudiced attitudes that contributed to a great deal of suffering for several people, some of whom are present and some, conspicuous by their absence. But he had the grace to repent, not only in private, but publicly from this very pulpit. In Philippians three, we read Paul's admission that he, a pastor, had more to learn. *Not that I have already obtained all this, or have already arrived at my goal, but I press on* … Your Pastor, Alisdair Mullins, was humble enough to admit this as well.'

Okay, the book stems from the aftermath of the Rachel scandal, but why rake it over?

'I tell you now, I bitterly regret that I was occupied with other matters at the time, that after discovering what had gone on, I moved south, and immersed myself in medicine, marriage, and family life. That I did not return to First Truly to share in what my father went through.

'My own involvement in the tragedy had blinded me as well. But now, I see.' Yes, dabbing your eyes. 'With my father's repentant, guiding hand gone, his public confession has had no impact here at all. It's as if he had never made it. Clearly to have their pastor admit he had been wrong was an embarrassment to people who wished for nothing more than to carry on the same as ever.

'And so, First Truly Reformed, successful as it appears, is no advertisement for Alisdair Mullins' beliefs from the time of his repentance until his death, and it is a place that I am now leaving with relief and little intention of revisiting.'

Max closes the Bible, stalks down those pulpit steps, shoulders back, head held high, arrogant as Alisdair. The congregation's silence is total.

I feel terrible: so much pain, such a public show. Max never talks about stuff to me like this. Why here, and why in public, so humiliating. To both of us. Arms around Alice like we're sheltering from gunfire.

Max strides right past us down the central aisle and out of the building.

Alice fights free. I move to grab her, she ducks away, climbing over legs, feet, and bags faster than I can follow. Fee stands aside, letting us past, but Ian, his wife, Alex, and Alex's girlfriend all rise to sing *Amazing Grace*, now being played by the organist. All of them in my way. Kirsty stumbles up too, tears running down her face, and begins to sing.

Erin grips my arm. 'Don't. Alice is okay. Let her go.' At a touch from her mum, Chloë nods, understands, and slips out to join Alice. Erin holds Cam by his shoulders, 'Leave it to the girls.'

My hands are fisted. Heart pulsing like crazy, fury fighting compassion. Isn't every hostile eye here on me?

'Jenny, stay and sing,' Erin hisses. 'Max is okay.'

I stay. Fury wins. Erin thinks she knows Max better than I do, furious that I can feel ashamed to be here.

'*Tis grace hath brought me safe thus far, And grace will lead me home.*' We sing, we bow our heads and we speak the prayer on the service sheet, as if nothing was wrong.

Max

SAME AFTERNOON

Rachel's getting into a small blue car as I walk into the open air. The driver, who I can't clearly see, slams their door, revs the engine loudly, indicates, and zips away.

Probably best not to speak with her again.

And then something cannons into my back: Alice. With Chloë not far behind. 'She wanted to find you so Mum told me …'

I have that picture of Rachel in my head, as the whole congregation erupts onto the gravel, buzzing like a hive of bees. Jenny, tottering in her high heels, makes straight for me, 'Max: what the hell were you doing in there? God, are you mad?' She touches the black fascinator perched on her head, 'is it falling off?'

'A eulogy for Dad,' I say. 'An honest *message*, as he called them.'

'Why couldn't you've given them what they wanted? Even if it was lies? What about me?'

She takes off her specs, and brushes her eyes. Tears. 'I gave them the message he was trying to: which they needed to hear, before they self-deceive and lose the plot again. What about you?'

'They'll cast me as the secularist, the bad influence? *Comprenez?* How can we stay, and shake hands and drink tea? You never *think!*'

'Shush: it'll all be fine. Mam knew all of it already. Erin's on side.'

'Erin? Your Mam was embarrassed: you embarrassed her.'

The sweat pours down my back: maybe I did get it all wrong. It seemed right and obvious at the time. After spotting Rachel outside last evening.

'Max? What? Did you hear me?'

'Jen?'

The girls, who'd moved off into the crowds, rush towards us. 'We saw a butterfly, coming out!' Alice cries.

'Really?'

'Really! A yellow one. It was on the wall, drying its wings, Chloë showed me.'

'How—wonderful,' Jenny says, in a flat voice. 'Max, are you coming?'

'Where? We have to go and have tea, they're our guests.'

'Max, it was a brimstone, I think.'

'Mummy, can Chloë and me fetch Zoë?'

'Max: we can't. *I* can't. I'm taking the girls away. I'm not running off: it's a protest, I am not staying here to be the focus of their hatred of what I stand for or they think I do.'

I'm stunned. 'I—You read the book—?'

'Why the hell blast them with criticism? All they needed was to hear about their lovely parental pastor, who cared for them like God does. Love indestructible, or whatever? Couldn't you have stuck with that? Like the slide show? Then tell *me* what you thought and felt, at home?'

'What've I said that you didn't understand?'

Someone's arm is around my shoulders: Erin. 'Maxie-boy, great stuff. You gave it them. So, you coming to join us all for tea?'

'Piss off Erin, out of my marriage.' Jenny, chin stuck out and fascinator quivering with rage on her head, insulting my sister, is incredible, and out of character. I grab her by the arm.

Erin, stunned as I am, says, 'Sorry?'

Jenny pulls her arm free. 'As if you haven't noticed who's been his closest friend and mate for ten years?'

'Zo-zo was crying. You didn't fetch her. A lady came to find you.'

We're all brought to our senses: a small solemn group stands at our feet. Alice and Chloë are presenting us with the child we seemed to have forgotten while we adults ranted. They have Zoë by the hand, one each side, protectively. Zoë's cheeks and her long eyelashes are wet. But being centre of attention, she beams happily at the three stunned, enraged, unhappy adults.

Chloë says, 'Jenny, have you got a tissue and I'll wipe her face?'

Erin moves back into a group of her old friends from First T.

I ask Jen, 'D'you believe in lies? I thought better of you. You never read any of the book, did you? I thought we came here to face this together.'

'We'll see you at home,' she says, taking a child by each hand. 'You can tell your Mam, Alice needs to get back to school tomorrow, and Zoë'll sleep better in her own bed.'

POSSIBILITIES

Daze

OXFORD, ST HILDEGARD'S RETREAT CENTRE, SAME DAY

Daze walks the completed labyrinth in her bare feet, eyes shut, feeling the rough-textured edging tiles, and the smooth, tiny tesserae, following the twists and turns. Yes. It'll work for those who can't see. She sits, cross-legged, in the centre, resting her mind on a phrase: *don't be fazed if your thoughts wander: that's what thoughts do.*

She gets up, returns through the labyrinth, fetches her smokes from her bag, pulls open the double glass doors, and steps outside.

It's a gold, blue, and green summer day. Yellow roses clamber up walls, trees hiss gently in a warm breeze. The lawn's equipped with benches, but Daze prefers the ground. In a secluded spot, sheltered from the house by a clump of flowering shrubs, she sits, lights up, inhales. Warm enough, sunny enough, balanced. Daze lies on her back, watching the clouds.

Then, bummer, she's aware of people, talking. The nearest bench is occupied, a bush obscures the bodies but she spies two pairs of feet. One wearing a slightly scuffed pair of boat shoes: David. The other well-worn sandals, the toes bare, nails painted crimson. These feet are small, but not young. The woman's denim skirt hangs almost to her ankles. Etta.

Etta's relocation of loyalty is interesting. What's she discussing with David? The homeless project, which segues into experiencing homelessness. David shares a few scraps about falling in with a crowd who invisibly occupied the benches in an airport terminal long-term, masquerading as international travellers. Daze knows a little of how that ended, and is pretty certain he won't tell Etta everything. He describes how they lived on the scraps and leftovers from the coffee shops and how—his voice drops, Daze can't hear. She crushes the remains of her ciggie into the ground, then wriggles herself stealthily nearer, until she's right behind them, squashed flat behind the bush. Its thin branches poke and scratch her.

Etta's describing giving people an ear, while making and serving soup. 'All they want, you know, someone to care. I know I can give that caring. I know it, like here, in my heart?'

There's a silence. Daze imagines Etta's hand-on-chest gesture. David's canny enough to be wary of Etta. Who adds, 'Oh, I got references, if you need 'em.'

Etta can sew, knit and crochet, paint and draw. Her origins are obscure, but her looks underline a story of poverty, and hard work. Daze leans forward, and shifts closer: a large twig snaps, she freezes.

They're too engrossed to notice. David's asking Etta how come she upped and left the women's refuge where she was happily settled, helping to care for the traumatised offspring of the women who'd fled domestic violence. Gently he probes. 'You'd got your NVQ's, you were qualified in nursery care: what made you leave?'

Daze wonders: did Etta do something wrong? A crime? Did she have to run away? Hah: David will find it out. He is quietly coaxing. She's cunning, isn't she? She'll lie. Will he perceive that?

Daze risks holding aside the veil of leaves. Etta's sitting slightly sideways on the bench: Daze can see her face three-quarter view. She's not looking at David, but at her hands. They're spread on her knees, and she smooths one palm with the fingers of the other hand. Daze knows those hands: small, square, roughened by work, but skilful.

'This is something I could do for my girl: like God's shown me. Directed my eyes.'

So, she's had a kid, then? Dead now, perhaps? 'How about, we start at the beginning: you tell me about your girl, and why you feel God is involved,' David says, slowly, very quiet.

'Well you listen, Dave: I have to think back and tell you—Begging pardon,' (as she lays a hand on David's knee, of all places) 'it's horrible. What men do.'

A story Daze has never heard unfolds, first with silence, then with great sobs, and words Daze can't decipher, since Etta covers her face with her hands.

Shit, Daze thinks, as Etta snuffles, sobs, and eventually blows her nose. And David murmurs about acceptance, and taking her time. But here at last is Etta's story.

'My Da, it's awful really, he had to pay off a debt, an' he couldn't, so what did he do? He let that bugger, the man who he owed money to, *have me as a wife.*'

Intriguing. Daze has heard of women being sold: but not recently, and not quite like this. Etta wasn't exactly sold, but pretty nearly.

'I was fifteen. God almighty, I was a kiddie who wanted to go to school an' that. Though marriage was a lark: dress for the ceremony, my sisters envious, status. But he was old. Thirty-seven, he was. Got some kids of his own, and—rough, you know.' She pauses. Daze imagines. 'I ran away. After the wedding night. I didn't want that again. I told Lucille—my sister—I can't, I won't, have him do all that to me again, an' we took off. He'd have had Lucille, rightly, she was older. But he fancied me—' More tears. 'I was good-looking, back then.'

Lucille? 'We, me an' Lucille, we needed to get away far as we could from Dad and my husband. We went north. On the road, we met up with some New Age travellers. This guy, he had a van, the three of us drifted together. Jack. He was going our way, offered to help us, keep us safe an' that.'

Jack? Oh My God. *Jack?* And Lucille—Loose? Daze's mouth is open, like a fish's: her cousin Shane's parents? Jewels—Juliette—Julietta—Etta? Her mouth is dry: she closes it, and swallows. Not—my mum? My mum could be *Etta? And that's why she hangs around me like a wasp on sugar?*

No: same name, no reason same person. She could be treating *me* as the lost daughter?

'We went north, further and further, we ended up on a boat to the Western Isles. One thing about Jack McShane—'

Daze is sweating, mouth dry, throat tight. Etta's still talking, 'wasn't so nice: he bought us food and stuff, helped us out a lot, but we had to pay him for it. You get my meaning.'

Jack McShane. Jack made the girls pay for their food and a roof with—. She and Shane are more than cousins? Jack, the swine, had sex with both girls he brought to Val's commune—is *that* how I—?

Val never told Daze any of this. There was the Romany stuff, but this …

Daze's hands want to cover her ears. Or stop Etta's blabbering mouth. God, I had sex with my half brother? Well, almost: it was IVF sex, it was sperm through a tube.

But Etta her Mum? She looks at those small, square feet with the crimson nails. Was the pretty girl in her photo *Etta?* With the long dark hair and the daisy chain, and the princess look? Etta and Jewels, they are the same person?

What to do? Wait for her to go away, then grab David, and—but I shouldn't have been there, listening … Hardly a *dah-dah, here I am,* moment, leap from the bushes, *hello Mum it's me …*

Max

ON THE ROAD HOME

Own goal, Jenny: leaving me to travel with my sister, who you resent.

On the journey south Erin's congratulations continue in the car. Why hadn't one of us said all that sooner?

'She dragged far more attention to herself by putting the girls in the car and driving off home like that,' I say. Then hear Erin's account of Mam and Dad's life over the past nine years, confirming all my suspicions, and my regrets. 'I should've spent more time with them.'

'Max, whatever: Mam totally understands.'

'I expected Jenny would. Her reaction stunned me.'

'Didn't you share what you were thinking of saying? You realise you came over a bit like Dad. Jenny needed warning.'

'I clearly asked, please read the book. We hadn't a moment … We never discussed it again. But going home without consulting me was needless.'

'You should have *shared* the book's contents rather than—'

'At one time—'

'Okay.'

'Och, listen: there was something else.' Seeing Rachel was the most important prompt. I find (with Erin's bairns totally absorbed in their hand-held computer games in the back seats), I can mention to Erin what I couldn't to Jenny. 'Rachel. She was there.'

'*Rachel?*'

'Outside last night. I escaped from First Truly to breathe, last evening, while you two were busy. Rachel was hanging about across the road, leaning on a wall. I knew it was her, though she's changed a bit. She'd Nat, the wee adopted bairn, with her. Seeing her gave me a fright.'

'I can imagine. How was she?'

'She half wanted to know what First Truly's like now. She told me about her life. She's back nursing, with Nat in special school, and a flat of her own. But the scars are there. She looked too old. For whatever age she is.'

'The scandal was nine years ago. She's only—maybe thirty-two? They encourage us to marry so young.'

I plunge into discussing what inspired my rant, as Jenny called it. 'Remember the nice girl Mam, and even more Dad, had wanted me to marry? Who was then snapped up by their school's headmaster? I couldna' keep to a bland speech about the nice pastor and his congregation of wonderful Christians after she'd told me what they did to her. How she was first persuaded to behave as if nothing had happened, and then edged out of the church. Did you not hear that from Mam?'

Erin admits she heard something. 'I knew they were patting it all back into place. They have to, it's their religion.'

'So you bloody colluded?' I hiss the words, seeing we've small ears in the back.

'Max, calm down. No, I didn't know much, and I thought about it and—maybe I was wrong, but I thought you and Jenny had a good chance if nobody rocked your boat with what was going on up here. And I was pregnant, with deadlines to meet before maternity leave. I'm sorry. God, I am sorry, it's nearly ten years ago now, but I could've done better.'

I'm absorbing Erin's words. She says, 'Max, speak, please: I said sorry.'

'Mam?' I say.

'She does what he says. Did.'

'Mmm.'

The miles flash by, till we both recover, and we can talk more objectively.

'Don't you hate everything fundamentalist religion does to women? I knew I must alert them to Mam's enormous influence and contribution to Dad's work. All his best work was inspired by her. She made him see how he'd colluded in Colin's attitudes and the unconsensual sex, if not the violence.'

'They're made to accept that's women's lot.'

'Rachel's moved on, but she's in no-man's-land legally. She can't get Colin to give her a divorce. He doesn't believe that marriage can or should be dissolved by a lawyer.'

'That's appalling. It's outdated. It's slavery.'

'It is.'

We travel in appalled silence, till Erin says, 'It's why we've married out, so to speak. And maybe why Kirsty—'

'Kirsty?'

'Kirsty's love life is complicated. But the boyfriend's not a reformed Presby, whatever.'

'Right. And I'm not to ask?'

'Got it. For now.'

'How old's Nat? Didn't they discover he has fetal alcohol syndrome?'

'He has. Around ten?'

'I guess Rachel's a great adoptive mum. But—lost years, lost friends, lost faith. And you didn't share about seeing Rachel with Jenny?'

'Rachel's friends at the women's refuge are more honest than the ones she had here. No, I didn't tell Jenny … Don't you hate the screw-ups we all make?'

'Based on our cherished beliefs. Or someone else's. Yep.' Erin's mouth closes tight.

We speed silently through south Yorkshire, until a voice from the back says 'I know we're not nearly there for ages, so can we have some chocolate?'

'Grandma's packed us a picnic. We'll stop soon to eat.'

Daze

THAT EVENING

Daze sits on the roof of the *Ironic Lady*, swinging her legs and drinking cider. The sunlit canal water below is greasy and slovenly: long thin willow leaves and twigs, which fell during a sharp shower of rain, float by. Her life may be canal water, but she is nothing like a twig, or a dead leaf.

She takes up her sketch book and begins to draw. The bent willows: gnarled, sinewy, twisted, split, strangled with ivy. Beyond the willows is a fence: beyond the fence, a junkyard of twisted, rusted, metallic things. Between the willows, elvish creatures peep out: a hand here, a leg and foot there, a wizened little face. After a while, she notices that these faces are more memory than imagination: skewed features, ears too low, upturned noses, wide apart eyes, drooping eyelids. But the bodies are healthy, slim, and lithe.

Okay, she's read that old research on the malformed baby. Everyone concluded that both she and her cousin Shane inherited a genetic flaw, shared by her mother and aunt. But no blood tests were taken from either woman. So there's no certainty about who passed on the—what was it—*translocated* gene? Translocated … moved elsewhere. *Whole or in part*, to quote the printed account of Persephone.

Suppose Etta and Jewels *are one person?* Suppose the translocated gene was Jack's, not Jewels's? Suppose Jewels—Etta—doesn't carry the broken gene. She and her sister Loose both have sex with Jack. He passes a duff gene to both their kids.

Can she imagine Etta and Des as a couple? All this is madness ... But, she has to know. She seizes her cell phone and dials the Sennen number. Caro answers: 'Daze! How lovely to hear you!'

What a lie.

Caro says the house is empty all summer.

'Hey, I was gonna come down an' see you all!' Daze returns the lie.

'Oh, sweetie, I'm sorry. Your father's booked through July and half August, teaching wannabes on summer schools and tramping art groupies around galleries. And I promised Mummy I'd accompany her to Nepal, so now they've given me the job of checking out some health care scheme there.'

Bugger. But they'd probably lie about Etta anyhow.

Could Etta be made to take a blood test?

Daze slides carefully down the roof, and goes inside to find the metal box where she keeps documents. Take another shufti at the birth cert. Mother: Juliette Loveday Potter, born Symes. Why she hadn't twigged Juliette, Etta, is a mystery: her normally sharp brain let her down. Father, Desmond Potter. Hah: they lied then … People lie all the time, don't they? Especially, to survive. Like if they've had sex with more than one guy and got pregnant. Des was obviously the one more likely to take on a baby. He's a soft enough wuss. Etta's a shocking little liar. All that God-stuff to get herself a roof over her head at Ruth's house, and then sucking up to David.

Loveday: sounds like a Hardy heroine: how about changing her own name to Loveday Potter? Or Daisy Loveday? Or even Loveday on its own, like that violinist, Kennedy?

Her moods continue to swing. Disgust at Etta's behaviour and who Etta is. Admiration for Etta's spunkiness. Anger with snobby Caroline. Weak Des. And bloody Etta, who'll be up at Hildie's, and Daze doesn't want to go there now, 'cos she'd have to see her.

Caution: do not even think about parents!

To get her head together, she'd drop right out, maybe even visit sweet Harriet in Melbourne. But Caro's suggestion's less expensive. Go home, rootle all through the attic, get in some surfing, live and breathe Cornwall. Maybe even invite David, and pick his brains? He's mentioned he has friends around Penwith.

Max

COMING HOME, LATER

As we get going again after our picnic, Erin flicks on the radio: symbolic of keeping her own counsel. I'd definitely made my own mistakes, not sharing what I intended to say in the eulogy. Or that I'd spoken to Rachel. Should I expect sympathy?

But she thoughtfully drives right into Oxford, and up to the house. Letting me out, 'Okay? Positive thoughts, Max, and stick with your convictions. You might apologise to Jenny for treating her as a lesser being?'

'A lesser being?'

'I know you didn't mean anything. I'm a Mullins kid too.'

It's after ten: I find Jenny in the study, seated at the desk. Back to me, she says 'I heard the door. The car needs petrol tomorrow.'

'Jen, can we talk?' I glance over her shoulder, at the computer screen. She closes the file.

'I don't know: can you?'

'I need to apologise.'

'You do. I got implicated as an outsider, responsible for you not spending time with your closer-than-close family since we've been together.'

'Mmm. Erin said similar stuff to me.'

'You talked about me with Erin?'

'She offered me a ride home, and was decent enough to come to the door ... Bairns in bed? How did you manage the journey?'

'As well as you would. We had a great time, story tapes, and no arguing; tea at a service station was junk food, they found that a huge treat. Alice invented a story for Zoë and me. Okay, it was extremely derivative, and I could've used some silence, but she's only five. I don't see them enough. They shared their chips with me, so kind to Mummy!'

'Jen? You're not—are you crying?' Dad has messed us up, again. This whole thing's been a disaster. I kneel by the chair, wanting to move in close. 'I've done it all wrong, haven't I?'

She leaps up; the chair whizzes on its wheels; I recoil; Jenny, keeping her back to me, heads for the door. 'I'm off to bed. Work tomorrow. Oh, and I charged our meal to the travel and holidays credit card.'

'They—my family didn't blame you for *anything*.'

'Really? What about perfect pastor Ian?'

'Ian's way too perfect even for the family. Anyway, he's wrapped up in being a dad at age twenty-two. Erin's full of insights, she said—'

'I don't want to hear.'

Jenny

FRIDAY 20 JUNE

Today starts well, first Rich chatting in a friendly mood about Danielle's progress, then moving to the great news that we're submitting the conference paper to *Nature,* and a discussion about peer reviews. His whole demeanour's positive. I feel confident. My contract's bound to be renewed.

But after the disastrous service, I went straight to look at Dad's Vangenics site. I might just succumb: get away from here, and—sort myself out without Max.

Without Max. The awful thing is, I don't hate him.

After work, I pick up the kids, and we dash round the supermarket on the way home. They're fractious, so I pacify them a little at the greetings cards stand, suggesting we choose one to thank Grandma. Then Max appears home inexplicably early. So we've ended up all sat round the table together, sharing a rather horrible thin-crust commercial pizza.

Zoë sits looking at her plate. 'Grandma's pizza's nicer, isn't it?' says Max.

Alice reaches over, fork in her hand, 'I can eat Zo-zo's.'

'No. You've lettuce left there: look.'

'Why not?'

''Cos it isn't yours, okay? Eat your lettuce and get down, Ally.'

Max takes Zoë's plate, and cuts the rubbery-topped pizza into smaller triangles. 'I-sosi-lees, E-quilateral', he makes a sing-song description of their shapes. She giggles. He adds 'Uni-lateral.' I snigger. She lets him pop the pieces into her mouth.

Max's dark fringe falls across his eyes: Max and Zoë match. My insides twist up: what if we separated, and I took the kids to Vancouver?

But who would the girls themselves choose?

'All gone!' Zoë slides off her chair.

I begin to clear the plates. Max is flipping the pages of his *British Medical Journal*, silently absorbed as if the rest of us weren't here. I'm about to try to communicate, at least to ask if he had a good day, when 'See Grandma's card?' says Zoë, trotting up with a smile, and plonking it in front of Max.

He takes the card, looks at the front, opens it and scowls at the words inside. 'Lilies are funereal,' he announces, folding it shut.

'Well, that's what it is, a sympathy card.'

'It's a sympathy card after the event. And did the bairns understand what you were doing?'

'I didn't talk about—listen, she might appreciate the thoughtfulness: the words were about the one you miss who's close as a breath or something.'

He groans.

'Least I can do, after you rubbished me on Tuesday.'

Where did that leap from? I want to bite it back. Max ignores it.

Alice empties out all the Lego. She begins fitting bits together, humming softly, till a winding Lego wall curves and spirals on the floor. 'Is that a snake, Ally?'

'It's a labby-rinse, silly.'

'Oh-ho, who taught you?'

'I copied it. From Auntie Daisy?' She walks her fingers around inside. 'That's me walking it.'

'Are we done with this meal then?' Max pushes back his chair.

'I was going to serve I.C. but seeing everyone's got down—where've they gone?'

They're both flat on the kitchen floor, on their tummies, watching a spider skedaddle towards the laundry room.

'Evidently research scientists: observational fieldwork on Arachnida,' says Max.

I'd have laughed, back when—instead, my throat closes up and swallowing down that feeling I haul them to their feet, snapping 'Bedtime! It's late!'

'There's no need to apologise to Mam, Jenny.'

'What? I've got to get them in bed.'

He moves along behind us, as if the girls hadn't ears to hear it all. 'If you'd read the book, you'd have understood everything. You'd have supported me. Mam knows. Dad put it all in there, but he was so marginalised that he couldn't put it to the congregation. He was too unwell. I was at fault—whatever his grim mood was, I canna' explain everything while you—'

'Me what? I'm just too busy. Now we're submitting an article to *Nature*, the most important interdisciplinary scientific journal publishing original research, in case you don't remember. I have to do more experiments and God knows what to make the peer reviewers happy.'

'If you'd have read the book—'

'Just help with the kids can you?'
Why did we have them? Why are we here?

Max

SATURDAY 21 JUNE

It's a beautiful evening: sun's out, clouds are clearing to a blue sky, the whole world smells freshly of rain.

'I'd rather be playing tennis,' says Jenny, as we walk down Parks Road, on our way to the Holywell Music Room. We're passing the University Museum. I turn to look at her, and she adds, in an angry tone, 'You treated them badly. Even if the congregation needed to hear that stuff. You moved without warning from some nice memories of your Dad to a spiteful attack on how they've not changed their attitudes since discovering Colin and Rachel's violent marriage, and hearing your Dad's confession about his dealing with it wrongly. You presented yourself as Mr Perfectly-tolerant-and-wise. They'd come to show loyalty. To pay respects. Not to be criticised. I didn't know where to put my face. They'd naturally assume I put you up to it. Can't you admit you're sorry?'

'I said nothing that'd make them blame you. We're off to have a nice evening. Why did you drag the subject up?' Why do women go on and on, spoiling life for themselves as well as us?

'I came to be pleasant, mingle, show my appreciation. Fit in. Your speech compounded their distrust. *He married a secularist. She's poisoned his mind.*'

'What I said wasn't meant to do that.'

'I can't see how you thought it wouldn't. An attack on their religion?'

'I don't know. I just didn't.'

She stops and blocks my path. 'Okay, tell me I've spoilt the evening. But we must discuss this.'

'Keep your voice down—'

'I wasn't shouting.'

I glance around: a small huddle of tourists have looked up from studying what looks like a road map. Let them not now ask us the way somewhere. 'You've made that group of tourists stare.'

'All I said was—all I want to know is, why?'

'Because I didna' think—'

'That's right, Max, you never think!'

'Because I didn't believe they'd see it that way, or pull you into the equation. It was about my parents, not you, or us. About Mam and Dad. About how the congregation ignored his change of heart, and her sacrificial contribution to his ministry. Hand over control to the assistant pastor. Buy a big TV screen to beam out the words of the songs. Send away Rachel, the innocent partner in a dysfunctional marriage that hit the headlines. It was all me, my thoughts. Not you. Me.'

'Right. You. Not us. You're so selfish you let me take all the flak. What's more, they don't even know how little influence I have on you, or what you think and do.' She reaches into her bag, pulls something out, shoves it at me. 'Here's your concert tickets—note I had them in my bag in case you forgot—I'm off home.'

'Wouldn't you—'

She begins to walk away, then turns, throwing words over her shoulder. 'No. See, Max? This is the way home.'

I grab her by the arm. She can't do this. 'I hoped we'd enjoy the evening. You brought the subject up.'

'Oh yeah! Evening out? The first violin is your senior partner's daughter, and the programme includes a twelve-tone experimental piece written for adapted, or augmented, or—I forget, but something weird's been done to the piano?'

'We're his guests. It's *prepared* piano.'

'I'm not prepared to spend the time. With it. Or you. You're the musician. Let me go!' She shakes free.

'How can you be so petty? Who was it made me listen to Dad's confessional tape?'

'Don't blackmail me!' She runs down South Parks Road towards the science area.

'Where're you going?'
'Anywhere. Not the holy music room!'
She is crying.

Jenny

HOME

I send the babysitter away, and leaf through some notes at the kitchen table—then he, Max, is back in my kitchen, poking about in the cupboard where I keep drugs. 'Headache pills?' he asks, without saying hi.

I find the painkillers for him. 'Here. Not many left. Good concert?'

'No.' He takes two with a glass of water, and slaps the glass down on the side. 'Futuristic plonk.'

Then he fishes the programme from his pocket. Glances at it, chucks it in the bin. 'Though his lassie plays well.'

'Your boss? You apologised I wasn't able to make it?'

'I murmured darkly. They know you're a busy research scientist. He's no' my boss, Jenny.'

'Your senior partner. Dr What's-it. Kettle boiled. Tea?'

'Jenny, if you're half interested in what's going on for me, I was throwing out the sympathy cards they all sent, this evening.'

'Sorry, who? Earl Grey?'

'Patients. Anything. Not peppermint.' He notices the post, lying on the kitchen table. *Pulse*, his GP magazine '*at the heart of general practice since 1960*' lies in its plastic wrapper amongst the letters and bills. He picks it up, scans the headlines.

'That was kind,' I say, 'You never told me. That they did that.'

'They're people—och, they're patients—' he puts the mag aside as I approach with the tea, 'who—thanks, ouch, mug's blazing hot—'

'It's got a handle, use it. So they sent cards? How did they know?'

'The grapevine's very effective. Plus I was gone on compassionate leave.' Max pulls a kitchen chair out and sits at the table with his mug. He opens the brightly illustrated magazine: trying to end the conversation?

I say, 'You should be glad they cared.'

He looks up, making eye contact, frowning. 'Jen, when I first joined this practice, when Dad was alive, a form of fame, even glory, had arrived before me. Patients, people you'd recognise from HPC if I told you a few pointers, which I won't, turned up with a kind of shy, knowing, conspiratorial smile, to join my list. People who could've found a good doctor nearer their home would request to join. You ken my meaning?'

'The faithful who'd heard your Dad speak at conferences?'

'Alisdair Mullins's son: he'll think as we do. He's one of us.'

'Heavy. Like Dad's fertility following. I do know it's worse for you—but—'

'I hate,' he bangs his fist on the table: the mugs shake, 'being the blue-eyed boy that I'm not. I hate their misdirected kindness.' Bang. 'I never wanted,' bang, 'to uphold the image of the locality's safe GP who shares their morals and beliefs. I'd prefer to be me.' Bang. 'Does any of that answer your questions?'

'I—think we have to be who we are, don't we?'

'And you know who that is, do you? How'm I supposed to think?'

He's so aggressive, my aggression boils up to meet his. Else I would cry. 'I wouldn't get sour about people sending cards. You know what? You're more like your father than you realise.'

'Is that true?'

'You've a following. It weirdly includes Daisy: she thinks the sun shines out of your bum. She's told me how concerned she is—'

'You stop there, Jenny!' Max jumps up, chair scrapes back noisily, falls over backwards, journal comes flying through the air. It lands briefly on the table, skids down the runway, and is away again, sending a plate crashing to the floor.

Silence. Slowly several letters and bills slide from the table, landing on top of *Pulse* and the broken plate. A pencil follows behind.

This is Alisdair, blindly throwing the microscope.

Max turns and leaves the room in two strides. Slowly, I stand the rejected chair back on its legs, and sink onto its seat.

I'm dazed. Torn apart. Lay my head down on the cool table top. Sati's *'Je te veux'* begins. His playing is beautiful, and ironically composed. It stops mid-phrase.

Creeping to the living room door, I peer around it. Max is bent double on the piano stool, shoulders heaving. Okay, he's crying. Daze would know what to do. I'm confused.

Upstairs, Zoë starts up.

Jenny

SATURDAY 28 JUNE

It's not been the best of weeks. I don't understand Max and I don't understand me. To get out of the house, I take the girls to buy new shoes, which they need, whatever rumpus is going on between their parents. I park at the Angel and Greyhound car park. The only space is under the bloody lime trees. Right away Alice exclaims, 'Grandma's car!'

'Where?'

'Grandma fish-car!' Zoë points.

We're right behind an old navy blue Audi, with a small silver fish symbol on the back. Can it be Alisdair's tenth anniversary present from his congregation?

'Granny-Granny-Granny!'

'Where? There are lots of—cars like ...' But it is Fee. In a typical A-line blue denim skirt and flowered blouse, walking briskly towards that car, keys in her hand, and in the other, a plastic carrier bag. *St Andrews Bookshop.*

'Granny!'

I can't pretend she's not there: all I can do is open my door, dive in through theirs to unloose them from their car seats, and put on a brave face for mum-in-law.

The girls, freed, dart forward. 'Alice, Zo-zo, hold my hands! You never run off in a car park—do you?'

'Only to Grandma!'

'Jenny, pet, and my wee grandchildren. What a lovely surprise.'

'Fee—Max didn't say anything.'

'I don't think Max knew I was here. How are you all?'

'Shopping for shoes. They keep growing, don't they?' Do I sound bright and positive? Shall we avoid the awkward subject?

'They certainly do.' She smiles, as if nothing is wrong. What was it Max said, about her knowing all along the kinds of things he'd say at the service?

'Granny, I got all my spellings right! That's a gold star.' Alice stands on one foot, gripping the other and hopping round Fee. 'One wrong is a silver star. We all get a blue star for trying. What's in your bag? Can I see?'

Fee obliges, holding the top of the bag open. 'Books. Grown-up books.' Alice peers inside.

'I was so sorry we had to rush away. Did Max explain? Alice needed to get back for school.'

'Jenny,' Fee lays her free hand on my arm. I stop her speaking, in case it's something I can't bear to hear, by saying, 'Max was a bit up-front, wasn't he? I didn't—' And then, she stops me.

'I didn't mention coming here, because I'm on silent retreat. We're not supposed to socialise. I'm in town only to buy a book we were recommended, which had sold out on the bookstall. And the new Tom Wright.'

'Please—' It's like my mind hasn't registered what my ears perfectly well heard, as I blather, 'Aren't you allowed out for tea? Or supper? There's a lovely new gastro-pub—'

'No, though I'd love to. But I'm here to spend time with the Lord. To see what I should be doing in the future.'

'It's not because of what Max said, is it? I saw the first version of that speech: I've no idea why he rewrote it.'

She pats my arm, gently, 'Another time, pet. I mustn't break my retreat. You needn't tell Max unless he asks. He'll understand.'

It's a brush-off. It hooks my anger. 'He's full of grief and won't let me in. I felt so bad about the eulogy.'

'Really?' Her eyes widen. 'You shouldn't, Jenny. I knew it was all Max, none of it was you. You remember, I'm praying for him, and all of you.'

A pious reply's as good as dried breadcrumbs to the thirsty. How can Fee be so cold? 'Max isn't usually cruel. He's hurt all of us, especially you.'

'I don't think he was. Max and his father had a complex relationship. But they loved each other.' Her voice quavers. 'Alisdair loved Max and wanted God's will for him. Max was so gentle with his father, in the last days.'

I hate grown-up tears, and want to stop them falling down her cheeks, 'I'm sorry, I'm sorry but I didn't incite him.'

'Oh Jenny.' Her hand on my arm. Her arms round me, while the contents of her bag—earnest religious books—whop my bottom. 'Life is so hard sometimes, isn't it?'

'Yes.' We cling. I don't deserve to be held. It's Fee who's waking up alone, me who's making a mess of my life without even trying.

When we let go, 'I'd better say goodbye to the girls.'

'They love you. How can tea be wrong?'

Fee crouches to their level, and takes their hands. 'Now, Grandma's on a journey, so she can't come and see you in your house today. Another day, soon, we'll visit. Won't we?'

''Nother day.' Zoë echoes. Alice stands staring.

'That's right, another time.' Fee stands, brushing dust and dried lime flower wings from her skirt. 'Soon.'

I try polite objectivity. Though what I want is a lesson in how to reconnect with Max. Before it's too late, and I've decided to—take a job far away to further my career? 'And you're staying where?'

'St Hildegard's,' she smiles, as if it's the obvious, and best, place. 'Then off to London lunchtime tomorrow, to see my girls.'

I'm astounded. Fee hurries to mitigate, 'It's beautiful at Hildie's. But not remote. I needed space to be alone with the Lord, far away from First Truly ... So, we'll be in touch, won't we Jenny? And when I go home, I'll send the children a surprise something.'

God is more important than her family. And home? She'll be moving out.

'Yes. We must let you go. Thanks for—staying to chat …' I load Zoë into the buggy. She squirms with reluctance. 'Say bye-bye to Grandma!'

*

It's a miserable trudge, then, up the Plain, over Magdalen Bridge, a sea of bright carefree people surging towards us. 'C'mon Alice! You want new shoes don't you?'

'They've got ice creams!' Alice says, as a group of students licking cornets emerge from the punt station.

Cornmarket heaves with teens, tourists, and street vendors. A guy with a mouth organ, busking in a doorway. *Big Issue* sellers with dogs. Some tourists stop us and ask me to take their picture. Remembering Max's interest in the homeless people, caught by sudden guilt, I double back to the seller, and buy a copy of the *Big Issue*. He wishes us a good weekend.

We are served, in the shoe shop, by smiling Saturday salesgirls who ooh and aah about the pretty sandals we eventually buy. At least that was easy.

'Yo!' It's Shaz, with Charlie, crossing the road towards us, shoving through the crowds. 'Hey, time for a coffee?'

'What?'

'Time to chill?'

Upstairs in a coffee shop, with a window seat looking down on St Michael's Street, the girls with ices, and milkshakes, I try to smile over my cappuccino. 'How's life treating you?' I ask Shaz.

'Eliot's off visiting his friend who's in rehab. How's you? You were away, weren't you?'

'At Max's father's memorial service. It was ghastly. The congregation had adored him. The whole event was a 1950s vignette. Women in Laura Ashley dresses preparing the tea, quiches, meringues, and masses of homemade cakes.'

'Northern spread! And Max did the speech? He'd be good.'

Keeping my face straight, 'Max was up in that pulpit—like a pastor himself. He—used the eulogy to critique the congregation's attitudes, it was embarrassing. Then Erin, his favourite sister, was all over him, Congrats, Maxie-boy, as if he's still at school, and so—excluding. Of me, I mean.'

'Partner's sisters can be horrible. At least Erin sounds half normal. Eliot's sister Lizzie is—' Shaz glances at the girls: they're busy messing with their straws, blowing bubbles in their milkshakes. 'Don't.' She bats Charlie, 'What did I say?'

Charlie giggles.

'I said, Do Not Do That, it's dangerous, you'll choke.'

'No I won't!' But she stops.

Shaz leans close, 'Eliot's folks are one of those medical dynasty families. Although Eliot's adopted, he's fitted in. He worked like stink to be a doctor like they wanted. Lizzie, his sister, rebelled. She's Gussie and Jocelyn's biological child. She got into med school, she could do it, but she didn't want to. She developed a habit.'

'That's awful. Force a child to do things ... Max never tells me stuff. Colleague's family and all that, I suppose.'

'Gussie and Jos, I hate them.' Shaz hisses. 'Jen, they're not human. They're like something from a medical soap. I try to keep Charlie away: but to be honest, they couldn't care Eliot's got a little girl. Long as she carries on the tradition. Gussie's like, gin in one hand and something on medical politics in the other, "Hi Charlie how about I put a cartoon on the TV for you?"'

'They sound ...worse than the Mullinses. Alisdair, on his terms, loved his kids. Don't get me wrong, he walloped them. Yes, really. It's in their culture.'

'It's abuse.'

'It is. Max's brothers are frightful, Ian and Alex, the heavenly twins.'

'And Kirsty who's always asking advice?'

'You remember. The middle one. Fee—' I can't speak. Fee let me down. Fee has rejected me now? I have to hate them?

'Yes?'

'Oh, families can be shit can't they. The Mullinses are like aliens, from another planet. Max and David, what's that about ...? So, did Lizzie escape medicine? And quit the habit?'

'She works on a farm. She doesn't see the folks. Charlie, finish that ice cream: look, it's melting.'

Charlie opens her mouth like a fish, Shaz spoons a couple of teaspoons in. Alice stares. Charlie and Shaz laugh.

Zoë lays her head on my lap. I stroke her cheek. 'Someone's hot and tired.'

'Not me!' Charlie says.

'Not us!' adds Alice.

'You and Max okay? You looked a bit—walking down the street—'

The question makes me feel weary. 'Actually, if we're finished, maybe we should get back.'

'You doing anything this weekend?'

I gather our shopping, and swallow down more sharing. 'There's a party. Leila's a colleague, Tim and Max are old friends—'

'Party should cheer you both up.'

'Can't be worse than the Memorial Service one!'

'Hope you didn't have to help?'

'Those women did all the tea stuff. I felt I should've contributed a cake or something.'

'I wouldn't worry. It's their thing, they're probably retired.'

'I—look, thanks for suggesting this, I was dropping. See you, maybe at school?'

'PTA—can I suggest you now?'

'Like hell—I'm not retired.'

'Nope. Enjoy your party. Go, girl!' Shaz waggles her fingers goodbye.

'What's retired?' Alice asks, as we tramp back to the car.

'It's when you don't work any more.'

'Like something's broken? Like my wind-up music box?'

'Not quite. Not at all.'

With a family like his Eliot might've caught my meaning.

Max

THAT EVENING

'Max could you get that? It'll be the babysitter.'

I dash to open the front door, and exclaim cheerily, 'Etta! Come on in. Jenny's almost ready. She'll update you on the girls. Meanwhile, you know the house but I'll show you where we keep the tea and coffee.'

Etta traipses behind me into the kitchen, where I show her where everything lives, while fending off her inquisitive small talk with my chat. 'So how's life treating you? I know Jenny appreciates you stepping in when Katerina had to leave us. And coming to mind the girls.'

'Always happy to help,' Etta says.

'We appreciate it.'

'Oh, *Big Issue*! You mind me reading yours?'

'Sure, please do.'

'You know I'm up at St Hildegard's now, cleaning an' that?' A hint she's moving on, leaving us? Would solve a problem. Never wanted things to drift this way. 'You seen their labyrinth?'

'I heard they'd commissioned one. Oh, here's Jenny now …'

Jenny bustles in, cocooning herself in a pink and gold pashmina, sharing with Etta that the evenings can be nippy, despite it being nearly July. I remember to extract the bottle of white wine that's been cooling in the fridge.

Will we now put the problem of Dad's memorial service behind us? As we walk towards Tim and Leila's there's a growing beat in the air, and as we turn their corner, it really blasts. There's a line of expensive parked cars. Laughter, and the babble of voices, bounces over the hedge. The music changes. 'Hey, Motown!' Jenny says happily, 'They're a bit vintage, aren't they? Mum and Des play this at their parties.'

She grabs me, and dances a few steps. From Leila's house, the scent of Mediterranean cooking fills the street.

'Cyprus,' I say.

'Memory lane, example two. Are we getting old?' I laugh. Jenny's hand brushes mine. I take hold of it, closing my fingers over hers, and slightly swinging our arms. 'Oh no—the wine. I forgot, Leila's mother's over—maybe they don't—when she's here?'

'Tim didn't mention his mother-in-law. Or the party being an alcohol-free zone.'

She shrugs, 'Intellectuals are always less religious. Leila's mother's a very high-powered university lecturer.'

'Otherwise, I'll hide the bottle in their hedge to collect on our way home?'

The party crowd's noisy and uninhibited. We shove our way into a joyous, crazy, mêlée in the garden. Tim's busy at the barbecue where lamb chops, and kebabs, are sizzling. Leila, in an electric blue outfit, circulates, laying out salads and dips. Several couples have brought children along: the children weave in and out of the crowd, eating sweetmeats and bumping into everyone.

When dancing begins later, buffet tables and chairs whisked away, Jenny starts teaching a bunch of women some lively steps to that pulsing Motown beat: 'Listen? This is my song. Anyone else born in 1965? It's your song too!'

Happy, bright and clever, the mother of my girls who's the reason I spent so little time with Dad in his last years: Jenny is so beguiling when she's like that. I am so proud, and so turned on, as a group of us stand around clapping the rhythm. And the women bounce around, squealing, laughing, and singing along, *Needle in a haystack, boom, boom!* Their kicked off shoes lie in a muddled heap. They remind me of Toulouse Lautrec posters as they dance, high kicking and bumping bottoms. Until they fall into each others' arms, breathing heavily, laughing. Definitely not an alcohol-free party. And no mother-in-law as I've noticed.

Leila is clutching her head, 'Tim, everyone, we must do something! The neighbours!'

Tim charges inside. The music slows. Jenny lassos me with her pink pashmina.

'Max?'

'Och, it's you.'

'It's me.'

I slide my arms round her. She is hot and breathless. There must be twenty of us on this terrace, slow dancing, shoulder to shoulder, bum to bum. Mostly doctors and research scientists.

I want to take Jen home and have her to myself. She looks up, our eyes meet. 'I was talking with some people working with transgenic mice. Their research might eventually mean we could visualize synaptic circuits by genetically labelling neurons with multiple, distinct colours. It's at an early stage but …' I risk kissing her mouth: she responds, and briefly her tongue explores inside mine. Then she pulls away to say 'but then that song—music is much better don't you think?'

'Than?'

'Discussing our work,' she smiles, leaning in. The heat of her body, the beat of her heart.

*

Etta appeared distressed as we stumbled in the door: was she brushing away tears? We absolutely agreed, almost by telepathy, to phone for a cab to take her home.

I see her into it. Warm fuzzy party feelings even make me rather over-solicitous, leaning in to squeeze her hand, once she's settled. In return, she searches my face with her big dark eyes.

Jenny is in the hallway: we fall into a protracted cuddle, far more intimate than for a long while. Then she says, 'Etta left you a note. Someone phoned.'

'Mm?'

'Etta left you a note. You'd better make sure it's nothing.'

The now-scrunched up note is folded in four. Inside, Etta's carefully written *Your Mum called and wanted to speak to you. Please call,* and the official St Hildegard's number.

Mam at David's?

'Nothing serious?'

'No—no. Surprising.' Slide my arms around Jenny pulling her close again, 'Mam's in Oxford.' Her body stiffens: from softly erotic, fitting herself against me, to tense, and wary. 'Is that a problem? I needn't call till tomorrow. It'll be good to see her, away from the Manse.'

'You won't like this: we met her in the car park, today. Total surprise. The girls couldn't understand, nor me: she was like, I'm here but I'm not here, I can't visit with you.'

'*You* saw her? Today? And you said nothing?'

She wrenches herself away. 'Silent retreat, she said. Telling you was pointless. Anyway, *she* said not to.'

'Why?'

'I s'pose it hurt ... She won't visit. She doesn't talk to me, but seems she'll talk to you ...' She flings herself up a few stairs, then leans over the banisters, '*Holy hypocrite.*'

'I'll not have you call her that.' The put-down's what Dad would've said, she looks stricken. Desperate, longing to swallow back the phrase, I leap upstairs towards her: 'Jen, baby, I'm sorry. Mam doesn't shun people, and she's no reason to shun you. I canna' think why—och, you should've told me directly you came back—' She moves away, rejecting my advances.

'No? You Mullinses are so secretive. You've all closed ranks.'

'Och, Jenny, please ... I'll call her tomorrow and we'll sort it out. Look we canna' stand here bellowing like this, we'll wake the bairns and then there'll be a stramash ...' Certainly will, both of us dishevelled and half dressed as we are. 'Will we go to bed now and—we're dead tired, there's no point in arguing.'

'Is there not? And what for? I shan't fall for your seductions to deflect how I feel. Like I did before. Remember: when our cell cultures disappeared? In Cambridge?'

'Why the hell bring that up? I remember you were upset and I came over and took you away to cheer you up and cook your tea. Old news, Jenny, water under the bridge.'

'Is it? Tea? Your word not mine. Our cultures—not cells,' she waves her hand, trying to express something, 'socially, we're too different.'

'So you're too posh for us, lassie? Mullinses not good enough for you?'

'Just—too different. I—I've been thinking anyway. Dad's been—he's been hinting there's a job for me if I wanted it. I—'

'*What?* I have heard everything now. You do that and—' I stop myself. Somehow. Though I would do it. I would. 'So it's all about you.' I say, quietly. 'And you call me secretive.'

'It's reasonable. It's experience. Vangenics have massive funding. I don't agree with all his ideas but—'

'Stop there. It's breaking all your promises.'

'To whom? I've not signed anything that says I have to stay in academic science.'

'Marriage vows? *Our children?*'

In the silence which follows, I force myself to walk away. Down the stairs, into the study. She doesn't follow. Riffling in my bag, I know where to find a short-acting drug that'll knock me out a while. Because I am too angry to trust myself around her. I swallow one capsule, and look at the other in my hand: decide that's going too far. I'll stay downstairs, on the couch in the family room, and she can do whatever she likes up there.

What I shan't allow is for her to take the bairns with her wherever she imagines she's going.

Maybe none of this is real?

Jenny

SUNDAY, 05.30

My thoughts swooped and whirled: Why, why, why, they asked. Why the hideous pricking of jealousy? Why accuse Max of collusion? Why throw Dad's offer in his face?

And then, a quick burst of the kind of sleep that does nothing for you: and waking up to a cold bed, no Max, and the hideous reality that all those things really happened ...

I've come to hate my life.

In the bathroom, my mascara-smudged face taunts me from the mirror. Oh, horrible memories ... this all began at the Ahwahnee, the evening with Wil, the fax about Alisdair ... I don't hate myself, or Max. I hate what we are together.

Silence wraps the house: the children sleep.

The idea seems so logical: my workplace never sleeps. Science is global, and twenty-four seven. Experiments don't keep regular human hours. People work late or arrive early. So, remove myself until Max (presumably in the spare room) has talked to Fee, and then ... do something about facing each other?

So here I am, downstairs, and shoving my feet back into those strappy sandals I wore last night, grabbing my bag, finding my keys aren't in there. Diving through the family room to the kitchen, am stopped by a sound, a loud, quivering snore: Max, flung out untidily on the sofa, his shirt undone and twisted sideways, a cushion fallen over his face, and the picnic rug from the car—he must've fetched that in—rumpled up on the floor.

God: he stayed down here?

The breathing continues noisily, he doesn't wake. He took something to blank out? Now my brain plays a nasty trick: me waking at dawn our first real night away together, reaching for my camera, taking pictures of Max sleeping, naked, sprawled across the bed.

My legs buckle: what a cow I've become.

Yes, I know. I have to get away. Creeping, I ease my keys off their hook, sneak a cereal bar from the cupboard, and slink away, locking this sleeping family inside their nice house.

The sky is beautiful, a clear blue. Birds sing, tears flow. I am lost. I sniff the tears back, unlock the small car Max uses for work, and drive through the empty streets, to where I belong: the science area. Rich mentioned he's away for the weekend, I park in his allocated space.

Safety is the biochemistry building. Along our corridor posters and charts of our research are pinned to the walls, witness to our busy, hardworking, lively group. Felicia's recently pinned up a graph showing her first results. When she did that, it made me happy.

All around, equipment hums, everything is rational and objective. An open door and noises from a side room indicate one of the postgrads is here. 'Hi Jenny!'

'Hey, Felicia?'

'Yeah: my little sister's staying, so I crept in early before Mum wakes. I'll need to get back by eight-thirty to do all Mum's morning stuff. But see, if I passage the cells now, then when we've got Mum up and done, we'll all go somewhere. Easier to do a day out with someone else to help.'

Family evidently staying. I'm not capable of chatting. 'Lovely day for it,' I call, heading for the lab office.

Crunching my cereal bar and sipping a strong coffee from the machine, I try reading my e-mails. A gull, perched on the window ledge outside, gazes in. He's so beautiful and sleek, makes me smile. Then my mind presents another sight: I see Max on the sofa. And I'm getting a memory of Dad on the sofa at our home in London: real or imaginary? I don't want to think about it.

Where are those naked photos now? Do I want to know?

I screw up the wrapper from my cereal bar, and chuck it towards the waste bin. Scoring total accuracy, it falls inside with a plop.

Can't sit still thinking.

I switch off my computer, find some gloves, go into the dirty lab—thank goodness, Felicia's gone—and take some cell cultures from the incubator. Isn't work meant to cure emotional pain? Are these samples, glowing fluorescently, demonstrating what we think they should, and showing that our hypotheses are correct? Viewing them in the tiny dark microscope room perfectly suits my need to hide away.

But thoughts are powerful, and intrude. The family, and the congregation, are so wrong. Those observations about the behaviour of his weird sect were all Max's own. Who made sure he listened to his father's repentance sermon? Me. I can't be Fee, obedient and suffering.

He chose me over Rachel the submissive. I was born fighting. All I did was help Max to be true to himself. He hardly took convincing: if not me, he'd have found someone else equally sceptical and she'd have wanted a career and ... he explained himself how Rachel's attitudes repelled him.

On the microscope slide, the cells go blurry and merge into each other.

I shouldn't wipe my eyes on my lab coat, but what else is there?

Max didn't believe his father had really changed. His fault he's devastated by his own decision to minimise contact.

Fee understood our relationship. Told me that she knew Max would never stick with fundamentalism. So why alter his eulogy so it became like a horrible betrayal?

Oh, that vile woman at First Truly, doing a few last twiddles to her flowers—'The photos Nick's prepared brought a tear to my eye ...' What rubbish. How typical of the way the women talk there.

My cell phone goes off in my bag. Hurry, hurry! A text, a text! I ignore it.

The office phone rings. Ignore that.

Try to think ... Fold my arms on the desk, lay my head on them.

*

I must've dropped off: and meanwhile, a paralysing possibility has crept up. Like someone whispering in my ear. Do I now really want to work with Dad? Surely I only threw the idea at Max because we were having an argument?

When we re-met, I had so wanted two things. To work with Max, intelligent, caring, and fun, driving me crazy with every kind of desire, clearly desiring me after four years apart. And to *prove myself against Dad*. Who had the sheer gall to take over as Clinical Director at the Drey, at the same time I arrived to study in Cambridge. Unavoidable to hide the fact that I was the controversial Dr Guthrie's offspring.

Daze's baby provided the opportunity to do both.

Do I really want to cut Max out of my life?

Another text. *Bairns frantic. Told them Mummy needed time out. Now in Parks, with picnic. Join us?*

I go, lethargically, and for the kids.

Max plays vigorously with them, kicking a ball, rushing about. I've got that picnic rug now, and I lie on it under a tree, watching the cricket match at the other end of the grass. What was it Alisdair used to say? *'Keep the team together!'*

The sun shines. Wanly, for June. I roll myself up in the rug, shivery with misery.

Max doesn't try to talk. And I can't.

Is this whole thing really about him?

Or—about me?

Max

MONDAY

Arrive very late. Rush through crowded waiting area to sanctuary of my room.

Inside, pause to run my eye down the list. Hoping most of these will be minor ailments and worried well. Let nobody present with potentially serious symptoms, the kind they'll be upset about. Or worse, with something that's all tangled up in a relationship problem. The surgery is not a confessional: and I am a human being, a worn-out cynic with my own worries.

Can't concentrate: sit breathing slowly, trying to blank it all out. The questions: was my ironic response, *Will I take the Discovery then, seeing I'm to do the school run today?* lost on Jen? As she shoved the bairns, their bags and lunches, their outdoor clothing and her garbled information on their social diaries, into my arms?

Between patients, some images slide themselves into my consciousness: repeatedly, I dismiss them. Zoë's tears: understandable. Alice, totally out of character, clinging tight as a limpet as we enter the breakfast club. The woman in charge, kind but unknown to Ally.

Thank goodness she suggested I hung about. Alice and I sharing a bowl of porridge.

A fine explanation of her own behaviour Jen gave, blaming their principal investigator or whatever's his official title. Richard Woods. *He's got me pretty much leading the group of us who're slogging along with the extra experiments required by peer reviewers before we can publish in Nature.*

Future looks bleak. Is it psychological breakdown? Mam'll have to wait. I'll not ring today. Why she's here I don't know. Or want to know.

Did Jen realise my shock when she took off yesterday, leaving no indication where she'd gone? Leaving me the car with the kiddie seats in it as a silent hint that I take charge of the children?

S'pose it hurt ... if she'd stopped at saying that ... instead of adding *holy hypocrite.*

Jenny

SAME DAY

Another cool, grey, morning. Where's summer?

Glad to let Max do the school run, leaving Alice at the breakfast club with some money to pay her teacher, because her mummy is too busy. He believes my mind is so much on preparing our submission to *Nature* that I'm impossible to live with. He said it, not me.

As I arrive, Rich pops his head out of his office, 'Ah Jenny,' he looks at the clock, 'early start, busy? We need a meeting. Tomorrow—maybe after lunch?'

I nod, 'I'll come to you around when?'

'Two-thirty do you?'

He withdraws his head, and closes his door.

Having given him a good impression by walking in at eight (and goodness, what's made him arrive so early?) I hear him in his office, jabbering on the phone. What does he want? We've done really well for him this year. Our work, his kudos.

Maybe a nice opportunity to discuss progress?

I schedule a catch-up meeting with Felicia. So I can update him on my mentoring. Admit I'm actually enjoying it. We talk through whether she'd be ready to proceed to a D. Phil. in a year's time.

'Graduate studies are quite a learning curve to begin with, aren't they? But I've worked out about where to follow my own initiatives ... And using the new electronic stuff in the library ... Rapt about Medline,' she smiles.

Rapt about a bibliographic database of life sciences and biomedical information? We laugh. As we finish, I remember to ask about her rowing.

'Had to give it up: no time to train. Life's a bit too full-on back home.'

'Yes, research does eat away at the social life—and the sports life. At least keep up some exercise, and don't abandon your friends?'

She takes a breath, about to speak, then turns away, 'Okay, thanks for all the advice. I'll see how my results are coming along at the end of the academic year then?'

'Yes. I—when stuff doesn't work, I try to remind myself that even experienced scientists can still have problems with their experiments. You're doing really well.' Felicia disappears to find some articles in the Radcliffe Science Library.

Living with Uncertainty. That's me right now. Putting on the confidence act. Even to myself. Steadied myself a bit since yesterday ... Though I can't stop seeing that image: Max in a drugged stupor on our sofa ... and I left the girls with him ... at least he dragged himself awake and looked after them ... I threw that book into my bag, before I left home. I'd better try to read it. What can Alisdair say that Max admires?

Lunchtime, in the deserted lab office, I unwrap my sandwich, and open the book. If any of my colleagues do catch a glimpse, I'll say I'm reminding myself why taking religion seriously can damage your critical faculties.

That's pretty much true.

The motivation for writing about something which your peer

group spends its life avoiding must be to flag up its approach and take precautions. I glance down the contents page. A chapter suggesting readers might try accepting uncertainty, welcoming it, treating it as a challenge, or an opportunity. *We can't make an omelette without breaking eggs: has your quest for certainty become a lock and key on the doors of learning? Life is a journey, and on the journey, as we travel, shouldn't we learn?* Interesting he's asking this.

'Applying the wisdom we gain from experience is what moving forward is all about.'

Moving forward? Do First Truly people move?

'There you are! Jenny, I was looking for you—' It's Leila. Startled, I grab at a journal lying by my desk, and shove the book between the pages. Wave it at Leila. 'Ah! It's you that nicked the lab copy of *Nature*!'

'Sorry. Did you want it?' Convenient it was there. She didn't see, did she?

'No need. You're obviously busy.'

'Actually you can have it in a minute,' I say, 'I'd better go. I'm—off to collect some more blood samples from the hospital after this.'

Not quite a lie. I'll collect the samples, but first ... A thought is forming: if anyone understands Max, and what's going on, it'll be David. I'll go via St Hildegard's. Fee's in London now, isn't she? To *see the girls*. I think, sourly, of Erin.

Then smile at Leila, 'Oh, and did I say, thank you for a lovely party. Great food, and the music...'

She rolls her eyes, 'Tim's idea: he collects old singles, and insisted we must play them! Max told me he was born in Cyprus?'

'Mmm: his dad was in the RAF. So that music was vinyl? Anyhow, must rush,' I can't discuss Saturday evening, though what happened afterwards wasn't their fault. I slide the book free without Leila seeing, '... do have the journal.'

*

I arrive at St Hildie's through a side gate. Cycling towards the main building, passing the wheelie-bin area, I remember how at the pancake race someone tossed their pancake spectacularly and it landed atop one of the bins. Almost grin: but a woman wearing denims and an overall appears from a doorway, carrying a mop, and one of those plastic hold-everything trays with a handle, stuffed full of cleaning materials. It's Etta.

Can't smile and chat, all happy: I zoom back down the drive to the church. Hoping she didn't notice. I lean the bike on the church wall, shove open the door (very heavy, and it creaks), and step inside. The door scrapes slowly along the stone floor, taking its time, finally closing with a bump and a click. I'm now enclosed in incense-scented darkness. How does it feel? When we came for the carol service, it was magical: hundreds of candles, and masses of excited people. Today, it's 'silent retreat.'

No footfalls, nobody. The stillness tries to absorb me. My innards contract. What could Fee find here? First Truly people hate and fear darkness like it has power and personality. At the service, Max more than hinted that it was her who told Alisdair to get realistic about women, marriage, and submission. So how come she finds help here?

My eyes begin to adapt. The sun comes out, shining on the stained glass, and casts coloured patterns on the black and white tiled path that leads up the main church. There's a statue of Mary, with a rack, three rather stubby candles burning in it. I can feel her blue painted eyes staring. How ridiculous.

Her candles gutter in the draught.

The draught? I didn't leave the door open. There's someone down there! In the open doorway, occluding the light.

David.

'Hiya—someone in here?' He stops, peering into the darkness. 'Hey, Jenny? Is that you?'

'You gave me a fright!'

'Were you looking for me?'

'I thought you might—'

'C'mon outside: this place never lets in enough sun. Hey, I hear Max made a bit of a splash at First Truly.'

David's cut to the chase. He holds the door open, and steps aside for me, replacing a pair of shades as we exit his church and strike out into the sunshine, side by side. The sun is surprisingly warm, after the cold grey morning.

How do I begin? 'I felt for Fee. She adores Max. How could he do that to her?'

David takes a long breath. I almost hear his brain ticking, searching for the answer. 'Yes—' he says, slowly. 'But, Aunt Fiona is a toughie: and her adoration—' He stops, and re-starts, 'Jenny, let's talk, talking often helps. The stone Max threw must be causing some concentric circles in that pond.'

'And ours.'

I need to be careful: I'm not up for David scrabbling his way into my mind, like some counsellor. 'Fee said she was here on silent retreat: we met in the car park, casually. She hadn't mentioned visiting.'

'That bothers you?'

'Well no, she can do what she likes. Seemed out of character, though.'

'In what way?' David leans towards me, hands in his pockets.

'Don't get me wrong, but, Hildie's isn't First Truly. It's kind of monastic. I mean, Daze's always up for anything Goth. But not Fee.'

A clock dongs once, the quarter hour. Three fifteen. A beat passes. David slows, almost stops walking. He grins, 'I enjoyed working with Daze. Jen, you haven't seen the Labyrinth, have you?'

'I've had descriptions. Alice calls it a laby-*rinse*.'

David laughs. 'Daze was inspired. Come and see.' His insistence includes a jerk of the head towards the main buildings, and touching my back, his arm around me for a second to turn me the way he wants me to go. Down a path through the shrubbery, across an open expanse of lawn, dotted with guests, to the modern extension, fronted by a terrace with benches.

'I wanted to talk about Max.'

David takes a step back, and gives me a look. It penetrates. He says, 'I'm happy to,' and does the busier-than-you thing, glancing at his wrist where he wears a nice, surfer's-waterproof-type watch,

'There's someone I have to see—give me ten? Then I'm all yours.'

A woman a bit older than me, elegantly built, casually dressed, comes walking towards us. Evidently not the person he has to see, but David greets her warmly, and draws me towards her, 'The artist's sister, come to see our labyrinth. Jenny, this is Midge.'

David's deftly caught one of the obedient Community to dutifully entertain the visitor. I shake the proffered hand. Reluctantly, seeing I didn't come here to be sociable.

'Jenny takes wonderful photos,' he smiles at Midge. 'I'll leave you together.' He turns and almost jogs away towards the retreat house.

'So Jenny, have you come far?' She leads off more slowly in the direction David went.

'I live here. I work in the University.'

'Ah—not another artist then?'

'No—no, biology. You?'

'Horticulture: I'm helping restore the walled garden. Your sister's inspirational. Daisy took our rather blurred vision of a labyrinth and ran with it. Here we are.'

This is unfair! Immediately, standing in the doorway, I'm conscious of amazing colours, as well as a scent of paint, and newness. The blue mosaic labyrinth makes me gasp: it curls around the floor, large enough to almost cover it. Its edges are rough cream-coloured tiles, and what remains of the floor between it and the walls is huge smooth tiles, in a warm, glowing orangey pink. The centre is shaped like a six-petalled rose. The only two unglazed walls are decorated with appliqué hangings, or curtains, in shimmering abstract designs which have the same colours as the floor and labyrinth tiles.

Did Daze design and make this amazing, beautiful decor? Did making Alice's wings inspire her?

Midge, the community woman, explains, 'Daisy suggested she'd use tiles with a rough surface to distinguish the main path from the edges … You see, we walk with our shoes off. If you can't see with your eyes, you can feel through your feet.'

'Oh—yes. I see.'

She smiles. 'So: would you prefer to walk it on your own?'

I hadn't thought of walking it. I wish she'd go away. Maybe then I could think straight.

Max

THE SURGERY, MEANWHILE

A knock on my door, and here's Steffie, with a temporary resident's form she plonks on my desk. 'Sorry, your afternoon list had a cancellation, so we slotted this one in ... She's outside, having a smoke. D'you want me to send her through?'

I give the form a cursory glance: then reread the name properly. Swallow down some unsuitable remark, and smile brightly, 'That's okay, I'll fetch her.'

I head through the waiting room, and out into the warm, bright afternoon. Beside the rose bed, Daze is standing on one booted foot, her other leg bent and her other foot pressed against the wall. A bit like a heron in a lake. Wearing her usual black bat-like clothes, and wreathed in nicotine. The seductive stench of it drifts over as she exhales.

'Daisy Potter?' I call formally, as if from the waiting room. She turns, inhaling another deep lungful of destruction.

And exhales 'Max', along with the smoke. Drops the ciggie and grinds it into the concrete. 'An' I am entitled to be a temp res aren't I, seeing as I'm livin' on a boat?'

'Oh I think so, yes. What's up Daze?' Here's hoping the pattern of nice routine consultations won't be broken by this one.

'A lot is what.'

'Don't tell me now: wait till we're inside?'

As we enter my room, the sun lazily casts a bright rectangle across my desk. 'For starters,' Daze begins, 'can you untangle the bumf Jenny gave me on the Persephone genetics?'

I close the door. She's had that information since before Christmas:

why wait six months before asking? 'There's something you don't understand? Did you bring the documents along?'

She's brought them in an army-surplus canvas map-case. A few questions and I realise she understands them perfectly well. But she's edgy as a nervous cat. 'Let me see your hands, Daze?'

I hold them loosely, palms up. Cold, and damp. 'These feel like frogs. There's something else on your mind.'

'Yeah.'

'You begin: I'll try to help.'

'Thought of you 'cos who else—like you were fucking kind about Persephone, an' you saw her. It's about your cousin, David? An'—Etta—?'

On cue, the fire alarm shrieks into urgent, blasting, action. Daze's hands fly to cover her ears. I can just hear her saying, 'Fucking sirens are all we need.'

Chimes with my own thoughts. Don't need Daze today, with a problem which might affect my personal life.

I rise to my feet, and cross the room, acting cool as if fire alarms happen every day. 'Don't go, I'll see if it's a real one.' I poke my head out of the door. People have leapt from their chairs, dropped magazines, grabbed their children. In the centre of the waiting room, Steffie stands making *calm down* movements with her arms, 'Everyone stay calm. The engineers are here testing the system.'

'Bloody system,' complains an old man wearing a hearing aid.

There's a gap in the noise. Eliot comes running down the stairs. 'Nothing doing?'

'Apparently they're testing the system.'

'Great. I just sent mine to the loo to produce a sample,' he grins.

The old man shakes his head. 'Seems even the people who work here got took by surprise.'

The senior receptionist appears, 'So sorry we didn't warn you—' she beams. Her last words are drowned out. The district nurse pops her head out of the treatment room, signalling in the old man with a wave of her arm.

I return to Daze. 'No need for panic.'

'God, you might've warned me,' she says.

'Testing the system.'

'Great.' A few more blasts, and the siren falls silent.

'Mm. So, where were we? David and Etta? Spill, and I'll listen.' The siren's given me time to recall how kind she was just after Dad died. And Jenny's remark: *'Daze told me how concerned she is about you.'*

Hugging herself, Daze walks about the room, describing how, hiding in a bush, she overheard Etta telling David a heart-rending story of abuse.

'I've been looking for Mum *for like my whole life.* If bloody *Etta's* my *mother:* you see, Max, don't you? She's a right pain, she's a user, and she was giving me the creeps, turning up, hanging out, wanting to be with me. Couldn't she have like *told me?* Straight out? Is that like normal?'

Daze is entitled to horror and panic. If true, it's an extraordinary story. Enough to freak anyone. Calm and compassion is necessary. 'If Etta has a good reason to believe she's found her daughter, and that's you, I imagine she's as scared as you are.'

'She's the mother. S'up to her.' Daze bites her thumb.

I hunt for inspiration. Daze's supposition—that Etta must lead the way because she's the mother—is a cop-out. As perhaps is my chosen response, 'What do you want to happen, Daze?'

She runs her fingers through her hair. 'I don't bloody know. She walked away, didn't she, at Glastonbury?'

'Suppose you were able to ask her about Glastonbury?'

'I don't want to even see her!'

'Could you ask your father?'

'Dad let her go. Proves he's useless.'

(Will I *let* Jenny *go?*)

We discuss ways Daze might check Etta's story. She points out the genetic data about Persephone. She finds what knowledge she has of her mother's family convincing, though horrifying. 'Val said Roma: so even if not, probably travellers? Would there be documents? Liar: calls herself Etta, hides her, like, real name … clever, she thinks herself.'

'Daze, you can't know why she left until you ask. Though she may not want to tell you everything. She's been sussing you out: d'you think she may've learned to trust you, a bit?' Biting at her thumbnail, Daze regards me. With distrust. 'Remember when we came to discuss the Scottish dancing at the Fun Day? My father died a few days before?' She nods. 'You gave me a big hug, and offered hospitality, and were very kind. You knew exactly what was needed.'

'Yeah.' Daze grins, half-looking at me. 'But, you're not Etta. An' we haven't an agenda.'

'True. But you have the skills Etta may not have?' She studies the carpet. 'Otherwise, it's asking your father.'

She shrugs. 'Looks like he's as bad as she is.'

'You'll only know if you try. Remember her disappearance would have affected him as well. Think how he might've felt. Expect he may be reluctant to look at his own past.'

'Maybe.' She pauses, then looks brighter. 'There was no blood test, none she had, when the baby was investigated, so we don't know for certain she's the shit gene carrier do we?'

'You and Shane have the same translocated gene: and your mothers are sisters.'

'So? They both had sex with Jack.'

'Daze,' I say gently, 'Try talking to your father.'

'Well, I was looking for her, an' she's found me. Great,' she sidesteps with a non-sequitur.

'You aren't saying that as if it is.'

Daze shakes her head, assuming naivety on my part. 'You don't get it, do you? Think.' She stands and makes for the door, opens it, turns back. 'My portrait, me and my mother? Juli*etta*? *Symes*? ' She walks through and away, leaving me a thousand thoughts.

Her rejection of Etta has hooked my grief about Dad: I'm almost tearful. Her presence had already hooked the agonizing screw-up in my marriage. Don't think about it.

Think about Daze. Etta, *our cleaner*, inspired that shocking crucifixion she was working on, the first time I met Jenny's family? A child, nailed to a cross which was, quite obviously, a woman ... Daze was seventeen ... the pain these two must have is unimaginable. No surprise some people are gunning for the social institution of the family.

Ironic, patients come here thinking the GP is a fount of wisdom—while his wife thinks he's a plodding, embarrassing idiot.

Not so idiotic: used to getting a grip, presenting a cool and caring front ... almost but not quite ruined this time by Daze's visit.

Of course, I shan't breathe a word to Jenny.

Jenny

ST HILDEGARD'S, SAME AFTERNOON

'Coffee up.' David depresses the plunger. 'With or without?' He holds up the milk carton: it's totally skimmed.

'With,' I say.

The kitchen's svelte, organised, and domestic, with a Raeburn and smart appliances. But as we walked through to his flat in the older part of the retreat house, I had a surprise: a bright yellow surfboard mounted, horizontally, on the passage wall. He didn't ditch that along with the lifestyle.

'Max says you're more like brothers than cousins.'

David hands me my coffee in a mug with bluebells on, and pulls out a chair for me. 'Shall we sit?'

I sit. David hitches his fine behind on the tabletop, and adjusts his neat trouser leg to accommodate the pose. He swings his leg. 'Tell me a bit about your impressions of the family: you obviously didn't expect Fee would come on retreat?'

'No.' I study the tabletop. Pine remains almost fashionable, and has knots and interesting lines. 'They're very different. To mine. Though Fee was very welcoming—you know how she is. Almost too many cakes?' David smiles, and the smile becomes a nice laugh.

'And now: or maybe, fill me in about that first visit?'

Seduction: I know I shall spill all. He's close enough to've been inside the circle, and then he's been treated like an outsider. 'First, can I explain how I came to be there? Max and I—actually no, it's down to Daze, really. How ironic. If she'd not wanted to do a clever art installation, and produced a dysmorphic child, I wouldn't ever have seen the Manse...'

The whole thing unwinds like string from a ball, everything that took place in the few weeks after my finals exams in Cambridge. Being Daze's birth partner; witnessing her pushing out the horrific, premature baby; Max being the on-call paediatrician; me being the over-curious, embryonic geneticist. 'Embryonic?' asks David.

'Oh, I was just, well hardly, qualified? I'd worked with embryos, in an undergraduate way. And with Dad being a fertility doctor, I— possibly read up more about chromosomal abnormalities than I needed to, doing my degree course? I was well up for finding out what caused the strange phenotype, and I knew Max had been interested, earlier, in possibly doing similar research. We wanted to work together.'

'Right. And—how did this lead to the Manse?'

As I tell the story of the lost cultures, of the excuses and the explanations from Rich, and from Wil, I try to make David understand how I must've pushed aside what I should've thought. That I really knew that something underhand had taken place. Wil wasn't someone who'd happily clear up other people's messes, unless infection might result. Okay, my insistence on sailing so close to the wind probably meant that someone had to stop me. But, why not simply take me aside? And talk? David's quiet listening draws all my suspicions out of me. The plot I've constructed, with Max as colluder and seducer.

'They produced no evidence. I knew Professor Nicholson had warned Max about conflicts of interest. Then Max was there, outside the lab, that evening—Max—whisking me off for a meal to make me forget ... We nearly—we got back together, and he invited me to meet his family. I mean, they lived in Northumberland. How convenient. Just a shortish train journey further north was Roslin, where I was going, anyway, for an interview.'

'Mmmm: it all fitted, didn't it?' David's one of those men who oozes everything a girl could want and will always be unavailable. If not, that gentle voice would've sounded too patronising for me to stay a moment longer.

'The visit was from hell. I think you pretty much know how it panned out. How Colin attacked Rachel. How we found her. How Alisdair admitted he was at fault—all that teaching about women's submission. Fee was amazingly supportive of me. But now, the memorial service's hardly over, and Fee's at St Hildie's, yet ignores us. If she's angry about the eulogy, she needs to believe I didn't put Max up to it. I was gutted. On her behalf.'

He's silent.

'Okay, I was also gutted for myself. You're back from Oz. You're family ... Does Max share with you? He doesn't open up to me.' David's wrap-around shades are on the top of his head: coolly, he takes them off and lays them on the table. 'Talk to me! You are so laid-back annoying!' I spring up, coffee spills from my bluebell mug. 'Max won't talk to me. Fee won't talk to me. What about you?'

He regards my het-up ranting face through his gold-rimmed specs. 'If it helps, I think Max does find putting his own stuff out there to other people hard. We were all raised to notice other people's needs, it becomes a habit. But, I wonder if—Uncle Alisdair's last book, did you take a look at that yet? I've a copy, Max brought it back for me. He must have one?'

'I gave it a glance.'

'If you could give it another ... you might find it quite revealing. Quite helpful? And another thing: people who come here, they do it to step off the daily grind and slow down.'

'Fee should've done that long ago. He exploited her.'

He furrows his brow, 'Ever thought life is a bit like a journey?'

'Never. What's that to do with this?'

'Well, some people do. And for a journey, we all need a map. You might think about pilgrimage. Going on a journey to discover the map for your life.'

'That's back to front. You use a map for the journey, you don't take the journey to find the map.' Confident I've nailed him.

'Is it?'

'Unless you're talking about trailblazing.'

David smiles, 'Touché. So maybe, a voyage of discovery? Got some holiday due? Take your bike? With Alice on the back? Just, go—somewhere.'

'Impossible. I'm leading a team, we're revising our presentation to submit to a journal that's probably the most prestigious in our field.'

'Oh, well.' He raises his eyebrows, 'Not the time to slow down and notice things. Though a map can always help you find the way. If you want to, later on?'

Permission offered to walk away from my success, my ambitions, and my status. Actually, the idea's so tempting I must give it the brush-off. 'Get real. Even without the submission to *Nature*, I've still got a responsible job, a raft of research questions, and a student to supervise. And Alice is in school.'

'I met Alice and Max, going into school today. Bright kid, seemed to be in touch with mum being rather busy right now ... Anyhow,' he holds up his hands like it's not his fault he mentioned total irresponsibility and drop-out, 'that's a suggestion. Up the river—or the canal—or along the Ridgeway?'

'Now I know you're joking.' How disturbing: he saw Ally and Max. Does he mean to imply he read our situation, and sees more than I'm telling him?

'No. You might discover you and Max are travelling the same road. If you found a map to follow. Rather than staying put and trying to draw your own.'

'Are you telling me how to live my life? Did I come here to hear this?'

'Probably.'

'Probably which?'

'Probably both. Or the one you least want to listen to. Jenny, another thought. Try listening to yourself a bit. What you are saying, to Max?' He pauses, then does the watch thing again, 'I've got to go: there's a group about to arrive, a retreat on meditation—. Take some photos, real art ones—if you go.'

I sling my bag onto my shoulder, grab my coffee mug, rinse it, and dump it on the draining board. 'I'm sorry if I wasted you time.'

'Time's only wasted if you think it was. I'll see you out.'

'I can find my way.'

'The door has a funny lock. I'll undo it for you.'

David takes me out of the building another way. We emerge through a white painted lobby and a side door. Guarded by the wheelie bins. 'Thought you'd prefer to slip away without passing the labyrinth again. Someone may be walking it.'

Actually, I wanted another look at it. And to get a photo. Was David being ironic? Was he having a go?

He does see into me. Painfully clearly.

'About Fee. Underneath the pastor's-wife surface there's more ambiguity than you'd expect.'

'That interests me.'

'It's all in that book. About uncertainty.'

'It is?'

'I have to go!' He turns, waving.

At least he listened. It was like a mirror: my whole motivation for starting to research the causes of Daze's deformed baby was very mixed. Effectively, I am totally responsible.

Somehow, I pull myself back to the present moment: I'm supposed to be collecting some samples the hospital have for us.

Daze

TUESDAY LUNCHTIME

Daze's destination is Parks Road, hoping to find some ideas in that goldmine of weird Victorian attitudes, the Pitt Rivers Museum. Ever since moving to Oxford, she's been fascinated by its architecture, and determined to pay another visit. A suitable place to distract her from obsessing about her betrayer, Etta the child-dumper.

She stops to take a few shots of the museum building. There in her lens is Jenny Four-Eyes. Sat on the grass. Alone. Doing nothing? Does Jen ever do nothing?

Daze crosses the grass, flings herself down alongside. 'Look who it is. S'pose it's lunch time, and they've let you workers out?'

Jenny startles. 'Mind out!'

Daze shifts herself: 'So sorry: careful where you put down your specs next time!'

'Yes, lunch: hummus sandwich. Tomato.' Which Jen now pulls from her bag, and unwraps. Replaces her glasses on her nose. Meanwhile the bag topples over and deposits several balled-up damp tissues and a paperback book on the grass. Jenny shoves it all back, hiding the book's author and title from view. 'What are you doing?'

'Looking at the museum. How's my nieces?'

'Lovely as ever. Bundles of joy.'

Daze hears a drop of cynicism, and probes. 'No more angel stuff?'

'Wrong time of year.'

Daze considers the tissues. Had Four-Eyes been crying? Interesting. 'They loved the Fun Day didn't they?' she muses. Then, 'Max?'

'Mm.' Jenny mm's through her sandwich. Then, so-obviously perking up, changes the subject. 'Where've *you* been?'

'Working for Max's cousin. You knew that. Cool or what?'

'Yeah. I saw your work. I was amazed.'

'No need for the sarcasm.'

'It wasn't. I was amazed. I was like, that's incredible. Did you—do all of it? The hangings, as well as the floor?'

'It's a total experience, isn't it?' Daze feels her mouth and eyes smiling with spontaneous pleasure. If tinged with triumphal ripples of *told you so*, seeing Jen's always been the stepsister you have to beat. 'Of course, the idea's grown from Alice's wings. I wanted to use that fabric again, exploit its ethereal possibilities.'

'Un-Goth.'

'Goths aren't all about darkness. You'd be wrong there.'

'So, David's got his labyrinth: what's he like to work for?'

'Not your type.'

'Not yours surely?'

'Sporty, spiritual, and annoying.' Daze, hoping to score further over Jenny, introduces an ambiguous story. 'I like it that he hung out with the monks.'

'Monks?'

Grinning, Daze says, 'Dave's born-again experience: monks who cared for AIDs patients at weekends, and were super-compassionate. It impressed him.'

'That's why he went back to the faith of his fathers?'

'They were Buddhists.'

'Oh. More your kind of thing then. You staying in touch? With David?'

'You're curious about him, aren't you? Listen, you, you and Max, going on holiday somewhere soon?' Daze pulls out her ciggies. Offers one to Jenny, mainly to provoke. Jenny waves them away. 'You know I gave up. And made Max.'

'Always the cell scientist.' Daze lights up. Inhales. Blows smoke through her nose. Crosses her feet and pretends to admire their small neatness in her new black ballet-style shoes. Her mind reverts to Etta: really her mother, Julietta? If so, what a liar. Jewels? Judas more like.

'Mum says the house is empty: are you going down?'

Daze hauls her mind back, what were they talking about? 'Say again?'

'Sennen,' says Jenny. 'We're there in a couple of weeks. July?'

Daze leans back on her elbow, watching a line of tourists entering the museum. 'Ants,' she says, nodding at the line, 'don't you think? You going to Sennen? All of you?'

'Seeing neither of us booked anything else.' Jenny fishes around in that huge bag of hers, and extracts a bottle of water. She twists the top and drinks, then takes out an apple, polishes it on her shirt. Tosses it hand to hand a few times.

Obviously acting mysterious. Wickedly grinning, Daze says, 'We might be there together.'

'God,' Jenny laughs.

'Might be fun, retro, both of us? Re-live the old days?'

Jenny looks dubious. 'Possibly.' She tosses the apple up and catches it.

'Can I have that, the apple, if you don't want it?'

'I may do, later.'

'Memory test: what d'you remember: first thought, first day you came to Cornwall?

'Me, when we moved to live. Dark, cold, musty cottage. Mum pulling Harriet into her bed. Me squeezing myself in with them. You?'

'Coming to have tea in your house. Dad with a spanner, looking under the sink, and your mum making me a toasted sandwich. The TV was on. We didn't have one.'

'What was it? On TV?' Jenny says, and bites into the apple. Daze wonders if she would have, if she hadn't asked to have it.

'Magic Roundabout. You sat so I couldn't see,' says Daze.

'I'd've moved a chair, to be closer. I couldn't see unless I was really close ...'

'I moved it back. We shoved it about till they came and got cross.'

'You had two of us to cope with.'

'Harriet was a push-over.'

'Really?'

'I ate the stuff she didn't like off her plate: your mum didn't see. There was a sea mist, remember? We got stuck at your cold damp-smelling cottage, and Dad made a tent out of blankets in the living room.'

'And then?'

'They got in your mum's bed, the springs creaked.' Daze grins, as Jenny blushes. 'Later they married and we all lived together in a little shoe house. I've a photo somewhere: you, me, and Hat, in sleeping bags on the floor.'

'We were innocent. I didn't think about Mum and your dad that time. I did later. I almost miss those sea mists that wrap you up like a blanket: going to school in a mist, couldn't see our hands.'

'Mist wet on our faces. Picking blackberries on our way to the beach. Being surfers before the lah-di-dah people discovered Sennen.'

'Yep.'

'My board's still there, in the attic. How about yours?'

'I'll look. At least no Mum. When we go, she always suggests stuff. You know, play the granny role: *Why don't I babysit and you two go into Penzance and have a meal ... better, go over to Exeter for a couple of nights in a decent hotel and I'll field the kiddywinks.*'

'I wouldn't know.'

'Sorry.'

'What for?' Daze says, though they both know. Daze struggles to her feet, pretending she doesn't care or feel any envy that Jenny has kids. 'Yeah, well, no probs, I have to go anyhow. D'you know if they allow photography in the Pitt Rivers?'

Jenny shoves stuff into her bag, the water bottle, the sandwich paper, the apple core. 'Daze, I have to tell you something you won't like. Then, you can kill me.'

'What? Family stuff?'

'No. About the egg donation. There's been some research—'

Daze holds up her hand. 'Stop right there. I'm cool.'

'You haven't heard what I'm going to say.'

'I don't need to. I'm into something else.'

'But you wanted a baby: we talked about it, you came over to the lab, you gave the impression this is why you came here, it's all to do with—'

'Forget it, okay?'

'No, I've put time into this: I got near enough to egg donation I was looking at the process, and working out when I could do it, and ... everything ... You can't fling away my taking you seriously.'

Daze, stung as if by wasps, throws her pain about Etta back on Jenny. 'I'm bloody not! I'm trying to tell *you* something. I'm like not interested! So you can take your research and shove it up—'

'No. Daze, I only wanted—' Jenny cuts in, sounding like her mum Caroline. Daze knows how Jenny looks when she's trying not to cry.

Whatever the details, she doesn't want to hear. She wheels round and starts walking across the neat grass, set all over with groups of picnicking museum visitors, towards the building. Then stops to throw her parting shot, "Bye, Four-Eyes. By the way, Sennen's my house, ultimately. Dad's house.'

Jenny yells, 'Did you come here to make trouble?'

Daze feels the truth of this. And the root of the problem, 'What do you know about me?'

She's perceived that, like her, Jenny is really unhappy about something else. Otherwise, why chat hysterically about when we were kids?

Suddenly her phone rings with the insistence of an arriving text message. She grabs it, and turns it off.

If David's asking for the precise address, well, if she doesn't know he's called, how can she answer his question? And if he doesn't know where to go, maybe he won't go at all. 'Cos actually, having suggested he comes down sometime, she's not so sure: he might try to get her and Etta together. To suggest forgiveness is the way to go.

Max

TUESDAY EVENING

After teaching a session at the medical school, I'm crossing the car park, and my cell phone rings. The caller's a haranguing, frantic female. 'I had to find your surgery number and convince the receptionist, who was locking up, that I was genuinely searching for someone, a parent, to fetch your daughter. She gave me this—listen, Alice is very sensible, but I still had to be Sherlock Holmes.'

Alice's voice joins in, from far away: 'Daddy?' I reach my car, as the phone is passed to her. 'Daddy? Are you coming to get me?'

'Yes, I'm on my way.'

'We had spaghetti. They have to go to bed now.'

'Yes. Can you give the phone back so I know where you are?'

Driving to the address in Farndon Road, I recall that Jen had mentioned they both had a play date after school. But I wasn't asked to collect them, was I?

As I push the bell at the house, I look down from the front steps and can see Alice is in the basement kitchen, playing with two ginger kittens. Feet scurry, and her friend, wearing pyjamas, opens the door, Alice leaps out into my embrace, and behind the little girls appears a pregnant woman with wild ginger hair. 'Very, very, sorry,' I say. 'I was unaware Jenny hadn't picked her up. I don't seem to be able to get her on the phone at the moment.'

'What a relief! All's well that ends well,' says the gingery woman, 'here's her reading book and jersey.'

'And my lunch box! Daddy, we have to find Zo-zo.'

'What's her friend's name?'

'Something like—' But Alice is vague, turning round and round, forehead furrowed in thought, but not really knowing. Ginger hair is trying to say goodbye and close the door, but then she relents, goes down the hall calling to some unseen child about violin practice, and returns with a list on the back of a flyer about an art exhibition. 'I've scribbled a few suggestions for you.' Evidently she knows more than I do who Zoë's friends might be. I put out my hand for the list: she hangs onto it a moment, studying me, so I'm forced to accept what a useless incompetent family we appear. Jenny's doing!

Alice tries to read the list, written in a large, rounded, posh-school, hand. Ginger hair adds, expression changing slightly, 'Don't I know you? Aren't you the—gosh it was you—we went to your surgery before, well, before we moved. I hadn't connected you and Jenny!'

Have I ever seen this woman before?

'Frankie Southern: you confirmed my pregnancy and sent me for a scan. That was Imogen—Alice's friend?' She grins, pleased to have identified me, even if I have no idea about her. 'Actually, I suppose you'd better come in and use our phone.'

Alice stays close by, but Frankie corrals her daughter, guiding her upstairs, talking teeth cleaning, and spellings. The sound of a stringed instrument being tortured with a bow comes from the back of the house, as I use the hall phone, weary, sweating with apprehension, and ready to pile on the apologies. What if none of these families have Zoë? What if Zoë's friend's mummy belongs to a quite different circle of Jenny's acquaintances?

On the third try, we're after someone called *Lucia Lopez (Maths Institute)*, and Frankie's voice comes over the banisters, 'Imogen thinks it was Lucy's mummy if that helps!' just as a heavily accented voice says 'Hello?' down the phone.

I explain the whole thing as a mix-up, and discover that Zoë's happily listening to a bedtime story, in a block of overseas graduate flats.

When we get there, pounding up several flights of concrete steps, me ready to again apologise for abusing hospitality, Lucy's mum hasn't seemed to've worried at all. 'Jenny is late, I give them something to eat. They are very good, I think? Zoë is very sleepy so I read to them.'

'Yes, she is good, and she loves a story. I'm so sorry about this. Jenny's obviously had a long day and, well, we got mixed up about collecting. Thank you. Can you say thank you for your nice tea, Zo-zo?'

The flat is very small for a family, the furniture basic, supplemented with bright rugs, and large numbers of books and files. The living room leads onto a balcony, where I spot Lucy's dad, smoking, and typing on a laptop. He turns and waves. I do know him: our practice run a weekly surgery at his college. Last time I saw him, didn't I suggest he cut down the cigarettes? Lucy, or Lucia, gives Zoë a big hug as they part. Her mum offers us all sweets from a bowl. I am enormously relieved by this family: time is not a problem for them.

We start down the stairs. I notice now that Zoë is wearing a necklace of red beads. Are these hers or should I give them back? Alice says, 'I don't know,' and Zoë, grasping them, insists, 'They're mine!'

I call Jenny's phone. She doesn't answer. We're passing the science area on our way home, so I call again, from outside her department.

This time, she picks up. 'I have had to rescue our children's friends from keeping them overnight,' I say. 'It was humiliating for me to admit you had forgotten them. I had to fudge up excuses for you.'

It is more than that: it's painful to discover that she's fled to her small, cool, scientific world, when my personal resources are so low.

Jenny

EARLIER THE SAME AFTERNOON

'Ah, Jenny,' Rich says, walking into the lab. He's been gone all afternoon: hours. Why? I was here promptly at two-thirty. And after those two words, as I smile and look ready and expectant, he asks me to wait, and shuts himself in his office.

A crisis in another part of the department?

A couple of postgrads had their heads together earlier, and dropped their voices as I passed. They kind of looked like their conversation might be about me. A few others of the team have given me looks: if they think he favours me, they're probably wrong.

Though would be nice to think he does.

I return to my desk, and continue fiddling with things I can't get on with till I have proper time. It's amazing Daze's abandoned the baby idea: a relief she's not mad that I'll not donate. For God's sake, why did I ever think I should give her my precious ova? She even talked as if my offer came without personal cost. Shattering when you realise how someone can shrug off stuff you thought was important to both of you.

Maybe David was a bit right about some things? Maybe now I can sort out priorities. Especially if Rich is going to tell me about the funding. No reason to worry what this chat's about. I'll read Alisdair's book, and when we're away I'll make sure I listen to Max, and … Things will sort out.

David's right about Fee.

For a guy, he's quite tuned in to feelings.

He didn't have a go at me ...

I glance at the clock. Nearly five-fifteen? Now I remember—going cold—that I must collect my children from their friends by six. Come on, Rich!

Burble, burble from his office: he's on the phone. Max did the school run again: I'm on my bike, we'll have to walk home, Zoë in the baby seat and Alice ... Shall I leave the bike and we'll catch a bus?

'Jenny!' The door opens, and Rich stands just inside, calling me across the lab. I smile.

He doesn't.

'Sit,' he says, indicating the visitor's chair, and going around behind his desk.

He sits, swivelling the chair to consult his computer screen. He looks down on me in the low, minimalist, armchair. He tents his fingers. 'Well, Jenny. How is the mentoring going?'

I try another smile. 'Felicia's doing well now.'

'Yes? Though she should hardly need serious mentoring, of course.'

'Well she was rather trying at first.' I risk humour. 'But now, well, she's really trying. To do her best work, instead of trying my patience.' Grin. From me.

Not from him. His eyebrows raise. 'Really? Even with your inattention, your D. Phil. student is now trying, as you put it.'

My stomach drops as in a too-fast lift. This is going wrong. Jenny, what did you learn at David's? I thought he'd noticed Felicia's initial classic silly mistakes, and extra time off. 'Is this about her shaky first term in Oxford—she's fine now—'

'You failed to pick up on her distress and check its possible causes.'

'She's a keen rower. I—assumed she was spending too much time training.'

'It seems you've not troubled to discover Felicia is a young carer. Her mother has multiple sclerosis.'

Oh my God. Visions of Alisdair's disabilities. Of Fee's dedication. I wasn't aware. 'Any time off Felicia has taken has been to do shopping, take her mother to appointments, and other necessary tasks. She and her mother moved here so that Felicia could continue to care. Shortly before they arrived, her mother had an episode—but insisted Felicia mustn't give up her chances—'

'And I didn't—think to inquire.' Past phrases crowd back into my brain. She talked about *getting Mum up*. That a day out would be easier with her sister to help. That *life was too full-on at home*. But did she explain? Should I have asked? Max would've done. Carefully. Caringly. Well, I can't look stupid in front of Rich Woods, can I? 'I mean, you can't *probe* into a person's personal life—can you?'

'There are ways, if you have a new graduate with good qualifications, who appears quieter, more lost and lonely, than seems normal.'

'Did she complain—about me—to you?'

'I saw the situation. It's resolved.' He takes a deep breath. 'So, moving on, about you.' Rich looks thoughtful, leaning back in his chair, his hands loosely held together, doing eye-contact. Reminding me that my contract's up for renewal, asking me what kind of a year I think I've had.

'Not too bad, actually really good.'

'Really?'

'The conference … and we're up to speed on repeating those experiments, everyone's very enthusiastic, and helpful.'

He picks up, and flips through, a file. Mine? He frowns as he delves among papers which must relate in some way to my employment here. Surely giving supervision is the only way I've failed? What about my marvellous success playing the Dr Woods substitute in America?

So bothered, I'm missing what he's saying: '… your time in Cambridge, and realising people often work better when they're living in the same city as their partner, I brought you over when the lab moved. I've tolerated your producing two children with the accompanying inevitable loss of your input through maternity leave, your desultory attitude towards timekeeping due to childhood illnesses, nursery and school hours and functions, your less than enthusiastic appearances at Team social occasions …'

I can't believe it! Or find words: mouth opens and shuts again like a frog after a fly. I've tried my best to be there for meetings, even those ghastly get-togethers he arranges in local pubs for *bonding*. I worked my butt off writing my talk and attending the conference in lieu of him, presenting our work in front of world respected scientists.

I feel so lowly here: I rise, and cross to the window, trembling inside. I do not understand. 'I—I've taken less maternity leave than is my right to have. Max has commitments that mean he's not always there in the evenings to attend school functions and parent evenings, so it has to be me. But when the conference was coming up I put our meeting about it before seeing Alice's first school play, with a speaking part.'

Outside, the sky's turned a deep hostile grey.

'OK: the conference. Jenny, you should know by now that consorting with the—the private sector labs, especially if you have relatives working for them and that is known, it's not only not done. It's foolish.'

'My father?—I didn't tell him anything that wasn't said from— what I mean is, he only heard about our work from the presentation, and public debate.'

'Hmm. Also, I never received the hotel receipts from your trip. And that was because, I've since gathered, you stayed at the Ahwahnee in rooms *booked by your father for your use?* Have you any idea how that appears? Plus I have had to cover the cost for the cancelled accommodation.'

'I know how it looks. But he's my Dad, we don't visit much. And he's impossible to—to—'

'To?'

'If I say, refuse, it could imply what it doesn't. His *hospitality* wasn't refuseable. His probing, if he'd tried it, would have been.'

'How do we know that? And could you turn round, the light from the window—so I can see you again.'

I turn, again noticing that big folder on his desk. My personal file? 'I know it. I'd never be disloyal to us. Our lab. Our work. Our reason for existing.'

He snaps the folder shut.

'I'll find the receipts and pay you back right away. Only slipped my mind because—because Max's father died while I was away and—Rich—Dr Woods—I can do the work, I'm not—a shirker. What about the contract?'

He stares. 'Jenny, it's nearly the end of the school year. Perhaps you need some time off. In fact, I'm telling you that you do. While you're away, think through what you really want from a career in science.'

'Isn't that obvious? From what I did—' I lean over the desk, emphasising, 'for us, for you and this lab—presenting our work?' Suddenly, my upset and fury's really kicking in: 'And what about what you did to my cultures—back in Cambridge—why destroy them and ruin the work I was doing? Why not simply get someone to decently explain to me why it was unwise, with a conflict of interest, to even start?'

Shit. What made me say that? He looks menacing. He moves towards the door, holds it open. 'Jenny, I think you had better leave my office. I have a letter to write to human resources. Go and clear your desk and then, wait outside: there will be a copy for you.'

I'm rooted to the floor. 'Clear my desk? Like you're saying—'

'There must be things there someone else can get on with. And the clutter you all accumulate.'

He means it: everything's imploded. I slide through his door, eyes watching my feet. I happen to be wearing pink Birkenstock sandals. I keep them here to wear while I'm working. My trainers are in the office. Far too casual, them and my jeans and pink T-shirt.

I know, I know: I walk past everyone and their eyes are on me. Eyes drilling into my back. I want to vaporise. To disappear up my own backside like that oozlum bird.

I make it to the lab office, grab my long grey cardie-coat from my chair, and bolt towards the lift, feeling in my pockets for a tissue.

The building rocks and spins: someone I know might be in the lift, so I grab the handrail and stumble down the stairs, specs misted over. By instinct I find the women's loos, bash open the swing door with my shoulder, and almost fall across the floor towards a cubicle.

Its door swings closed behind me. Alone, where nobody can see. Even so, I lean on the door to shut them out, staring at the mouth of the lavatory pan, and the absurdly worded notice about putting nothing but toilet paper down there.

My busy life has been snatched away.

My cheeks burn, the salty tears on them itch. How did I do wrong? How could I have not done what I did? Why did I do those things?

Once long ago I lurked like this in a loo. I'd got me and Daze into trouble at Mum's surgery. We'd been lying on the grass outside, spying on a consultation through the basement window. I knew *that* was wrong. When we got caught, Daze cried and threw up her school dinner. They looked after her. It felt so unfair: Daze wasn't part of our real family. I bunked through the waiting room, and hid, sat on the loo, reading a leaflet I'd grabbed. It was about periods. I must've been about eight or nine then? Feels the same.

I decided then that I'm a strong person.

I think I'd thought Daze would be in trouble, but Mum would let me off… Of course she didn't.

Yes. Now I'm over thirty, I have a doctorate, I have two small children.

I'm being pricked all over by a thousand porcupine spines, not knowing whether I'm wrong or they're wrong. I'm so angry I could scream! Why is this happening? I'd resolved to be nice to everyone. To develop empathy…

I'm a strong person, my own person.

But I can't stop myself crying.

A frightful thought: has Dad netted me now, through my acceptance of his offer of a room at the Ahwahnee? Did he plan that? To put me in a place where I'd need his wretched job?

How hateful… surely not?

Someone opens the outer door, and calls my name.

Leila has brought me my letter. Leila, though I didn't know it, stayed late, waiting to see me after the explosion. She knew it'd be a bad interview: but she didn't warn me.

Did he tell her not to?

Max

A LITTLE LATER, OUTSIDE THE LAB

'Did you actually know you'd worked past the time you were supposed to collect them?'

'Would I have done that, by choice?'

'I don't know: you tell me.'

Trembling, white, chilled, she whispers, teeth gritted, 'Just take them home. Just do it!'

'Jen, what's wrong?' A long silence. She brushes her cheek with her hand: another tear falls on it. 'Jenny?'

'Let's pretend nothing, for the kids. Okay? Everything is all right. I've got a couple of boxes here: we'll put them in the car. I—'

'Yes?'

'Nothing.'

Something is very wrong: but I play the cool Mullins way, and for once, she does as well. Whatever made her forget the bairns can wait. We emerge, each with a box, from the department of biochemistry. We pretend.

At home, after the stories, and the goodnights, we go downstairs. She heads into the living room. I follow. Hunger gnaws at me, hunger and a sense of black gloom. 'I had to talk with Rich, and I got late,' she says. 'He made me late.'

'Okay.'

'Collection slipped my mind because—I had a lot to think about.'

I slowly let myself down onto the fat arm of an overstuffed chair. Ready to listen. To try to coax out the monster from the maze. 'This sounds like something I need to know more about.'

'I saw Daze today.'

'You finally told her your decision?'

'She popped up as I ate lunch, on the grass in front of the University Museum. So I told her.'

'How did she react?'

'No sweat, she said. She's *moved on*. Like she never really took my offer seriously.'

'Okay. I'm—sorry.'

'Of course, Daze was the one who was there after your Dad passed away. You shared about your father with *Daze*. Ever since I was at that conference, you've cut me out.'

'You were thousands of miles away.'

'You said don't bother coming back.'

'Where's this going?'

'Your eulogy was nuts. You won't admit it. I've struggled with how your family works, and made a relationship with your Mam. You ruined it. In those ten minutes.'

'Nuts? D'you want to hear me say that hurts? Because, it does.' I hear myself shouting like Dad making a stramash about some Biblical principle we've violated.

Jenny recoils, bending over, defensive.

My anger fades. 'Jenny, no—no, Jenny—I'm sorry ... I'm—och, my father had ruled all our lives, even from a distance—'

'And now you've marginalised me with your rationalisation.'

'What rationalisation?'

'About your guilt that you should've spent more time with him. After he was dead and you couldn't?'

'I think you're transferring your anger onto me.'

'Medic-think. I hate it. D'you ever do proper feelings?' She crouches, and reaches for something on the floor. A Barbie, pink dress over its head, high heels and no underwear. Kneeling, she smooths down the torn, flimsy dress. Where has my wonderful girl gone? She is small, pathetic, and defeated. This is what feelings tell me.

'I looked at your father's book. About uncertainty. I decided I wanted to read it.'

'What did you think?'

'Not what I expected.' She shrugs, and stays where she is, on the floor. Something frightful has happened, and we aren't near the bottom of it yet. 'Certainty is like, *the facts*. Why we repeat the experiment ...'

'Why Galileo was vilified for saying the earth orbits the sun? His opponents' certainty about what they *thought* were the facts? Which meant they feared accepting his results.'

'So *I've* got my facts wrong, have I?' Jenny snaps.

'Not necessarily. It's human to look for certainty. In science, or religion, or relationships. None of these guarantees unchangeable certainty. If we *live with* uncertainty—open, receptive minds ... You've not said what happened at your lab earlier. Something awful? I need to know.'

'Rich fired me. That's it. For accepting Dad's hospitality, having babies, and screwing up as a supervisor. Among other misdemeanours. He got me into his office and told me I'd done everything wrong. And that was after Daze had revealed what an ungrateful cow she is. No surprise I forgot our children, was it?'

'Och, Jenny, that's awful. Did he really say... Come here, lassie. You can't think I don't—'

She covers her ears. 'Don't—. My whole life's in question. Don't say *anything*.'

Jenny

WEDNESDAY

The abyss is too deep to gaze down: I shall fall in.

I am in bed, I notice the curtains of the spare room, and the way the light is different at the back of the house. The front door bangs: voices fade.

A cafetière of hot coffee, a jug of milk, a mug, on the bedside table. I turn away: lumpy throat, tears, I can't touch work subjects, or even think of Max. Everything hurts.

But *I am a strong person.*

So by lunchtime, I've thrown together what we need for our pilgrimage, found my Chapel House keys, told the head teacher at Alice's school and the manager at Zoë's nursery that there's been a family crisis. The main thing is to stay focused, not do anything silly, keep the kids safe.

I bring them home, explaining we're off to have adventures. We select toys they can take. 'Where?' they ask.

'Glastonbury.'

Don't know why I said that. Have to stick to it. Good. Because we can approach Cornwall slowly, and it takes all my concentration to drive.

Glastonbury is fairyland for Alice and Zo-zo. Shops with fairies in the windows. Thai style curry supper in a café. A bed and breakfast, where we have a family room but the girls are suddenly frightened, and pile into my bed.

Zoë sleeps, one arm flung out sideways, the other around her now-raggedy toy cat, her thumb in her mouth. Alice curls against my side, as I read to her. I don't hear what I'm reading: I hear the awful things Rich Woods said yesterday. The heaviness of her head eventually indicates Alice is asleep.

I can't face anything. I am a strong person. I can't be so wrong: can I?

Sleep isn't for me: I keep the lamp on and pick up Alisdair's book. *Sexual reproduction: how wonderful, and how risky ... The amazing intricacy of cell division: like spinning yarn, the cell replicates the DNA ... How uncertain the outcome is for the new beings, which must live inside their mother's bodies, nurtured by the equally amazing system that exchanges nutrients and waste products, while they grow. Have you heard of Hox Genes?*

Weird: that's my conversation with Fee, nine years ago. Almost word for word. Either she told it him, and he was impressed, or ... Max's hints mean he thinks she ... Flipping further into the book, then searching more carefully, I find more. Seams, in rock formation. Gold thread shimmering in a sari.

You can't make an omelette without breaking eggs: and we must sometimes break the eggs we have in our hands in order to make the omelettes we enjoy on our plates. Distinctly domestic.

Max is right: *'It wasna' his usual'*: not his father's typical, extremist, one-sided, bigoted rant. *Religion has acquired a name for causing disputes and even wars. Fear for our own futures, or uncertainty about having the Truth, and nothing but the Truth, has beaten back the higher good of listening to others, seeking to understand them, and showing love. Can we learn to live with this uncertainty: is there a different kind of truth, which we've been denying?*

What is truth? Does it exist?

Max said there were *proofs of Dad's book on the little desk that Mam uses*. Seems Fee and Alisdair don't always tell what they'd call the truth.

Max

LATER THAT DAY

Does psychosis fit the bill? Should I have acted differently last night?

Rich gave me such a hard time, I've gone away to think. We're all okay and going to Mum's, wh. is empty. Don't say anything. Jyx

It is propped against the fruit bowl, and the fruit bowl is on the kitchen table, and the fruit bowl is empty.

The house, which should contain my family, is empty.

The Discovery was gone when I turned into the drive. Dread drives me to hunt further. Small pink bikes and scooters in the shed, but gumboots and macs gone from the laundry room, and upstairs duvets, and cuddly animals from little girls' beds. Clothes, toys, books snatched from cupboards, boxes, and shelves. Jenny's half of the wardrobe is bereft. Our tent and sleeping bags have disappeared.

Her laptop. Her toothbrush. Her spare spectacles. And what's this, forgotten, dropped on the floor? I pick it up: her contraceptive pills. *Dr J L Guthrie Mullins* is printed on the pharmacy label. She uses both surnames to her doctor?

Suddenly it feels wrong to move her things about. I replace them in the bathroom cabinet.

I see her everywhere, tearing about the house, flinging things into bags and suitcases. Distracted, she'd grasp her hair, pull it into a ponytail, throw open drawers looking for a fastening. She can be meticulous, focused, and organised: but she falls apart under the pressure of family life. Under the horrific thought of being a failure. Did she shout at the children, or behave calm and controlled? What did she tell them? Did they cry? Did they ask for me?

Has she taken food, has she thought ahead? Did she do this like a holiday trip? Tell anyone she was going? Shaz? Daze? Leila?

Leila's her closest colleague. Leila's sensible. I try their phone. The answer machine picks up. I replace the receiver. Can't put this into a message. Shan't try Shaz.

Sudden weakness, must eat.

No cheese in the fridge, no bread. There is her favourite semi-skimmed milk. I eat Weetabix, shovelling it in, hardly tasting its childhood memories, though remembering that dryness at the centre of each soggy bite. I pour myself a dram and down that.

What's got into her? How could she have done such wrong that he sacked her? How could she not have seen any danger in accepting Guthrie's hospitality in the US? I was afraid she might get ticked off for that, but I never imagined it would be viewed seriously enough to lead to this.

Jenny's last few run-ins with me flash through my brain: raving that I'd lied to her about the cell cultures ten years ago. I have never lied to Jenny. She knows that.

I didn't tell her I'd seen Rachel: but she didna' give me a moment of time, taking against the eulogy, misinterpreting everything. So with that, and raking up old issues, the cell culture business, *does* psychosis fit the bill? Is she delusional, and should I contact … Who?

I phone again, 'She took the Discovery: she took the kids.'

'Do you know where she is?'

'I know where I was told she is.'

A pause, then Leila says, 'Jenny came out of Woods's office like a zombie, and cleared her desk. He—he had a letter for her. I took it to her. I can only imagine the contents.'

'I picked her up. I had the kids in the car. She told me bare facts, and went to bed ... I gave her something to help her sleep. This morning I wanted the kids to have normality, took them to school; went to work ... what should I have done? I came home and found this ...'

'Give me your mobile phone number: you have one? I'll call if she contacts me. You keep in touch, Max.'

Yes. Relieved by Leila's offer, I act like the irrational pastor's son I am, and sitting on our bed, head in my hands, earnestly ask God to protect her, and my children. So used to God that I'd miss him if he really weren't there: though hardly ever think about him. Though no good reason, if he is there, anywhere, that he should rescue us from this.

The book's gone. *Living with Uncertainty*. So she's going to read it? A positive sign.

I remember Daze's visit to the surgery.

I remember finding lovely, quiet, Suraya more than merely a good student, and wishing Jenny was more like that. You mayn't do anything, but the temptations are there. I've failed my own choice, my feisty wife, by expecting her to be quiet, submissive, and controllable.

Jenny

THURSDAY AND FRIDAY

We go to see the fossils at Charmouth's Jurassic beach. We are careful. We can't afford to slip, hurt ourselves, lose any of our party. This is important.

Mum brought us here. A breezy day, the Easter holidays. She explained how the blue clay was full of the remains of creatures from the Jurassic seas of 180 million years ago. Me with my very first camera, totally absorbed, taking shots and shots of, as I tell Alice and Zoë, 'Curly-wurly ammonites.' Wanted to be a geologist for a bit after that.

Rocks have a safe truth.

Remembering's fatal. I want to be alone. I want to cry. Swallowing it down, brushing tears away, I tell Alice how a little girl found a fossil dinosaur here, a long time ago. 'Was she a Joo-rassic?'

'No: that was a very, very, long time ago. This was, just a bit ago. Before Granny, before Great Granny.'

Alice bends to pick up a stone. 'No fossils in it,' she says, throwing it away. 'We might find a dinosaur,' she adds hopefully. 'But I don't think we will.'

Next day, we cheer as we cross the border into Cornwall. Though Alice groans as I remind them, 'It's a long way yet, on slow wiggly roads.' Zoë joins in as Alice begins the inevitable 'Are we nearly there yet?' We stop off at Bodmin, we find a café that serves cream teas all day. We stop again in Penzance, to buy basic provisions and stretch our legs looking at boats in the harbour.

Finally we're at Chapel House. The key is under the usual flowerpot. It's like letting myself in after school. Propped against the wall in the porch are two windbreaks and three umbrellas. On the mat there's a fat A4 registered letter. *Dr Jenny Mullins*: care of this address.

To ignore it, I consign it quickly to the windowsill.

Familiar scent of the open-plan living area: floor polish, coffee, and whiff of oil paint and Sans Odor escaping from the studio. Mum's left local cheese, bread, butter and clotted cream in the fridge, honey on the table, a bottle of wine. For Daze?

Des has left a cartoon of all of us on surfboards. Will I try?

The kids stand in the living area, with uncertainty. So do I. The three-piece suite isn't the one I remember: they've bought one in black leather. Granny Ianthe's black and white, silver-framed photo of my grandfather, her lover, is out on the bookshelf. I reach out, take it down, and stare into his face. Clever, handsome, intense: eyes to catch your thoughts and penetrate some intriguing puzzles of biochemistry.

Genetically linked.

'My grandfather,' I proudly told Max when we stayed at Granny's London flat. He was so impressed.

Pangs of regret, as I replace the photo. My throat tightens. Someone bats at me. 'Mummy?'

'Yes?'

'*You said* we'd go on the beach.'

Forcing a smile, 'I did. We will. Now.'

'Why're you sad?'

'My home, when I was little.'

You can't fool a child. Brushing away a tear, while she stares, unconvinced that this is about history.

I haul our luggage from the car, ferret out beach towels and swimmers. Off we go, leaving bags, cases, and furry toys on the living room floor.

Max

FRIDAY EVENING

Leila phones again, to say she's heard from Jen, who's arrived at Chapel House and seems to be keeping in touch.

Jenny wouldn't let me into her pain.

She has our children with her.

She hasn't flipped. I decide to trust her.

It all began, or at least escalated, because Mam was at St Hildie's. For her own reasons. Blaming Mam is unfair, but even if visiting us wasn't in her plans, it would still have helped if we'd known she was around.

I've a long empty evening: I'll walk up there and see if David can shed light on what could've caused a misunderstanding between her and Jenny.

As I arrive, the place looks deserted. I push open the main door. Sounds and smells a bit like school dinner fill the passage: clattering cutlery, chattering voices, cooked vegetables. Clearly it's supper time. I beat a quick retreat back into the grounds, where the doors into the Livingstone Lounge stand open. Around the walls, someone has attached shimmery hangings, like shower curtains. They make it strangely like a wet room.

What purpose would there be in walking the labyrinth? Is it, as my Presbyterian mind says, futile? It's certainly against First Truly's rational, anti-ritualistic principles. It's romantic nonsense.

But I enter, and step onto it. Momentarily, it becomes a coiled snake: then it is a path again.

Your word is a path, a lamp to my feet.

'It is a journey, a pilgrimage.'

It is a pattern on the floor.

'It has a calming rhythmic effect.'

'It's a passage between two worlds.'

'It's ancient technology that mimics the journey of life.'

Inwards, around, outwards, within. This is supremely juvenile. But I do it.

At the centre, I sit, profoundly weary, on the floor.

The circular centre is maybe a metre and a half across. Whatever I do not believe about it, there are effects from walking a flat spiral shape. A kaleidoscope of wrongs presents itself.

First it spins; then it slows. Is it psychosis? Or something else? 'Women's highest calling is marriage and motherhood. Women are best at home with their children.' Dad's ideas, not mine. Are children and science research incompatible?

This thing is Daze's artwork: how is she now? After our talk? And Jenny's announcement?

Can't help her right now.

Daze, and Etta, saw me as a receptacle for their pain and sorrow. They're family. I have to pass them on. Find the right therapist.

Jenny wanted me to be generous towards my family. Did my eulogy betray Dad's confidences? What did he always want? To lead his congregation in the ways of God, as he saw it.

'Hey, mate?' Startled, I spring to my feet. It's David. They've finished eating. 'Anything wrong?'

'Och, so only something wrong would make me go round this thing?'

David shrugs, hands in pockets, waiting. 'Not a Mullins thing, is it? Or ... There's a party here for a couple of days' meditation, about to come in here.'

'I'll be away then. But, to answer your question, I gathered Mam's been staying. She's all right, is she?'

'A bit of time alone, to think, away from the Manse. Actually, after her retreat she went to visit your sisters. She's back tonight, breaking the journey north. You want to drop by?'

'She's not part of your meditation group?' I smile.

'Oh no, mate! A bridge too far.'

Somewhat reluctant to open up the subject of Jenny's behaviour, I follow David's directions to the room where Mam's staying. Going along the corridor I glance through an open door. It's a small guest kitchen. There's someone in it, filling a kettle at a sink: Mam. She turns towards me.

'Max! What a nice surprise.'

'David told me you were back, so I came up. I'm sorry I didna' call you back before.'

'That's okay. I went to London to see Erin. And Kirsty. David suggested I spend another couple of nights here on the way home. And as God had laid it on my heart to visit you and your family,' (I wince inwardly at the phrase) 'are you all well?'

'Jenny's taken the bairns away to her mother's house. I'll join them later.'

'I'm sorry to miss them. I was about to make some tea, you'll join me, will you? Downstairs is rather crowded and noisy.'

There's nowhere to sit but a stool and a flimsy chair. After a few pleasantries, I stand leaning on the counter, hanging about like a teenager, unsure whether to confide or not. Mam, busy with taking down mugs from a cupboard, asks, her back to me, 'Is there anything I should know about?'

Whew: straight to it, Dad's style. Though without hostility in her voice. How could I have forgotten that to First Truly parents, their adult child is always a child? And, of course, when God lays something on the heart of your mother, it's hard to get away from the subject. Don't rant. Keep dignified. 'You're referring to the eulogy? I—decided honesty was needed,' I say, as she waves me away from any attempt to take over the tea-making.

'You know, pet, Rachel hasn't been with us for a while now.'

Why's she begun with that? 'I saw her–briefly–outside First Truly the night before.' It slips out, before I bridle my tongue, though knowing perfectly well those parent-child barriers, so carefully put in place. Underlined by professional training: me the doctor, Mam the pastor's wife.

'I see.'

'Mam, Rachel hasn't been with the congregation physically, and we both know why. Despite Dad admitting his counselling mistaken, they edged her out. They preferred to see Colin's violence as some kind of permissible response to Rachel's lack of submission. The idea's medieval.'

'Yes,' Mam breathes. I know Mam wouldn't have been the perpetrator, or in any way to blame. She sits on the flimsy chair, then touches her wedding ring, and begins turning it.

'Whether she's within the community of believers, in any sense ... Did anyone try to find out? I thought not. Well, anyway, Rachel's back nursing. Nat's in a special school, he's happy there. She mentioned someone whose love is healing, in her life, as she put it.' Mam's eyes remain fixed on the symbol of her marriage. Then she covers her face with her hands, so I add, quietly, 'I'm sorry. Not for my eulogy, if it hurt you, but for hurting you with words aimed at others.'

'Max, you haven't. We're in agreement.' She leans towards me, reaching out. 'Max, pet, you spoke the truth. It was touching.' I take her hands in both of mine. They're warm, and papery dry. 'I wasna' ever angry.'

'But I have to explain this: Jenny was terribly upset by what I said. That's why she took the bairns home, and didna' stay for the tea.'

'Oh!' she exclaims.

'It was all her—or us—she didna' read the book before the service, and so, she wasna' prepared for what I said.'

'And that is why ... Max, I am sorry. Poor Jenny. What can we do?'

'I think it's for me to mend it. Somehow. I should've thought. The service, and the eulogy, opened up everything which happened that first weekend she visited. Dad's sermon, Colin's hostility, Rachel's-injuries–she'd never encountered domestic violence in reality ...'

'Oh dear. The memories havena' healed then.'

Something drops onto my hand: a tear. It sears me, like something molten. Hesitating a moment, I drop to my knees and reach out to her. Our tradition shuns intimacy, but now we cling together. It feels almost *adulterous* to cross this boundary: the system counts me as an interloper. Mam belonged to Dad, we belonged to her, Dad belonged to God. When did Mam last let go of her emotions? When did I, to her, to anyone? Except in anger?

All our pain is the legacy of Dad's preaching. Such a tragedy.

At last, 'Remember *Beatus Vir*?' I say, untangling myself, and stepping across the kitchen to tear off sheets of kitchen roll for us to mop our faces. She glances up, puckering her brow, then smiles in recognition.

'That solo? Right before your voice broke? Your father came to hear you, seeing the text was from Scripture.'

'And the music by Monteverdi.' I laugh quietly, the tension eases. '*Blessed is the righteous man, who doesn't walk in the ways of the wicked?* We boys in the choir had a translation, though with Dad being a pastor the text had been hammered into me. I used to wonder about that weight of responsibility laid on Dad, and everyone, by the need to be righteous.'

'Yes,' Mam nods, and smiles.

'And so, *Living with Uncertainty*? Mam, look at me?'

She responds almost inaudibly. 'We wrote it together. He was terribly concerned to give them the message God had laid on his heart.'

God has laid a lot on our hearts lately, I think. It's how we religious fundamentalists step away from trusting our own judgment. The thought makes me cringe: making God responsible, so our thoughts, our instincts, become justifiable.

'And so: Jenny? I wish I had known she thought you'd hurt me. I could see she was unhappy. But so are you. Though you're good at hiding it.'

'Yes. Part of the home training.' Undo the first knot (our imposed taciturn attitudes), and the string untangles, knot after knot. 'Yes, any problems are not Jenny's fault. It's me.' I pause, then decide to share more. 'That evening, your first visit here, and you called us? We were out. You spoke with Etta, our babysitter?'

'Etta? Oh – yes, that day I'd met Jenny. She poured her heart out. Very unexpected.'

'That situation's worrisome. I've been told both parts of the story.'

'Max, I have been there, as people say. As had your father.'

'Their—rift— it's no' the same, of course, but it's helped me understand, a bit. It's helped me with this difficulty, me and Dad. Understanding how we—how I—I so regret how I treated Dad.' Mam startles. I plough on. 'Something terribly broken between us was never mended. Now it can't be.'

She sighs, and shakes her head. 'You and your father.'

Yes: and Mam and her pastor husband who she consented should rule her life. And how did she bridle her tongue all those years, and has she now the courage to publicly escape? Head held high?

'I must go,' I say, seeing as she starts to rise from her chair that she feels this intimacy's gone far enough. 'It was good to see you. Jenny took the book with her. I suspect she's reading it, at last.' That is all I shall say.

We hug, but awkwardly, and say goodbye.

On my way out, I slip into one of the clean but drear bathrooms: pink suite, window looking onto a blank wall, vase of dried flowers by the sink. I'm thinking of things we didn't mention: David's return, David's changed life, David's family. What grabs him about running a retreat centre? Will Euan and Margaret ever accept his lifestyle?

Silence and secrecy collude with lies. Truth breaks open the possibility of healing. *Nothing is more perilous than truth in a world that lies.* Where did I read that? A book Jenny borrowed from Leila. By a perceptive Egyptian feminist.

Jenny

SAME DAY

I found my wetsuit and bought little ones for the girls. We've spent our days building sandcastles with moats. We've dug rivers and dammed them with stones. The girls, zipped into their black suits, caper every day in the lacy edges of the incoming waves, squealing with pleasure, watching the elegant surfers, excited, imitating, on the sands, that ballet out on the waves. Carl and Ellie, who I knew at Cape Cornwall school, are running the village shop and post office: Ellie minds the girls so I can swim. I even do a spot of body boarding.

Feels like longer than a week. Every lunchtime, back at the house, I sit the girls down with kids' TV that Mum recorded and left us. Muppets and Sesame Street. While they watch, I potter. And I check in by phone with Leila. It's like being on bail. Or what Granny calls in limbo. Leila can pass messages to Max. I avoid involvement.

I found pictures of us in Mum's photo album in the bookcase. Me and Max giving a dinner party at his Oxford flat. Sam Skull, who we kept from Max's student bone box, is on a shelf, watching through his shades. It felt awful, thinking of those years when I was living in Cambridge, like we weren't married, doing my PhD and visiting for weekends.

Where are our real selves now? And where's Sam?

Today, our holiday was meant to begin. Today, might Max suddenly turn up?

Today, I phone but Leila's out.

I wander into Mum and Des's bedroom. If Max arrives I suppose we'll use their waterbed. Halfway through making it, shaking a pillow into its case, I catch sight of myself in the mirror. I look distinctly better for the bodyboarding. And for ignoring thoughts about work, Rich, the conference, my career.

The usual keys aren't in the dressing table drawers: when I pull, they open. Even that bottom one, where we imagined Mum kept her secrets. What's really in there?

My curiosity's not disappointed: a bundle of stuff tied with a black ribbon. I undo it.

Hilarious photo: Mum and Dad. He's in a tux, she's in an ugly long dress, sleeveless, shiny fabric, stiff little bow at the front of the waist. Jackie Kennedy 1960's. With backcombed hair. A college ball programme? Order of proceedings, and menu. Chicken, of course. On the back, in Dad's writing: *Hey, Carrie-Ann, many thanks for a splendid evening, and letting me play. Yrs always, Johnny G.*

Blimey: embarrassing. She kept all her old sixties singles, so I know this one goes, *Hey Carrie-Ann, what's your game now, can anybody play?* Tease my aching brain: by— by— —the Hollies! Stupid name for a band. Play? Did they? Have sex? When, where, first date, late date? Date of song? Looking again, it's not an undergrad ball, it's some kind of medics' reunion. 1967. Revise my scenario. *Yrs always*: how sad, he'd left by '71 or '72.

Always knew Mum still has the hots for Dad. I think of them back then, he still loved her. I was around already. The sex could've become Harriet: I grin.

And reach back into the drawer: more photos. My God, Mum's got *these*? Our first trip north: Max, sleeping naked, all relaxed, before we reached the Manse and everything went wrong ... I let *Mum* have them? No: she nicked them from my room.

I feel deeper into the drawer ... shouldn't, mustn't.

But she took my stuff ... I can look at hers.

A brown envelope, dry, friable. Stuffed with documents. What's this? Mental hospital, in Edinburgh? Did Mum work there? *Juliette Loveday Potter*. From Somerset. Sectioned. A med school friend who flipped? If Mum's got this, they must've been really close?

Potter, Juliette—light-bulb moment, obvious! Jewels: *Daze's mum*. Des and Jewels were married? I never knew that. Or about a mental illness. I've uncovered something significant, kept from us. This feels dangerous. Where is Jewels now? Did she recover? Does Mum know?

'Mummy can we go now?'

'Mm? Zo-zo?'

'Can we go to de beach? Whas dat?' She leans over, staring at the documents in my hands.

'Boring work, darling.' Realize I'm white lying. Like Mum. Quickly, I stuff everything back inside the envelope, replace it, close the drawer. 'Yes, the beach. Muppets over?'

'All gone!' Zoë claps her hands.

Max

SATURDAY, A WEEK LATER, READING STATION

Changing trains: me on the down escalator, a crowd of teenagers, chattering like birds, on the up. Like Jacob's ladder, or some kind of an allegory. Silly hats, bedding rolls, backpacks, obviously on their way to a festival, obviously weekend hippies.

Never-ending containers rattle through at speed, blasting us waiting passengers on the platform with noise and a powerful slipstream of dusty air. Wonder what the girls will think of their presents, wish now I'd bought a newspaper ... The Penzance train's due in ten minutes: if it's crowded, and I have to stand, that's own fault for a snap decision. So, shall I beat myself up? Jen's got the family car, and if we can't go in two cars, and two directions at once, on this holiday, then maybe we'll learn about compromise. Which I had thought I knew about, but no.

'Hey, you! It's me—hey Max?' Heartsink moment: why Daisy, and why here, now? Part of her amazing talent for turning up where you don't want anything more to go wrong? Daisy, with a shy grin. Huge backpack perched on her tiny frame. And clutching a take-out coffee from the station kiosk. 'Hey, you're not—going to—?'

'Joining Jenny and the bairns. Caroline offered us the house, apparently it's empty for a month. You?' I ask, trembling inwardly with anger and despair, sweat breaking out, hoping my face doesn't show my true feelings. Too late, I fix a smile on for her.

But she obviously knows, and she's obviously equally appalled. 'Oh sh— I see, yeah, well, sorry an' that but I'm going all the way, too. Penzance train?'

'Sure we'll manage. Sorry. Jen took off with Ally and Zo-zo last week, so, well, we're rather taking over the house and—'

The tannoy coughs into life, a woman's crackling voice announces the train's been delayed by cows on the line further up. 'Right cows they must be ...' Daze laughs, I don't, then 'Sorry, I know, poor humour,' she adds.

'Och, it's just me, not yet in holiday mood,' I offer.

'Be nice to see Ally and Zoë, though. Never mind you and Jen,' says Daze, and opens her coffee. A second later, 'Ohmygod, they boiled it!' she exclaims, shattering a reassuring picture my mind had produced: Alice and Zoë, hugging my legs, looking up with big smiles ... What'll Jenny say, as I walk through that door? What is it we want from each other? 'What's the temp above boiling point. Is there one?'

'Sorry? Say again?'

'Doesn't matter.'

Fact is, this is my real self: the self which shared a bit of me with Mam, the self she and Dad trained, distorted, whatever they did. The one with the Mullins genes. The one who let Dad down in his last days. Daze is trying to talk to my work self, full of confidence, even compassion, and bright ideas for solving other people's life problems. Left that behind. Hoping to find the home self again. Still puzzled how to link these two up, and then offer Jen whatever it is she needs. Me? Or that job at Vangenics? Sweating again, did she really mean she'd go, trample on whatever's left of her idealism and work for Guthrie?

Rescue her from precipitous thinking? Not me, right now. Put on a face for Daze, or somehow find a way to disappear? Disappear, definitely, once the train arrives.

'You okay, Max?'

'Mm. Yes: Daze, didn't Jenny tell me you were going to do some surfing with David? Is he down there?' David's been away since that day when Mam was staying at his place: on holiday, someone said.

Revelation about the parents' collaboration on the *Uncertainty* book was useful ... but is Jen reading it?

'I might've. I haven't heard from him, if he's going,' says Daze. With a guilty look, like she knows something. I probably have one on my own face, as I recall how generous Daze was after Dad died, and can hardly wait for the train to arrive so I can dive into it, and be lost amongst the crowds in there. 'Look, Max, I'm gonna find a smoking carriage when it comes in—isn't that the train? Winding along down there?' She points up the line. 'Or the hungry caterpillar, coming to eat us,' she adds with typical Daze humour. In another mood, I'd laugh with her. Then as I pick up my bag, she grasps my arm for attention. 'Listen, when we arrive, I've got mates to see, you go on ahead?'

Jenny

SAME DAY, LATER

Mid-afternoon, it's hot on the beach. Though the surf is high, and there's a stiff breeze off the sea. I keep the girls close, away from the breaking waves, as slathered in suncream, toes in warm, granular sand, we stand in a row, holding hands, watching the surfers.

Daze can do that: ride the waves, confident, elegant.

Whatever the facts, Jewels didn't deliberately abandon Daze. Did she have a psychotic episode at Glastonbury? Sparked by smoking pot? Or something stronger? Does Des feel responsible? *Was* he? Social services might've taken Daze into care. She was lucky Des kept her. She was lucky Mum annexed them both.

'Mummy?' Alice nudges me. She points out an athletic-looking guy who clearly knows exactly what he's doing. 'We know him,' she says, as he gracefully arrives on the shore, and picks up his board.

'We do?' I shade my eyes.

'Auntie Daze made him the labby-rinse.'

'Alice, that can't be him: he's in Oxford. Miles away. It's someone who looks like him. In a wetsuit, people can look like somebody else.

C'mon, time to pack up and go home.'

Alice capers ahead. I have to pull gently on Zoë's hand to make her move. In her other one, she's grasping a long shiny brown piece of bladderwrack, trailing along the sand. 'C'mon Zo-zo, and let's leave the seaweed behind.'

'I want it.'

'Oh, bring it then. But it'll dry out and smell horrible. It likes to live in the sea. Alice!'

'Put it in the bath?'

'Yuck, no! Alice?' I look round, and there she is, with him, running to keep up with his lopey strides.

'See, Mummy? He's Uncle David, isn't he?' Alice smiles. She really did recognise David.

'You weren't wrong,' I say, as my heart sinks. Why the hell's David everywhere I go? Why here, on this beach?

'Jenny! So are you all here?' Hair plastered to his head, body outlined by the wetsuit, surfboard under one arm. Hardly priestly.

'All? Just me and the kids.'

David grins, 'Pilgrimage? Is Daze around? She mentioned coming down. I thought that was this week? But great you guys are here.'

I retie my sarong, gather our belongings and ask David 'Did Daze invite you? To ours?'

'No—no, she said she'd be at her parents', and possibly we'd join up for some surfing. I'm visiting friends.'

'Ah. Nearby?'

He gestures. 'Towards Land's End.' Then looking at that waterproof watch he wears, 'I must be getting back. We're off to the Minack later: Shakespeare. Cambridge Dramsoc seem to have a yearly slot. You must know it well?'

'Yep. It can be great, in the right weather. I never know what Daze is doing, can't help you there.' I know I'm grinning like the Cheshire Cat, while wishing I could, like that cat, disappear.

'See you again, perhaps?'

Shall I tell Daze anything about Jewels's mental illness? Or first ask Aunt Val why she never mentioned it?

*

I've literally dumped the beach stuff in the laundry room and dropped my car keys on the kitchen counter when a taxi swings into the drive: the girls hear its engine, run to the window, and shriek, 'Daddy's here!'

My stomach tenses. The excited kids fling themselves at the front door, jumping up and clutching at the latch: 'Hurry up Mummy!'

Relaxed single-mummy time is gone.

As I reach over them to undo the lock, I know what it'll be. A version of *Are you okay ... I was worried ... You took Ally out of school—what message does that give ... Jen, it was all me, screwing up.* No: it's me: here hunting my map like David said.

The door's open, the girls rush to hug magical Daddy. Yes, for a second I'd almost wanted to stand across the doorway, keeping what's been our paradise to ourselves. But as he sweeps up Zoë in his arms, and almost staggers as Alice embraces his legs, I know I shouldn't have. *They're so happy.*

'Jenny?' He looks weary. His eyes search my face, *Is the wee wifie okay?*

We hover, almost kiss, don't.

He lowers Zoë to the ground, turns, picks up his luggage, and strides into the living room. Alice trots behind, hauling a plastic carrier from a baker's in Penzance. Max plonks his bag in the middle of the rug. Alice looks in the carrier. 'Buns,' she says, plunging in her hand. 'And this.' Holding up a pot of Rodda's clotted cream.

'You been all right? Gave me a fright, disappearing.'

'Yeah. Having a ball with the kids. Really. God, what should we do?'

'Act normal till after bedtime. Then,' he stops, and flicks his fringe back with the sweep of a hand, 'let's take it slowly. A lot's happened these past few months, hasn't it?'

'It has. You—you—'

'Jen, I need to warn you: I met your sister on the platform.

Changing trains, at Reading. Daze. She was on her way here.'

I shake my head, 'Figures. She mentioned coming down: I'd forgotten. And you know who I met at the beach? David. He seemed to think Daze was going to meet up with him. For some surfing.'

'Och, we don't need him down here as well!' says Max.

'Why? You and David—could be funny if—' I try, hoping maybe we'd laugh?

'No, it's not.'

'Right, *All me*, as you so often say.'

'I do not.'

'Do—' I mutter. Aloud I say, 'Can we have civilized cream tea, please? For the girls?'

We're in the garden, on the picnic rug, with a tea tray, doing a family-time routine with fat scones, cream and jam. Grins were pinned on while making tea and finding the rug. And all too soon, a small figure ambles up the path, with a huge backpack.

'Look who it is! Grab a mug and join us,' I say, as if nothing's wrong. And add, evilly, 'Guess who I met at the beach? David. He was expecting to see you.' Daze's hand flies to her mouth, and 'Omigod!' flies out of it.

'You'd forgotten you'd been so generous with our old home?'

'F-word, f-word, I was swanking about, it was late at night—oh *pants*.'

Daze's reaction is so satisfying. Almost smug—actually, really smug—I regain some self-possession. And with it maybe some confidence that I can do this, even if it is a pain to have everyone here. And Daze ... When do I mention my discovery?

I know I'm turning into Mum when I find myself looking in the fridge for inspiration and announcing, 'Nursery supper, people, lots of cheddar cheese, loads of milk, pasta in the cupboard, it has to be macaroni cheese. Max, if there're any of Mum's lettuces that haven't bolted, go cut 'em for us?'

I put a couple of bottles of Des's wine to cool. Daze goes down to the village to buy fruit for dessert. Nice to have a willing servant sometimes, and she'll liven up everything and divert stuff from Mullins-type angst. Even babysit? We could go and turn over our problems at the First and Last Inn, long as the pub's not jammed with old schoolfriends from Cape Cornwall or Penwith college. Seeing I'm the reverse of an enviable (or more like, stuck-up) success right now. Not the star pupil in the Penwith College newsletter.

Shall I share the Jewels discovery with Max, pick his clinical brain over what to do?

'Strawberries!' Daze bursts through the door, sooner than I expected, 'fresh an' local, an' I saw Carl and Ellie have that now?'

'Wow, indeed. Huge ones! You were quick.'

'I got a ride home. From—*ta-dah*—David!' Oh God … I groan it *inwardly*, as they say, so as to remain polite. 'Come on through!' Daze calls over her shoulder. 'I found him at the shop,' she says, popping a strawberry into her mouth.

'Hey, aren't those for us, then?'

'Sure. The rest of them. Anyhow, Dave's Minack friends got their days mixed up. I made him agree to join us. He's brought some drink and a cheesecake.'

'You're okay about my crashing your evening?'

'Sure.' It's odd: I behave normally. Well, almost. I've poured myself a big glass of white wine to sip as I cook, more Mum-like than ever, and that's already helping. 'Fine, fine: more is good. Nice of you to contribute.'

David and Max have a can of Stella each while we sort dinner, though they eye my wine glass as I refill it. I offer some to Daze.

'Don't mix your drinks, boys,' I say, 'I need you to behave, with the kids sitting down to eat with us. Max, where's that lettuce?'

Max ambles off to the veg patch, taking his can and ignoring David. Back with two half decent lettuces, he comes up close behind to give me a hug: I don't move away. Are we acting the relaxed family thing a tad too well? Zoë hauls Uncle David off to see her bladderwrack, floating *temporarily* in the bath. Alice brings Max the fossils we found at Lyme Regis. The lovely family-type stuff is a fragile dream: like I imagined things would be, and they weren't. Zoë throws a wobbly, and with the tension, the brittleness, the toddler tears, the scent of wine and macaroni cheese, it's like I really am my mother. Getting along with all these people I don't want to be with, just like Mum when Des brought home his arty-blokey friends without asking first.

Whatever: I remember they had some fun evenings. We're gonna have a fun evening, before any family truth-telling begins.

Daze

SAME TIME, SAME EVENING

Trouble in Paradise, and it's fucking uncomfortable to live with. Anyone can see the shedloads of efforts being made to hide the cracks. Kiddies pick up the atmosphere, there are tears about eating leaves. That kills the conversation.

Daze remembers her thoughts on the station: a fun element is needed to break this atmosphere. Let's revert to student lifestyle, at least for this evening? Max and David are doing kiddies' bath time and Jenny is stacking the dishwasher. All far to seriously grown-up. 'I've discovered Mum and Dad have joined the Bridge Set! D'you play?' Daze says brightly.

'What? Like do I read the *Daily Telegraph?*'

'You might. I don't know what you do. What would Mum say? *It's a skill like any other.* That's about what she'd say.'

'What's your point, Daze?'

'I don't do points.'

Daze fetches the cards, and moves to the dining table, where she sweeps aside the salad bowl (one leftover floppy leaf drowning in vinaigrette and tomato seeds), and half the cheesecake, (top stained pink with strawberry juice). She knocks the three packs of cards on the tabletop, to tidy them, then builds a skyscraper. 'Now *that* is cool,' Jenny says, clearing the remains and wielding a cloth. The tower tumbles. 'Oops, spoke too soon! Sorry!'

'Earthquake!' Daze grins, gathers the cards, and repeats her building on the floor.

Max returns from kiddies' bedtime waving an envelope.

Jenny reaches to grab it away, Daze tips back on her heels as Max and Jen collide over the card skyscraper, which topples and scatters on the sanded and polished floor. 'Shit!'

'Sorry, again, Daze.'

'Gonna open this?'

'No I am not! This is my holiday.'

David, putting away the cheesecake, speaks into the fridge, 'Yep, Jenny is having a jubilee.'

'A what, David? Can you leave the strawberries out, we might want them later?'

He dumps them on the coffee table in a clean bowl. These are really some of the largest I've ever seen, Daze thinks, eating one. David explains, 'A Jubilee Year: nobody works and everybody celebrates.'

Daze imagines a three hundred and sixty-five day carnival, something like the Notting Hill crossed with Penzance's Golowan, with twelve Mazey Days, one for each month. 'Oh, more that! Where's the idea from?'

'D'ye no ken the Old Testament,' Max and David chorus, in broad Scots accents, 'Leviticus chapter 25 verse 10.'

'God,' Daze groans.

'God clearly doesn't want me to open that big envelope.'

'Let me see: who's it from?'

Jenny takes a swig of Max's Stella, carelessly put down before he took the children upstairs, 'I don't care.'

'Children!' Daze speaks like a teacher.

'They're not crying are they? Did you read them something scary?'

'Me? I *am* scary.' Max roars like a lion, Jenny flicks him with her cleaning cloth.

Daze sorts the cards into piles. She places the three packs on the artisan coffee table, a 'wood or tree' gift made for Caro and Des's fifth wedding anniversary by one of Des's craftsmen friends, a woman who lived over towards Zennor. Caro, who's never liked the thing, often says how she'd prefer it if the woman had given them a tree to plant.

'One each,' says Daze, tapping the piles, 'Almost. Now what could we play with these?'

'Rummy?'

'Tame. Bridge? Jenny needs to learn.'

'Too young for bridge,' David jokes. 'It's an old man's game.'

'We used to play at med school. We had our own rules.'

'Now *that's* cheating.'

Max and David start some argy-bargy about card games and board games in their families, and how Max's bonkers Dad's attitude was inconsistent, since he was a minister of the True Church. Daze picks up the wine bottle and holds it to the light, surveying what's left. 'Shall I clear this up?'

Nobody replies, so she tips the remains into her glass, then takes her drink, pulls an art book (reproductions of Hieronymus Bosch) from the bookshelf and curls up on the sofa. Until they all do something more diverting, she thinks. Hiding her face in the book, she thinks again about Max and Jenny: Max would actually be a pain to have around twenty-four seven, since he's full of bright ideas, based on the vain hope that people want to be good.

She listens to what they're saying.

Max says, to David, 'So you saw your father: how was he?'

David says, 'Stripping wallpaper.'

Daze, without looking up, comments 'Stripping? As in Poker?' Thinking, this is could become the silly fun lightening up we all need. Pissed, we'll do a bit of bonding, tomorrow we'll all feel too silly to fall out?

'Poker? Did you ever? Have you?' David asks.

'Guilty as charged,' says Max.

'It was before my ordination.' adds David.

'It was after my medical degree,' Max divulges.

Their badinage is quite amusing, but their togetherness seems to annoy Jenny. 'Are you two Tweedledum and Tweedledee or something?' she asks.

'No, ma'am.'

'Shut up, Max! So am I the only one who's missed out?' Always serious, Daze thinks. Names for them two: *Always Serious* and *Bright Ideas*.

'Looks that way, pet.'

'Okay: if that's what the company wants. But—for cash or what? Or—' Jenny walks towards the kitchen area, passing that Habitat room divider Caro bought 'because you can get in its drawers from either side,' Daze remembers. 'Buttons?'

'She doesn't still have that button tin, does she?'

Jen sweeps back into the room carrying her glass from dinner, and another wine bottle. 'She has. Remember school shirt buttons: they always came off?'

'As our boobs grew,' Daze says in a dreamy voice, and puffs out her chest like a strutting hen. Then very brightly, swinging her legs down off the sofa, 'Ordinary poker's a kids' game. How about Jenny's idea. Strip poker?'

'Was not!'

'Who mentioned shirt buttons?' Daze asks, having fun.

'Who mentioned stripping?'

'Listen, nobody here, 'cept Max, is wearing a shirt with buttons,' Daze remarks.

'You'll no' take that off my back, lassie.'

'Chance'd be a fine thing.' Daze murmurs, as, seated on the floor, she shuffles and deals the cards. She puts the remaining ones face down in front of her and indicates to gather around.

Max

SAME TIME

David looks at me: I raise my eyebrows. Then glance from him to Jenny and back again. I guess we're both wondering the same thing.

Let the girls go ahead, play along, and face the consequences? Or, break in before things hot up, wearing our heavy judgemental boots, spoiling the fun? Or rather, spoiling the set-up Daze constructed, in this strange, hyper-emotional atmosphere, everyone with unresolved issues, nobody mentioning anything. *Nothing more perilous than truth?* Truth is—irresponsibility is—liberating, once in a while.

'Okay: Jen's bet,' Daze announces.

Jen bets two fives. David hands them over. As rounds continue, we all lose at least a shoe, Jenny's kicked off both, and everyone's at me to remove my socks since nobody else had socks on when we began.

I get up and fetch two more cans from the fridge, where David stashed them, pull the rings, hand one to him, and taking a swig of mine.

Jenny says, 'Don't we get any?'

'Up to you.'

She doesn't move. She has a glass of something by her side. The game proceeds, now collecting an argument around whether the girls are unfairly weighted by an extra garment specific to females. Daze claims she neither needs nor wears anything of the sort. Jen, bold and giggly, responds 'News to me, Sissy.' Evidently pissed.

Skinny Daze certainly is, I imagine counting the ribs. Though decent boobs she does have, as she boasted earlier … 'Max! Shirt off mate!'

'Undo those *buttons*,' yells Daze.

'— one, two, aw, don't slow down—' Jen joins in.

'Hey, is this—' The women start singing, banging out the rhythm of the tune on the floor with their hands, so I stand to do the striptease better.

'Yeah, it's the real thing: Dr Mullins will now demonstrate how it's done.' That's David. Who's by the table, removing the largest strawberry from the cheesecake plate. And I'm back in the bar at med school on our graduation night, smelling the beer and sweat, gyrating, twirling my shirt, seeing our exam-ravaged, grinning faces: we've finally got the accolade *Dr* in front of our names, so now there's the terrifying slog of real work and responsibility to come— 'Go, Max!' Both women clap, stamp, sing and cheer.

'Go Jenny!'

She gets unsteadily to her feet, pulls her pink vest top over her head, twirls it, then starts unzipping her skirt, grinding her hips to the beat of our chanting, *'Ba-boom, ba-boom, ba-boom-boom-boom!'*

For a few seconds, Jen and I seem to be dancing together, booming and grinding and bumping behinds, till my rational self nudges a few thoughts about decency, orderliness, and bad behaviour, and notice Daze pointing, 'Hey, it's Max and Four-Eyes doing the—' as Jenny, skirt fallen to her ankles, steps on some of the cards, slides, staggers to right herself, topples, and falls on top of Daze.

'Whoops, a *daisy*,' she laughs from Daze's embrace.' We all laugh, the two women giggling and tussling.

My brain cools down as I remove the wine bottle from the area lest we break it: funny, I thought Daze finished that up, but it's about a third full. I take it carefully to the kitchen, come back, and find David's suggesting Jen puts her skirt back on. She wipes her hands across her eyes, and tries to argue, 'What's different? You've seen me like this already, pink gingham two-piece, on the beach?'

David shakes his head. Jen says, 'For God's sake, why hang out with us if you aren't gonna join in? You're spoiling the fun! Got a party trick?'

'How about juggling? I learned it on my travels,' he replies.

'Okay, show us. Demonstration.' He swigs some Stella, then searches around for something suitable, 'Got any balls?'

'Aw, *David* ...'

'Seriously. You must play tennis? Or oranges: apples and oranges?'

Daze grabs two apples and an orange from the fruit bowl, and adds a couple of big strawberries. David shrugs, laughs and begins juggling them: he's really rather good. Daze and Jen take up their song again, clapping along with the beat, dee-dum, dee-dum, *dee-dum-dum-dum* ... David gets faster and wilder and then, suddenly, he loses his rhythm and all the fruit splurges on the floor. 'Awesome,'

Daze says.

'Yeah, used to come in handy.' David tosses one of the strawberries into the air, catching it in his mouth. We clap. He does it again. This time, something goes wrong: he's struggling for breath.

He's bending over, gasping: Daze's singing and laughter stops abruptly, Jenny half-rises, 'You okay?'

Dave's face is puce, he struggles to breathe, speechless. *He really can't breathe.* 'Get up man! C'mon, stand up! Can you stand?' I get behind him, thumping him hard on his upper back. One, two, three, four, five: nothing. *Bugger*: I try the Heimlich manoeuvre, which evidently works well, compresses the lungs, and exerts enough pressure that the outsized strawberry, lodged in the trachea, flies out of its hiding place, and David slithers to the floor gasping, panting, and actually drooling, unable to speak. Jenny crawls over, and wipes his face with my abandoned shirt. At last, 'Uh, oh, thanks for that, mate. Thanks for—bruising my diaphragm, or whatever ... you ... did.'

After all this, we're very sobered up. Some of us, a little unsteady, devise a bed for David on the sofa, since we're not in a state to drive him back to his friends, and he's not in a state to walk it. Though Daze insists 'Have my bed: I love sleeping on sofas.'

'She's a natural sofa-sheeper. Shofa sleeper.'

'Bed, Jen?'

'Mum an' Dad's. Too many people,' she shakes her head. 'I never had to do that. I learned it, once.'

'Too many?'

'Visitors. Have to share.'

So we end up together, rolling around in Caro and Des's waterbed, 'Innit horrible?' she says. 'But you saved a life there. Congratulations.'

'Are you okay?'

'I worried, a second, 'bout you an' David.'

'I love it when you go all rotate—rhotic—Cornish. Like tonight.'

'Shurrup, Max. Sleepytime. An', Alice saw your dance. You know tha'? She was ... on the landin''

'Oh *no* ... I ...'

'Ssh, Zo-zo's on the blow-up.'

Unencrypted, that might read, 'No sex please'?

Max

MORNING

The bedrooms at Chapel House were once the chapel gallery. I'm always touched, and amused, waking where the Primitive Methodists worshipped. Today dazzled by all this whiteness: Caro and Des's long and narrow totally White Company bedroom: white walls, bedcovers, carpet, curtains, blind, and low, sloping, white ceiling. Only relief is a couple of abstract paintings, in white, grey, and turquoise.

White, bright, headache, tongue like a desert. Remembering last night's absurdities, shame creeps up behind. With Jenny's parents away, we behaved like kids.

Turn on my side, thinking, actually, it's funny.

Jenny is a hump which, when poked, groans 'No', and moves further under the dazzling white duvet. *'Looking for self-fulfilment instead of loving service?'* A horrible phrase from one of Dad's awful Christian Marriage books. It drifted by, as I looked at her. Both options sound equally unpleasant. Oh, God, here we are, trying to mend things.

I sneeze: the duvet's strongly scented with washing powder. It's an incentive to stop lazily lurking beneath the covers. Slowly, first poking out one foot, then rolling myself out from under the stifling white mound. Stand, plod to the window, let up the blind. Makes no difference: we're encased in white sea mist. Which gives this excruciating quality to the light.

Is that Tchaikovsky's *Nutcracker* playing downstairs?

Remembering Zoë, I glance at the floor beside the bed: the blow-up mattress's disappeared half underneath. No Zo-zo. The sheet, pillow, and duvet tangled and topped by her *blankie*. Painkillers first, then track down bairns. In the en suite, cursing blister packs, I struggle two capsules from their foil, and swallow them down with a handful of water.

Chapel House is a clever conversion: from the narrow gallery outside the bedroom, you look down into the living area, and now, covering my ears against the top-volume *Dance of the Sugar Plum Fairy*, what I see is a ballet class, and what I smell is coffee.

Alice, wearing swimmers and a frilly skirt, is the teacher. Daze, wearing what my granny'd call a petticoat, is one pupil, Zoë, in nothing but underwear, with her chewed, stuffed-cat toy clasped to her chest, is the other. The living room's been tidied: cards stacked, cans and bottles removed, dining chairs set in a line. Carefully holding the backs of chairs, all three bend their knees to squat, then rise and repeat. Then Alice commands, *'Straight backs at the barre!'* and *'point those toes!'*

My head throbs. My heart goes out to Daze, amusing our bairns. My watch says half past ten. Jen must be wrecked.

Sea mist is about it. Lost in a mist. Missing something. I head for the family bathroom, not ready to face Jen, or any of them, yet.

Jenny

A WHILE LATER

Much too bright for morning. Brightness penetrates my head, brightness is part of the pain. Max let the blind up!

He's gone … somewhere… He took Zoë? *Eleven thirty?* I have to get up! There's a houseful staying.

But he left me a full glass of water. Like in our spare room he left me a jug of coffee. Lean on my elbow, sipping water. Last night we danced, we danced that thing they do at strip clubs, bump and grind. Me and Max were funny. Max was fun.

Carefully, I replace the glass on the table, push back the heavy, humid duvet, swing my feet to the ground. Mum's water bed, how she raved when they bought it. It's like sleeping on a jelly. Gosh, I slept in a bikini top did I? And nothing else?

Outside, a sea mist, blank, white, and luminously bright. Eyes dazzled, I head for the shower. Thank you Mum for leaving your citrus shower gel, it's amazing, with the wonderful warm water running through my hair, down my body, definitely rain on a desert.

Finally at her dressing table, in PJ bottoms and a baggy top. My reflection's haggard. Definitely haggard, though suntanned, and own fault, Jenny. A touch of make-up might help. I didn't bring any. What's Mum got? Foundation? Mascara? Concealer, for under my eyes?

Foraging, now. Oh bum: no girly stuff, she must've taken it along. To Nepal? Whatever... Bend over, feels like a lump of concrete collides with my frontal lobe.

But my curiosity kicks in: on my own, can't hear anybody, take another look in that bottom drawer? Juliette Potter, sectioned. Kneeling on the rug, pulling that bottom drawer open. Evidently where they kept documents they didn't want us to find. Delving far back, pulling out what? An envelope, inside, a folded official-looking paper. Marriage certificate. Desmond Potter and Juliette Loveday *Symes*.

Symes? Juliette Symes, became Juliette Potter ... is... can't be... could be? *Etta Symes?* Daze's mum? *Our* Etta? Our *cleaner?* Am I crazy? Is this possible?

Daze's birth certificate would have Juliette *Potter*. Wouldn't she have made the connection? Or does she only have a short one? Oh, she was born in Scotland: are they different?

Do I want to get involved?

Yes: with painkillers and coffee.

Better put this all back. Tidily.

Should I *tell* Daze? Or confront Des, when he's back from teaching summer schools?

Downstairs, I open the door, take gulps of the cool air. Sunshine slides out of the mist, beaming a lemony light. The drive's empty. Great, Max has taken the kids somewhere. And thank God, David's car's gone as well. Come in, shut the door, listen. No music: Daze's out. I've got the house to myself.

On the hall table, that large envelope's been joined by two others. One to both of us, very neat handwriting, maybe Ruth's. And, horrifically, a typed envelope from work. Shudder. Leave that all for later.

Actually, I'll make some coffee, and take it Des's studio: it's comforting and practical, even though I do feel rather odd about Des right now. And I'll open that first envelope and read whatever's inside. Can't believe Jewels is Etta.

Surprisingly, first time I've been in the studio, this visit. Motes of painterly dust slide down sunbeams, there's the familiar whiff of oil painting. Now, here's all Des's stuff, his signature predictable seascapes, the tourist-targeted paintings he turns out easily, and despises. Not his real work, which is much darker, and more mysterious. Do those relate to Julietta Loveday Potter? Breakdown, capture, consignment to an institution?

What really happened? Can't believe he'd abandon her. Did he know when she came out of mental hospital, did he care? If not—can't think about it. Without knowing, can't judge him.

Etta's our *cleaner* ... a woman who was homeless. Max talks about homeless people, rejected by family, who've had mental illnesses, who've—. But she's such a survivor. She's talented. Wonderful animal masks.

Daze painted that crucified child scene, herself and Jewels ... is that Etta? Singing while she irons?

Shivery thought: Etta in charge of our children.

And another: do we really know Des? *Does Mum?*

Scary thought, that.

I must do something ordinary. The bluebird tin's in place on the usual shelf, the cassette player's on the window sill. Feeling very much at home, I press play.

Ouch! Nearly drop my coffee as Carl Orff's *Carmina Burana* blares out. *O Fortuna!* Turn the volume down! Des used to press 'repeat' to play that one over and over. *Oh Fortuna! 'Fate crushes the brave.'*

Right: now... stomach's feeling empty. Does Des still stash gingernuts in that bluebird tin? He does. 'I find crunching up a gingernut aids thought,' he'd tell me. 'Crunching up two is even better. Have one? Help with your homework.'

Dozy Des and Jellybean? Really? I eat a gingernut, then another. And then—he takes up with Mum? I eat another one, crunching and amazed.

I sit at the studio table: I'd work on physics and chemistry at one end, Des would mark art history essays at the other. Seemed so ordinary. Not like being in some bohemian novel, or an edgy play, where a guy marries a Roma woman, then—. Can't be, isn't so.

Daze'd be hanging out in some Penzance cafe with her crowd. Hat would be in here with us, unless she had some sporty team practice. I miss Hat, my real sister ... Des is meticulously tidy: I'd better get rid of my biscuit crumbs. I shunt them along the table into my palm, drop them into the waste bin. I wash the last ones off, drain my coffee, rinse the mug, and set it on the draining board. Even the studio sink is shining and clean.

So, envelope: what's inside? A sheet of yellow American legal-pad paper, folded around another envelope. Inside that, a strip of negatives.

The paper isn't just wrapping, it's a letter: '*Hi there Princess, You were truly impressive at the Conference, and sadly you were not for me. I've an apology to make: I've sat on this too long. Don't blame your esteemed leader at the Woods lab among the dreaming spires, or the saintly Max. I confess: it was indeed yours truly, back in June 1988. I think now it's time I sent you these (enclosed) ...*'

I've stopped breathing.

I know the handwriting. Wil's admitting what he did and why? '*the grapevine'd picked up on Max being paeds on-call for a very dysmorphic newborn. I overheard that he and you had some cultures in our incubator ... one thought led to another, took a shufti. They were weird. Assuming you'd be busy celebrating Finals, I thought, you and I could work together ... Those buggers didn't let me: they limped along then died. At least I got some shots first ... If you look you'll see what I saw ... Max knew nothing, fault is all mine. Anyhow, unwise to proceed (you'll understand what I refer to) and you're clear of having ever made an unethical move, which better suits you'*

What a cheek. And he stayed shtum that evening I tried to get it out of him in the US. What a coward. He's finally confessed, but only after I've accused Max of lying and shouted terrible things at Rich.

He thought it was *unwise to proceed*. At least he's as curious as I am. Though he waited nine years to send me his findings. Grimly funny?

The letter was posted in Ireland. He was visiting his little boy, was he? Conveniently, there's no sender's address. I want to hit back, no chance.

Shit, shit, shit. He doesn't admit it, but was he jealous? He nicked our stuff, moved it to an incubator in another lab, and when the cultures died, covered his tracks. With or without Rich Wood's knowledge?

Wil's a *creep*, inviting me to be unfaithful on a work trip. He's well capable of nicking his pupil's work, to present as his own initiative. How cheap novel is that. And what would Nicholson have said? Where did Wil think he could present it, that nobody would follow the trail back to me?

Furious, I use all my energy to scrunch and screw the vile yellow paper into a ball. Chuck it across the room.

Makes me feel better. At least I know. At least I have the option: crawl to Max, and say sorry. Crawl to Rich: can I have my job back? Oh yeah, some hope.

'Fate crushes the brave.' Why let it? I'll take the negatives into the dark room, have a squint at them under the enlarger, maybe print them out. The pictures might be worth having.

Illegal or not, the work Max and I put in on that deceased, dysmorphic fetus was done properly. I would've liked it to be us who found out about the translocated gene. Daze hadn't even known Shane used his own sperm for her IVF treatment. He told her he had access to the clinic's sperm bank, and she believed him. So thanks to his heavy recreational drug use, Persephone's DNA had additional genetic damage.

Pointless to be angry with Shane, the bastard.

In the darkroom, everything's where it's always been, and neatly labelled. I prepare to make prints. When the negatives are in the enlarger, as the images begin to appear, they look much as I'd expect. I wish Wil had sent undeveloped film. Developing is best. Seeing your pictures for the first time. So exciting. So magical when Des taught us how.

*

'... cheesecake?' asks a voice. David, again?

'In here. We shouldn't be disturbed: it's off limits for under fives. Another shot of caffeine and something for the blood sugar?' Max. The heavenly twins.

Hell. My hands ball into fists. It's meant to be us, down here. Not a house party.

'D'you always talk like a medic?'

'Och, Father, I am a sinner: I canna' talk like a priest.' Oh, *ha ha*, fooling about, predictably.

'That's crap.'

'Crap? Are we not all sinners until we're saved?'

Someone plonks something down. 'Cafetière...'

'Wait, I'll move this pot of brushes ... And shift the sketchbook... Des is pretty meticulous, better make sure we're careful about crumbs.' They scrape chairs across the floor, witter around, till I hear forks clattering on plates. My head pounds. Could scream at them caging me in, and upsetting my trying to think.

'So, he's accepted your presence in the family. *That* is not crap.'

'Both the religious and the sexual lifestyle.'

'I'm staggered. What more is there for you and him to discuss?'

'The weather? Mam's golf handicap?' Max laughs. I can see them out there, flip as always. Is David sat on the edge of the table, swinging his leg? And Max, running his hand through his hair, which flops back over his eyes, to where it was before?

I don't want to snoop, but I'm forced to. A prisoner unwillingly hearing through a partition wall.

How easily they talk together.

'I honestly think he missed me. Once your father was—not gone, but a tad less capable of belligerent arguments over the finer points of doctrine, he allowed himself to feel it. Your Mam encouraged me, you know the way she has. Once the memorial service was over she was able to escape from the Manse and came straight down to St Hildegard's.'

Oh. If Euan's got over his objections to David's sexuality, can any areas of Alisdair's control remain?

'Aunt Fee thinks Hildie's is a sanctuary. It was quite touching. Nobody at First T would dream she'd be spending time at a liberal Anglo-Catholic set-up.'

'Mam's a remarkable person: not enough people know that. She's always been the cannier of the two. Only apparently a submissive wifie.'

She seemed to be, standing up for me at the Manse, that first weekend. So why so cold recently, in the car park? I agitate the paper in the developer. Overhearing is getting worse, but I can't waltz out with, 'Hi guys,' as if nothing's wrong, 'any cheesecake for me?' Not until I've worked out how to apologise. Shit. I can't squeeze through the tiny window and escape, like I did when Daze locked me in years ago. And could kill myself for stupidly accusing Max of collusion. Would he do that? To help along a creep like Wil?

David's talking about Fee's visiting Hildie's: might I understand now why she went? And ignored us?

'I suspect that trip became more than she first intended. We were walking in the garden, talking about the family. Then instead of me being any help to her, she began encouraging me to stop waiting for Dad to change, to get in there and seek him out. She's clever at avoiding that judgmental pity which silently conveys you're no more than a reluctantly accepted sinner.'

'I hated that attitude. I knew it was screwed even when we were kids. You see now how Mam almost made sense of First Truly's God—'

It sounds like Max is getting worked up about the culture of First

Truly. He'll be walking about, looking out of the window. Be useful to learn how David handles this.

'—Mam wasna' angry with Jenny. Jen got it all wrong. Mam knew from the start what I meant.'

What? Fee wasn't blaming me for my influence on Max?

'If my silly lass had read Dad's book—it was the basis of the eulogy. My only request was she read it. No. She'd no' see reason. So inevitably my speech caused a stramash in our house. Hell, David, Mam was his co-author, and if Jenny had read the book, she'd have understood. Everything.'

My suspicions about those phrases in the book weren't wrong. Fee's more than capable of writing that book herself. But she wouldn't. She'd prompt from behind. She'd quietly suggest. I remember her saying, 'Sometimes you have to be subtle as a serpent. But with it, be harmless as a dove. You see, Jenny, if you come head-on at someone ...' Oh shit. I'm learning about me, not Max. My lack of empathy, my academic arrogance, my putting work first. My Dad's culture.

'The service was supposed to be honouring my father. Would you believe *Living with Uncertainty* wasna' on their bookstall?' Max hasn't finished with the eulogy. 'I was in First T, browsing through their slick leaflets, and it hit me: Nick's taken over. Okay, Dad was fundamentalist. But he had dignity. Nick's morphed Dad's church into some kind of minority group country club. I thought—at the time it seemed right—to tell them how screwed their version of faith, hope and love is. Jenny was meant to understand. She'd applaud, I'd feel smugly proud and happy.'

I needed to know all this. He should've told *me. Though maybe I should've realised it was important to him. We've been together long enough: I've been tuning out and trying to pretend Max doesn't have emotions.*

'Rachel was there, outside.'

Rachel? Why not tell me? Afraid I'd be jealous? So unlikely.

'I'd a great surge of anger, hearing what her life's like now. Social housing, dragging herself up from nowhere, all her old friends ignoring her.'

That's awful.

'The other night, at your place, Daze's artwork, that labyrinth—'

'You had walked it when I found you there?'

Would Max do that?

'I began by trying to control it by insisting on rational thoughts: what is its history, that kind of thing. Then wondering what it does to the brain, leading you off towards the centre, twisting you back on yourself. But I gave in, and followed along where it took me. You think it's deceived you, you've almost arrived in the centre, it returns you to the outside. Suddenly you're smack in the centre when you least expect. I sat there a while.'

'So, what did it say?'

He hung around in the stupid labyrinth feeling—plunged inside the well of his grief. On his own. At David's place. Because I screwed up, and wasn't any help. How ... awful.

When *my* father walked out I ... just wanted him back. Everywhere felt cold.

'It was difficult to hear, for an ex-Presby like me. You ken my cynical side, Dave. Maybe it does take you on a journey. I wondered about the mistakes I'd made. It was too hard for me to believe Dad had really changed after that Rachel business. I doubted he had. And then comes the book: his last. The dangers of literalist reading of texts. The pitfalls of ramming home scriptural truths with threats. Amen to that.'

'So up to then you couldn't believe he was any different?'

'I don't know. He maintained the gruff exterior. Hell, I hoped but I didna' risk to test it—I thought, good, he'll leave us alone now and I'll damn well leave him alone—no opportunities for his wee chats when we'd visit. It was a shock when I went up there, to be with Dad, the last days, he suddenly shared his vulnerable side. That was difficult to take. I'd thrown away the chance to really know him, by then, no time to develop a relationship—I can't forgive myself. Jenny hasn't a clue ...'

I brushed aside that moment when he almost managed to talk about Alisdair's softer side. Scared of his unhappiness, scared of his regret, of his tears.

I can't deal with death. It's never happened near enough to me. I don't understand grieving.

I should do. Pictures of those families I met at the conference flood into my head: they grieve all the time. I thought—I realise I think—that Max deals with suffering on a daily basis, so why's he got a problem. He should've known. I couldn't deal with Rachel, could I? Max was always adequate and in control. I came home from America and he'd gone down like a deflated balloon.

It's like a laser, searing into my inner eyes. At last, stuck in a dark cupboard, with a bath of chemical developer and no escape route, I'm being forced to hear and visualise how Max felt, in the very worst way.

'I expected she'd empathise. Like she did when she made me listen to Dad's public apology. She was quite perceptive. Back then. Who empathised when Dad died? Her crazy stepsister.'

'There's more to Daze than meets the eye.'

Evidently. She's overtaken me in the empathy marathon.

'Today's women are raised to expect a lot more than playing the supportive family role. Jenny's not wrong, it's me. I should've known the perils of adopting a normal lifestyle, beyond the confines of First Truly. Jenny's ambitious, and why not?' Max begins banging the table as he makes his points. 'I love clinical work, including its routine side. It's as vital as hers. But she resents that Dad's example of the alpha male type led me to reject being a high flyer. We both love the bairns—'

David interrupts, 'Basically, this year's been devastatingly hard for both of you. All badly timed with Jenny's big career break in the middle there. Either event stretches you to the limits.'

Yes.

He's choking up and I'm stuck in here, listening in.

I don't know how to deal with the accusations I made. I'm not that concerned about the prints: only about Max.

And Rich.

It's all well over, anyhow. And my successful career. Why do we all do stupid things? Possible perfect life, ruined. Own fault.

They shift about, a chair scrapes on the floor.

A tear's fallen onto the bench: I dip my finger in it, write an M, and realise I'm indulging my own grief.

Crying won't help.

Max's recovered a bit. 'You know, there's a side of Jenny that's not unlike Mam: she wants to cut through the crap to the heart of whatever it is we call being human.'

I might want to cut through the crap, but I'm not at all like Fee. Not as understanding. Not as honest.

'Been there, done that—not giving you any advice,' says David. God, I see why they're close. David's not pushing points home, not a crowing know-all. 'If Daze is still around, ask her to field the kids this arvo, and go somewhere? Stuff can change: not too late?'

'If and when Jenny's back with them.'

Back? *With them?* Heart stops: they're out there, and they think I'm somewhere with Alice and Zoë, so *who are our children with? And where?*

Max

A MOMENT LATER

The dark room door bursts open.

'You stupid guys! Wasn't it obvious: I was here, the kids weren't? Where've you been?'

'What? *You were in there?*' She heard everything? Shame, confusion—even relief?

'Well I haven't just climbed in through the window!'

'No, no. But your car—' says David.

'Why didn't you—'

David, calmly, stops whatever I was about to say, 'We went to the Penzance Tesco. Thought you were at the beach.'

And I know, don't I, that Jen would've been too embarrassed by my show of feelings to open the door on that conversation.

'*No kids and no cars! David* mightn't add it up, but you—. Obviously I assumed *you'd* got them, Max—'

'I didn't—'

'Think? You never do!' She pauses, hand to her mouth. Sorry she said it? Then adds, '*I* might've been shopping in Tesco.'

With everything she's heard fresh in my mind, how do I deal with all this? Dad, horribly calm, would admonish her for jumping to conclusions. Referring to God's care and protection. But I'm saying, 'Yes, I was surprised you were evidently up and out already, driving off somewhere to entertain them, after I left you mumbling in bed about being allowed to rest after last night—' Dad would leave that to explode later, with a sermon to his family. Actually when really roused, he was more passionate than me: he could throw things, and bellow.

'You never thought, Jen's *wrecked*, *Daze's* taken the car?' she asks.

'Blimey, but she wouldn't be insured to drive your vehicle,' David says.

'She doesn't think like that. Daze can and would drive anything,' Jenny snaps.

'So where're your keys?'

'I—left them somewhere—kitchen table?' She dashes about. 'Max, we don't know anything right now—,' running her hands through her hair, 'Oh God, God, God—.'

The kitchen's central island is piled with bright stripy bags, the shopping we simply hauled in from David's VW and dumped there. Fish fingers, sausages, Cheerios, pasta, fresh veg, tiny lunchbox fruit yogurts, which I failed to pack away. David starts silently, methodically, finding homes for everything. Normally Jenny'd snatch it from him or dictate where it goes: now, she's too busy despairing that she doesn't remember whether she hung her keys on the key rack or not, hunting in drawers, shifting things about on the counters, looking in cupboards. 'It's only been us here—totally focused on kiddie stuff, I wasn't a bad mummy—Why the hell go shopping?'

'To help, because everyone's descended like gannets—'

'If you'd asked me—then you walked in from the supermarket,

made coffee, found stuff to eat, how could you, without wondering where everyone else was, where the children were?'

'Because I was selfish enough to want to talk through stuff on my mind, that I couldn't share with you?'

'I know—I heard—' Her shoulders sag. 'We all got pissed and now we've lost our children—' This is a vulnerable Jenny, devastated by events piled onto what she's had to hear from me. Instinct calls for holding her in my arms: fear keeps me away.

David's almost finished tactfully stowing the shopping, most likely in all the wrong places: he turns to catch my eye. Jen, beside the sink, is crying into a little blue garment, 'They can't be at the beach: I found Zoë's swimmers on the floor here.'

'Jen, we'll find them.' She lets me hold her: she buries her face in my chest. 'And then we'll sort a few things we both know about.'

'Like your mam never hated me—' she wails. 'Like I said terrible things—'

'Let's think logically: Daze is a good driver and she knows the area. Look at me? We have not lost our children,' I say with conviction, 'they didn't wander off alone, they have not been taken by a stranger. Jenny, you're a scientist: let's keeping working with facts. I have kept quiet when I couldn't speak, and screwed up, but we'll deal with it all later?'

'I am so sorry—'

'Jen: I know. I'm—our muddles didn't make this happen.' I'm hoping that's true. I'm working on how I see Daze: not as an annoying stepsister, but spontaneous, yes, a bit damaged, but less self-absorbed than you might think. 'Daze acts on impulse, doesn't she. So where might she take them? Around here? To have fun? Let's make a list. Pencil? Paper? What are they wearing?' I loosen my hold on Jenny: she doesn't jump to it as fast as I'd expect. I'm always doing that: expecting she'll make snap decisions.

'I was asleep,' she says, 'How could I act so dumb? We need to know my keys are definitely gone—'

'The Discovery has: QED?'

David plumps something on the table. 'This flyer—'

'David, you're the expert are you? No kids, but loads of—'

'Shit about God stuff?'

'Sorry. Pray if you must. Though, I found out what happened at Glastonbury—Daze's mother had a psychotic episode—'

I grab an immediate answer, 'But we never knew that before, Daze hasn't ever had mental health problems, has she?'

'Well, no she hasn't. She's—'

'Daze is her own person, but let's assume for now her mother's medical history's not relevant, and she's taken the girls to whatever's on David's flyer because she thought they'd enjoy it. Simplest explanation first?'

'And prayer, as your mam-in-law says, isn't empty words. Practical action's built into prayer. In my experience.'

'Okay: flyer's for some festival thing. I remember this: it's quite new. Lafrowda's a big parade day with sideshows and events—she probably has gone there. I've never been.'

'Sounds beaut to me: the kind of place she'd want to go herself, and take some kids along,' says David.

'It is. It is. Let's go then?'

'Jen, you can't just—you're wearing pyjamas—'

Daze

SAME TIME, ST JUST

The streets are decorated, the girls each have a balloon. Daze, recalling how she cheered everyone up last night, and even got David arsing around, feels good today. Gosh, Dave juggled fruit. And nearly choked himself to death! She grins to herself. The sun shines, the air is soft and balmy, people are smiling, the Etta thing's on hold. It was nice to meet Max at the station. Even if he was miserable, and she has to share her house with them. This is her good deed for him: take the kids, then they can have some couple-time and sort themselves. While she shares her good mood with her nieces.

Crowds are assembling on the green behind the clock tower. 'That's the *Plain-an-Gwarry*,' she tells Alice, 'it's a kind of stage. They acted plays there in medieval times. About, I dunno, maybe King Arthur?'

'Or King David? He killed a giant in Grandma Fee's story.'

'Arthur's story's better: Arthur was a western king, he lived right here in Cornwall. In a place called Lyonesse.'

'Lioness?'

'Not the animal. A place.'

'Oh.'

Zoë pulls on Daze's hand, so hard that her red balloon bounces, on its string, into Daze's face. 'You said, ice cream?'

Daze bats the balloon away, 'Poof—yes, ice cream. But first, let's look around a bit more. My friends said they'd be here, what colours were their costumes?'

'Rainbow! With big hats and eyes and masks and scary bits!'

The sun, now the mist's burned away, is very hot: she could do with a drink, water would do. And the music's very loud: you have to shout to be heard. The hands in hers are very sticky. She's too small to see much. The crowds surge them along like seaweed carried by the tide.

But she is careful: she won't let go of them. Even if she is a bit high from smoking weed with her friends while catching up each other's news, and now feeling the pangs of hunger that inevitably follow. She stops at an organic pastie stall, and insists on buying three, though Zoë takes one bite, then keeps asking 'Auntie Daze, you carry my patsie?'

'Oh wow, isn't this fun?' Daze leans down, and carefully breaks Zoë's pastie in half. 'Better? Now, I'll carry this bit while you eat. Look, there's a stall selling lemonade. We could have a drink. And listen: drums! That'll be the procession, we have to see this!'

Zoë passes the piece of pastie to Alice, 'You eat.'

Alice takes Zoë's pastie, and drops it for her, over a garden wall. 'What d'you do that for?' Daze snaps. Children are so unpredictable. What a waste!

'She's fussy. Daddy says take no notice. Mummy says it's *tenshunseeking*.'

The swirly crowd almost carries the girls away from Daze, who grabs them both, 'I said, didn't I, hold my hands!' Gosh, you have to keep your eyes on them. Two kids, not enough eyes to watch both. The drums beat louder. As they pass a litter bin, Alice feeds it the remains of her pastie. Daze decides to take no notice: she's spied amongst the crowds the headdresses her friends were making: a fish, a lobster, a jellyfish.

She lifts Zoë up to watch the lively procession. 'Look! Isn't this just awesome?' It's a miracle: the mist rolled away, the sunshine, music and dancing has transformed the dreary grey town into a total experience of colour, sound and excitement. First the band, and then the costumed people with banners and balloons and masks, waving and nodding and dancing. Daze bebops a bit to the music, jiggling Zoë, who laughs.

'Can't see,' Alice says beside her.

'One moment,' Daze looks around. Maybe someone else could lift Alice up? She can't manage two of them, and Alice is sturdy and heavy. A family with a baby sleeping in a buggy, and an older child sat on the dad's shoulders, are beside her. Daze tries to attract the mother's attention. Could she lift Alice up?

'Sure, if she'll let me. Great, isn't it?'

'Alice? This lady—Oh my god—' Not enough eyes to watch them both—she's disappeared. What to do?

Jenny

THE ROAD TO ST JUST

I said sorry to Max: it slipped out, obvious, and easy, because—? Because Daze took our children without asking.

I stare out from the front passenger seat of David's car. We're going with what Max said: my hands ball into fists with anxiety, I tell myself to trust his judgement. Hoping that Daze acted on impulse, nothing more.

When we park the car, David insists we look at his street map and split up to search. Max heads for the Plain-an-Gwarry and Market Square, David's covering the library and surgery area, and then Market Street. I take the church, cafés, British Legion place, and anywhere else where people may be eating or looking at displays or exhibitions. 'Meet up at that marquee—see, the Methodist Church is doing cream teas in there? In half an hour?'

I push through crowds in holiday mood, kids with balloons, ice creams, burgers, and dive out of the way of people in bright costumes with banners and musical instruments. Ordinarily it'd be huge fun. But the cheering and noise, smiling and colour, pushing and capering, is just irritating. Everyone's so happy.

The church might be running a crèche, or serving coffees and cakes. In fact, it's bleakly empty, a flower festival laid out but nobody here. I pause for breath, glancing around, noticing an ugly wall painting of a man with a sword.

Alice

Alice can't see, feels too hot, drops Daze's hand to struggle out of her jersey, since Daze isn't helping. Or holding her up to see.

She tugs the jersey off, then begins pushing forwards, moving fast. The crowd of legs, skirts, buggies, and dogs on leads opens out. Once she can see the marching musicians and costumed people, she stops to watch, spellbound. The bright colours shimmer in the sunlight, the masks are even more amazing than anything Etta made for the Fun Day. The procession people laugh and sing: the crowd cheers. It's like the Fun Day, only huger, and louder, and it draws her whole mind in, like being in the play only more so. Quivers of excitement run down from her head to her toes.

But then, the procession's gone, the crowd thins out, she finds herself alone. Except for a few people who aren't her family. And where's her balloon?

A cold, empty, feeling wells up inside. Her hands go sticky, her legs go wobbly. She wants to cry, but stops to think. How did we get here? Where is the car? Which road was it in? All the roads look the same, but wasn't it past that shop that smells of oranges? She decides on a road, and begins hurrying along, wiping away tears with her jersey, which she clutches close like a soft toy.

There's another crowd, standing watching something. Alice walks into it before she realises. She sees scuffed trainers, and a pair of legs in denims. A voice says, 'Ally?' As she looks up, the legs fold and the voice crouches down. The face smiles, and the arms are ready to hug. 'Daddy!' He's solid and real: he has a familiar scent. She nuzzles his chest as he hugs her.

'Ally, is Auntie Daze here? And Zo-zo?'

'She's with Auntie Daze.'

'Yes? And where are they?'

Alice shakes her head. 'I lost them.'

Jenny

In Market Square, a cheerful crowd's breaking up. Max isn't anywhere to be seen. I head for Cape Cornwall Road, to check the tea shop, darting through the people, apologising for tripping on a buggy, and knocking into a woman with a trundly shopping basket, a tiny white dog looking over its edge. The bell rings as I open the teashop door. The place is packed with people, consulting over cardboard menus, sipping tea from china cups, eating buns.

A woman at a corner table half rises and waves at me. I do a double take. She is, she really is—Max's Mam.

'Fee—?' I stagger across the shop, amazed.

'Jenny!' My mouth opens, but Fee holds up her hand, 'I've seen Max. He has Alice safe, and he knows Zoë is with Daisy.'

It's like the sea's swept over me, knocking my breath away. I swallow anything I'm about to say. Then as I try asking where they all are, Fee gives me a look, and indicates a chair.

I stop, and sit, on its very edge.

'Now you know the little ones are safe, I've some explaining to do. I wanted to visit, that day we met in the car park. It was very hard to say no.'

Must see the kids, really know they're safe. 'You can't—' I'm hardly sitting, legs ready for the off, like I'm in a race. Though even as I reach 'can't', I know it sounds rude. Fee's offering to spend time. With me. I can feel the glow of my shame. Fee is one of those real people: okay, she's religious, but she's also honest and open. I've heard Max's explanation of the book, and all my mistakes and unfounded imaginings.

'Maybe you could stay and drink tea,' she says, 'though if you need to reassure yourself Max and the children are fine, I understand. I'm here to visit you all, if I may? So we have plenty of time.'

I settle further into the chair.

'What about—'

'Oh, they've eased me out of the Manse: they're busy updating. I didn't want to watch that. Alex sorted out the movers, and I've marked what I'm keeping.'

'Isn't that—difficult?'

'No: Alisdair and I had decided what we'd take if and when we moved. And I'd a feeling you might imagine I was cross when we met in Oxford. So, when I decided to extend my time away, I came back to St Hildegard's. But you were all on holiday. Then, God's ways are strange: someone needed to come all the way to Cornwall, and was so anxious, I realised I could drive her, and save her the train fare, and visit.'

'You really wanted to see us?'

'I really did, pet. So, what's wrong?'

Dry mouth, my eyes fix on the teapot. The wretched, unwanted, and now too familiar tears are still lurking, and have another try. I blow my nose, swallow, pick up the little menu card to gaze at.

'I know you're anxious, but your children are safe. How about a scone and jam? Another pot of tea, and a plate of cakes?' Fee's speaking to the waitress, who has her pencil poised over her notebook. The waitress waggles her pencil at me: she was in my year at Cape Cornwall school. 'I remember you! Jenny Guthrie!'

'Suzy? You stayed then?'

'I came back. This is our business now, mine and Robbie George, remember him? He gave up fishing, an' sold the boat. We've got two boys, he wants to see 'em grow up. So what'll it be? Cream tea?'

*

Smiling, Fee shocks me with her honesty. 'I find what Nick's done at First Truly quite strange. The big screen, and several other things. As I think you do? And I realised you had a problem with the Memorial Service.'

'It wasn't that, it was me—'

Fee lays her hand on my arm, 'Jenny, take your time.'

'I heard what Max said, and I heard it wrong. I thought you'd have heard it like—like I'd incited him to have a go, attack everything you believe in, instead of saying how—how good a pastor Alisdair was. And that you'd blame me. For corrupting his mind with secularism.'

'Mm, we can't know how other people hear things. Can we? I understand what you thought. Max could've discussed what he was planning to say.'

'It was awful of me.'

'No, you were afraid for my feelings, which was considerate—and generous. Max is so like his father. You have to accept that, but he has to learn, if he can, to involve you much more.'

Like Alisdair ended up sharing writing a book? I try again to imagine the two of them discussing it. As Suzy arrives with a tray: tea, another cup, scones, dishes of cream and jam. Alisdair must've genuinely dropped the grim attitude. Shall I mention *Living with Uncertainty*?

Maybe not yet. I say: 'Would you like another cup? Shall I pour?'

When I hand her tea over, Fee smiles, puts it down carefully, then takes my hand. 'D'you know, pet, trying to help people by second-guessing what they need, I've acted far too much on what they didn't,' she laughs.

'And me.' She's so right: egg donation was my biggest unwanted second-guess idea to date.

'Mm,' Fee says, though not in Ruth's way. Ruth's way indicates disagreement, silently imploring, *let's drop it there, shall we, before we fight.*

'When I was at Hildie's—a place I knew I would not meet anyone who knows me, except David—David showed me the beautiful artwork your stepsister made for the Community.' She pauses, looking at me as if I should be picking up on that remark. 'Not my kind of thing, but I can see it's useful, these days, to have a visible symbol of healing and wholeness, one which crosses cultural and religious boundaries. David's very perceptive. He indicated Daisy may've found healing in making it.'

My turn to say 'Mmm.'

'Max worries about his family. He cares so much about you, Jenny. And your precious wee girls.'

Inside, I squirm, and cover my confusion by spreading jam and cream on a scone. My throat is so tight, can I actually eat it? I wish she'd say more about Daze, or anything, rather than me. Why is she specially interested in Daze?

'Daze made amazing wings for Alice when she was in her class play. She's very skilful.'

'You're also very skilful. Max is concerned for your work, which he knows you believe in passionately.'

'I—can't discuss that.'

'No need to discuss it. As long as you each know how the other feels.'

I can hear distant drumming, moving nearer.

'Actually, we—might try. To talk. Max and me.'

The drumming passes the window, accompanying a long line of bobbing heads, flying banners, bizarre paper creatures, laughter, shrieks and whistle-blowing.

When they've moved down the road a bit, Fee asks, 'What do you want?'

I know the answer, 'Perfection. I've always wanted perfection. For all of us. I've wished Max would make more of himself, use his curiosity and his good brain.'

'And what does Max want?'

'What he has. Or maybe—what he had …' I slump back into my chair, unsure why I haven't left this embarrassing meeting. Or been too proud or resentful to respond to Fee's questions.

'Jenny, your tea will be cold, pet.'

'Sorry? Oh, yes.' So as not to look rude, I sip tea, then try a smile. Fee smiles back. Then, she looks at her watch.

'Is that the time? You'll have to excuse me. I need to find the person I brought with me, I'm not sure what she's doing and we're expected back for supper where we're staying. But I'll see you very soon: remind me of your parents' phone number? May we drop by?'

I scribble down the Chapel House phone number. Rising to her feet, she insists on paying the bill, then we hug briefly. I'm never quite sure whether Fee believes in hugging goodbye, but she doesn't hug just anyone, casually.

She hurries away, the bell dinging as she closes the shop door.

Daze

A LITTLE EARLIER

Daze holds Zoë's hand tightly, as they cross Market Square. Her eyes swivel this way and that: two kids is too many for one person to manage.

It'd looked like a good idea: take the kids, she'd have some fun, and they'd enjoy the festival too. Wouldn't they? While everyone else sorted themselves. When she saw Jen's keys on the kitchen table, that seemed like a sign. She'd use the Discovery.

But now she's lost Alice, she's going to be in real trouble.

'Et'a!,

'What?' Daze leans down to hear, 'Say again?'

'Et'a—Et'a!'

'Zo-zo!' The voice, the clothes, hell! Unmistakable. How come she's here? Bizarre. Life gets worse. Etta, of all people, crouches between them and escape, wearing a stupid carnival hat, black topper with a label, 10/6d. A Mad Hatter hat. 'Yes, it's me, come all the way to see you, Zo-zo.' She looks up, removes the hat, 'Know that patchouli scent anywhere. What *you* up to, Daze Potter?'

'What you fuckin' up to?' Daze imitates. 'I know what I'm *up to*. We've lost Alice in this crowd and we need to find her. So I dunno why you're here but—'

'Oh, I'm here with news for you. What you'll be very interested to hear.'

Daze thinks she can guess. Drama queen stuff, to come chasing her down here and then make an announcement. That is so Etta. While she's worried about Alice, and encumbered by having to haul a three-year-old wherever she goes. 'You came all this way to tell me what you couldn't in Oxford then? Right now, I can't deal with it, hunting Alice's doing my head in.'

'Oh you'll be very interested, in what I've come to say. When we've found that little madam.'

'You take this one: I don't care where. No, I do: go and sit in that cake shop and buy her an ice cream and don't move. I'll find Alice,' says Daze.

'How?'

'What you mean, how?'

'You psychic?' Etta mocks.

'No, you old phoney.'

'Who brought you up to speak like that then?'

'Caro Potter: after *you* dumped me like a parcel!'

'You watch what you say my girl—or I shan't tell you. I don't have to.'

For a moment, Daze, imagining what she thinks is the news, and the truth, manages silence. Then: 'Well whatever shit you're here for, I need to find Alice.'

'She's over there, look.' Etta takes Daze by her shoulders, and turns her to look. Alice is indeed across the road, hand in her father's, dancing on the end of his arm like a berry on a bush touched by the wind.

A stream of relief flows down from Daze's brain, through her arm and body, to her tingling feet. She doesn't let go of Zoë, who hasn't seen Big Sister and Daddy yet. Instead she turns back towards Etta, so's Max can't see her face and hopefully won't notice her at all. Big trouble's brewing for when they all get back to Chapel House.

'So: your urgent message. What brought you down here, and how the hell did you know where to find me?'

'Flyer on the table, wasn't there? I love a festival. I know you do. I knew where you'd be.'

'Table where? You been in my boat?'

'Nah: posh place, used to be a church. Chapel House, isn't it? We called and knocked and nobody was in, so we—I, Mrs Mullins's too polite—looked through the window, and we could see it.'

'So you're here with—? You a pal of Max's Mum then? Did I know?'

'You said there was a cake shop: this news is worth a cuppa and a cake. Or a nice cream and jammy scone. Little soul there could do with something to eat, couldn't you, precious?'

Daze feels her arm jerked, as Zoë does two little jumps towards Etta. 'Payback time for the fish and chip suppers?'

'Worth a tea,' Etta says, 'Look, here's a tea tent. I left Mrs Mullins in the cafe, she don't like noisy bands and clowns, she said she'd just read quietly. So, seeing we're gonna be noisy with Missy here, and I s'pose there's only the one café in a place this size, we'll have to put up with the tent. Hope it's the WI: they make good jam.'

Inside the marquee, Etta swivels her head around, *clocking*, as she says, the clientele. A couple are leaving a table. Etta instantly plumps herself down at it. 'We'll sit here. Cuppa tea, hot and strong, and there's cream and scones, I can see people eating. Mrs Mullins, nice woman, thoughtful. We had lunch on the way down, sandwiches from out of a picnic basket.' Daze slides into the opposite chair. Etta jumps up and lifts Zoë onto her lap: Zoë looks up at Etta's face. Etta says, 'Milk or juice, then, Missy?'

'Listen—I think we're meant to queue,' says Daze.

'You go then, you know what we want. Two cream teas? And a milk: that's in a glass, half full, with a straw?'

'Right, you hang onto Zoë, tight, then.'

As she queues, Daze watches Etta and Zoë: *that could've been me.* That might not've been me. It wasn't. But what if it was? Her tongue sticks to her soft palate. She tries to remember things, scenes. But they won't come. Etta's coarse, greying, black hair, frizzes out from the brightly patterned red, purple and blue scarf tied around her head Alice-band style. Jewels. Really?

'Now, listen,' Etta leans across the table, a few minutes later, as Daze dumps their tray down. Her hands holding Zoë are plump. Hard manual work has leathered them. She's not free, beautiful, like Jewels.

'Just what were you doing coming here? You didn't *make* Fee Mullins bring you? Or did you?'

'Nah. Couldn't make that one do anything. Not *make.* I come all this way to tell all of you what I learned.'

All of us? Daze's voice comes out strangely strangled, 'I heard you: talking to David.'

'Right Miss Know-All: you tell me.'

'No, you tell me. Or I'm out of here. Tea or no tea. Sorry an' all that.'

'What did I say?'

'You fucking know!'

'I bloody don't! I come to tell you about the scam that robbed you of your arts centre plans—'

'What?'

'*I knew I shouldn't've trusted them nutters!* And here's David, now—'

Max

SOME MINUTES LATER

There's a kerfuffle at one of the tables as Alice and I enter that tea tent run by the Methodists. David's part of the group, being harangued, apparently, by two women.

Daze, and—Etta? So does this mean Etta's come all this way with news that'll prove she's Daze's mother? Suddenly, the group opens out, a small figure emerges, rushes forwards and cannons into me: 'Daddy, Daddy!'

'Zo-zo.'

I sweep her into my arms for a big hug. When I look again, David is demonstrating for us to join them, 'Hey mate, over here!' and Etta's making a thumbs-up sign.

We all gather around their table, the girls hanging onto me each side. Will we all discuss Daze and Etta's grand meeting, and realise how each of us knew a bit of the story?

Daze grabs my arm, 'Max, listen to what's happened—'

Etta interrupts, 'It was me as found out, and Lady Muck here was terrified my news was something bad about herself!'

'Shush, Ma, they're all looking, hey?' The news has evidently united the two of them, and Daze is accepting Etta's her mother.

'It's about Keith Taylor—' Etta says, 'the bastard!'

Alice and Zoë, realising this is grown-up talk, creep their hands towards the plate of scones on the table. Etta bats them off, 'You learn to wait, my girls!' She turns to me and David, 'He's done something important enough to bring me all the way down here. That is, when Mrs Mullins came looking for you and your family, Dr Mullins, and I knew you was on holiday, she offered me a lift. Seeing people we were after were all in the same place, give or take.'

'Mam?' She'd only said she was here because she was worried about us. She didn't mention she'd brought Etta.

'I dunno more than she was looking for you all, an' when I said what I said, she thought we'd come down together. Nice, wasn't it? Right, David. I know you mayn't like what I did, but, seeing it affects you—' Etta reaches out, and grasps his arm. 'What you need to know is, I was cleaning in their conservatory, what Keith uses as his office like. And, I know I shouldn't have, but I was moving stuff to dust, and the computer suddenly woke up and on the screen was this plan thing. And, as my eyes were like on it as it came to life, my eyes read some words—*then came the dawn*—'

Impatiently, Daze takes over, '—what she's saying is, she realised how creepy Keith used his influence in some evil, nefarious way to sway the council's decision towards the Hildegard homeless plan. Not because he cares a flying fuck about the homeless. Or because he didn't want an arts centre in the old print shop—though his type's not bothered if there's nowhere for community arts to happen. He did it because he totally wanted to help a group of the Headleigh Parish crew to take over Hildie's, and *put a heterosexual in David's place. I told you* he's homophobic.'

David looks a bit shocked, but says nothing.

'Keith's a council employee. He obviously got access to information he shouldn't have,' says Daze.

'He bent an ear, has to be. He snooped about. I began to think those two were up to no good. Too friendly by half.' Etta emphasises, nodding, while spreading jam and cream onto the split halves of a scone. She hands a half each to Zoë and Alice. 'There now: eat up, don't drop it on the floor. I paid for that.'

Daze makes a face, like 'Crikey, and she's really my mother?' or is it 'No she bloody well didn't'?

Etta says, 'He wasn't thinking to stop there. They want to take over Hildie's for themselves. Run it, like. They'd have both the properties, by working to change Hildie's from the inside. Seems backwards to me. But why they've moved there, isn't it?'

David looks even more shocked. 'Parasitical wasps. It was a clever ruse.' He clutches his forehead, shaking his head. 'Give the place to St Hildegard's, then work to gain both properties, while completely altering the use and ethos of Hildie's from the inside. If it's so, it's a very serious allegation. We need to be certain.'

'Parasites: always disgusting,' Daze adds. My thoughts entirely.'

I lay a hand on David's shoulder, saying 'Keith Taylor: remember I warned you the faithful from HPC who began coming along to Hildie's might be trouble?'

'They wasn't going to run it as Hildie's no more. They'd change everything to suit themselves. I don't know as Anthony Field-Plowright was at the bottom of it. Nice man. I would hope he wasn't.'

Daze grabs David's other arm, 'Look, I'd got that place, fair and square, for my arts project, and then, mysterious reversal! So you'd better believe her, however she got the information. Okay, agreed, I know you'll have to go through the proper channels but, it was totally weird how that decision was changed.'

'Etta, thanks for alerting me. I'm hopeful we can sort this. And Daze, more apologies. Looks like your dream studio was nicked, and given to us, in a most unfair way. Oh, and Daze—I think you brought more than the kids into town today? Max'll need his car keys if he's gonna take the family back to Sennen.' He opens his hand, palm up, 'You did come here in the Discovery?'

'Nice car. Yeah, parked around behind the church, my mates' place.' Daze lets go David's arm to fish in her bag, then drops our keys into his outstretched hand. David passes them to me. Daze says, 'Max, you'd better find Jenny wherever she's gone. There's a Lafrowda ceilidh or something tonight, and I said I'd help with refreshments so I'd better split now.'

David grins, 'Right. All done. I'll see you all back in Oxford some time. Arrivederci, all of you, and best to Jen.' Turning to me, 'Walk with me a moment?'

Seeing Etta's in charge of Alice and Zoë, I walk with him. He sighs. 'Bummer, important stuff if it's as she said. Pity I'll have to abandon this holiday. Obviously I'll be checking the facts before anything further can happen. Though I suspect she's right. Keith was far too concerned to enter into everything at Hildie's as soon as they arrived, including sides of our work which had nothing to do with the homeless project.'

'It's an insult, as well as corruption in high places.'

'Par for the course? Bit small-town, odd to find in Oxford? Maybe not?'

'You okay?'

'I could be bloody furious, if its true. I'll hold onto any negative emotions till I get through the initial enquiries. And keep a cool head for the Bishop and Field Plowright. The Committee will be on my side, whatever.'

'Call if you need me. And many thanks for listening, earlier.'

We've reached the entrance, where people are trying to come and go. And, Daze's followed us, 'I'll give you the council's letters to me, all the dates and that—the creepy bastard won't get away with it.'

'Thanks. I'll let you know if there's stuff you can do. Meanwhile, don't break your holiday for me. I'm driving straight to Lands End. Make a few phone calls, pick up my gear, and off back to Hildie's to talk to the Management Committee and a few other people, try to sort this.'

At this moment, I spot Mam entering the marquee. Glancing around, 'Max! David! Oh, you're obviously busy. I'm looking for someone. Etta? Is she in here?'

'She certainly is,' says David. Etta's smiling like a cat with cream, while the bairns sit eating scones and swinging their legs. Hearing Mam's voice, they twizzle around, 'Grandma's here!'

David turns back, and waves, 'Ciao!' Daze heads off towards a group of people with banners and musical instruments.

'Ciao!' Alice calls, opening and closing her hand as she waves. 'Chowchow!'

Jenny

Fee was lovely. All those perceived misunderstandings, disappointments, and resentments were mine. I was too busy to read Alisdair's book. I was horribly prejudiced, too sure I knew already what was inside its covers.

The sounds of carnival hit as I open the shop door, and find Max, Alice and Zoë, waiting quietly outside.

The girls explode into hugs and squealing. A horrible self-awareness grips me.

Understating, 'Fancy seeing you here,' is all I can manage.

'Granny's here,' Alice says.

Zoë says, 'Can we go home?'

'Good idea,' says Max, and Zoë gives us each a hand. We swing her between us. Alice walks close to my side, brushing her hand, deliberately, against my leg as we walk.

Max stays quiet, but friendly, normal. He doesn't want to get into explanations. He's being ultra-Mullins. Am I forgiven? 'Daze admits she did a risky thing. She's left the car behind the church,' is all he says about the day's crazy happenings: Daze's behaviour; my ranting; my hearing, from the dark room, everything he and David said.

I hold back any 'This was all your fault' or 'Typical Daze, like rules don't apply to her.'

We collect our Discovery, note that Daze didn't destroy it in any way, and bounce along the twisting road to Sennen, all of us silent with our own thoughts. 'What—?' I begin.

'I'm thinking about the Blue Lagoon,' Max says. 'Fish and chips'd be brilliant, wouldn't it? Eaten on the beach?'

'The seagulls'll steal our supper!' Alice exclaims.

'Eaten inside, then?'

'An' jus' us?'

'Just us.'

'David gone back to his friends' place?' I ask.

'Long story: tell you later.'

*

Kids in bed, Max and I have opened that letter, addressed to both of us.

...the Council recently identified some problems in the department where Keith works, and afterwards he felt that the right thing was to resign. We feel that the Lord is calling us to make a fresh start, and are very grateful that Keith's already found another post. We're busy preparing for the move. Jonathan and Sarah will be going to new schools, which is of course exciting as well as a bit challenging.

I am very sorry to have to ask you to find other solutions for Alice and Zoë's care after school/nursery. I have enjoyed having them for the past few years. I think they have enjoyed coming here.

So, this is goodbye, and wishing you both and the girls all the best in the future.

Yrs., Ruth (Taylor)

I'm astonished. 'Oh. My. God. How can Ruth play down what *Keith's* done as some *departmental problems?*'

Max shakes his head, 'She shouldn't. But this letter confirms he was central to the scheme.'

'And she's sticking by him? Colluding, abandoning her job, taking their kids out of school, and moving house?'

'She's joined to him in marriage. *Where you go, I go,* stuff.'

'I'd never do that,' comes into my mind: but the thought that I'd go to Canada to work for Dad, rather than sort our relationship, stops me saying it. Instead, 'that's shit,' I say, 'he's criminal, as good as.'

Max gives a great sigh of agreement. 'It is, he is, but it's the way they deal with it.'

'And she claims it's all God-business—that is such a lie, that is so—evasive, ridiculous, insulting. To our intelligence, to—'

'They're kidding themselves, she's kidding herself so she can cope.'

'You were getting at that mindset in your eulogy. Only you were too polite ... it's a frightful cover-up.'

'It is. It's an abuse of the language of faith. It's not unknown. A cover-up which they hope will convince, or be accepted by, everyone who doesn't have all the details. It'll satisfy their extended family and friends who won't delve deeper.' I'm beginning to understand the thinking. 'If you're a perfectionist, you can't afford to fall short,' Max adds drily. 'She can't live with shame, but if they move away—'

'So she's been cold and formal. Ruth was a friend. I'd thought of her that way.'

'And now she'll hope never to see you, never to speak to you again.' Something flashes through my mind: how Max wrote a dreadful, cold letter to me and tried to disappear, when we'd first been together. It was only walking straight into each other, four years later, at a symposium, that meant we're together today. 'She'll try to rebuild her life. She can't leave Keith. It's painful for her as well as us—'

'Though she's the one who's kindly dropped us in it: I wouldn't do that. What point does their faith have if they're such twisters—you never trusted her, did you?'

'Straightforwardness isn't a characteristic of that kind of fundamentalism. Neither is wanting to look as if you're the one who did wrong. I felt nervous about getting too closely involved or indebted to her because I know how things are likely to happen when anyone screws up.'

'You're the expert. I don't know why I didn't listen. Okay, Keith isn't violent, but Ruth's colluding with this abuse as much as Rachel did with Colin's.'

'I agree. She doesn't see it like that.'

We're both silent. Then, 'there's more to this,' I say. 'Keith put David in the wrong, made him upset Daze, and turned them into enemies. Of course, he made out that he was doing something his God wanted. That's sickening. If there is God, an arbiter of all things moral, he's hardly likely to approve of Keith.'

'I'll make no excuse for Keith: it is what people do who imagine a God who has favourites.'

There's no more to be done: a chapter of life has closed. 'No surprise they talk about moving on,' I say, desperate to somehow put this new problem aside, and accept that Max can actually know better than me sometimes. 'You—like gingerbread don't you?'

I go into the kitchen, and begin getting the ingredients together to make gingerbread people for Alice and Zoë to decorate tomorrow. I try not to bang the cupboards and drawers as I close them, and I read the back of the tubes of pre-made decorative icing twice. Pink, white, orange, green. We'll do it while the tide's in, then go to the beach. I can help them play and learn like Ruth does, at least while we're on holiday.

Don't think about all that.

But I do. Ruth let us down.

What'll David do about his homeless centre? That'll be interesting.

Why would Ruth add her surname to her signature, as if we didn't know her properly?

The way they do things. I should've known.

I have two trays of gingerbread people in the oven when the phone rings. It's Fee. 'Jenny, a word. You may wonder where Daze has gone.' I hadn't: she has loads of bohemian friends down here, but I say, 'Yes. Not with you?'

'You know—you mayn't know yet—Etta came down with me, in order to speak with David. But Etta and Daze need to talk.'

'They do?' *Julietta Loveday Symes:* I've had no time to say anything, but if Etta really is Julietta Symes, has she told Daze?

'I think they have a few things to say ...' Fee's voice kind of trails off, and the kitchen timer buzzes loudly, 'I have something in the oven!' I squeal. 'One second!' And I drag out the trays, and put them on the counter. There's a wonderful gingery aroma, as I seize the phone again. 'Daze and Etta?'

'They've gone to a ceilidh, part of the Lafrowda. I think you should expect Daze won't be back tonight. So you'll have the house to yourselves. How are you and Max now?'

So frustrating: Fee won't say more, she doesn't believe in what she calls gossip. 'We've lots to talk about, while Daze is away.'

Once we say goodbye, I move to the counter, and start sliding a fish slice under each of my gingerbread people, and placing them on a rack to finish cooling. I realise what Ruth's avoided. The tearing apart that's landed me where I am.

There's one gingerbread person which cracked in half. I reach out for it, and perch on the edge of the table, nibbling one of the halves. 'Who was it?' Max says, from behind me. He touches my hair. Tentatively, like he expects rejection.

I turn, reach out, and touch his hand. 'Your Mam. To let us know Daze and Etta have gone to the ceilidh together.' I put the other half of the gingerbread person in his hand. 'These are nice. Why would they do that?'

'They both enjoy dancing,' Max says with a shrug.

'Could it be possible she's found her mum? D'you think—Etta—or is that too bizarre? I told you I found something about her—about Julietta Symes Potter—having a mental health problem, the year Jewels went missing from Glastonbury.'

Max hands me the other envelope, the one I don't want to open. 'How about this, you need to open it.'

I carefully tear the envelope open, and unfold the letter, printed formally on what feels like extra crisp paper. My hand shakes as if the thing is dangerous to hold. 'Rich is asking me to send him hard copy of the article for Nature. He says nothing about my employment situation.'

'It could just be a hunch, but possibly, your future there mayn't be as bleak as you thought?'

'Maybe…' I can't think about it right now: is Rich generous enough? Do I want to remain there? Change of subject needed. 'I've a hunch you know more about Etta than you're letting on?'

'One good thing. After what Keith did, David offered Daze a commission, and they've become friends.'

'Mmm. And that labyrinth is stunning.'

Jenny

A FEW DAYS LATER

We're all stunned, except the kids. They act like, Why shouldn't Daze's mum turn out to be someone we already know? Or Uncle David have been there on the beach one day, and disappeared the next? Why shouldn't the grown-ups have been dancing with half their clothes off? Why shouldn't Granny Fee come on our holiday again, but mustn't be told about that dance?

Alice and Zoë are so accepting, they keep us sane.

I don't know where Daze's staying, but she's still around when we're into our second week. She sends a message: *Everyone be at the cliff top car park, at five twenty-two am tomorrow. Arrive before sunrise. Wait for the sun, then look towards the beach.*

We park on the big green field above Sennen beach. It's empty, except for us, and a lone dog walker. The sky is paling from black to navy to faded denim. Despite being summer, it's chilly waiting for the sun. We sit in the back of the Discovery, drinking hot chocolate I brought in a thermos, and munching croissants. This is so *cosy* it's not true.

The girls are wriggly. 'This is exciting. Like Christmas, isn't it, Ally?' says Max.

Alice gives him a wiser-than-you look. 'No, it's not, you're silly, Daddy. That's all cold and shivery. With candles.'

'So, where's the sun, then?' I say.

'Coming up: see, over the village? In the east? So now we can see, off we go.' I know the stony beach path so well. It slopes steeply between high walls of blackberry bushes. We walk single file, me first, the girls between us, Max in the rear. Sometimes it's too steep, and Max carries Zoë. As we reach the soft, sandy bit, with the wooden steps, Alice pauses, 'There's a laby-rinth down there. Look.'

There is a huge labyrinth drawn on the sand. The tide's far out, the beach is empty, Daze is nowhere, and there's something she's left in that labyrinth's centre. As I realise what it is, so familiar from all the years we lived here growing up, the old annoyance with Daze bubbles into my throat ready to burst out. She's devised a game. I turn to speak to Max, and there are Fee, and Etta, coming down the steps from the promenade.

Fee waves. Etta waves, and points: Daze, in a wetsuit, is emerging from the sea, surfboard under her arm. Alice and Zoë squeal as they run towards Daze. 'You're a mermaid!' shouts Zoë.

'No, I *know* you're not a mermaid!' Alice laughs.

'Okay: this is easy: we each pick a stone, and carry it with us as we walk the labyrinth. The stone's whatever you want it to be. When we reach the centre, we each cast our stones into the lobster pot.'

Cheesy or what? I have spent about ten days trying to sort my life out, feeling a right wuss, I don't need this. But they all begin looking for the right kind of stones. I'd better join in. I find a nice stone, speckled granite with pink and yellow bits against the black. It's been smoothed by the sand and the sea; it feels heavy in my hand.

Daze is telling the meanings of the labyrinth, even Fee's listening respectfully, and so am I. And I keep looking at Daze and Etta, wondering what resemblance I can spot: they take sly glances at each other, when they think the other one's not looking. Obviously wondering the same thing. Etta nods as Daze talks about how 'walking the Labyrinth allows us to focus our thoughts, helps us see clearly our personal and professional lives. It gives the opportunity to think through our goals, talents and abilities, make decisions, and evaluate progress.'

Yeah: she learned that from a book!

Whatever, suppose it does help? It can't harm. I step into, or onto, it, and walk the thing, astounded to find myself doing this, behind Fee, who's behind Max, who has Zoë by the hand. And Alice, who is taking exaggerated steps. Behind me are Etta and Daze. When I get to the centre, I stand there a while, letting my mind stop spinning: *where will it stop?* Working for Dad? Finding a replacement for Ruth? Rich finding a replacement for me?

Slowly, I leave the centre, and walk back, noticing how as you get near the edge the first time, it takes you back towards the centre, before throwing you out suddenly and unexpectedly.

I stand looking at it, and the little group of people I shared it with a few moments ago. I notice I still have the stone in my hand. *A labyrinth is not a maze.* Maybe we've been guided through, and given some wisdom in there? We'll see. The girls separate from the group, and run, jumping at the lacy edges of the incoming tide. The sea licks the edges of the labyrinth. Zoë bends down, Alice leans towards her and says something. They both run, Zoë dragging a strand of seaweed, towards the labyrinth, laughing and scuffing their feet in the wet sand.

QUESTIONS FOR BOOK GROUPS

1. 1996/7 is a 'labyrinth year': Daze makes a labyrinth for David. But in what way is this a labyrinth year for Max and Jenny?

2. Jenny starts out believing that Daze is in need of some kind of 'help to happiness', but how do you understand Daze? Are she and Jenny co-dependent?

3. Max has been raised to keep his emotions in check, and private, and to always be available to others. How is this affecting his marriage?

4. What do the children contribute to the story as a whole?

5. Daze's attitude towards David changes dramatically fast over New Year's. Why might this happen, what has motivated Daze?

6. Jenny assumes that, when they meet in the car park, and Fee says she is 'on retreat', this is an excuse and a rejection. Is this assumption valid or believable?

7. A labyrinth takes you into its centre, and then out, supposedly changed. Have we seen any of the characters reach a better place?

8. In the last scene, Jenny is still carrying the stone she took into the labyrinth with her. What do you think the stone might symbolise, and has Jenny learned anything lasting from her labyrinth year which will help her move forwards?

PRAISE FOR
Baby, Baby

BY MARI HOWARD

'A great story that unpacks some fantastic dilemmas about life, love and science. Highly recommended'

'You won't forget these characters once you have met them'

'This is an exciting, fast-moving story, almost a whodunnit! It's also a book which takes personal and ethical dilemmas seriously, and examines them through credible, complicated characters'

'A fascinating story, encapsulating many of the tensions in 1980s society'

'I grew fond of the well-crafted characters while reading this book: with a great plot to drive it and a background of points to make you think, it is definitely worth a read'

'Smart, savvy writing that took pains to get the science—and religious tension—right. A really good and thought-provoking read'

'The more I read the more I wanted to read and the conclusion was masterly and redeeming'

'We often criticise fundamentalism harshly and critically without perceiving the bonds of love which link family members in spite of the strange codes which dominate their behaviour. This book explores the good and the bad with honesty and depth'